A VERY ANG...
WAS CHEW...

"Call yourself a soldier, Le Sal?" he demanded. "You're in big trouble, Mister! Look at the goddamn battle board! You're the target, and the bogey is at five o'clock!"

Then I couldn't see or hear the computer-room reality, just my warlord chewing me out and pointing at the board. A klaxon horn was blaring raucously.

The scene snapped off. I was in an arena surrounded by the planet's six best warriors, all skilled in an art that combined the fluid ritual of *aikido* with the abrupt attack violence of *choy li fut*. They were supposed to kill me slowly, to entertain the emperor and his extended family. I'd been caught in the bed of an assigned daughter—assigned to someone else, who had then hired these six to kill me.

As the warrior at five o'clock moved toward me I reversed the vector of his stiff-fingered jab. . . .

JOHN DALMAS AND ROD MARTIN

THE

PLAYMASTERS

BAEN BOOKS

THE PLAYMASTERS

This is a work of fiction. All the characters and events portrayed in this book are fictional, and any resemblance to real people or incidents is purely coincidental.

A Baen Books Original

Baen Publishing Enterprises
260 Fifth Avenue
New York, N.Y. 10001

First printing, January 1987

ISBN: 0-671-65610-4

Cover art by Stephen Hickman

Printed in the United States of America

Distributed by
SIMON & SCHUSTER
1230 Avenue of the Americas
New York, N.Y. 10020

To:
the Cat Girls and
Mama Kitty,
who helped,
and
to Puk and Buc,
whoever they may be

ONE

Ahead, the waxing moon hung nearly half full above the Pacific, and looking over my shoulder, I could see lights on Santa Catalina Island, forty or fifty miles south. But I gave none of them much attention; the Pacific Coast Highway west of Malibu was familiar territory, and I had a lot on my mind.

Primarily: How did a fair-haired boy like me get in a jam like this?

The "fair-haired boy" tag had been pinned on me by a competitor when I'd been awarded an eight-figure contract by the air force. "Well," he'd said, "General Decker's fair-haired boy has struck again."

"Decker's patsy" would have been closer. He'd probably planned all along to kill me once the research was completed. I'd just hurried him along a bit by finishing ahead of schedule. Now I'd have to nail his ass to save my own.

My attention went back to my house and the dead agent in the rec room. I'd actually killed a man, casually and without fear, my only feeling professional satisfaction. Talk about out of character! The electronics industry had been my area; I'd left war to the army.

My headlights caught a sign marking the junction of county road N29, and I turned north on it into the low coastal mountains. A jet was waiting near Thousand Oaks to fly me to D.C. I glanced at the note on the seat beside me, a pale rectangle in the darkness. The signature on it was Dorothy Anderson. I couldn't help grinning. "Dorothy" was appropriate—she'd been doing the Oz number on me for the past six weeks.

The road curved through high-humped grasslands, with live oaks meditating here and there in the night. This far from L.A. the city glow didn't amount to much,

1

at least looking northward, and I could glimpse stars through the windshield. A story by Robert Heinlein slipped into my mind—*Glory Road*. Scar Gordon hadn't had the foggiest idea where his road was leading, and I wasn't very damned sure about mine.

But it was a beautiful night to start. I found myself smoothing out, and enjoyed the rest of the drive.

The airport was large enough for private jets, but quiet, with only a few lights visible in a hangar. A row of tall Washingtonia palms along the approach road greeted me from a distance. Up closer I got a look at an eight-foot chain-link fence. The guy at the gate looked stoned, and he didn't ask any questions: My overpowered Irish import was credentials enough.

The pilot was waiting beside the twin-engined jet—a Cessna, maybe $5 million worth. As I got out and swung my car door down behind me, he walked over. "Mr. Ambers?" he asked, looking me over.

I don't fit most people's image of a self-made millionaire, unless the millions came from playing cornerback or left field. I hadn't, but I looked as if I could have.

"Right," I said. "And you're Stu Rogers." I handed him the note with the "Dorothy Anderson" signature.

"Come aboard then, sir. I've checked all systems and we're cleared for takeoff. I filed a flight plan for Las Vegas as instructed; we'll change course after we're east over the San Gabriels."

I climbed aboard and buckled in while he closed the door. As he passed me, heading forward, he pointed to a small counter with a hot-drinks dispenser, and beneath it a miniature refrigerator. "Help yourself to drinks and sandwiches after we level off," he said.

I leaned back and relaxed. A sense of loss rose up, but it was a small one that vanished quickly. I'd abandoned my company and my house, and there wasn't even much prospect of coming back to pick up my stainless steel road cruiser. In return I'd gotten my own glory road to follow, plus the most—multifaceted, shall we say?—playmate on this or any planet. And the damnedest *cat* you can imagine.

The engines took life, and pretty shortly I felt us lift

off the runway. I wasn't out of heavy trouble yet by any means, and the next three thousand miles were in the hands of a man I'd never met before: Stuart Rogers, my pilot. But considering who'd selected him, I was willing to let Stu take care of things for a while.

I let my eyes close, and my attention went back to before the beginning of this crazy situation. Back to before the two wild days of—I guess you could call it deprogramming. Back even before the accident. At age nineteen I'd gotten impatient with college, and quit in my sophomore year of an electronic engineering program to start my first company, Vidtel, with $1,300 borrowed from relatives. Vidtel was in the video game business at the right time, and I sold out at the right time, too.

With the capital from Vidtel, and with a few of the key people who'd been with me more or less from the beginning, I'd started HOLEX, which manufactured holographic displays for the DOD—the Department of Defense. Once that contract was going smoothly, we began research on advanced holographic systems, with an eye toward a future holo-game product. It was the research in that area that led to a breakthrough, and some juicy R&D for the air force.

I'd had a small but well-equipped lab between my office and the board room, to make my twin functions of research and management easier. That was where the "accident" happened. The test that night was an attempt to reduce the power requirements of a holographic display system by standing wave collation— SWAC, we called it.

It had worked in the very first test—worked too well. It was a private test. The output was to be a duplicate of me, assembled with a collation of very low-power standing waves. I'd stood alone in front of the iconoscopic scanner. So far so good. And then it, the holographic copy of me, opened its mouth. All on its own!

"Good evening, Jan."

My goose bumps must have shown through my shirt.

"Don't be afraid," said the holo-me, "I won't be here long. The collex phase lock isn't complete, and besides,

I have no cursor. *You're* the cursor, in that icon."

You're the cursor in that icon? That didn't make any sense to me at all.

"Should I tell him?"

This time my mouth was talking! Talking without my volition! I'd gone nuts!

"I guess you'd better," said the holo-me.

"Hey, you!" my mouth said. And this time it was talking to *me!* I could sense it.

"That's right, you!" it went on. "You're the cursor and I'm the icon. Like Abbot and Costello: We're a team. Been one for years. I do the work and you get the credit."

"And you haven't gone crazy." This time it was the holo-me talking again. It was impossible, all of it, some weird effect of the electrical field on my brain. Abruptly I turned and left the lab, shaking my head to get the cobwebs out, and went to the concealed bar in my office for a large brandy.

Or it might be that I was asleep and dreaming this, or that someone had wired a practical joke into SWAC. That was it! A practical joke! And when I found out who. . . . I poured a double shot and turned, and there was the holo-me, *in my office now,* sitting on my desk with one leg dangling. It had followed me! I almost fainted. It was supposed to be affixed to the magnetic net in the rig.

Yet there it stood. "Jan," it said, "we need to talk. Why don't you offer me a drink."

My hand shook, actually shook, as I poured another and handed it to—him. The holo-clone. That's what it was; it had to be. I'd cloned myself holographically!

He swirled the glass and sniffed it, and I recognized my own motions in his.

"Not as good as we drank in Switzerland last year," he commented casually. "Or did the fireplace and the blonde make it seem better? Mood can't be discounted entirely."

I lowered myself onto a seat and sipped the brandy, feeling calmer now. So I was crazy. I'd ride along with it and see what happened next.

Then a voice spoke inside my head. "We're not crazy," it said. And after a pause, "Sometimes it's necessary to repeat yourself to the aborigines. You *Cursor*, me *Icon*."

I sat warily, afraid to think, waiting.

Then my vocal cords started up again independently. "Let's look at the basics. You, the one who's listening, *you* are the cursor." It was speaking very calmly, soothingly. "You are the cursor, and I . . . To avoid getting complicated, let's just say that I am the three-dimensional standing wave pattern of an icon pulse; you refer to me as your body. And he"—my hand, with no help from me, indicated the holo-clone—"was *not* cloned from you. He was cloned from me."

I didn't know whether to cry or what. Then nothing more happened, and gradually I became aware that the room had become still, in a way that I had never experienced stillness before. The silence was absolute. My hand was still out in front of me in a frozen gesture. Again, warily, I shifted my attention to the wall clock; its sweep second hand stood unmoving. I wasn't breathing. I felt slow panic form, but there was no sense of suffocation, and my shoulder wasn't getting tired with my arm out the way it was.

Time had stopped! *Everything* had stopped!—everything in the outer world. *But my mind hadn't*. Subjectively, time was still moving! Now that was interesting.

Then my body laughed, and so did Holo-Clone, a duet of laughter in close unison. The second hand was moving smoothly again, and I could feel my body breathing.

"See what life would be like without an icon?" my mouth said. "We're your connection to physical reality. You cursors need us to have any fun." My voice lowered then, murmuring to me conspiratorially. "I'll let you in on a secret, though. We icons need cursors to appreciate it."

Something felt very funny all of a sudden, and we laughed together, the three of us, long and hard. When we'd finished, my feeling of sanity was back.

"You guys really know how to shake a guy up," I said. "But how come you never let me know before,

Icon? Does anything like this ever happen to other people?"

"Damn seldom. Icons aren't in business to scare their cursors into the cuckoo nest. Besides, it's the icon they'd put in the straitjacket. But with you—I've got my reasons for coming out in the open like this. And SWAC set you up for it; you were expecting a holo-image, so it wasn't the shock it might have been."

We took Holo-Clone to dinner, him and a set of identical twins that I—that Icon and I—knew. The girls assumed that Holo-Clone and I were twins, and were surprised that I'd never mentioned him before. I implied that the work he'd been doing for the government was so secret that he'd had not only to drop out of sight, but as nearly as possible out of existence. But that was over now, and he'd just arrived unannounced from Japan.

Then I got another surprise: Holo-Clone spoke Japanese fluently, or at least freely. And it occurred to me that if he was a clone of Icon, then Icon should speak Japanese, too. And if Icon and I . . . But I couldn't.

Icon chuckled inside my head.

The next morning, after breakfast on the terrace overlooking an unusually bright and clear Pacific, the twins kissed both of us goodbye and went off to work. We turned and started into the house.

"It's about time for me to disassemble," Holo-Clone said as I held the door for him, "but before I go, I want to thank you both for a really great night. You'll know it was great for me, because when I've gone, you'll have my memory of it." Then, before I could ask him how that could be, he went two-dimensional, rotated sideways into a thin line, and vanished.

He was right. I drove to work sorting through twin memories of last night's twins, and arrived knowing exactly what I was going to do about the Standing Wave Collation Project. In my office I called in every scrap of work and paper in the plant relating to SWAC, and personally destroyed it as classified waste. As the team members brought the things in to my office, I could sense Icon doing something to help them forget about SWAC, and I wondered if he'd done things like that before, when I wasn't aware of him.

"Not really forget," he corrected me. "I wouldn't want to leave any weird blanks in their lives. I'm just blurring it up and making it all seem disinteresting. Right now they're losing the details, and they just won't think about it any more. Ask them about it tomorrow and they'll tell you it dead-ended—didn't pan out. Had to be that way; otherwise, it wouldn't have been trashed."

When the models, diagrams, reports, and data in the computer were all beyond salvage, or at least interpretation, I buzzed Dan Kearney, HOLEX's administrative vice president and my oldest associate, and asked him to come in. I also called Legal and asked them to send over the stenographer we used for contract talks. She was beside my desk and ready when Dan arrived.

"What's up, Jan?" he asked.

"I'm resigning, and as owner of all the voting stock, I'm appointing you president of this place, beginning tomorrow. I'm also selling you all the voting stock; we'll set a payment schedule you can handle with no sweat. Have Legal set that up, too. All I'm holding on to are my patents." I smiled pleasantly; Dan's eyebrows had climbed halfway up his forehead. "Any questions?" I asked.

"Yeah, one or two. First off, what the hell is this all about? Care to tell me?"

"I'm leaving to do some private research on my own—a kind I can't do here. Let's talk about the terms of the stock sale. I want to get this all taken care of this morning."

We did. Then Dan and the steno left and I cleared the personal items out of my desk. That done, I drove home to soak in the hot tub and decide what the hell I was going to do next.

And as strange as it might seem, I felt absolutely cool about the whole thing. I could always start another company if I wanted to.

*   *   *

The next morning I began the first day of my new research with a trip to a metaphysical bookstore I'd seen in Westwood, near the UCLA campus. It's one of those places where the owner is the only clerk and has to hang a sign on the door when she goes out to lunch. She was a pleasant, middle-aged woman, who beamed when I asked her to select a twenty-volume beginner's library for me. She began to make a list on an invoice form; it didn't take her long.

She added a couple of dictionaries. "These are very important," she told me. "Use them if you feel bored or confused or sleepy while studying. There'll usually be a word you didn't understand, back just before it stopped going well."

I was listening, but in the back of my mind I was wondering why she seemed vaguely familiar. She reminded me of someone, I decided. She promised to have the books delivered that afternoon. I paid the bill and started to leave. At the door, I stopped and looked back at her.

"How many texts should be included in a really good basic education on metaphysics?" I asked.

Something had changed about her, as if I'd caught her with her guard down. She'd lost her librarian mask. But she recovered smoothly.

"About a hundred. Let me know when you're ready for the rest of them, and I'll have them delivered, too." She said it as if reading twenty or a hundred books on metaphysics was just a pleasant summer project.

Then she turned away and I left.

TWO

My attention returned to the present and I looked out the window beside me. The jet had leveled off and was over the Mojave Desert. Unbelting, I found throwaway plastic plates and real cups in a cabinet, ran myself some coffee, then took a sandwich labeled "tuna salad" from the fridge and sat down with it—my third snack since dinner. But I did it more or less on automatic. It was review time, and mainly, my attention was still on the past seven weeks.

After my experience with Holo-Clone and trashing the SWAC project, I'd become a temporary recluse. Except for a break to sign legal papers and have a last round of drinks with my co-founders, I spent the next five days reading those first twenty books. I'm an extremely fast reader, but it still took eighteen hours a day to do it, with an occasional break for pushups or the heavy rope to pump some blood around. Not that there seemed to be any hurry to finish, but when I'm into something new, I tend to get into it pretty intensely.

Just before I finished the last one, the doorbell rang; it was a delivery service with six more boxes of books. The old girl must have been psychic, I told myself, but I didn't really believe that, in spite of having just read twenty books on metaphysics.

The COD bill was a lot more than I'd expected, but what the hell. The novice tends to be taken advantage of until he learns his way around. Besides, the service was remarkably well timed, and I owed her something for her hopefully expert advice.

When I opened the numbered boxes, I found a neatly typed list of all the titles, in the sequence to be studied, and after looking at the first volume, I decided that the bill had been too low. It was an original handwritten

9

manuscript from a monastery in the French Alps during the fifteenth century. The only catch was that I'd never studied French.

"Don't worry," Icon said in my head. "Fifteenth-century French is no problem."

"Yeah?" I thought back at him. "And where the hell were you when I was taking Spanish in high school?"

Thirty days and nights later, at about 4 A.M., I finished a volume and reached down for the next one on the floor by my chair. All I found was the rug. The stack was gone; I'd finished. Irritation flashed. Somewhere in there I'd expected to find some key data, or maybe one big datum, that would pull things together for me. Instead, I'd loaded myself up with seven weeks' worth of odds and ends.

I stood up, stretched, and tossed one very frazzled dictionary into the fireplace, then stood watching it burn. "Well, hell," I said out loud, "integration time."

"Wrong!" Icon replied. "Bacon and eggs time." I heard his/my stomach growl, and agreed, and we headed for the kitchen. While I was eating, I realized that this was my first hot meal in at least a week.

When I'd finished, I took a long shower, then went for a walk on the beach to begin sorting out the jumbled mess called metaphysics. There seemed to be a lot more noise than data. Luckily, I'd learned early to read the data without being bothered by the noise. Some of my best patents came from ideas I'd sorted out of the written confusion of other researchers. Metaphysics promised to be a real test of that ability; it had even more noise in it than economics or psychology!

I'd stopped to rest on the sand, sitting with my knees drawn up, my back against a big mass of rock that had fallen from the cliff, when three pieces of data came together with an audible click. No light flash, just a click.

Most reports of cursors moving away from their icons were about experiences in space/time, and usually involved people being drawn to some point in space and time without their control.

On the other hand, visitors to what's been called

Nirvana, God, the prime mover unmoved, the static, and lots of other names, had described reality as being two-dimensional for a brief moment during their transfer from the body to the static or god state. Some had called it "stopping the world," and said it was like holding on to and navigating in a two-dimensional realm.

All the visitors to the static area seemed to have the idea that they'd been invited to stay with the static—to join or merge with it. They'd wanted to, but something had drawn them back into the three-dimensional reality and their bodies, their icons.

As might be expected with my background, I viewed that in electronic, rather than religious terms. In a system of flows—electrons, gases, or fluids—a static zone will build up around the edges of the system. A static zone could be laminar, between flow layers, or it could be a stagnation, or simply neutrally charged.

By the time I pulled those three data together—about a second after the click—I felt a pop, and I was outside my body, looking down at it leaning loosely now against the rock. Another pop, and there was my body, stuck like a decal to a two-dimensional reality. At the same time, I sensed a darkness at the periphery of my vision. Then it occurred to me to increase the reversal of my cursor charge, and instantly I shot backwards very fast for a few milliseconds, after which my direction of view did a 180-degree flip-flop and I was at the static boundary layer. The darkness I'd sensed went two-dimensional and was gone. There was only a light golden stillness.

I felt for all the world like an electron in a TV tube—one that had lost its way en route to the screen and ended up stuck on the static discharge boundary layer. I started laughing to myself about the poor bastards who had come here and thought they had found God.

But that was short-lived; even we superior scientific types can be fooled. The quiet ended. I heard, or I sensed as hearing, a very clear, booming voice:

"WHAT'S A GOOD-LOOKING CURSOR LIKE YOU DOING IN A VIDEO GAME LIKE THAT?"

I jumped, figuratively speaking. The literature on

this sort of phenomenon hadn't mentioned voices, only urges. And the voice was friendly—loud but friendly— with a touch of amused laughter. I let go of whatever I was holding onto to maintain location, and the rate of getting there was duplicated in reverse. I was suddenly leaning against the rock with a loud ringing noise in my head.

"Easy does it," Icon said, "or you'll burn out both our fuses. Next time let the hammer down easy, okay?"

"Sorry."

After we'd sat there for a minute, recovering, he spoke again. "Well, go back and answer the man. Excuse me, the IT, not the man. Cursors like him and you don't have gender or sex, it's icons who have sex." He paused. "You can call him just plain *Great Cursor* if you want. And you don't have to be afraid of It. It won't eat you, although It'll invite you to be eaten."

Go back and answer the man, the It, the Great Cursor. Hmm. Without wondering why, and without knowing exactly how I did it, I repeated the polarity reversal process, and there I was back in Nirvana, or my version of it, anyway.

"Hi!" It said. "That was a quick recovery, my son!" He paused, then asked again: "What's a good-looking cursor like you doing in a video game like that?"

"*It's the only game in town,*" I said cautiously. He laughed loudly.

And that became our standard opening exchange for the daily visits I had with It over the next two weeks.

I'd been up all night reading a new addition to my library, and went to sleep in the chair about 6 A.M. Two hours later I woke up with an urge to drive to Hollywood. I couldn't see any good reason to, actually, or even any poor reason, but I gave in without arguing and left.

It was Sunday. I'd lost track of the date, but I did know it was Sunday. I drove around for a while and then parked to get out of the before-church traffic. Things felt strange to me—otherworldly, dreamlike— but I knew I was awake.

After a little I found myself in a park, and lay down to rest on the grass by an old orange tree. The place felt lazy, and I wanted to flow with it, but when I closed my eyes, I went out of phase and drifted slowly into the static discharge boundary layer to visit the Great Cursor. It was in the serenity mode, as usual, with all polarizations at zero.

"Hi!" It said as usual. "What's a good-looking cursor like you doing in a video game like that?" And as usual I answered, "It's the only game in town."

Like other seekers of wisdom and truth who had visited It, I was full of unasked questions about lots of things—such as who I really am, who we are, how It came to be there, is there any other destiny for a cursor besides attaching itself to icons . . . You get the idea. I was always primed and ready to ask them before going there, but after arriving I never seemed to get them asked.

The Great Cursor stirred. "Merge with me, my son, and be at peace," It said, the way It always did, the thought resonating a bit like some metaphysical "OM."

And again I found the offer easy to refuse. Just sitting there all day long, being It, watching other cursors move with their icons around the Reality Grid, seemed like no destiny at all. The static discharge boundary layer was an interesting place to visit, but I wouldn't want to live there.

"Have you used the wisdom I showed you the last time?" It asked.

"Yep. I can use phase locking to locate myself at other grid locations now when I reverse polarity, but holding phase with a scene is hard for me. I keep bouncing around a lot and seeing things that don't make much sense."

There was never any question about their reality; they were nice and solid. And they had a sense of internal logic to them, even if I didn't know yet what it was. That's what I'd been working on lately—trying to learn my way around in what seemed like the backstage side of reality.

"You must be able to control your out-of-icon travel

before you can begin your quest," It said placidly.
Quest?

It paused to let the idea sink in, then went on. "Since
you won't join me here, as most do who get this far, it
means you're a free cursor. You must make your own
destiny.

"Now, freedom can be a curse for cursors, or it can
be a great boon. There is a path for you to follow, and
the map for it is hidden within you. The key to reading
that map is your urge for wisdom and destiny. There
are many traps and pitfalls and false leads. No one, not
even I, can show you the way. I have observed many
paths, and no two are the same.

"But I can give you a hint—just one. *Do not seek
satisfaction.*"

It went silent then, and shuddered. It occurred to
me that I had never seen the Great Cursor stay out of
zero flux for so long. I wondered if that accounted for
the shudder, or if it had come from thinking about
satisfaction. I'd never thought of satisfaction as being all
that heavy.

While I waited for It to settle down, a scene from
The Wizard of Oz—the movie—floated by in a wave of
inner vision: Toto pulling the curtain aside to reveal the
phony wizard. I wondered why I'd thought of that.

When It seemed settled enough, I asked, "How did I
become a free cursor, and what does it mean?"

It waited a while longer before answering. "Hmm;
you do have a lot of questions! You free cursors always
want to know everything up front, which would spoil
the challenge of freedom." It paused again, as if considering. "I'll say just one thing more before I send you off
to begin your quest. Legend has it that a Great Maker
made the generator for grids and cursors, and then
divided itself into twelve Players, all totally independent. They began the play that you are now in."

For whatever reason, telling me this excited It again,
and It paused a long while to stabilize. A part of the
golden static energy field had become discolored with a
slow-moving wave of green. When the static boundary
had become smooth once more, It continued.

"Your auto-programming circuits have been disengaged," It told me, "and all the subroutines for satisfaction are gone. Your Player has disconnected you: You are free. Follow your own path skillfully and it may lead you to a place where you can program your own future. Fail and you'll become the slave cursor of a different Player, the one who designed your path."

It said one part of that a little more slowly than the rest, so that it caught my attention as strongly as what It had said earlier about satisfaction. "Follow your own path skillfully," It had said, *and it may lead you to a place where you can program your own future.*

For a moment It regarded me silently. "Go," It said at last. "You are now a Primary Cursor. That's PC for short."

As I was returning to my icon, where I'd left him under the orange tree, I heard It say after me, "And come back if you get lost."

Then I was back, merged with my icon, resting on the grass beneath the orange tree. I inhaled deeply the aroma of the park—a sea breeze had blown away the smog—and thought how good it was to be alive, here on this beautiful part of the reality grid called Earth. I'd forgotten the admonition not to seek satisfaction on the path, and felt a great rush of it through my icon and me.

But the feeling faded quickly as I thought of all the questions I hadn't asked; I always seemed to come away having more than I'd started with. The seven weeks since the accident had been filled with attempts to get some of them answered. After two weeks of visiting the Great Cursor, I seemed further, if anything, from the answers.

"I could have told you it would work that way," Icon said in our head. "Remember the wizard in *The Wizard of Oz?*"

"Of course I do."

He grinned with our mouth. "I think it fits It very nicely. Hell, It probably scripted the damn scene in the first place."

"Go back to sleep," I said. "I need to do some thinking—without interruptions."

For most of my life I hadn't knowingly talked with Icon, or recognized him for what he was. I'd always had the idea that there was only one of us. But after I discovered him as a being in his own right, he became the best friend I knew.

Another urge hit me then, like the one I'd had that morning, and I got up and followed it across the park— with Icon, who hadn't gone back to sleep. Things felt dreamlike again, surrealistic, but at the same time very real, as if I were walking through a vacuum in which a lot of the knowledge of life was missing. I'd look at something, and most of the concepts, values, connections I'd ordinarily have associated with it were absent! It was a *strange* feeling.

Near the center of the park I met a guy dressed in sackcloth—regular burlap. You can see almost anything in Hollywood, and I don't mean just in films, but I'd never seen a man like him before. He was giving out little wooden crosses.

It seemed to me I should know what this was all about, but the information was gone. *What the heck*, I thought, and took one. Immediately I got a strange feeling, a sort of rapture, but it didn't really feel like my rapture. It's as if it were supplied, along with the cross.

"Carry it up the hill," he said. "It's the key to Paradise."

Turning around, I found a hill that hadn't been there before. There are a lot of hills around Hollywood, but this hadn't been one of them. As I started to climb, the cross quickly got bigger and heavier, so I had to carry it over my shoulder. The path was hot and dusty, and Icon and I worked up a quick sweat that washed the rapture off in a hurry.

This definitely felt like the way to go, all right; there was absolutely no satisfaction in it. Not for a PC, anyway; some of the people sweating up the hill with me seemed to be doing fine. Finally, I got to the top, and the same man in sackcloth was at the head of the long line in front of me, collecting the crosses as the people filed past.

The air was stuffy, hard to breathe, and the line moved slowly. I felt as if I were going to pass out, but it never occurred to me to just put the cross down and leave. Finally, the man took my cross and directed me to some stairs that led upward, without visible support, into the clouds.

I climbed them, wondering why no one had installed an escalator. At least it was cooler in the clouds. I soon ran into the end of another, even slower-moving queue. Just above the clouds, the stairs opened onto a wide platform, half as big as a football field. The same man who'd given out and collected the crosses was there, too. Either he knew a shortcut or he was identical triplets.

This time he was taking up icons. He had some kind of hand-held apparatus to extract the cursor, and as the cursor emerged, the man touched the icon, two-dimensionalizing it. Then an assistant hung it on a hook next to the last one. The hooks carried them away on a conveyor like the ones in dry-cleaning shops.

I felt and heard an internal scream. "Don't send me to the cleaners again! Please! I hate that place, and I hate going 2-D! I hate it every time!" It was Icon. He'd startled hell out of me.

"I should have recognized this place sooner," he babbled, then, realizing I was confused, he calmed down. "I forgot," he said, and gestured around us. "You wouldn't know about these things. This is what paradise means to these people. But they never tell you right up front. That's part of their sales strategy."

"You mean—you've been here before?"

"Oh, Lord!" he groaned. "Too many times."

All of that went on inside our head, of course. I nudged the lady in front of me and asked, "What line are we in?"

She turned and scowled angrily at me, as if I were crazy, then turned away. Obviously the rapture hadn't lasted for her, either; more likely it had turned into something else. I stepped sideways out of line for a better view and saw the cross-giver or his triplet handing a new, snowy-white, 2-D icon to each cursor as it came up to him. The cursor would merge with his new icon, which was still in 2-D, then move sideways through a very narrow door, no more than a slit. I got the notion that it was narrow like that so no one could sneak in. But it could work both ways; it also occurred to me that once you went in like that, maybe the icon went 3-D on you. Then you could be stuck in there for eternity, maybe with time off for good behavior.

"Icon," I asked, "what goes on on the other side of that door? Do you know?"

"Not firsthand. They never let us street people in there. We always get two-dimensionalized, reconditioned, and sent off to storage to wait for our next cursor. But I've heard it's dullsville: no screwing or anything like that. Hell, those icons they're giving out don't even have any organs for it. The story I've heard is, you get a cloud and a harp, and spend your time floating around on one while you play the other."

Rumor or not, I didn't like the sound of it. "Hold on," I said, "I'll be back in a jiffy," then reversed polarity. Free of Icon, I popped through the slit door and beyond.

There wasn't any solid ground in there at all, just space all pink and gold, with little silver clouds floating in it. And a lot of cursors, each in its snowy-white icon, all three-dimensional, sure as hell. I have no idea how many; they extended as far as I could see, gathered in large and small groups. All of them were facing a beautiful, opalescent glow, playing their harps and singing. And exuding a rapture you'd hardly believe! I mean, if rapture's what you want, that would definitely be the place to go.

It seemed to me I'd heard about this place, but I couldn't remember what. Being a free cursor, I relocated myself close to the glow to get a good look. Maybe I shouldn't have been surprised, but I was. The source of the glow was the Great Cursor! It looked at me.

"Hi!" It said. "What's a good-looking PC like you doing in a video game like this?"

I knew It was going to say that. Before I could

answer, It added: "I didn't expect to see you here; I didn't think you were the type."

I didn't know what to say, but It made it unnecessary. "You'll have to excuse me," It said. "I can't talk to you any more just now. It's my adoration time." Then It took Its attention off me, and I relocated myself back outside the slit door with Icon, who was almost to the head of the line.

"Do you have any idea how to get out of here?" I asked. I had the distinct feeling that we couldn't just turn around and go back down the stairs the way we'd come. For one thing, there wasn't room; the stairs were straight and narrow and full of people. I could always relocate, of course, as a free cursor, but I didn't want to lose Icon. We were buddies, and besides that, it seemed to me I'd need him.

"I think so," he replied. "I think you'll be able to relocate both of us when I'm 2-D. When the guy 2-D's me, you knee him in the groin—just think it—and I'll give him an electric shock at the same time. Then you grab me and we'll get out of here across the two-dimensional reality. I'll remember how to go 3-D again."

I did, and we did, and he did, and we woke up standing in the park again. My earlier feeling of surrealism was gone, and things felt normal again. The hill that shouldn't have been there wasn't any longer, but the guy handing out crosses was; I decided his icon had to be a clone. He tried to get me to take another cross, as if he'd never seen me before, but I told him no thanks, and we walked away.

"I'm hungry," said a voice inside my head. "You buy the steak and beer, and I'll handle the dessert."

Sure enough, it was evening already. I'd wakened under the orange tree just after church let out and somehow spent the rest of the afternoon climbing hills and stairs and waiting in line. I should have stuck with 2-D video games and stayed away from holographic labs, I told myself.

It felt good to be in a familiar environment again. We went into a steakhouse not far away and ordered up; what the hell, I told myself, a little satisfaction couldn't hurt. And sure enough, Icon arranged for dessert: Our great-looking waitress invited me home with her.

What with one thing and another, and another, when we did get to sleep, we didn't wake up until nearly noon. And even then we didn't get up right away. As our icons lay in relaxed satisfaction, the waitress cursor and I floated up into some sort of seventh heaven of our own. I told her she was a fantastic playmate, and asked if she wanted to keep her sex life at play or shift into the marriage mode.

"No marriage for me," she said. "It doesn't fit with a lot of my other plans. Or yours, either. Let's keep it purely play."

Later, after lunch, she told me a raunchy joke I can't remember, except for the line "kiss my grits," which she delivered in an imitation of a waitress in a TV sitcom. It surprised me; this waitress didn't seem like the kind who'd tell raunchy jokes. Then she kissed me goodbye and shoved me out the door, saying, "Go now, and get back to your quest."

I'd gone half a block before it got through to me—she knew about my quest! And she'd also been the first cursor, except the Great Cursor, ever to speak to me outside the icon. I ran back to her place, but no one answered. That seemed impossible. I'd only said goodbye to her two minutes earlier. I tried the door, and it opened, but there was absolutely no waitress there.

A strange feeling of déjà vu washed over me. Something very peculiar was going on, I told myself. My attention went back to the urge.

THREE

At least the grid stayed familiar—the same old world, the same LaBrea Avenue running north to the green Santa Monica Mountains nearby—but I was feeling odd again.

I followed the urge down the street and met a bald-headed young guy dressed in an orange robe. As far as I could see—and I looked him over carefully—he didn't have any crosses, so I listened to his spiel. It didn't take long to realize that he wanted to help me on a journey to visit the Great Cursor.

"No, thank you," I told him, "I just got back from there."

I continued to follow the urge, and was starting to wonder if it was a bum steer when I found myself standing in front of a reading room. The urge nudged me toward the door, so I went in. There were no crosses or orange robes, the word *science* was prominently displayed, and there were racks and shelves of books. A very handsome elderly lady came from behind a desk and asked if she could help me.

"I want to find my path to the cursor reprogramming facility," I told her.

She looked at me until I began to squirm. When she spoke, her voice and the look in her eye were somehow familiar.

"Your path," she said, "is back to the park for a nap under the orange tree." Then she turned her back on me and returned to her desk, where she began to work on some papers. I took her advice and went back to the park. The grass under my orange tree was vacant, so I laid down and closed our eyes, but my attention was still on the elderly lady at the reading room.

"Take a nap," I told Icon. "I'll be back shortly." Then, popping out with reversed polarity, I relocated to the reading room to see the lady scientist. There was something I had to try there. How had she known about the park and the orange tree? And why had her look seemed familiar? On top of that, I was sure she'd read a lot of the books there, and probably a lot of others, and it seemed to me that some of them might be helpful.

I pulled her from her icon, which went to sleep with their head on the desk. What I needed to get, conversation wouldn't handle, even assuming she'd "talk" outside her icon, so I went for a little cursor tête-á-tête in the meld mode. In about five minutes I'd absorbed her whole lifetime of dedicated reading. Not that I could have told it to you, but I felt it inflowing, knew I had it. It would be there if, when I needed it. Then I put her back into her icon.

Some technique! I thought, and wished it had occurred to me before. It could certainly save a lot of path time. Some really strange things had gone on with me since the holo accident, especially in the past twenty-four hours, but this one made me feel as if I were coming along pretty darned well.

Icon was under the orange tree where I'd left him, and woke up as soon as I moved in. He proposed that we go look for the waitress again, but I told him he'd have to wait. The quest urge was stronger than ever, and somehow I knew it was *mine*, not something imposed on me by the Great Cursor.

We were enjoying one of those sea breezes that makes for some cool clear June days in L.A., so I walked down the north side of the street to enjoy the sunshine. Things looked and smelled real enough, but I still had that feeling of walking through an idea vacuum. Only I was getting used to it by now, and it felt simply different instead of actually weird.

It also told me that something strange was likely to happen.

Ahead of me about a block, a large sign caught my eye: INSTAMAB, with a spaceship logo at the top. When I got there, I found a smaller sign above the door: "Institute of Advanced Mental Abilities, Hollywood Introduction Center."

"Institute of Advanced Mental Abilities." That had to be what INSTAMAB stood for. Vaguely it seemed to me that I knew about this, too, like the day before with the crosses, but I couldn't remember. The only thing that came to me was a single word—"Menties."

The word and the feeling both passed when a salesman emerged from the door and stepped in front of me. He was about twenty, with thin lips, tousled blond hair, and the confidence briskness of the well-drilled. I knew right away this was going to be the strange experience I'd been waiting for, because his lips weren't in sync with his words. When I looked at his mouth, it was hard to follow what he was saying, so I tried to look past him and just listen. It wasn't as easy as you'd think.

"Come in and get a battery of free commensality measurements," he said, "and we'll fit you with a Kobold Mind to define your operating parameters and explain everything that's happened to you since the beginning of the universe." At least that's what he seemed to say.

The Kobold Mind: I got the notion of a new computer with some interesting programs thrown in. "I'm not interested in the beginning of the universe," I told him, "but I do have a problem. I'm looking for the cursor reprogramming facility, and no one seems to know where it is."

He seemed delighted. His mouth took off in one direction, but the words came out more or less like this: "You've come to the right place. Our latest model PC, the Kobold Mind, can solve any problem you've got or ever will have. With it, reprogramming your life will be a snap. You can be the kind of cursor you always knew you could be."

Or words to that effect. I knew the computer people had been making advances hand over fist lately; maybe his company had come up with a breakthrough. And he'd said it was a PC; it might be fun to play with a personal computer after years of working with high-capacity, superspeed, mainframe models.

"Sounds interesting," I said. "Maybe I should get one." I'd look over the documentation and play with it—see what it could do.

He ushered me inside. It was a strange kind of computer store. I didn't see a single computer, just an old black and white television, but they did have a lot of books. He drew me a cup of coffee, told me he'd have someone with me in a minute, and left. While I sat there, two grim-faced people walked through, looking as if they owned the place. They were wearing what looked like some sort of space uniforms—dressy-looking silver-colored jumpsuits with miniatures of the INSTA-

MAB spaceship logo pinned to their collars. One was a girl who looked about eighteen years old; she had enough braid and ribbons on her shoulders and chest to impress Admiral Halsey. This place was starting to look stranger and stranger.

A minute later another young woman, this one wearing civvies and a near-genuine smile, came out and led me into an office. She was nice, but she had the same speech problem as the sidewalk salesman. On the wall behind her desk there was a large photo portrait of a man. I was sure I'd known him somewhere—known him very well indeed—but I was equally sure I'd never seen his face.

"Is that the president of INSTAMAB?" I asked.

She looked blankly at me for a moment, then followed my gaze. "Oh," she said, "that's our founder. He's the one who established the institute."

I was still having trouble with the out-of-sync lips, but I was still interested, so I decided to follow through on this. Hell, I could afford it easily enough.

"I'll take your best model," I told her.

She asked something then about signing up for the full program. I didn't really follow her words, but I thought I knew what she had to be saying.

"Right," I answered. "I'll take all the programs you've developed for the Kobold Mind."

Her smile became very genuine; she positively beamed. Quickly she wrote up the sales ticket, then led me out to a chunky cashier with chestnut hair in a bun on top, and handed the ticket to her.

The cashier stared suspiciously at me. "That will be $120,000 with discounts," she said. "Check or credit card?"

I heard her clearly enough, but I said it anyway. "A hundred and twenty thousand?! For a PC?!" I'd expected something more like two thousand—ten at the outside. "Before I go that high," I said, "I'll need to see your system specs and have some time to play around with the equipment. That's an awful lot of money for a PC; your competition doesn't charge nearly that much."

The salesgirl looked stricken, and kind of slid back

into her office. But not the cashier. She jumped up and ran out of the room yelping somebody's name that I didn't get. Obviously I'd broken some deep taboo, and the place for me was out of there. But before I got to the door, a very large guy in uniform stopped me. His demeanor said military police, and while he didn't have an armband, he did wear a white hard hat shaped like a helmet liner, and carried a nightstick like MPs do.

"What did you do to that girl?" he asked in a very firm voice.

I asked Icon, "Did you do something I missed?"

"No, but I'm going to do something to this MP if he slaps that stick against his palm one more time."

Just then he did it again, and Icon did something too quick for me to see. I grabbed the guy as he started to fall, and let him down gently so he wouldn't be injured. Then Icon and I hurried out.

Back on the sidewalk, I looked around, then continued walking east. The California sun made the boulevard bright, and the concrete felt nice and solid and dependable beneath my feet—very this-worldly. Maybe, I thought, that INSTAMAB place and its Menties wouldn't have seemed quite as crazy if there hadn't been the problem of the strange way they talked. And if they hadn't wanted $120,000 for a PC! That Kobold Mind must be pretty powerful.

About two blocks farther on I met another member of the same group, in civvies, handing out free tickets for commensality measurements. Her smile was very warm and genuine—no mean trick with a perfect stranger. And I had no problem at all understanding her; her words and lips were in perfect sync.

"This is for you," she said. She was holding out a ticket to me. I reached past it and took her hand.

"I was just at your introduction center back there," I told her, "and signed up for one of the new Kobold Mind PCs with all the software. But when the cashier told me it cost $120,000. . . ." I let it hang there. She let me keep her hand, and laughed a friendly laugh. Her eyes were marvelous, a clear sapphire blue.

"You seem to have misunderstood," she said. "Buy me a coffee and I'll try to explain our program."

Without waiting for an answer, she led me to a nearby café. Once we had our coffee, she asked, "What's holding you back in life?"

"Right now," I answered, "I've got two things on my mind. First, I'd like to know more about this Kobold Mind and maybe buy one. And second, I have a nagging feeling that I know you from somewhere. You're very beautiful." I reached out and took her hand again. "You probably think that's a line, and I guess it is. But it's also true."

Her eyes were bright and alive, and her answer was light. "You're joshing. Did my chief send you here to check me out or something?"

I gave her the Boy Scout sign. "No, on both counts. An urge sent me this way, and curiosity and your eyes brought me in here. Have you used the Kobold Mind?"

Her eyes were tan. I would have sworn they'd been blue a minute before. Then she laughed, and it didn't matter what color her eyes were.

"The kobold mind," she told me, "isn't something we sell. You've heard the old programmer's saying? 'Garbage in, garbage out.' Well, the kobold mind is the garbage content of the unconscious mind: the part that causes you problems."

Not a computer. I began to lose interest in the subject, but I had to keep her talking—see if her eyes changed again, and maybe recall what was so familiar about her.

"And our programs," she was saying, "have nothing to do with computers. They're to help you get rid of all the stored garbage that makes up the kobold mind."

I could see little energy beams, like light beams, from my body to hers, and decided that Icon must be doing something to her. She was beginning to glow, and her voice, friendly before, was starting to sound fond.

"Would you give me a demonstration?" I asked. "About how it's done?" My original quest, whatever it was, had been overridden by one more in line with Icon's interests, and meanwhile, I'd missed another change in her eyes. They were hazel now, not tan.

"A demonstration? Here? I can't do that. We're not allowed to give demonstrations in public places." Her voice sounded rather stern, but her eyes and aura were otherwise.

Another new development! I was seeing auras now! Meanwhile, she went on talking, but I stopped paying attention because visuals, memories of other faces, came floating between us, totally distracting me: A teacher I'd fallen in love with when I was sixteen, a waitress with a story about "kiss my grits," an elderly female scientist telling me to go to the park, and an eight-year-old girl who let me play with her black cat in the park one afternoon when I was ten. They all seemed to have a connection, but I didn't have an inkling of what it might be.

I stood up, interrupting her, and took her hand. "Come with me," I said, "and I'll show you how to float from your body and be a primary cursor."

She looked, smiled, and got up. There was something about the smile that went with the beautiful eyes and the voice: It was familiar, and somehow I had the notion that my quest was coming along just as well as Icon's. Out on the sidewalk once more, she said, "Come on. I have the keys to a friend's apartment. It's a lot closer than Malibu."

She led me up a cross street toward Franklin Avenue. I didn't remember mentioning Malibu; as a matter of fact, I'd almost forgotten that I lived there. Well, I told myself, ride along with it. Things seem to be going in the right direction.

The apartment building was in the luxury class, and the armed security man at the door nodded to her when we went in. Apparently they knew her there. The posh apartment was on the eleventh floor, the living room occupying a corner of the building, with glass doors on the south and west sides opening onto a balcony with planters. The view was excellent, southward across the Los Angeles Basin and west along the Santa Monica Mountains, with the Hollywood Hills looming greenly close by to the north. The Washingtonia palms along Whitman Street reached almost as high as the balcony.

When I turned and stepped back into the living room, she was standing by the sofa with nothing on. For a moment I just stared, unbelieving.

You have to understand, I'd never particularly attracted women. I looked as if I might, but I never had. My money attracted them, when they found out I had lots of it, and there'd been a few who'd seemed to be attracted to me without benefit of wealth, but I'd never had a lot of sex appeal. And now this was the second really lovely girl to make a move on me in less than twenty-four hours who couldn't have known I was rich.

Believe me, she was worth staring at. She had a lovely athletic body, and as I stepped to meet her arms, I discovered her eyes had changed again; they were a light gold, harmonizing perfectly with her golden tan. Then I was too close to notice.

After an incredible half hour, she lay beside me with her head on my shoulder, her blue eyes on mine. "Now I'm ready to go flying with you," she murmured. I reversed polarity and helped her from her icon. Together we drifted to the ceiling and viewed our bodies now asleep on the couch. Then, without my intending to, we did a cursor meld. Within a few moments I had all her data about kobold minds, and a certain amount of other stuff she gave without my asking.

When the meld dissolved, I thought for a moment she'd disappeared. Then I saw she was back in her icon. She lay there looking up at me with those black eyes. Black?! I'd missed it again! The impish grin on her face seemed to say she was waiting for me to realize something. I did; it was among the extra data she'd given me during our cursor meld. I got back in Icon and bolted up off the couch. She was already on her feet, backing away, laughing.

"You're not!" I said. "You weren't! You couldn't be." There weren't words for the realization that was sinking in more firmly by the moment.

"It's her again!" Icon was saying. "It's her again!

Catch her, turkey! Or at least say something! We've really got ourselves a winner!"

Catch her? With the realizations buffeting me, I could hardly stand up. I leaned against the end of the couch, looking at her where she stood behind a chair by the balcony doors. And as I stared, groping for words, she changed. Not just the eyes. The athletic figure and impish coed face became a marvelously beautiful mature woman, her hair long and black, her eyes gold, a face that could have belonged to the never-seen mother of the eight-year-old I'd met at the park, long ago. Her bearing and aura suggested a Greek goddess—a real one.

She stepped toward me, and said something completely out of character for her appearance. "Wanna kiss my grits?" The waitress! Another step and the voice became elderly: "Your path is back to the park for a nap under the orange tree." And another: "I have the keys to a friend's apartment. It's a lot closer than Malibu."

Malibu! I *hadn't* mentioned Malibu!

My knees were starting to give way. This, on top of everything else that had happened over the last two days, was overloading my circuits. Now the additional data she'd given me in the meld came flooding in in full, overwhelming detail. I blacked out and fell over the arm of the couch.

I woke up to find her kissing me gently. The goddess mien had softened and she was wearing loose silk lounging pajamas. When she saw my eyes open, she smiled and straightened.

"Well," she said, "did I pass the screen test? Or do I have to run the rest of my repertoire by you?"

"No! No more repertoire! You've got the job and anything else you want. Just hold still for a minute and don't change." I was actually, literally shaking.

She laughed infectiously, and I managed a smile. "Shall I call you AC, for actress cursor?" I asked, trying to cover my shakiness with wit.

"No," she said, softly. "Call me DC, for director cursor. I'm a Director of Playground Activity in this place you think of as the Reality Grid." She helped me up. "Now be a good playmate and turn your back. There was one more me you saw a while ago but couldn't confront."

Carefully I turned away, and after a moment felt her hand on my shoulder. I was afraid to look, to see who she might have become.

"Don't be afraid, Jan. I'm not going to change this time. Not physically." Surprisingly, she chuckled then. "I just want to be here to catch you when you faint." Someone else had talked like that—not just the voice but the style, the subtle timing. Gooseflesh crawled from my scalp to my feet as a perfume invaded my nostrils, one I hadn't smelled for twenty years.

"Jan Ambers, would you do me a favor and help me pack tomorrow?"

I didn't faint, but I felt a long-hidden grief begin to well up in me, and tears started to run down my cheeks. That had been my first love, not my lover but my love, my teacher when I was sixteen. I hadn't cried when she moved away, but I'd felt lost, really lost. Devastated. And I'd felt it again, more desperately, two years later when I spent the whole summer trying to track her down. Now she put her arms around me, her cheek against the back of my shoulder, and held me until the grief had flowed off and I began to chuckle.

I reached back and pinched her lightly, and she laughed, buffeting me gently above the ear. We ended up back on the couch in each other's arms, still laughing. "Think of the best playmate you ever had," she said.

There wasn't any question: the salesgirl who had brought me here and the waitress. They'd each been marvelous.

"How sweet of you," she said archly before I could answer. "Both of the me's you've seduced lately. I suppose you're too sated now to be interested any more."

We started tickling then, and quickly graduated to something better. Satisfaction had become more important than any urge to find a cursor reprogramming facility. Afterward, resting, I began to wonder if the Great Cursor was as wise as I'd thought.

She read my mind. "It's just a little mischievous," she said. "It likes to put people on. You're still on your quest, incidentally, right here on this couch, and you've passed your first tests with flying colors. Most people, going through what you've been through lately, would be trapped somewhere, insane."

I lay there very satisfied indeed, not wondering or worrying about what was beneath all this—what it all meant. Things were going along beautifully, wherever I was headed. Two days earlier I'd been wondering, "Is this any way to run a video game?" Now all I could say was, "Wow! What a way to run a video game!"

FOUR

We awoke to the sound of a lock being turned; I'd forgotten the apartment wasn't hers.

"El, is that you?" someone called.

The voice was female. And my Greek goddess's name was El.

"I know you're here," the voice said. "And I see a man's clothes! I know who it is, too."

Then, pretending to pout at the lack of response: "Is that any way to treat your favorite monitor cursor?"

Monitor cursor? So her friend knew about—things like that.

At the last words she emerged from the entry hall and stood in plain view, looking around as if she didn't see us on the couch—even though I was a vivid pink. She was a nice-looking middle-aged woman who could have passed inspection in any Marine Corps outfit. Then she vanished right in front of me, replaced by the biggest black cat I'd ever seen! Bigger than any black panther—in the two-hundred-pound category. More like a black Mato Grosso jaguar.

And I wasn't a bit scared. The feeling was fascination.

After what had happened to me lately—especially today—my self-assurance was way up. Besides, I'd have felt it if she was a threat to me.

The cat looked directly at us. "Everyone gets to party but me," she said with a mock mental pout. Her words were in my head, but not in the same way Icon put words there.

"So you connected," she went on. "And obviously he made it through all the tests. Well done to both of you—to all three of us." Then to me: "Welcome back."

She moved to El and nuzzled her, taking her scent with small motions of her nostrils. Then she turned steady yellow eyes on me and paused. I sensed a question, a request for permission to approach, and I nodded. She put her nose to my chest and licked me with a raspy tongue, then stepped back.

"I'll go make us some coffee," she "said," and padded to the kitchen. Now that, I thought, would be something to see, unless she changed form again.

El smiled at me, her eyes watchful. "Do you remember your name?" she asked.

"Sure. I'm Le." It came as easily as breathing. And saying it seemed to shake loose old memories, letting me know they were there but not demanding examination.

Now Icon laughed in our head. "You're starting to get the picture. This isn't our first visit with these two, not even in this lifetime."

That's when the connection occurred to me. But the last time I'd seen—Monitor Cursor, she'd only weighed six or seven pounds. It was one day when I was ten and met a girl with a black cat one Saturday afternoon in the park. I'd been on my way to play second base, but it had seemed perfectly natural to stop and play with her instead. El and MC had walked me home afterward, and said goodbye in a way that meant *see you later*. I'd caught billy heck for missing the game and staying out after dark.

We'd pretended to be children. And for me, anything beyond that pretense had been done behind a cloak that separated reality from appearance. Now I could see it; then, I couldn't. Then we were just two children and a cat, playing in the park.

But before I could remember what had really happened, I'd had to experience Holo-Clone, and meet the Great Cursor, and undergo the deprogramming of the last two days.

I looked at my last conversation with the Great Cursor. Somehow, just now, it was hard to accept what It had said about satisfaction. I didn't even feel particularly worried over what It had said about becoming a slave cursor if I failed in my quest.

El, who had looked at the memory with me, chuckled and kissed my nose. "Old DUO-HEX—you think of It as 'The Great Cursor'— is a bit of a tease," she said. "All cursors are free. It was just joshing you about being a slave if you messed up. There aren't any human robots or real slaves in this reality. Some appear to be, but only because they selected that mode to experience."

MC's voice—human voice—interrupted from the kitchen. "Coffee's ready. Come with or without clothes."

I wasn't inclined to stand nude inspection before a female marine drill inspector, but before I could get to my pants, El had my arm and was leading me to the kitchen. She was stronger than I would have imagined.

MC had changed into black lounging pajamas. She'd changed in some other ways, too. The face was basically the same but seemed younger, and the body slimmer. She didn't look like a female drill instructor any longer, or at least less like one. Either one of these women would make Lon Chaney seem like a clumsy amateur.

While we had coffee, MC reported on her day's activity, but a lot of what they said went over my head. The gist of it seemed to be that MC looked after several associations in the community who were approaching a nexus in what she referred to as their "game programs." Her job was mostly to observe without interference but make sure that each player had a choice when the nexus arrived. From what I could make of it, it was like helping people at a crucial moment. They could continue the game, go back three spaces, return to "Go," or give up games altogether and just play for fun.

That part of it I could more or less follow, but then they began making plans to handle a problem between two master gamesmen, whatever those are, and suddenly I found myself getting sleepy. I got up to move about, and the ever-practical Icon led me directly to the fridge. That reminded me that we hadn't eaten all day.

I dug out the makings for a ham and cheese omelet. They talked while I cooked, and ate while completing their plan. I tuned out their voices, watching their faces without listening to their words. They were both beautiful to watch.

"That was delicious," MC said when she'd finished. "You'll make someone a good houseboy, and I think I know who it's going to be." There was no putdown in the way she said it, though; her laugh was friendly and her direct gaze light and easy.

"Don't tease him too much," El said. "He's still recovering from two rough days of reality shock." She turned to me and took my hand. "People are always free to change, but they seldom do unless they feel forced to, or unless some shock wakens them to the possibility."

"The biggest shock to me, just now," I said, "is that I feel really comfortable being here with you two. Your shock treatment worked. Two months ago if I couldn't explain something, it simply didn't exist."

She reached and took my hand. "You're doing great, dear. But we've kept you very busy the last two days. Go home and shower; sit in that hot tub for a while and let the kinks soak out. We'll meet you there after"—she paused—"after MC and I finish our task for the night." Then she squeezed my hand and got up.

It occurred to me that I'd completely lost track of my life these last few days. I didn't even remember where I'd parked my car.

"It's in the garage downstairs," MC said, reading my thought. "I picked it up from the police impound yard this morning."

I started to ask how she knew it was mine, and why the police would release it to her, but decided not to. Then I started to ask El how she'd known I lived in Malibu, but before I could get it out, she answered.

"We had that house built for you about ten years before you bought it from us."

I stared at her as I recalled the strange circumstances that led to my finding the place. It was the exact house and setting I'd been dreaming about since high school, on a bluff overlooking the ocean. My first tour of it had been a déjà vu affair, even to the color of the bedspread in the master bedroom.

"I suppose," I said, "that you ladies have an invisibility mode?"

El smiled slightly. She also blushed, which surprised me.

"And you visited me there in your invisibility mode?"

This time she laughed out loud.

"You damned well bet we did," said MC. "And when you took up with that redheaded Amazon type, we knew something had to be done quickly. Otherwise, you'd never have been able to return to us; not in this lifetime. The decision would have been beyond your ability to make."

I remembered how that affair had ended, with the redhead running from the house nude, carrying her clothes and yammering something about witches and black cats. Once she'd stopped to try putting on her slacks, then screeched and ran again. I wondered now if she'd picked up some pinch marks on the way.

"I hadn't meant for you to know how that had happened just yet," El said. "It was a pretty drastic scene. But something did have to be done, and hints weren't working."

"Is there anything you two *can't* do?" I asked thoughtfully.

Both faces went immediately sober. "There's an awful lot we can't do," El answered. "Basically, there's an entire . . ." She stopped in midsentence, as if she'd almost said something she shouldn't. "Look, darling," she went on after a moment, "there's a lot you need to know, but we can't just dump it on you. It'll come in some pretty heavy lumps as it is, but it'll have to be in something like a reasonable sequence; and right now we don't have time. We two have too much to do in the next few hours.

"So why don't you go home and take that hot bath. This witch and her faithful familiar will see you at the stroke of midnight and show you what we do for a livelihood."

I left, and found my stainless-steel, butterfly-door jalopy in the basement garage, where MC said it would be. Ever since I'd bought that overpriced Irish import, I'd had the urge to design a real car, but it did have its good points. And on the drive out to Malibu, I had time to reconcile some of the multitude of realities I'd experienced lately.

FIVE

After a long soak in the hot tub, I showered and dressed and fixed Icon's favorite dinner—Icon's and, by extension, mine: steak and beer, with fresh rolls. It wouldn't be much of a life without Icon. By 10 P.M. we were satisfied on all counts. *Yeah, Great Cursor,* I thought, *or DUO-HEX, I'm satisfied beyond all belief.*

I imagined I could hear him laugh softly, with hardly a ripple in his static boundary layer.

I went into the living room and turned on a fire in the large rock fireplace; it gives a nice cozy effect for after-dinner brandy and reading. I was eager to get into a book that had arrived while I was gone.

It was actually a package of page proofs for my first subsidy publishing venture. It had been waiting in my mailbox when I'd stopped at the gate. The book itself was still at the publisher's, waiting to be printed. A friend of mine, traveling in China, had found an ancient manuscript in an old Himalayan temple in Chang-tu, near the borders of Tibet and Bhutan. Somehow he got the idea that I'd want it, although at that time I couldn't have cared less. He'd managed to copy it on film, which he'd smuggled out of China in his shorts. It reported on a metaphysical research project that had spanned three lifetimes for the monk-author.

Max had gone through some interesting rationalizations of why he'd taken the trouble and risk, considering he couldn't read it and had had only a brief oral description of the content through an interpreter, while I'd explained spending the time and money to get it translated and published by telling myself I didn't want to disappoint Max.

Since then my attitude had changed.

I'd talked with the translator enough to get a rough idea of the subject. Very rough. What it came down to was, the monk had studied cursor travel away from the icon, and various techniques for verification and control. The translator had found it a lot more interesting than I had, and had tried to tell me about it while I'd tried to be polite. But I hadn't paid much attention to him.

Now, scanning through the page proofs, I could see that I might want to retranslate it eventually, using electronic concepts. One of the chapters was really on cursor stabilization at selected space coordinates of the reality grid. The original author, centuries ago, had come closer to that than the translator had. In the opening chapter, where the translator had first used the terms "soul" and "body" he'd footnoted that the actual Tibetan words meant literally "luminosity" and "pattern."

He had my interest now, for sure. As I finished scanning and prepared to start reading Chapter One, a strange thing happened. Instead of seeing the book in my lap, I saw a man seated at a table covered with large loose pages of handwritten script. I found myself reading from the original and understanding it better than I could the translated version.

Then the scene vanished, and a sort of reverse déjà vu came over me, as if it were me at the table knowing that someday I'd be reading it over my shoulder. "Don't blame me," Icon said, rousing from some reverie. "You and I weren't together then. And besides, Tibetan is one of the languages I've never learned to read."

The scene came back now, with the long-ago me sitting at the table writing the final words. The scene vanished, and the air whooshed from my lungs. I'd been holding my breath watching.

Himalayan goosebumps ran across my scalp and down my body as the realization hit me: *I now had the memory of those three lifetimes*. I didn't need to read the book—I had been, *am*, its author. We had called the place Sanmakan. *Sanmakan*. The sound of it sent more chills down my spine.

"You're feeling too freaky," Icon complained. "I can't daydream with all that stuff going on. Why don't you watch TV or something."

I laid the book aside and turned out the reading lamp to begin a reverie of my own, but the feeling of a presence interrupted me. I opened my eyes and there stood El, with MC in her cat form, between me and the fire. It occurred to me that the gate and doors were locked.

El jangled a set of keys and withdrew an electronic gate opener from her purse. "We held these little goodies back when we sold you the place. We witches like to operate mundanely whenever practical."

MC had walked over to take my scent while El was talking. "Ah," said MC mentally, "the flavor of Sanmakan. He's ready for more, El." Then she walked away, maybe to smell out the house.

"See what good care we've taken of you?" El said. "And all those years without one word of thanks, or even hello."

I stepped to her and kissed her. "Thank you for looking after me," I told her. "And most of all, thank you for taking me back again."

She returned the kiss, then stepped back and looked me over. " 'T'sall right, duck," she said in mock cockney, "you ain't so bad; there's worser'n you." Then we sat down sidesaddle on the sofa, facing each other.

"Why did I get the idea that the Menties were selling kobold minds instead of getting rid of them?" I asked her.

"I'd put a spell on you," El answered, "so you could hear the other side of what people say. I took it off when I handed you the free ticket later; I sure didn't want you to hear the other side of what I was saying or thinking."

"That explains the weird change in reality. But what the heck is actually going on with the Menties?"

"To solve a problem, there has to be a problem or problems to solve. So the solver must first create the problem, or more often recreate it. And, of course, you have to replace any that you actually get rid of. That's the usual function of organizations: to help one create new problems or take old ones out of mothballs."

I suppose my noncomprehension was showing, because she continued. "You've read Elbert Hubbard's *The American Bible*. He said that doctors tend to create the illnesses they claim to cure. That was close. Mostly unknowingly, doctors pray for illness, and patients are the gods who answer their prayers. Organizations carry it beyond that level—to the point of engineering, promoting, and enforcing problems. I'm sure you've noticed how their solutions provide a next generation of bigger and better problems. Call it a game of posing and resolving problems."

She could see I still wasn't getting it.

"Okay, let's take something you know about, like a battery. It has three poles: the anode and the cathode and the third pole—the base of the battery—which is neutral, and holds the other two apart. Reality, and the mind that fashions it, both work the same way, with three poles or terminals. In play, the charge is light enough that we let go of the third pole and let the sparks fly. In sex we call that orgasm."

She took a sip of brandy. "Does that make any sense?"

My nod was pretty tentative, so she continued. "When a player decides to give up playing in a simple sense of fun, and accepts the rules of a game, things change. The rules include precepts of position, activity, and reality, which are a part of the plan for any game. To satisfy the rules, the game player has to create, actively create, three positions—one each for win, lose, and watch. That's part of the enforced rules.

"From another point of view, the positions are problem, solution, and watch. The problem position can be the win position or the lose position, and so can the solution position. It depends on— Let's not get into what it depends on yet.

"Today at the Mentie introduction center, you *saw* one of the positions talking and *heard* another one.

"Of course, what they're doing isn't a game, it's work. Most of them would get very upset if you accused them of playing a game. They *know* that their activity is senior to any game. Actually it's the other way around: games are senior to work. In a true game, one knows the rules. But in work—which is to say, in the activity of a problem-solving group—the rules and the script are too remote to observe."

"But," I protested, "groups, organizations have rules. I don't know about scripts, but some of them have whole bookcases of rules and regulations, there for the reading."

"Those," she said, "aren't the real rules. They're after-the-fact rules, and lots of times they're broken more than followed. The real rules are out of sight, even to boards of directors. Those are the rules we're talking about now, and if you break them, you're busted."

"You mean a worker and organization member is ignorant of two-thirds of what the hell he's doing?"

"That's close, darling," El said. "Actually, at one level he does know, but at the aware level he has to occlude it. It's required—a rule of access to the grid. Don't feel bad about it though, really. It gives people something interesting to do, and to experience. Noncreative work would *really* be a bummer without that pretense."

"Then how did I manage to do so well in business—I mean, really well—if I didn't know the basic rules?"

"First of all," she said, "you haven't been operating at the level of *work*. What you referred to as your work was really creative play. And your corporation wasn't an organization in the true sense: It wasn't creating and solving problems—problems of supply or consumption or health or behavior or communication, ad infinitum. Or even *problems* of electronics design! You had an association of players—highly skilled players at electronics, at marketing, at management . . . Without analyzing it, you didn't hire anyone who didn't fit that description, so the rules of work and organizations didn't apply to you. And you had fun and success and money galore, and came up with gear that no one else came close to."

I got excited listening to her: that was exactly how it had worked! "By golly, you're right!" I said. "And I never thought about it before. I never worried about industrial espionage, even if the DOD did, or in keeping score or beating anyone. I was just having fun creating new electronics gear!"

"Exactly. And that's one of the main reasons you were so accessible to us. It's also why we had to run off that redheaded Amazon; she'd have changed all that. She couldn't have understood play for fun, even as a concept."

MC looked in the door. She was being a woman again, wearing slacks, a blouse, and an apron. "About those steaks in the refrigerator," she said to me. "I hope you weren't saving them for anything in particular, because right now they're being broiled. Rare. And the potatoes are about done in the microwave. If there's anything you need to do or finish before you eat, you've got five minutes tops." Then she disappeared again in the direction of the kitchen.

She'd taken me completely by surprise. I hadn't even had time to think of something clever to say, like "thank you," before she left.

El got up and took my hand. "Time to stop talking 'bout business anyway. After supper I'll show you another aspect of mine, and an old Hindu remedy."

"Remedy for what?" I asked.

"For talking too much."

It worked.

SIX

I awoke before morning from a bad dream, where El, in this instance a Hindu goddess, was being attacked by demons rising up out of a pit before a white marble temple on the side of a high mountain. The demon bodies were made entirely of black rubber, and they carried twin-bladed weapons that looked like slender pickaxes. I fought them with a long curved sword, but they couldn't be killed. Cleft torsos, severed limbs— anything with a means of dragging itself around— continued to fight. At the last I had several of their blades in my body. I looked over my shoulder at the goddess. She had a pained look on her face as one of them struck her with his pickax. At that she went two-dimensional, rotated sideways, and vanished. Then I woke up.

El was sleeping beside me in yet another version, a version somehow more beautiful than all the others, and with an aura of playfulness one expects only of a child. I wondered if this was the real El, and then wondered what I meant by the real El. But this version stirred hidden memories somewhere inside me.

I went right back to sleep, nonetheless. When I awoke again, it was full daylight and she was gone! I felt a double surge of panic: first that the black rubber people had taken her; and second, that El really didn't exist at all, that I had only dreamed her.

Then I saw her note on the nightstand, and the dread evaporated.

Good morning, playmate,
Yes, Jan Ambers, our Le, we are real and we
don't intend to let you get away so easily this time.
MC (we need to stop calling her that) and I are

off to duty. You needed some more sleep, to get the other side of that dream. Meet us at the Hollywood apartment for lunch.

Love ya,
El

I almost remembered Monitor Cursor's name as I read the note, but it slipped by too fast. As I left the bedroom, the clock read nine-fifty. I showered and shaved with an eager anticipation I couldn't explain.

All the way to Westwood, driving in on Sunset Boulevard, I was trying to pick up the other side of that dream El had mentioned in her note, but found nothing at all. The rest of the drive was spent looking at auras around the cars, amazed at the state some people were in. The trip went quickly, and I soon turned into the underground parking at— Damn! Missed it again. At what's-her-name's apartment. The attendant was expecting me.

I went up to the eleventh floor and rang the bell at exactly noon. The two women who greeted me were recognizable in face only. Their clothing and auras were very much in the business mode, like international banking executives. As I walked in, El's aura changed, and she kissed me with warmth and love. "We used that disguise to make ourselves believable," she said, "for some game players—international bankers—we wanted to outfox."

"You both look pretty spiffy, as my grandpa used to say. I'll bet it worked."

MC was grinning like Alice's cat, and I knew that part of it was due to my still not remembering her name. "I almost got it twice this morning," I told her.

MC laughed and kissed me on the cheek. "It's only a little tease. You can call me anything at all; just call me."

When she hugged me, I sensed both her power and her fondness—her love.

"We have to eat and run," El said. "Our crisis isn't over yet after all, and we need to be on location to handle things as necessary. If we can help them move in the right direction now, we'll save ourselves a lot of trouble when the real crunch hits."

I had no idea what the real crunch would be, or when, and it occurred to me that maybe I wasn't ready to know yet. So I just ate and listened, and admired them. Any banker would be pleased to do business with them, at least until afterward when he checked his wallet. Their total poise said they felt very much in control of the money game.

Some of the million questions I'd thought of earlier, to ask when I saw them again, began to line up for asking, but before I could get the first one out, El smiled at me, and the questions all evaporated. I was left with the dream about the black rubber demons, and the feeling of despair and wretchedness that had followed it. I'd failed her, seen her die, and even if it had been just a dream, it felt terrible.

She patted my hand. "Le, good playmate, you don't need to worry about protecting me, because no one ever dies. Even those who merge with the Great Cursor, as you call him, actually continue as independent entities. They re-enter the reality grid at once; it's just that they're cloaked with serenity and forgetfulness. And you and I—we may have been apart for a while, but we have never been lost to one another, and never will be. You and Dak and I are truly forever."

Dak! Realizing she'd let the name slip out, El said a curse word under her breath in a language I hadn't thought of for a long time, then turned to Dak. "Sorry. I concede the bet, but I'll let old moneybags here pick up the tab."

"From the looks of you two," I said, "I'm the pauper in this place. I don't even have a job these days."

They both laughed, then got up from the table to leave. El kissed me and said, "Whichever way this play goes for us, we'll be back no later than 5 P.M. Then we should have some uninterrupted time to tell you about what's going on."

Their mode of exit startled me. As they approached the door, with Dak in front, it became a black rectangle. I don't mean the door swung back or slid open or

anything like that. It simply became a black rectangle!
And they walked through it. When they were gone, the
blackness vanished. That sure as hell wasn't mundane.
A whole catalog of reports on teleportation flashed
through my mind from the metaphysical literature.

I wondered how many more surprises they were
going to give me.

SEVEN

In the darkened Cessna, I roused from my reverie
enough to illuminate my watch for a look, then peered
out the window. We were at maybe twenty thousand
feet, I suppose, and in all the expanse of country spread
to view, I could see just two lights, which surprised
me, even at 12:27 A.M., Mountain Daylight Time. We
were probably over northwestern Arizona, or maybe
south-central Utah, the only places I could think of that
were so empty of towns and traveled roads.

I'd eaten my sandwich without paying much attention to it, and my cup was still half full, the coffee cold
now. Not that I've ever minded cold coffee. More often
than not, when I'd be working on something, I'd forget
I had coffee, and a cup would last me half a day. It
occurred to me that El might have stashed a bottle of
something in the jet's little fridge, but I decided this
wasn't the time for it. I needed to be as alert and sharp
as possible tonight.

Instead, I sorted through the remaining sandwiches
again. The tuna salad had been good, especially for
something wrapped in cellophane, but this time I took
chicken salad, went back to my seat, and closed my
eyes.

After El and Dak had disappeared through the "door"
to wherever, I'd spent the afternoon reading a copy of
the old 1946 science fiction anthology, *Adventures in*

Time and Space. I suspected it was no accident that it had been left lying on the coffee table, and wondered what particular story or stories they wanted me to read. When I finished, my candidate was Anson MacDonald's "By His Own Bootstraps." Not that I could say I'd consciously learned anything from it, but it was a real mindbender.

At about four-thirty El had reappeared, looking smug. I'd gotten hugged again, and kissed, or Icon and I had. Then we'd gone down to my car and started for my place at Malibu, taking the longer way, the Ventura Freeway, to avoid the gruesome UCLA crush-hour traffic on Sunset Boulevard. Although the Ventura at that hour wasn't a whole heck of a lot better.

Dak, El said, would be waiting for us, and yes, she'd be taking a metaphysical shortcut. It occurred to me that the black door might be a lot quicker and less hassle for me, too, but I supposed if we could have, we would have. El had said there were lots of rules, and lots of things even they couldn't do.

Neither of us was talking much, but the slow traffic didn't seem to bother El; she seemed happy and serene, and glorious-looking, as if the drive was a pleasure. And at that, the Santa Monica Mountains and the plantings along the freeway made an aesthetic setting, but for me it was spoiled by the mass of cars moving slow-and-go westward. It was a relief to get past Reseda Boulevard, where the traffic thinned a lot, and a double relief to turn off on the Topanga Canyon Road.

When we got to my place, El raced me to the house, gleeful as a schoolgirl, then hugged me good and hard. "Oh, Le, it's so good to have you back again," she said. "Up close where I can squeeze you like this." She kissed me, then leaned back and looked at me, speaking more seriously. "It was too damned long without you."

We went in and found Dak waiting to squeeze us both. Dak grinned at me. "It's great to have the team whole again. Clandestine meetings are never very satisfying when one of us can't know what's going on."

She gave us another hug, got one of us on each arm,

and escorted us into the formal dining room. The table was set and the candles were already lit. Dak sat down at the head of the table, with El and I close to her on either side, then poured champagne and proposed a toast.

"Here's to our coup d'état this afternoon," Dak said, "and to us foxes who pulled it off. But most of all, here's to our being back together."

We clicked our glasses and emptied them; the warm glow of love and companionship was like nothing I could remember. After Dak refilled the glasses, I proposed another toast.

"Here's to two very lovely and loving and as yet mysterious ladies who seem to have been taking good care of me for a lot longer than I knew."

We drank again, then Dak served dinner.

"I got the impression," Dak said as we ate, "that this room has never been used. All the tableware was in the original wrappings. I remember helping El pick this stuff out after she decided we'd better furnish the place for you."

"You're right," I said. "I never found the time or inclination to give parties or formal dinners. It was the kitchen, patio, or living room for me." I looked admiringly at Dak. "Frankly, I don't see how you put this feast together in the time you had."

She grinned. "We have certain, um, 'time-saving' techniques. For example, I got here in zero elapsed time through a procedure not available to your role. But even so, don't expect to see something like this out of me very often."

"Right!" said El. "We'll soon have you hustling your tail off; you won't have much time for formal dining, by which I mean sitting down to eat."

"I'm looking forward to that," I answered. "Now tell me about your coup."

"Hah! Well," El began, "it involved two masters of the money game. They were very near to war, which would have damaged both equally and destroyed much of the world's monetary system. All we really did was get each of them to break one of their own rules and work out a compromise."

"El's making it a little too simple," Dak put in. "Actually, those guys would rather have died than make a single concession to the other side. So she played a trump card, and made them an offer that neither could refuse. She promised to support one of them against the other in their war, which would guarantee victory, but she wouldn't choose her side until after the fighting started. And after it was over, she'd have me kill the survivor in a way that was particularly distasteful to both of them. She also convinced them that after they'd finished chewing each other up, she'd have control of both sides.

"Wow, I'm impressed!" I turned to El. "Did you let them feel Dak's muscles?"

El laughed. "I didn't need to. Anyone who's conscious can feel Dak's power—especially people in money games."

The food was so good, I wondered if anything metaphysical had gone on in the kitchen, too. I ate quite a bit more than usual, and should have felt stuffed when I finished, but I only felt pleasantly satisfied—that word again! When I put down my fork and wiped my mouth, I realized that El's and Dak's eyes were on me, casually, not so much waiting as expectant. And I realized I'd had an unlooked-at question sitting in the back of my mind.

"Why now?" I asked. "If we've been connected for so long without my knowing about it, why did you choose this time to—wake me up? And why was I out of touch in the first place?"

El had taken her shoes off under the table. Now she rubbed her bare foot down my shin and smiled ruefully. "I guess I'd better explain that to you."

"Do it," said Dak. "I'll put the food away and load the dishwasher. But then I've got to run; we cats are night people, with tabs to keep. You can unload the dishwasher later and shelve the dishes."

El and I went into the living room and sat on the couch before a fire, she folding her legs yoga style in a full lotus position. Then she looked at me. "We've been on a mission," she said, "the three of us, for a very long time. Each with a different role. Your role has been in the trenches, so to speak, which required amnesia and a broad gamut of other restrictions."

"You mean I've been working toward a goal, a mission objective of some kind, without knowing what it is?"

"At one level, you *do* know, you've always known. But at the operations level in the reality grid—that's right, you haven't known."

"And you're going to tell me now?"

She hesitated for a moment. "No. You'll find it out for yourself."

"Why not now? And why did you hesitate just then?"

Again her smile was rueful. "The rules of the game; the very definitely enforced rules. And I hesitated because—because you might *not* find out for yourself. You'll find out for yourself if things go right for us."

I looked at that. "Okay. So if I don't know the objective at the operating level, how could I work on it? There's something here I'm not seeing."

"How did It, the DUO-HEX, always greet you?" she asked, then, without waiting, went on. "You've designed video games. Consider the reality grid as being a video game, with you outside of it operating a cursor. But not with a knob or buttons—with intention, and with attention on your intention."

She was gazing into the fireplace, as if looking there for words. "English isn't the best way of talking about what happened to you," she said, "but let's see what we can do with it." She paused, then continued reflectively. "Games are played by a very tight set of rules, and even straight play—play at the level above games—has some rules. Any system must have parameters outside of which it will not function. Some of these were preset, and others got added later to make the old play fresh."

She was warmed up now, her words crisp and confident. "For example, time has two sides, and before a restrictive rule was added, everyone had access freely to both sides. Afterwards, the other side was reserved for the directors of play and games. Like Dak and I. A sort of neutral territory for observation, and for special meetings like we held with the bankers today."

She turned her eyes to me. "Does this make any sense so far?"

"It's starting to."

"Good." She unfolded her legs and leaned toward me. "Now that you're relaxed, I want you to go to sleep. Close your eyes and I'll show you a dream to illustrate the mechanics of consciousness, which are attention, intention, and awareness."

It wasn't hypnotism; what I went into was a true sleep, not a trance—but on request, and instantly. I closed my eyes, she put a fingertip first on one eyelid and then the other, and I found myself standing on a very flat yellow plain. In front of me, at an intermediate but considerable distance, was a blue wall, like the sky above a horizon.

"Don't look behind you yet," she said.

Her voice had no sense of location or direction. "I'm going to put a red circle directly ahead of you, just above the yellow plain. That's your target, your goal. Start jogging toward it."

I did, and realized I was wearing my running clothes. The yellow ground was slightly springy, like a padded outdoor carpet. The air seemed fresh, and rich in oxygen.

"Le," her voice said, "for this to work, you have to make reaching the ring your own intention."

I nodded and kept running without taking my eyes off the ring. It seemed a long way off now, and I intensified my intention. The plain was utterly featureless, which made it easy to concentrate on the ring. It also helped that the running was so easy; my breathing rate hadn't even changed.

"All right," she said, "you've covered half the distance. Now I'm going to introduce a distraction. Whatever happens, keep your attention on your goal."

A thing appeared off ahead, just to the left of the red ring. I couldn't make out what it was, but it certainly had part of my attention. It was no problem, though.

After a bit it began to move farther to my left, so I ignored it and kept running.

Soon, unaware, I'd drawn up almost even with it. Then it made a noise, and despite myself my attention jerked to it. It was closer than I'd thought—part Rube Goldberg machine and part living monster, on things like rimless wheels, wobbling along on about four spokes each, which were different lengths and had feet. El's upper torso was protruding from a slab of metal on the front of it, as if she were being absorbed. She was waving her arms and trying to scream, but no sound came out. Agony was plain on her face.

No you don't, I thought, *I'm not falling for an obvious trick like that*. I switched my attention back ahead—and the ring was gone! But I thought I could sense where it had been, or damned close, so I concentrated on that and jogged easily on. The mechanical thing seemed to be falling behind me now, making noises as if it were broken. When it seemed directly behind me, there was a loud scream from El. I flinched, and space seemed to spin. The thing was in front of me again, about two degrees to the left of the red ring, which now was on a green wall instead of the blue one.

Something wasn't right about that—blue, then green. But there was the ring, so I kept jogging toward it, and the thing moved to the side again. When it was directly beside me, the ring ahead grew dim and vanished again, but I was sure I knew where it was supposed to be, so I kept running, leaving the monster behind. Shortly there was another scream, an awful sound. The space spun again, and there was the red ring back on the blue wall, seemingly where it had been in the first place.

Then El appeared beside me. "That's enough running," she said. "The demonstration is over. Now I want to show you what happened."

I stopped, still not breathing hard. "Okay," I said, "show me."

She took my hand and we floated high up into the air above the monster. "You left blue footprints on the yellow carpet," she said, pointing.

They formed an approximate circle around the machine/monster.

"Come on, El," I said. "You're putting me on. First, I know I didn't run like that, and besides, I'm not the kind that runs in circles."

"Darling," she said, "everyone runs in circles on this playground we call Earth. And the only deception I used was to occlude your vision of the green wall until the moment you put the red ring on it as the space flip-flopped on you. That and lying to you about being halfway to your goal. But that's like life: One can't know where the end will be, and you can depend on someone lying to you."

I shook my head and pointed downward. "I still can't see how that can be. I know that thing was behind me twice, and the circle shows that it was always to my left. That's unreasonable."

"Your perceptics told you it was behind you; in this case, your sense of hearing. But on the reality grid, you create your awareness as you go, unknowingly, and your perceptions agree. Your awareness is basically the mean of your vectors of attention and intention. That's what causes people to lose track of where they're going, and eventually lose all memory of it.

"That's why you needed this dream: to regain your memory and your basic intention."

She waved her hand and the scene vanished. I awoke with her kissing me.

EIGHT

At 8:00 A.M., Dak woke me with a cold nose and a very rough tongue. "Get up, sleepyhead," she ordered mentally. "El has breakfast ready. But don't feel too spoiled; you'll be earning your keep soon enough."

She was in the black panther mode this morning, and her body had an aroma that reminded me of something I couldn't put my finger on.

"No clothes allowed," she added as she left. "And hurry."

I stepped in and out of the shower and dried off on the way to the kitchen, then wrapped the towel around my waist. As I walked in, Dak snatched it loose with one swipe of a forepaw. Happily, the claws were retracted.

"Careful, Dak, that's Icon under there. And one of our favorite parts."

"I never miss, except on purpose," she thought to me, and the kitchen thrummed briefly with a feline chuckle. El was putting a platter of fried eggs on the table. When it was safely down, I took her in my arms and gave her a good-morning kiss.

"Thank you, m'dear," she said. "And about the clothes, including terry cloth sarongs: whoever does your laundry uses fabric softener. It offends Dak's nostrils, in her human as well as her feline mode."

"Besides which," Dak said with her human voice, "a team as long together as we've been doesn't need to stand on formality. Let's eat now. I'm starved."

She was in her human mode, and once more I noticed that she appeared younger than last time. "I'll explain that phenomenon to you sometime," El said.

While we ate hearty portions of eggs and bacon, I asked El when and why I'd left her and Dak in the first place. "I still have no memory of anything before this present life, except for writing a book a few centuries ago as a Tibetan monk."

"We won't try to give you the full picture now," she answered. "Just enough to let you feel good about what's going to happen. On the *when* part: in a very real sense you never left us. We've been a team, the three of us, the entire time, actually, ever since the playground came into existence. And our function is to help keep the playground in place."

"Mine, too?" I asked.

She nodded, then paused to eat another bite and sip

some hot sweet coffee before continuing. "Occasionally a glitch occurs in the reality zones of group founders or warlords, and one of us has to go out to handle it. We either enter their reality or a zone next to it—narrow the reality gap so we can relate to them. But we can't just arbitrarily change anyone's reality for them on any level. The best we can do is barter or influence a change in their plan by direct action. And to influence war in its advanced stages, where 'war is hell' instead of fun and games—to do that, one of us must become a warrior."

"Okay," I said, "let's see if I've got it. To influence a reality, one has to create a pattern that's in phase, or nearly in phase, with that reality—create a phase lock so one can operate as part of that reality." Then it came clear to me. "Even if it means having to run around in circles for a whole bunch of lifetimes."

"Right," El said, "but only your attention went in circles. Your intention never faltered."

"But how the hell did I do it—whatever it was I did—without knowing what I was doing?"

"You knew. You always knew at one level. It lay there covered up, nudging you into the proper decisions, sometimes against your better judgment."

"How long have I been gone?"

"Let's just say that it's been 'oh too long and lonesome.'" She sighed and came around to sit in my lap. "Those of us left behind have it rough, too. Especially at critical points when we can't approach the traveler at all."

I grinned at her. "You mean there were times when I was safe from seduction by mysterious ladies?"

"Yes, there are times in the warrior phase when you're unapproachable." She said it with an undertone of sadness. "At times you would have slit my throat after a very unfriendly rape scene, when you were being a particularly savage barbarian. The slitting I could handle, but not the—unfriendliness. At other times, when you were with some groups, you would have roasted me at the nearest stake if I'd gotten within six feet of you, or maybe twenty. No reflection on you; that was the role you were in."

I was really starting to get the picture. "So when we do on-site work, we have to really be the part rather than just play it."

"That's it," she said. "Exactly." Then she got off my lap. "But enough of this sober stuff. Let's try out your pool."

Together we went out for a dip. El swam like a fish, with no apparent need to come up for air. After a good workout she got playful and nearly drowned me before she remembered I wasn't a fish yet. After that we lay on lounge chairs, drying and napping, mostly beneath a canopy so I wouldn't sunburn. Then she splashed me, and I jumped back in and chased her. The winner got kissed, and so did the loser. Now *that's* play.

When we got back out, we began my education again, reviewing the dream about the mechanics of consciousness.

"Okay," I said, "I think I'm beginning to see how it works. The awareness you mentioned is awareness of anything besides the goal, the intention. As attention diverges from intention, it spreads what you might call 'units of attention' or awareness, and these have a mode on a statistical vector midway between the vectors of attention and intention."

"That's right. It's analogous to peripheral vision being so sensitive. But of course, what we're talking about isn't vision, it's mental attention and awareness. That's why it's so much easier to remember something, like a forgotten word, if you don't try to think of it. You use a sort of mental peripheral vision."

"But there's still something here that I don't understand," I told her. "The flip-flop, where everything seemed to rotate a hundred and eighty degrees."

She nodded. "When attention is fully reversed from intention, you reverse directions. The person still has the same intention, but he's going the opposite way. For example, people intent on total freedom will eventually end up going toward total slavery, like the Marxists and various other social and political movements.

"But notice that I said *toward* total slavery. On this playground, or in this video game if you prefer, there is a prime directive that states: 'No Zeros and No Infinities.'"

I nodded. I'd pretty much come to that conclusion on my own, years ago.

"Now, just one more item," she went on, "and we'll be ready to salvage some more of your memory. In your dream, the circle you ran in had a time connection supplied by Icon—one of the functions of icons. You experience time as linear, but it's not. Tell him, Icon."

"She's right, old buddy," he said aloud with our voice. "When we completed the circle and it looked to you like the red ring was back where it belonged, it looked to me like it was about two degrees below the yellow brick road we were following. Time is a helix. And not only that, it's a different helix for each intention you ever mustered up and didn't satisfy. El must have done a little hocus-pocus for you to see the actual ring after the second flip-flop, to keep our dream from getting too complicated."

"According to that," I said, "an incomplete intention could never be viewed after the first rotation."

"Let's not say never," El answered. "You can and will handle them, but you'll need Icon's help to handle any intention you've had a flip-flop of attention on. As a generality, cursors can clear only recent intentions.

"And now," she said, getting gracefully from the lounge chair, "I'm going to leave you with that, and fix lunch." Then she walked to the house while Icon and I lay there admiring her walk.

The whole morning was gone, and so far, the girls had done all the real work. I wondered how long that would last. Then Dak came trotting out to the pool in the overgrown black panther version again and dove right in. Jaguars like the water. I thought of joining her, but I was dry, and decided I wanted to stay that way, so I followed El to the house.

She was in the kitchen, laying out sandwich makings. "You select a wine or fruit juice," she told me, "and I'll get plastic plates for two. Dak will be eating somewhere and someone else for lunch."

I took the cider pitcher from the fridge, poured, and

sat down to build my version of a Dagwood special, as my dad called them. This one involved Thuringer salami, hamburger dills, ripe olives, lettuce, tomato slices, Muenster cheese, and English mustard, between slices of sourdough bread. So it was going to ooze and drip all over me; in my bathing suit I was dressed for it.

"Is it actually possible to get that into your mouth?" El asked dubiously. "This is an aspect of you I wasn't aware of before."

"Of course it is," I told her. "I unhinge my jaws like a python. But I'd advise against watching; it's not a pretty sight. The aesthetics are purely gustatory."

It wasn't, she didn't, and it tasted as good as always. When we'd finished eating, El smiled across at me. "Let's dust off your war bonnet. It's time to make a warrior of you again."

"Again!? I thought I was through with that."

I truly felt aggrieved—even betrayed. It was as if I could almost remember things I'd done, or had had done to me as a warrior, and I'd decided definitely to have nothing further to do with the role.

But El only laughed. "Le, darling, you didn't burn your war bonnet, you just retired it for a time. Warriors have several options when the battle is over, and the one you selected was 'save it and wait.'"

"But I've never even been in a fight in this whole lifetime, do you realize that? Not even as a kid! I was even lousy in competitive sports, in spite of being big, strong, and well-coordinated. I just wasn't interested. And the only time I ever fired a gun was to test a set of little house guns I'd had custom-made."

El laughed heartily. "Little house guns! You have enough firepower in this place to take out a regiment of cavalry. A squad of infantry at the very least."

I grinned sheepishly. These girls had probably searched the place for more than dinnerware. It wouldn't have been any big project for them; they'd use senses not available to most of us, or maybe do it from the other side of time.

"It's kind of peculiar," I told her, "how I decided I needed protection around the house. The Department of Defense sent a security team to the plant to check out HOLEX. When I was introduced to one of them—I don't recall his name—I got the very definite thought that he would slit my throat, or anyone's throat, with pleasure. And more than that: I got the distinct notion that he *wanted to kill me.*"

After I'd said it, I felt that I still hadn't quite put my finger on it. El waited patiently while I frowned at the table.

"Could it be that he's supposed to kill me?" I said.

"How does it seem to you?"

"It seems like . . . Hmm. General Decker has learned that I trashed SWAC and left the company. So the next thing he'll do, if he hasn't already, is assign this guy to blow me away; he's Decker's hit man. Why he'd do that I have no idea, but that's the way it feels to me." I said it almost defiantly, because it sounded paranoid and I had no information to back it up. It was totally off the top of my head. But by the time I'd finished saying it, I felt sure of it, regardless of how it sounded.

El grinned at me. "Your war bonnet may not need much dusting after all," she said.

"I've got a better idea," I told her. "Let's burn the war bonnet and let Dak flex her power at those guys."

"Darling, that option's not available to us. Dak and I can't get into a battle, and we can't go with you when you do. All we can do is get you ready for it, as ready as possible.

"But I don't want you to worry about it in the least; in fact, worry is something you must not do. If you approach this battle with any worry at all, the result will be much worse than the slavery described by the DUO-HEX. You must be a superb warrior to win, and if you lose, we'll be apart again for as long as we were the last time. At least."

I stared at her, half exasperated. "If you said that to make me worry," I told her, "it worked."

"Exactly. Deliberately. You need to get all that out of the way before the battle starts. In fact, you need to get rid of those feelings even before we go to visit the founder of the Institute of Advanced Mental Abilities."

"Carlton Leonidas Masterson?" Now, with the spell off, I was remembering what I'd read and heard about the Menties and their founder. "What in the world do I need to visit him for?"

"The founder—the *present* founder—is someone we'll need as an ally after the first battle is won. He needs to retire his founder position, and you're the only one who can help him do that in time."

"Why me? Why am I the only one who can do it?"

"You need two new red feathers for your bonnet. That's one reason. And you are the only one who knows how to handle it. You."

She sat there calmly watching the confusion and unwillingness play across my face. "The only one who knows how to handle it?" I protested. "All I know about Masterson is what I've read in the papers and seen on television! And you know what good that kind of information's likely to be."

She shook her head. "You, my dear, are a founder emeritus of the Menties—a retired founder. And simply being retired from it is not a disconnection. You get your second red feather when you totally resign."

"Me? The Menties? What do you mean I'm a retired founder? That's ridiculous! I must have been—hell!—in grade school when the Menties were founded!"

"Sweetheart, the Menties, in one form or another, under one name or another, have reappeared in every cycle for a very long time."

Every cycle. I'd run into cycles in my metaphysical reading; the Hindus took them for granted. But it hadn't occurred to me they might be for real. Still, why not? Turn off the video game, maybe alter the program, turn it back on . . . That could be done with other video games; why not this one?

"And you're the only one who can help him," El repeated.

"I don't even know him," I insisted.

El laughed. "You'll see, dear. All founders would like to escape the ordeal of the second phase of their reign, where they have to covertly destroy what they built. Especially where the script calls for destroying it in the same lifetime, in the same persona."

"Sounds like what Hitler did for the Third Reich," I said. "That's a rough gig."

She nodded. "Exactly. Now we come to the hard part. I want you to remember that I love you very much, and anything you have ever done is okay and doesn't change that at all." She squeezed my arm as she said it, and moved closer to me. "But there's something we have to take care of now."

And right then and there I wanted to be any place else than in my dinette, because at some level I knew what was going to happen.

"Imagine a game," she said, "that ended so horribly you couldn't confront afterward that it had ever happened. Something that made you unwilling to remember, that formed a stone wall across any possible view of the past."

I felt a sickness growing in the pit of my stomach. The room spun 180 degrees, and I was face to face with an opaque wall of murky, roiling horror. I was moving toward it, and knew that I'd die the moment I saw what was behind it. Two themes went through my head from the metaphysical books I had read: "The debonair shall inherit the earth," and, "A warrior should enter battle as though he were already dead."

I steeled myself and went through the wall, stepping into a scene that blew me backwards. I wanted to turn and run but couldn't let myself. Sparks flew all over as I tried to focus my attention. When it settled down, I saw a version of El, saw the pain in her face, the blade in her chest, with my own mailed fist firmly on the hilt.

I stood frozen there, and cried away a long age of hidden grief, until the scene began to fade. Just as her image vanished, I heard a very happy voice.

"That's a take and a wrap. Put it in the can and let's have a party." It was El, and she said it as if we were talking in a large room someplace above me.

I felt another 180-degree rotation and my eyes opened on the present. I was on the floor and she was kneeling over me.

"Sorry, El, I didn't mean to be a crybaby about that."

"What do you mean, 'crybaby?' " she said. "I've seen people go up in smoke trying to edit smaller walls than that out of their past. Good grief but we cursors take our acting seriously! You and Icon did a great job."

She flopped down on me and giggled. "Now I am going to repay you for that shiv. I am going to unscrew your legs, and that's just for starters."

She tried. And maybe she would have, but Dak came in and broke it up. "Get dressed, you two," she said, "and take me to dinner. I need some friendly, too."

NINE

It was early for dinner—four o'clock—but Dak was pushing. She didn't say why, but I figured her reasons were good, and because she wasn't talking about them, not all right for me to know. But presumably they had a full evening lined up for me. Briefly, when that occurred to me, my stomach knotted with the sense that preparations were about over and the time of warring was upon me. But the fear was momentary; I was on a kind of warrior high.

My favorite place for dining out is an inn with genuine old Spanish flavor near where Sunset Boulevard meets the Pacific Ocean. At that hour we had the place to ourselves—just the three of us, plus a waiter and hostess—so we took a table near a fireplace. The atmosphere always made me think of the three musketeers and grog shops—a world for men, where the wenches had large bosoms, and soft bottoms for pinching.

Some of the historical novels I'd read had seemed too real to be simply the result of imagination and historical research. Now it seemed to me that their authors, probably unknowingly, had been drawing to some degree on past-life experience, and their effectiveness came from reminding the rest of us of some of ours.

Although I preferred my present company to any lusty wenches of the past.

We were having a before-dinner cocktail when those thoughts occurred to me, and Dak overheard. "It's a good thing you added that last part," she said. "My fanny still smarts when I think of what you and your cavaliers did to it."

The memory flooded back, and I laughed loudly. "Dak," I said more quietly, "you're wonderful," and getting up, I kissed her. "You still have a great-looking fanny," I murmured in her ear.

While we waited for our food, Dak told us about her trip to Africa for lunch with a herd of gazelles whom she loved very much and whom she visited now and then. As she talked, she showed us mental pictures of herself in the panther mode, running with the herd and playing tag with them until she was exhausted and lay panting in the grass. The herd came back and touched the recumbent black cat body with their noses, pawing her and saying, "Come and play some more."

"The herd master was there today," Dak said, and I got a sense of an entity whose responsibilities included caring for the herds, sometimes becoming a gazelle with them. "We did a ritual of retirement for an old buck," she went on. "My role was to cut the old buck from the herd and kill him. I almost had him on my first try, but the herd lent him power and he flew away from me. They like to win the first round, to make the fun last longer.

"In the next round, after I'd rested, he let me catch him quickly. When I'd pulled him down, I stood over him and said 'Goodbye till later'; then the herd master gave the signal and I made the kill. Afterward, I ate part of the flank as a love sign, him smiling down at me, while the herd stood round in a circle. Then the vultures and hyenas and marabous and jackals completed the ritual."

After a pause she raised her glass. "To the herd and to love," she said, "and to the love of play."

We drank, then sat in silence until dinner came. While we ate, a memory came to me of a gazelle who'd saved my life once long ago, in the Sudan. I'd been sent there with an army, which I lost in a great battle, and lay wounded and thirsty in the sun, when an old gazelle came and offered his body as food. He saved me. And it seemed to me that it was the herd master Dak had spoken of. Mentally I sent my thanks to him, and enjoyed the dinner with a new sense of value and appreciation.

"El and I found you recovering at the only water hole you could have reached," Dak said quietly, "with the herd master still watching over you. He'd led you there."

"That was a crucial lifetime for all of us," El added, "and if Dak's friend hadn't saved you, we wouldn't be here together now. It wouldn't be time yet. Do you remember who sent you on that mission to meet the ambush?"

The face of an Egyptian ruler came to view as he gave me the order to attack south. From my present vantage I could feel his concealed glee, and his certainty that none of us would come back.

"That's him," El said. "Dak and I meant to be there when he passed his zenith and went into the 'I must destroy my army' phase. But something unexpected happened, and he reversed signs ahead of schedule."

"That same warlord is in Washington, D.C., now," Dak put in, "well past his zenith in his present cycle, and just now quite insane. He's the general who gave you the SWAC contract—General Decker. And your knowingness about him was right; you've got him worried, and you can expect a visit from a hit squad."

That, I supposed, would include the killer ape I remembered from DOD Special Intelligence. And with Decker's resources and altitude as a member of the Joint Chiefs, he'd have no trouble coming up with a story to justify my death. Phony documents, photos— whatever it took—with all of it kept quiet on the basis of national security.

El broke my train of thought by raising her coffee cup and proposing a toast. "Here's to helping a certain warlord, a certain general, into early retirement."

I took a sip of coffee. "How come it was all right for you to tell me that about the enemy?" I asked. "Or doesn't that fall in the category of getting directly involved in the war?"

"It would have if you hadn't already picked it up

yourself," El said. "We can talk about data already available to you, and you'd already spotted Decker and his gunman on your own." She picked up her change from the service tray and left a twenty for the waiter. "Now let's go to your place and get ready to rescue one Carl Masterson."

The founder of the Menties. I had no idea how I was supposed to do that. But it didn't worry me. While driving home, I was surprised at how lighthearted I felt about the upcoming battle. Confronting the stone wall of what I'd done to El as a warrior in the past had worked wonders.

"That's the way to approach a battle," El said. She was marvelously lovely beside me with the early evening sun lighting her through the windshield. "And you'll be doing the general a service, too. Both he and Masterson are great men, and great creators, and no creator wants to prolong the agony of destroying what he created.

"Of course, it's only their inability to walk away that makes it agonizing."

Something almost slipped by me there, a question, but I spotted it. "Wait a minute. What organization did Decker create? Not the Joint Chiefs; they've been around too long."

"We can't tell you that," El replied. "You'll have to discover it yourself. Well done, though, on spotting the hole. Now you'll be alert to it."

She sounded pleased.

When we arrived at my place, El and I went into the living room for a brandy in front of the fireplace, and Dak went right back out on business, taking her short-cut through the other side of time, of course. We kicked our shoes off and relaxed.

"Now that we're comfortable," El said, "we have a couple of things to do before going to Mentie headquarters. First, we'll establish a new operating relationship between you and Icon. Reestablish an old one, actually. When that's done, I'll be able to take you to that 'cursor reprogramming facility' you were looking for. It's really the passport office, and the place where you stored some of your memory. We'll get it out of storage and get you a passport to the other side of time."

She took a sip of brandy and pulled her legs up under her. "Once upon a very long, long time ago," she began, "you had no icon. Your role hadn't required one. But to leave the world of play and enter a game that would put you on the path to becoming a warlord, you had to . . . split, so to speak, becoming two completely distinct individuals. You the cursor, and you the icon. Actually, that's a gross simplification, but it's a valid way of talking about it, and it will serve for now.

"After that, each of you had to overpolarize your favorite friends, Dak and I, along with some other things. You did that by loving us too much. You had to do it, and we had to let you. That provided the necessary basis for forgetting."

She sighed a long sigh and continued. "Don't mind me if I start to cry. It'll just be the residual energies of that parting flying off. When the love you gave us reached a certain level, both you and Icon were blown away from our secret place on the other side of time. You looked back once and felt the inversion of the heavily polarized love, the inversion that came with crossing to this side. That shut you off from us and from each other, and in a way even from yourselves. Certainly from your own true self."

None of this had meant much to me at any cerebral level, but it felt right. She began to cry and laugh at the same time, and turned for me to hold her. I kissed her face until all the grief was gone and she was laughing.

"Get some Kleenex for old slobber face," she said, and laughed a final "glad to be rid of that" laugh.

Without getting up, I handed her the box from the end-table drawer, and she wiped her face.

"When will I remember that?" I asked.

"Not until after the battle. There's a part of you that must remain isolated until then; otherwise, you couldn't enter into the warlord's reality as a warrior."

I took her word for it.

"Anyway," she went on, "in the process of leaving, you two not only forgot that you were ours, but that you were each other, as well. Even when you got together again, off and on, you didn't recognize your past history together. Icon didn't realize who you originally were, and you didn't recognize him at all, at any useful level of consciousness."

Icon spoke first. "Maybe so, but I sure as hell remember times when we were buddied up. And when we were on different sides and I lost parts of me to him in battle."

El jumped up and laughed. "Okay," she said, "I hereby officially declare your separateness at an end. Say goodbye to each other, because I am about to reunite you."

For a moment I must have sat there with my mouth open. I'd come to think of Icon as my very good buddy, and now he was going to cease to be at least as a distinct and separate being. It seemed to me we ought to feel sad about this, but I felt only the lightest shadow of that, and Icon, I think, none at all. At some level we both knew this wasn't the loss of a friend, but the regaining each of a part of ourself.

"So long, Icon," I said. We gripped our two hands in front of us and shook them, chuckling jointly to ourselves.

"So long, Cursor," he answered. "It's been good." El walked to the fireplace and turned toward us, holding out her hands for us to join her, then motioning us to stop when we were about six feet away—just before our personal reality touched hers.

She went two-dimensional and rotated sideways, then the line that was left merged to a center point. As something stirred in our gut, the room went 2-D and rotated. Or we did. And El was standing next to us in a shabby little office, a washbowl on one wall with a dirty water glass. A nondescript overweight guy in a rumpled white suit was sitting behind a messy desk. He needed a shave and his ashtray badly needed emptying.

For just a moment I wondered why she'd brought us to a place like this to see a seedy-looking guy like that. Then, "Hi!" He said. "What's a good-looking cursor like you doing in a video game like that?" The voice was all too familiar, though coming from that body it didn't resonate.

"It's the only game . . ." I was too confused by his appearance to get it all out.

"I'm not the Great Cursor here," He said, pointing to a plaque half concealed by the dirty coffee cup on His desk. "I'm only the passport officer."

El stifled a grin; stepping up to his desk she spoke loudy. "This place is a disgrace! An absolute pigsty! I shall send a monitor cursor to inspect it!"

There was a loud whoop and a pop. The human form vanished, and a golden dodecahedron floated in the air where He had been. A voice boomed through the small room: "I AM THE GREAT HE, THE GREAT SHE, AND THE GREAT IT. Or is that the great he-she-it? Damn it, El, I always get my lines confused when you're around."

There was another pop, and we were in a very clean modern office looking at a handsome middle-aged man in a white suit crisply new.

"There, kiddo," He said, "how does that grab you?"

Stepping around the desk, He hugged El warmly. "My dear, it's been much too long since you were here. And I'm glad to see you've kept your partner out of too much trouble." He turned to me. "You I won't hug till later. I wouldn't want to give you a big head before your battle." Laughing, He led us into another room, where He sat down at a console that looked identical to the one in my old office at HOLEX.

"It'll be nice to have this situation cleared up," He added as He began entering data on the keyboard. "This playground's been short on fun for altogether too long." His fingers flew over the console which, on closer inspection, wasn't at all like mine had been. For one thing, it had no keys, just coded areas. His fingers moved too fast to follow.

"What memory do you want returned to him, El?" He asked, then answered His own question. "Give him conditional access to everything since he gave up play for war."

As the input sequence ended, the wall above Him lit

up like a screen, with a gold-lined grid on it. What were to me meaningless varicolored blobs appeared, moved across the grid, and vanished. When the motion stopped, a series of markings appeared across the bottom, very briefly, and He hit one last tap on the input pad.

"All stored and ready," He said.

I stared numbly, because suddenly I understood. I mean, *I really knew what this was all about!*

El kissed him. "Thanks," she said.

"I hope you kids pull this off," He told us, and waved. The last I saw, as the room rotated, was the original scene, with the character in His rumpled suit like someone in an old Sam Spade movie, but this time He had a big grin on His face.

Then we were standing back in front of the fireplace. "El," I said, "this really *is* a video game, isn't it." And as I said it, the numbness ebbed away.

"Yes, in a way it is. But don't believe everything the DUO-HEX says, or all that you see around Him. Or It. It's a real joker. Like that console that started out looking like your IBM model and then changed into one It's more accustomed to. I've been in that same room and found a little old lady selling flowers: The console was a crystal ball She just happened to have in Her basket."

Suddenly I realized how very much alive I felt. In a spatial sense, Icon and I had been merged before, but as personalities we'd been separate. Now, with our personalities remerged, I/he/we were more vital than either of us had ever been separately. I grabbed El in my arms and swung her around. "This," I said, "calls for a celebration." Then I kissed her.

She kissed me back, and after a minute murmured in my ear. "You're right," she said, "but you don't have time."

TEN

So what we did was go out to my Irish import and drive east through the soft, late sunshine, heading in for L.A. to the international headquarters of the Institute of Advanced Mental Abilities. There I was supposed to resign my retired position and help the current founder resign his. We were halfway to Santa Monica when I turned to El, bothered by that. "It still doesn't make sense to me," I told her, "that I need to resign from a group I haven't been a member of, even if I was the founder of an earlier—version? incarnation?—of it."

"It will," she said. "Remember in your metaphysical library the science fiction novel titled *The Chronicles of Amber*, by Roger Zelazny?"

"Yeah. It reminded me of my old favorite, *Glory Road*. As a matter of fact, I was surprised at all the science fiction books in the box that woman sent me."

"That was Dak. She picked out the ones that applied to reality and to what we have to do.

"Both Zelazny and Castenada's Don Juan talked about using motion to make contact with other realities. Actually, motion isn't necessary, but it helps, so we're going to drive a crooked mile after we get into L.A., and while we're doing that, we'll take you out of your warrior retirement. Then, when we reach our destination, you'll have remembered yourself as a retired founder, and carry a little clout."

We exited the freeway on La Cienega and I drove the crooked mile under her directions. When we arrived at Mentie headquarters, we were wearing uniforms like the spacy-looking ones I'd seen at their Hollywood introduction center. At that time I'd thought they were pretty ridiculous, but now that I knew their background, I felt like part of myself had come home. I raised the car doors and we slid out to go and meet Carlton Leonidas Masterson, whom I now remembered clearly as my old buddy, Puk.

Being a founder of a problem-solving organization is the worst of all grid positions, which is why a warrior can win a red feather between battles by taking on that kind of gig. There never seems to be a waiting list for such founder positions.

After a certain point in the life span of such a group, the problems really start to outstrip the solutions, and things begin going to hell in the worst way. The poor damn founder takes a beating that makes being shot or stoned to death a welcome thing. But then, since death is no release, the founder stays on duty until the bitter end, when the group completely destroys itself. He has to orchestrate the whole thing like some Wagnerian Götterdämmerung, unless he can get someone else to take the job and commit himself to follow through on it. Or even less likely, unless he has the strength simply to walk away.

Loaded with gold braid as we were, El and I walked into the founder's office without even being questioned. "Hi, old shipmate and Great Mucky Puk!" I said.

His attention moved to me from the papers on his desk. He looked old and haggard, sick and crabby. His eyes, slitted from exasperation, were almost hidden behind folded, red-rimmed lids, and his response wasn't as quick as I would have expected from him.

"Huh! It's you!" He sounded grumpy instead of pleased or surprised. "I thought it was another one of those shitheads with the usual list of complaints, problems, and lawsuits. This damned place is really going to hell!"

I could tell he hadn't recognized me yet, but I'd used his old nickname, so he knew I was an ex-buddy from back down the time line somewhere—and who remembered. Like the quartermaster at the entrance and the yeoman at the desk outside his door, he ignored El, as if he couldn't see her.

"What are you doing here?" he asked. "Out of retirement?" He was peering at me with his narrowed eyes glittering hard; he nearly had me pegged. "Get tired of war games and looking for work?"

"I came to turn in my emeritus membership and make the retirement permanent. I'm resigning. The little woman told me to get my ass home and swab some decks. You know how women are. They'll let you out for a few lifetimes with the saber, but then they want you back."

When I said "saber," his eyes widened. "Le!" he said. "Well, I'll be son of a dung beetle!"

The word "saber" started him reminiscing about our ship being overrun by pirates; we'd stood back-to-back, killing them until the deck was covered with bodies and slick with blood.

"That was fun, all right," I said. "We'll have to do it again sometime. But I have to go now."

He looked a little sad. "Hell, I wish I could go, too. This outfit should have collapsed years ago; I set it up too damn well." Turning a faintly hopeful face to me he said, "Why don't you hang around for a while and help me scuttle it?"

"Puk," I answered, "I've got a better idea. Is Lom still with you? You know, the kid who never wants to be the founder—always fights like hell not to be drafted for it. Then, as soon as it passes zenith, *whammo!* He's in there all eager beaver, chomping at the bit for a juicy post as a demolition team leader."

"Lom?" His face took on an uncertain expression; he sensed that I had a solution in mind, but he hadn't spotted it yet. "Yeah, Le," he said thoughtfully, "he's still around. He doesn't remember, of course, but he's still demolition-happy: I've been making good use of him."

"Not as good as you could be," I said. "Remember that regulation about retired admirals being made honorary commodores? And how we used it to handle that blockhead CO we got stuck with in the Vega Sector during the Mortusk peace talks?"

Puk's eyes opened wide, suddenly in full gleam; he saw salvation standing before him. His hand slapped a key on his intercom so quickly that if a fly had been sitting on it, it wouldn't have had a chance.

"Yeoman!" he bellowed.

Talk about instant rejuvenation! Puk always did have great recuperative powers. He played the scene to the hilt. Twenty ranking officers were called in to attend the ceremony, a couple of them out of conferences. The hat he presented me had five pounds of gold braid and stars on it—enough to bring a Markabian dictator to attention. In minutes I had my full and complete retirement finalized and was awarded the posts of Past Admiral and Commodore of the Capellan Flotilla. They're strictly recognitional, honorary—they don't involve membership of any kind. For our purpose, the titles, gold braid, and hat were what counted.

After that game was over, he dismissed the others and called his yeoman. "Tell Lom to get his ass up here on the double," Puk said, then leaned back with a big smile on his broad face and winked. "I hope he remembers to set his nitro down softly," he joked. But when the yeoman announced Lom's arrival, Puk took on a very haggard look, slouching in his chair, and even let his mouth sag a bit.

"Send him in," he said weakly.

I was afraid he might be overacting, but he knew his audience. It was the sort of thing Lom loved. I could feel his suppressed glee when he saw the wasted look of his leader. He didn't even look at me, and I realized that, to him, El was invisible. I stepped forward and read him the riot act for letting his founder become so overworked.

"You're in big trouble, mister!" I finished. "You are, as of this moment, Acting Founder of this station, and you damned well better be in here fighting till the very end."

"Aye, aye, *sir!*" Lom snapped out. He was beaming.

El and I helped a decrepit Puk through the door. "You'd better get that man some R&R quick," Lom boomed after us, and the full authority of the founder was in his voice. The last glimpse I had of him, he was sitting behind his new desk, thoughtfully rubbing his hands, contemplating new ways to wreck the outfit.

I'd pegged him right: He was exactly the opposite of the rest of us. It was the early, rising limb of the group history curve he hated—the part where you take it as high as you can. He tried to avoid being made the founder of organizations because of what it took to create and organize and coordinate one in its earlier, expanding stage. Destruction was his bag. So we'd done him a huge favor; we'd put him in charge of the destruct phase—given him founder authority without demanding of him what he couldn't handle.

Outside in the parking lot, old, decrepit, worn-out Mucky Puk jumped two feet off the ground and kicked his heels together while bellowing a loud, *"Woo-hah! I'm free!"* Then he grabbed El and danced a brief wild polka between the rows of parked cars. After that he stepped back and looked at the two of us with the grin I used to know.

"El," he said, "you're a sight in that outfit." He cocked an eye. "You were in there all along, weren't you; I just wasn't seeing you." He gestured toward me. "And you damned well had a hand in bringing him here." He gave me a bear hug. "Thanks, Le, for bailing me out of that mess."

After that the three of us went down the street, arm in arm, to have a mid-evening breakfast and reunion.

Over an omelette, Mucky Puk, or Puk as he prefers it, told us how he'd come to volunteer for that founder position. He'd stayed in the warlord/warrior zone as long as he could—too long, in fact—and needed to take the fastest route out before he got too bogged down with penalties.

"I've got this great idea for a new game," he said, "and wanted to get back into a gamemaster slot. Doing a hitch as a founder was the quickest way to eligibility."

"You should have gone to Central America," El told him. "You could have been in and out in jig time. None of those military dictatorships last very long."

He shook his head firmly. "I never could stomach those founders who pretend to be warlords. They make me a little sick, and give war a bad name. Anyway, with the help of you two, it worked out okay. I got all the good side of it and didn't have to ride it out to the dismal end."

He reached across the table and shook my hand. "That was a stroke of genuis, Le, because this way everyone is happy. Even good old Lom!" He shook his head, the shaggy gray sideburns waving gently with the movement. "I think Lom has terminals one and two wired backwards."

We all laughed at the concept.

"Tell us about your new game," El suggested.

"Ah ha!" he said. "So that's why you came to bail me out and buy me a meal. You wanted the advance skinny! You playmasters are all alike: you want to know about the new games before they start."

"Stop teasing, Puk, and 'fess up," El insisted. "I want to hear all the details."

"I don't have it down to the level of details yet." He was grinning like a bear. "But I can tell you this: It'll take the place of war for those of us who like contests with hidden scripts. Plus it'll really add mystery to the game belt."

He sat back then, relaxed and beaming, to bask in our admiration, utterly transformed from the wreck we'd seen behind the founder's desk.

"What do you plan to do first?" I asked.

"First I'll find me a safe haven and write a novel." He punched my shoulder, a mock punch. "With the kind of recalls I have, it'll be a science fiction best seller. I think I'll tell the story of the Belserian war, but set it in A.D. 2500. I'll tell it from the viewpoint of the insurrection leader—good old Bucket Bottom, if you recall. Meanwhile, I can be working out the program for the new game."

"Sounds like fun," I said, and got up. "But we've got to run now. You just reminded me: I have to get ready for old Buc. He plans to have me assassinated."

Puk's eyebrows arched. "Watch that guy," he warned. "He's one of the best in the second part of the cycle. You kids have fun and stay in touch."

We left and found Dak waiting in the car. From her expression, there was trouble.

"What's happened?" I asked.

She answered with a question, gesturing toward Mentie headquarters. "How did it go in there?"

"No sweat. Puk and I are both disconnected from the Menties. I've got my red feathers and all the power I need to report to my warlord for a commission."

She nodded and disappeared without another word.

Something dangerous was going on, that seemed certain. While El drove, I used my new credentials—my two new red feathers—and projected myself into a metaphysical reality to see my warlord. Who's me, of course. I had to reclaim my war bonnet—my pattern as a warrior—which I might need as early as tonight, by the way Dak had looked.

Old soldiers never die, but warlords can sleep for a long time. I found General Le in a musty old office, in a uniform made up of pieces of uniforms from various past armies. A Norse battle-axe lay dusty on his desk beside a Gaelic *claidheamh mor*. He popped awake the moment I appeared, and looked up fiercely.

"What do you want, soldier? Don't you know better than to come in here unannounced like that? What kind of . . ."

I could have let myself run on until recognition dawned, but I cut him/me off and told him what I wanted. Grinning fiercely then, he gave me my commission: I was First Officer Le Sal, with orders to act on my own discretion to handle the insurgent group led by Warlord Buc, Old Bucket Bottom, just now a/k/a General Decker.

The prospect of action rejuvenated my warlord the way retirement had Puk, and with him his office. Before I left, the room had shifted from a dim old dustbin into a bright, fully operational ready room. One whole wall was a battle board, just now a map of southern California, with a flashing red aircraft symbol heading toward L.A. from the east. When I'd noted that, the scale and focus shifted, centering on an auto symbol just pulling away from my place near Malibu.

Which explained Dak's concern.

I was back in the warrior business again.

ELEVEN

My warrior skills felt as sharply tuned as they had been at my best, long ago. On that occasion, some fifty thousand men were killed or wounded—mostly killed— all but a handful of the whole damned Seventh Corps, as a matter of fact. But not me, and not Puk or Buc. The three of us, messmates and buddies, had come through without a scratch.

None of us knew why we were such hotshots, of course. Never even wondered. We just took it for granted.

I was pleasantly surprised now to feel so little discomfort—none, in fact—at warring with my long-time friend Buc in his current identity as General Decker. Mainly I felt the excitement and the challenge—the fun of it.

I'd expected an ambush, and as El turned into the driveway, I sensed it ahead. I was disappointed at the nonconfront of the warrior who placed it: Remote-controlled killer devices were not much fun to use, or to have used against you.

Don't confuse your times, I reminded myself. Old Buc might not have any Jhidda-class warriors handy, but he could make skillful use of what he did have.

And now I really remembered what *debonair* meant— that special kind of nonchalance that takes you into battle with a sense of being dead already, so what the hell. Then you don't spend attention on surviving, only on creating the desired result.

As a sort of bonus, a lot of the time you survive.

El stopped the car at the gate, about two hundred feet from the house, and I got out. "Stay here," I told her. I opened the gate manually, just in case, then stepped inside quickly, and out of sight behind the seven-foot stone wall that surrounds the grounds, hurrying along it through the landscaping to the underground escape tunnel that El had put in when the place was built. And I was the guy who thought it was ridiculous, back when I bought the place!

The hidden seal on the tunnel entrance was intact, which meant it hadn't been tampered with—not from the outer end, anyway. I raised the lid and headed for the house, trotting, imagining the turkey who'd set the trap sitting somewhere watching, wondering what the hell was going on. He'd have a backup device for remote detonation, and was probably considering using it. My assumption was that he wouldn't for a few more moments.

I reached the house end of the tunnel and threw the switch for the jamming device I'd installed to jam bugs. It ought to jam electronic detonator signals, too. The DOD security people had insisted that my house be "bug proof" and phone-tap proof, and had installed a jammer in the rec room. Later, after I'd bought the handguns, I put my own jamming device in the tunnel. Theirs was probably no longer working, but hopefully mine was.

I hadn't told the DOD about the tunnel. Having met Buc's hit man, I'd been careful about that. Now, if he just hadn't encountered it on his own . . . I felt over the exit area with my new warrior senses and found no booby traps, then sensed ahead for the next few seconds. It felt clear. I opened the door and stepped out into the basement rec room.

The 3-mm magnum—approximately .12 caliber—was in its secret place. It was one of a six-piece set I'd had custom-made. I slid it into my pocket, along with two extra clips. It's a small, deceptively powerful gun that would make an exit wound like a .38, and a clip could about cut a good-sized man in half. The real trick in miniaturization had been to design a small light-weight chamber that could handle the kind of explosive necessary to keep the cartridge case small.

I went upstairs cautiously but fast, and found one large explosive device by the front door, set to trigger when the door opened; there was one by every known entrance. I unwired them. They were set so that all would blow when any one of them did; the explosion would have demolished the house like a natural gas accident. It was a good thing I'd had the jammer in the tunnel; I could imagine the ambusher angrily jabbing his remote detonator switch.

El materialized on the couch with two glasses of brandy. "Hi, warrior," she said, sounding somewhere between Mae West and Lauren Bacall. "Got time for a visit?"

"A short one. Until our friend comes over to find out why his charges didn't work."

I hadn't much more than wet my upper lip when I realized something I'd overlooked: if the guy outside was who I thought he was, he'd helped install the security system. He'd have a signal detector, and would have noticed the jammer come on. At that moment he'd known I was inside, and that there was another way in that the DOD hadn't known about.

He must already be moving toward the house. If he was half as good as he ought to be, he'd find the tunnel entrance, which was not camouflaged but simply inconspicuous. I stepped into the hall to cover the basement door, and waited.

His fear announced his arrival. He'd become too dependent on remote devices for killing and had lost his sharpness for face-to-face action. As the top of his head came into view, I squeezed off a round into the center of it. I couldn't sense anyone behind him, but wasn't sure there wasn't a backup man outside, so I went down the stairs, stepping over his body, and secured the tunnel door. Then I returned to the couch, took up the brandy glass, and gave him a final salute.

"What about the body?" El asked.

"I'll let Bucket Bottom clean up his own messes."

Then Dak stepped through a black door and stood

before us with her hands on her hips. She had the aura of a drill instructor again, even though she'd have drawn cautious whistles on the street.

"I see you haven't lost *too* much of the training I gave you," she said. "How do you like having an operating channel to your ready room?"

Operating channel! Of course! I hadn't remembered there was one!

I put my attention on it—through it—into my ready room, my warlord office, and the scene came into focus. On the battle board, an auto symbol containing two red dots showed the backup hit men waiting for a report from their late partner downstairs. They were in a beach parking lot, next to its highway entrance. The aircraft symbol didn't show any longer. Instead, another auto symbol near Los Angeles International Airport indicated that the other team had landed and was heading north on I-405.

"What now?" Dak asked. "Are you going to meet them or scat?"

"Scat," I said. "I need to get to Washington and find Buc. But first, let's have a goodbye toast. I know you gals can't come with me."

"That's right," El said. "Buc would scream foul if we did, and we can't push our advantage with the DUO-HEX too far. Technically, Dak stretched the rules when she reminded you of your operating channel. We'll stay here for a while and keep those guys from tearing this place to pieces. It may be useful later."

Taking some cold turkey from the fridge, I made quick sandwiches, and we began a hurried snack: our last meal together, I assumed, until the battle was over. From someplace, the thought came that I had an unfair advantage over these hoods by having access to my ready room.

"Don't worry about it," El said. "They have warlord positions, too. And the script is still hidden; you can only know what they're doing as they do it."

"All real warriors use their ready rooms," Dak put in. "But most think of it as getting hunches or gut feelings.

Only those rare few in very good communication with their icons actually get visuals on it."

"You said the script is still hidden," I said to El. "What did you mean by script? Do you mean this whole affair is all predetermined? And I'm just going through the damn motions?"

"No way, José," El answered. "There's an open sort of outline script, with some more or less fixed events in it. But you create your own shooting script as you go, and the opposition does, too. You'll find lots of opportunities to pull off coups or screw up royally, and so will they."

Dak interrupted. "There's a private jet waiting for you at the new airport near Thousand Oaks—a Cessna Citation III. The pilot, Stu Rogers, is expecting you. Your I.D. and a note to the pilot are in your car, and I marked the airport on your highway map."

Judas priest, I thought, *what a pair! These two apparently know the script, at least such as it is, and provide locations, sets, and props. I won't even have to get around a bunch of airport police with my picture on their duty sheets.*

"Thanks for the appreciation," Dak said before I could put it into words. "We've done, and we'll continue to do, everything we're allowed to. For us it's relatively simple to set up the early scenes the way we've done. But from here on you'll need to do a lot of improvising, so don't depend on us."

While El and I finished our sandwiches, Dak left the room, bringing back my house guns, along with a briefcase armory. Then El left to bring the car up while Dak checked my warrior patterns. When everything checked out all right, Dak kissed me goodbye. "I put a little pocket money in your briefcase," she said.

We went out then. El was just getting out of the car, and I kissed her goodbye without pangs or reluctance; the warrior patterns were operating, sure enough. I drove down the short private road to the Pacific Coast Highway as the blip on my ready-room board pulled out of the beach lot; I wouldn't have to deal with them at all. And the CIA squad, or whatever they were, was still twelve miles away in Santa Monica. I was starting to feel the sense of adventure that goes with warriorhood when it's working properly.

I snapped out of my reverie twenty thousand feet above somewhere or other, with a clear view of my jet being marked as a target on the battle board. Actually it was shown as a large oval with a broken outline, not as a blip yet. Apparently they didn't have access to their ready room; they knew where we were headed but they didn't have our location or exact route. I went forward to talk with the pilot.

"Stu, are you picking up any unusual radio traffic ahead of us?"

"How did you know?" The suspicion was clear in his voice. "I just now picked up an air force fighter ordering a cargo plane to land—or else."

"I thought so. They'll be stopping every nonscheduled flight eastbound."

"I presume we land when they tell us to, right?" Stu asked. "Or do we set down somewhere first?"

He was wondering whether we were smuggling something, and didn't like the idea. "Stu," I told him, "I was hoping I wouldn't have to tell you this—on the 'need to know' principle. But from the time you took this job, you've been employed by a special task force of the Secret Service." I looked at him as if sizing him up. "Didn't you wonder why an owner would keep a plane of this value, and a pilot, on call, and use you so little?"

"Yeah, I had wondered. Especially when good charter offers were turned down. We could have been making money off this baby." He paused, his eyes hooded; he was trying to evaluate what I'd said. "I've been idle most of the time these last three years," he went on, "and I never met anyone except the two ladies, Ms. Anderson and her secretary, Dak—now there's a name—and all I've done is haul them around now and then, to some of the damnedest places imaginable. Where do they fit into this Secret Service task force?"

"What's your opinion of the two ladies?" I asked.

"Huh! Friendly and easy to work for—and *sharp*. And no way would I even dream of crossing either of them. Especially that Dak! I get the impression that they know what they're doing and get what they're after."

"You've got it," I said. "Exactly. Now, two weeks before we bought this plane, we discovered a plot among the Joint Chiefs to discredit the President and see him impeached, or assassinate him if that failed. By hearing this, you have just come under the Secrets Act, and don't you forget it. I am empowered to deputize you as a special field agent, and I am exercising that power now." I said it with all the authority that comes of necessity. "And what we'll do is fly on to D.C., or as close as possible."

"Hell, man, we can't fight F15's." He said it matter-of-factly enough, but there was a tinge of fear beneath it.

"We won't have to. That's what smarts are for. Before you were called to expect me, they learned I was on to them, and closed every form of public transportation to me. So you were activated as our contingency escape plan. The photos and tapes in my briefcase are the only hard evidence we have, and the President can't act without it. And while we've got him protected, he's treed, and he'll stay that way until we get this evidence to him."

"He's not the only one in trouble," Stu replied. "The Fighter Command has called a Stage Red Terrorist Intercept; I was in the Air Defense Command, so I know the code phrase. *No* one is getting through."

It was obvious that Stu was ready to resign his new post as deputy. "Is there an available field big enough for this bird between us and them?" I asked. "Or one even closer in another direction?"

"Sure. Five minutes east of here, at Jefferson, Missouri."

"Good. Put out a mayday to them for a paramedic team. Tell them your passenger just had a massive heart attack and you're coming in."

He was a good actor; he put just the right urgency in his voice.

"Captain Stu Rogers," I said when he was done, "welcome to the Service. When they take me off the plane, you stay with me and bring the briefcase. By all means bring the briefcase. But don't open it, and if someone else opens it, dive for cover. It's wired."

"Got it," Stu said, then asked, "what do I call you?"

"Call me Le. I'm Special Agent Le Sal."

"Okay, Lee. We'll get you to the President. We can't have our Pentagon playing Central America on us."

The resignation was gone, and he seemed pleased at the way things were developing. This Stu Rogers was all right—about what I'd expect of someone hired by a Ms. Anderson with a jaguar for a secretary. And while I hated to lie to someone I was going into battle with, the real story would be too unbelievable. Hell, I didn't know much of it myself, but I had a feeling that Buc wanted to trash the whole world this go-round, not just his army like that time in the Sudan.

As Stu turned to begin his landing approach for the Jefferson airport, I saw a signal on the ready-room board that I recognized instantly without knowing how. *My God!* I thought, *Buc's gone crazy!* "Stu!" I snapped, "abort the landing and head for St. Louis!"

What I had seen was a marker for a nuclear strike on Jefferson, Missouri! It would have to be an air drop, and it was hard to believe that even the air force chief of staff could get the air force to nuke an American city, even with a "small" tactical bomb, but no way was I going to land there now.

"Get the tower," I started to say, but somebody got us first. I was pretty sure it wasn't Jefferson, Missouri, and the voice certainly didn't sound like your usual air traffic controller. The guy was clearly angry, ordering us to land immediately because the paramedics were waiting.

"Sure they are," I said to Stu, "along with a bunch of armed guards to keep us in the plane until air force intelligence arrives to quietly shoot us. Tell the tower the owner is conscious now and insists on being taken to his own cardiologist in St. Louis."

Stu managed to get his message through the demands that we return and land, but the demands continued.

"How far till we get off their radar?" I asked.

"Too far. The F15's are already headed this way, and they're out for blood. Just before they heard about us aborting, they shot down a private jet that didn't yield quickly enough. It would take some very high orders to cause that kind of response."

"Then hit the hedges on this course and change our heading to south after a minute."

We'd already lost most of our altitude in our Jefferson approach. We shed the rest of it in a hurry. Stu was good. We were missing some of the larger trees by only a few feet; if we'd had props, they'd have had pitch on them. "Lee," he said, "I can lose them for a while this way, but we'll never make it to D.C. There's a ring of radar stations around it to protect it from low-flying aircraft. And I doubt to beat hell we'd ever get that far. If nothing else, we'd be picked up by the air force's recon satellites; at our speed, we'd be easy for them to pick out."

"How close to D.C. can you get me?"

"Not close at all. Not in this baby. We need something slower so we can hide in the light aircraft traffic. But I know a small field in the Ozarks west of Poplar Bluff, where we can leave this crate under cover and pick up a single-engine Cessna prop job. That's not too far from here. In a plane like that I can fly us between the trees if necessary, all the way across Kentucky. It'll be a rough ride, but you don't seem like the kind to lose your cookies. I should be able to get you to Charlottesville, Virginia that way, about a hundred miles southwest of D.C."

"Okay," I said, "that's our plan."

He changed course again and seemed really happy to be flying by the seat of his pants like an old-time barnstormer on his way to an air circus.

"By the way," I said, "when you drop me off, don't

head back west. Hole up in Bermuda or someplace else out of the country for at least three weeks. By then you'll be safe."

"I'll lay low," he said, "but it might be safer to leave this baby where we park it today. I grew up with the guy at this airstrip, and he's not on speaking terms with any feds. I could hide out for a hundred years in those back-country hills."

"Sounds good. And when you do get back west, run all the charters you can get until one of us tells you otherwise. All the money above overhead is your new salary. Once I get this situation handled, it'll probably be a while before we have another project."

"Sounds like a winner," Stu answered. "For me, anyway."

I closed my eyes and checked the ready room again. There were bogeys around St. Louis and Memphis, beginning to fan out west, north, and south. There were others around Little Rock, spreading north. They still hadn't spotted us, but they weren't too far off. All of them were observing radio silence, though that would change if we were spotted.

"How long?" I asked.

"About three minutes. You know, flying this low may create some complaints from farmers. Might be they can use those to trace us later. I've changed course a few times, but not by much."

He was flying without running lights, eyes intent ahead even as we talked. I wondered if he could find the strip, hedge-hopping at night, but he didn't seem to have any doubts, so I dismissed mine.

"You better buckle in now," said Stu. "That was Highway 60 we just crossed, and that's Cupola Knob ahead to our left. This landing's going to be tight; the field was never intended for an aircraft like this one."

He was right. He almost stalled it on top of the woods at the end of a runway that was longer than I thought it might be but a lot shorter than wanted. He set her down by starlight and braked as hard as he dared, and of all the crazy miracles I'd seen lately, maybe the biggest was that we didn't blow the tires and do for ourselves what Decker had been trying to do. As we taxied back to the lone hangar—a big tin shed, actually—a guy came loping through the dark from the direction of a travel trailer, an old overcoat flapping around his bare shanks. After we stopped, it took us about a minute to get out of our seats, we felt so weak.

"Stu!" The guy in charge of the place was staring at Rogers as we came down the steps. "Kee-rist! You crazy or sumthin', tryin' to land that thing here? Who the hell's after you, anyhow?"

"Answers later, Jim. We've got to hide this bird fast!"

"Okay. Taxi her 'round back and I'll pile some wrecks on her." Jim talked as if he was accustomed to hiding hot planes.

He was. There was a place just right for it among assorted partly dismantled aircraft and disorderly piles of parts. When Jim had finished with a small crane, the jet was sufficiently obscured that no one would ever spot her from above. She wouldn't be noticed from the runway, either; they'd just about have to go over by the junk to see her. The sky was starting to gray in the east when we went into Jim's "office," a table in the corner of the cluttered hangar that doubled as an overflow workbench. The Cessnas were all out on smuggling runs, hauling whiskey without benefit of federal revenue stamps, so Stu started dickering to rent the only plane available—a Cub. Ten minutes later we *owned* it. Although Stu was a friend of his, Jim didn't blush to demand the going rate for a new one, although the plane had been rebuilt more than once, its wings and tail sections still the colors of their original planes. Fortunately, Dak had stocked the briefcase with more than enough money for emergencies like this.

Prices are generally high outside the law, if for no more reason than the high risks of doing business. Actually Jim was easy on us, considering the position we were in; friendship did count for something with him.

I asked Stu if he needed food or rest before we left.

"Heck, no! Jim, how 'bout you throw in a quart thermos of coffee and a sack of sandwiches? Then we'll haul ass out of here." Just now he sounded almost as Ozark as Jim did. Jim, with a horsey grin, agreed, and gave me an old, oil-stained army field jacket as a bonus, to keep warm in the chilly dawn. We were off the ground before the last stars had faded.

In the back seat of the fore-and-aft-seated Cub, I closed my eyes and checked for bogeys. There were plenty of them, especially to the east, but they wouldn't be expecting a Cub until they found the jet. If they found it.

I went to sleep then, and after a while dreamed I'd been defeated and bound with chains. Old Buc was standing on a dais above me, laughing and slapping the side of his boot with his riding crop. He looked just like George C. Scott in *Patton*, but I knew who he really was. El was dressed as Cleopatra, and held a golden chain attached to a collar on Dak's neck.

Buc was telling what he had planned for the three of us during the first thousand years of our servitude. El would be his concubine, Dak his bodyguard, and I would serve him, fanning him while he dallied with El.

Some of the things he had planned for her were too much: I went berserk and broke my chains, then jumped on the dais and tore him literally to shreds. Then I heard him laughing, but the laughter wasn't Buc's after all, and what I had in my hands was the stuffing from a teddy bear. *Buc was someone's puppet.*

"Wake up, sleepyhead."

I was in that in-between state, not asleep anymore but not yet quite awake, still caught in my dream. The voice was El's, from someplace a long way off. I felt her kiss brush my lips and heard her whisper, "Heed the dream, and remember Dak's love for water."

I came wide awake then, to a bright Kentucky morning—green wooded hills beneath, and yellow sunshine. The cabin of the Cub was loud with engine noise, so I leaned forward and yelled in Stu's ear. "Fly straight for the coast," I said, "and land on the first beach you see."

"What happened?" he called back. "You have a premonition or something?"

"Yeah," I said, surprised at the question. "A dream."

He grinned over his shoulder. "I figured that was it. I just had one, too, and I wasn't even asleep."

"If you need some sleep," I shouted, "I can fly this thing for a while."

"No, no," he yelled back. "I wouldn't miss a minute of this. I feel like we've got an angel riding with us now." He pointed ahead. "We're coming to a little airfield at Corbin, Kentucky. I'm going to land there and refuel."

I grinned and gave him a thumbs up, then leaned back and popped a look into the ready room. The Appalachians northeast of our position were loaded with high- and low-altitude bogeys, so after we'd refueled, I told Stu to bear south a little; later we could fly her up the coast.

Somehow I wasn't worried. I felt confident of my skills, and at the same time perfectly willing to have things all come apart. And knew as I drifted off to sleep again that that was what debonair was all about.

I awakened with a start; Stu had reached back and was hitting my leg. He gestured out the right window. A chopper was flying alongside us, its pilot signaling us to land. It bore no service designation, but its rear door was slid back and a guy in coveralls stood facing us, holding an automatic rifle.

"No heroics here," I yelled to Stu. "Those guys aren't military; they're mercenaries. They'll shoot us down without blinking. Land in the closest pasture."

He looked back at me and nodded, then waved acquiescence to the chopper pilot. I reached into the briefcase, took out two of the little 3-mm handguns and handed them to Stu. "Put one in your pocket and hide one in the plane," I shouted, "and don't use either one unless I signal. If there's a chance to get out of this, I'll kill the guy with the rifle first."

I put another of the handguns in the sandwich bag. The one I'd been wearing on my belt I now tucked in my waistband, inside my jacket, dropping the holster on the floor. These guys would probably have a photograph of me, with orders to shoot first and bring in the carcass for verification. I had to stall them long enough to get an opening.

"Stu," I shouted, "they don't know yet that we're their target. I'm going to pretend to be an old fisherman who hired you for a trip to the coast for some surf fishing. Play along with me and don't be surprised if I look different."

He nodded understanding. He was lining up to land on a woods road, and the chopper was on top of us. I overlaid my warrior pattern with one that Brando would love to own—no, one he's had for decades—master thespian. I'd never felt more alive in my life.

TWELVE

Groping for a skill Dak had taught me once in another time and world, I concentrated on being a 70-year-old fisherman—a little decrepit, and slightly fuzzy-headed after a nap in the Cub. I felt my aura change.

The briefcase in my lap took on the appearance of a creel with a rod broken down and attached. In a way I felt the part, but only superficially. The old stained field jacket became a quilted down vest, open in front. If any of the men I faced had been rehabilitated the way I had, it wouldn't fool them, but that seemed unlikely.

In case my changes bordered on the illegal, I decided to drop the disguise altogether a moment before I attacked. It would do no good to remove Buc's puppet strings only to be overruled.

Meanwhile, Stu had lined up the Cub with a straight stretch of graveled road. Now he cut the engine back, dropped the tail, and set her down. As we bounced along the dirt surface, I leaned forward and gave him the rest of his instructions. "I have the briefcase set on delayed destruct, so don't worry about them opening it. Don't act unless you feel we can win. And one thing more: Are you a chopper pilot, too?"

"Right."

When we stopped rolling, the chopper landed a dozen yards from our right wing tip. I opened my door and peered out so they could get a good look at the old fisherman. The gunman in the door kept us covered while five others, including the pilot, got out, talking among themselves. Two of them, with rifles, posted themselves fore and aft of the chopper, weapons at a casual ready. Only the door gunman seemed poised for action. Two others, with holstered sidearms, were headed our way. The unarmed pilot was walking off to one side, apparently to take a leak.

That showed me our edge in unmistakable terms: These guys had stopped other small planes today, and I was obviously another wrong number. It was clear from their expressions and the way they walked and held their weapons, as well as by the pilot treating it as a rest stop. I could picture them all dead in the next few seconds.

The two with sidearms came to the Cub doors with nothing more in mind than looking at our papers, delivering the standard apology and cover story, and getting back in the air again. Could I kill them all without depending on Stu? I had no idea of how able he'd be in something like this.

No, I decided as the agent reached up to help an old man out of the Cub, *I'm fast, but no way can I get all of them before at least one of the riflemen squeezes off a burst.* I sent a prayer to Stu to at least make the one up front hit the dirt.

The guy's hand was on my elbow as I stepped down, and as soon as my feet were on the ground I dropped my disguise and crushed his trachea. For a moment they must have assumed I'd stumbled. That was enough. I held the sagging agent erect for just a second to block the rear rifleman's line of vision, then shot the door gunner and the guy up front. The guy to the rear was raising his rifle barrel as, hitting the ground, I snapped off three rounds at him. His rifle kicked with a *blam* as he went down with his face shattered.

Meanwhile, Stu had jumped his man and, lying on top of him, had his own gun in his hand and his eyes on the chopper pilot. The poor pilot. It had all happened so fast, he hadn't had time to open his fly. He was staring bug-eyed at us, hands just now rising above his head.

Then Stu got up; his man didn't. "A *wing chun* punch to the breastbone," he said. "I think he'll live."

My man wouldn't; he was already dead. I sensed over the pilot. "The pilot's okay," I said. "He just chartered himself and his bird to these guys for the day." I ordered him to sit on the ground and put his hands on his head. When I turned back, Stu was checking the I.D. of the unconscious man at his feet.

"Hey!" he said, "this guy's a civilian; at least he's got no military I.D. No federal I.D. of any kind, except a draft card. His name is Hedberg, and he works for an outfit called NORTEC, in Virginia."

"Huh! Must be a cover organization for the guys we're on to," I said. "Find something to tie these two up with and we'll put them in the chopper."

The pilot volunteered the location of a roll of electrical tape. While Stu bound them, I put two of the four bodies in the cub, opened the engine cowling, and broke the gas line. I put the other two bodies in the back of the chopper with our prisoners, after taking time to check their I.D., too: NORTEC again. By that time I had quite a bit of blood on my field jacket, so I took it off and threw it in the Cub.

I started for the chopper then, to ask for matches to start an agent bake, and Stu held up a flare gun from its pilot seat, so I climbed in and buckled up. He tapped his headphones, and I put on the other set. Now we wouldn't have to yell at one another.

"Where to?" Stu asked.

"Where are we?"

"About thirty miles northeast of Greenville, North Carolina, and eighty miles west of Mann's Harbor. I found out from the pilot that they've got a guy in Raleigh they reported to while he was landing. Raleigh's their search control center. The guy'll be waiting for a report that's a little overdue now."

"Good. Take her up. I'll blow the Cub and then report, while you fly us to the coast."

After Stu took off, he rotated till I was in position to use the flare gun. The pool of fuel under the front of the cub exploded; even though I was expecting it, I flinched at the force of the explosion, and its instant fireball. Then we headed east low and fast. I unplugged Stu's headset from the radio, loosened mine, and jiggled it as I talked. ". . . calling . . . was the guy, all right . . . real firefight for . . . kay, but the goddamn rad . . . their gas tank . . . king fireball two hun . . . it . . . it . . . home abou. . . . Over. . . ."

I'd put just a touch of post-firefight excitement in my voice. Not too much: Buc's people wouldn't be hiring anyone except professionals. I switched off the microphone and plugged us back into the intercom.

"That should buy us some time," I said, "but probably not much. I need to pick up a boat and get into Chesapeake Bay."

Stu changed our course to northeast. "This you'll love," he said. "Ms. Anderson had me fly her and her secretary to Norfolk last summer to set up a corporate R&R house on the bay. We picked up a new motor launch and a bunch of nonperishable foods and took them to what they called the 'cabin.' It's a ten-bedroom lodge, almost a mansion, on a secluded inlet near Reedville, not far from the mouth of the Potomac. We left the launch in the boathouse and had a bird pick us up."

"Great. Do we have enough fuel to get there?"

"Could be; I'm not sure. I don't have a feel for the fuel consumption of this bird. But I will before we have to decide."

I sat back and semi-relaxed—watched on my side for aircraft, with half an eye for the countryside of forests and farms. Soon I could see the Atlantic and a long offshore island to the east. After a bit I closed my eyes and put in a line with El.

"Thanks for the pad, and where the hell did you find this Stu Rogers? You guys not only run great stage and props departments, you've got a dynamite casting director, too."

"You're welcome. We thought the cabin might come in handy. Dak says kiss Stu for us. 'Bye."

That was short. I wondered what they were up to. Then I found myself laughing, imagining what would happen if I tried to take her advice and kiss Stu.

"What's funny?"

I covered. "You and your skill back there, and now this well-stocked hideaway. No one ever told me about either one. *Wing Chun!* What were you? Special forces? I'm beginning to think Dorothy—Ms. Anderson—sent you along with combat in mind." I paused for effect, looking at him appraisingly. "You're an agent, aren't you, Stu?"

"Not me. Not until you deputized me, back over Missouri. And all the Wing Chun lessons I ever had were one semester at the Air Force Academy. I'm surprised I could use it that effectively, especially after so many years.

"If she wanted someone along for combat besides you, she'd probably have sent that secretary of hers. I can imagine some poor bastard trying to mug her! I stumbled once, carrying a case of canned goods onto the motor launch, and bumped into her. It was like bumping into a tree! She grabbed me by the arm to keep me from falling, and my bicep was purple and green for a week from her grip! It was uncanny."

"I know what you mean," I said. "She made a hand-to-hand combat expert out of me."

I didn't mention when that had been, or where.

He checked the instrument panel. "They must have topped the fuel tank off not long before they stopped us, and it's holding pretty well. It looks like we can get in there all right, but we won't have a whole lot left."

"That'll be fine," I told him. "Take us in. And when

we get there, check the boathouse and see if you can find something to hide this bird under."

In back, the NORTEC man, Hedberg, was awake and trying to communicate with the pilot over the noise of engine and rotors. I tapped the center of my forehead meaningfully and pointed at the dead rifleman. Hedberg gazed at the bloody hole in the rifleman's face, and nodded.

A check of the ready room showed that all the air force bogeys were gone. The jet was still secure in its junk pile. They seemed to have bought, at least tentatively, the idea that we had been in the Cub. But a double band of lights showed all the ground approaches to D.C. covered. Old Buc and his string puller still weren't taking any chances.

Then, for the first time, it occurred to me to wonder why they were so concerned about me. It made no sense, *unless they knew who and what I really was besides Jan Ambers of HOLEX.*

Something about the name NORTEC was bugging me, too. I'd heard of it before and couldn't place where. I relaxed my search for it and there it was in my mental peripheral vision, in the fine print of our DOD contract for SWAC. The contract had a contingency clause that provided for bypassing the usual security channels in the event of a suspected leak or an unusual breakthrough in the research. A telephone number was listed, and if no one answered, we were to call an alternate number and report to anyone there.

I'd dismissed that as another bit of bureaucratic ass-covering. We'd never have used it; we wouldn't have even considered making a bunch of air force contract-administrators huffy by questioning their security measures. We needed their good will when the time came for the next review.

So NORTEC must be a private security agency of the one and only Lord Bucket Bottom—or his puppet master.

I laughed to myself, remembering how Buc had gotten that name. He, Puk, and I were close buddies, cadets for an outfit that hasn't been around for a long time. And although Puk was more or less the ringleader, he and I had looked at Buc as senior, because he'd served in the enlisted ranks and had four more years in service than we did.

We were on a cadet shakedown cruise, and all of us who used the cadet mess got dysentery our first week out. The heads were full most of the time, so Buc started carrying a bucket, just in case he couldn't make it through the long queue. We started calling him Bucket Bottom, and it stuck. Puk was teasing him about the bucket one time and suddenly needed one himself, but Buc wasn't lending his.

So I gave him the nickname Mucky Puk. One of his boots had had a medical transponder in it, which his accident shorted out. So he'd gotten called to sickbay to be checked out for diabetes; they'd kept him there until we made our first planetfall.

Boots. With a medical transponder. I got a gut feeling and ducked in back to deboot our passengers. Then I got carried away—we were over water—and pitched boots and cargo—everything but their clothes—out the door.

Stu had glanced back to see what I was up to, and when I'd come back forward asked, "What was that all about?"

"Just in case they were bugged," I told him. I relaxed and watched the ready-room board for a while, then asked, "How long?"

"We should be there any minute now," Stu said. We were over what I supposed was Chesapeake Bay, clipping along close to the water. Shortly he swung left into a narrow inlet between forested shores, and after a moment pointed. "There it is, ahead on the right."

Stu put us down on a large lawn between the boathouse and the mansion, next to a clump of old oaks. He trotted to the boathouse, and I checked the prisoners to make sure they were still secured. Then I made a fast reconnaissance of the grounds, ending at the house. Standing outside the French doors on the garden side, I spread my senses and felt no traps or ambushes, live or mechanical. The ready-room board had the place bogey-free, but it doesn't hurt to check for yourself. Then I went in, found the switch box, and turned the power on.

Back outside, I found Stu carrying a large bundle. "You're not going to believe this," he began, then paused. "Or maybe you will." Dumping the loosely rolled bundle, he gestured at it. "An army surplus camouflage chopper cover."

That Dak! What a props manager! Together Stu and I covered our bird with it.

We were taking our barefoot prisoners into the house when Stu remembered that the basement had a cagelike metal grating over the wine and food storage. The bars were like the heavy security gratings you can see over storefronts in some big cities.

Prisoners are a nuisance, but a basic part of the warrior's code is to never take a life out of combat. Prisoners could only be killed without penalty when they were first given an effective weapon and a fair opportunity to defend themselves. And I needed my pattern in good condition to keep my ready-room channel open; no code breaches for me today. So we put our prisoners inside the cage.

When they'd been secured behind the large padlock, along with a garbage can for a latrine, I had them back up to the bars, where I cut their bonds. "Help yourself to food and wine," I told them. "Someone will be by to let you out within the next three days."

They'd have to drink something, they had no water, and they'd be bored. Hopefully they'd start sampling the wines, and drink and sleep to pass the time instead of getting effectively ingenious and maybe escaping.

Stu had carried food and wine upstairs before we'd locked them up. He was in the kitchen when I got there, checking things out. "Stu," I told him, "go hit the sack. I'll wake you in four hours for a hot meal."

"You're the CO in this outfit," he said. "I'll be in the first bedroom on the right at the top of the stairs. Incidentally, the beds here are the greatest."

After he left, I realized that the prisoners had no tools to eat with, so I grabbed some forks and spoons, a can opener, and a cork screw, and headed for the cellar. They were about to break the neck off a wine bottle when I arrived.

I gave them the tools. "Eat well," I said, "and don't fret." I'd started to leave when a question occurred to me. "By the way, what did your boss tell you guys I'd done?"

It was Hedberg who answered. "The word was, you were on your way to sell the Russians a system for laying H-eggs that would make all launch vehicles obsolete and defense impossible."

"Huh! Well, for what it's worth, that's bullshit. I'm out to stop a coup your boss cooked up. Sorry about your buddies back there. The guy you work for is willing to waste a lot of people to take power here."

I left them staring, not waiting for questions.

Back in the kitchen, I set aside a canned ham, dried eggs, powdered cheese, and some soup powder with ingredients that ought to contribute to an omelet. Considering who'd bought it, I was willing to assume it was good stuff, and not something out of army surplus. Stu had brought up a gallon tin of stew, and I put that on to warm first. Another tin had two dozen brown-and-serve biscuits in it, and I slid them into the oven. No use going short.

While the stuff was cooking, I checked the ready room again and saw a broad-ranging aerial search going on in North Carolina. They'd already found the wreckage of the Cub, so I figured they must be looking for a downed chopper. The search corridor was between Raleigh and the Cub; the water approach to D.C. was still open.

I left the food to cook on its own and went out back to the boathouse. The launch Stu had mentioned was bigger than I'd expected—about thirty-five feet long, with six bunks. From the look of the engine, it was high-powered.

I felt the space and found the arms locker on my first pass, behind a false bulkhead that slid back with the press of a bolt head. It was a commando team's dream— the sort of thing you'd expect of Dak. There was even a small rocket launcher for surface-to-surface and surface-to-air missiles, with four of each type.

And a satchel charge with a timer on it. I wondered what that was for, and decided I'd probably find out soon enough.

"Thanks, Dak," I said aloud.

"You're welcome." Her response seemed so sonic that I spun around, expecting to see her standing behind me. She chuckled in my head.

In the main cabin, I found the boat's papers and a surprise: If they were genuine, which I doubted, the boat was registered as the property of NORTEC, and described as a test boat for marine security systems. There was also a master's license and a NORTEC I.D. card. With my new thespian talent, I could easily look like the photos on them; I was a master mariner again at long, long last. The only possible glitch that I could envision was if we ran into someone whose warrior patterns were in good enough shape to see through my illusions.

"How did you gals pull this off under Buc's nose?" I asked the air.

"Easy," came Dak's reply.

"Get back to the cottage," El said. "Your biscuits are about to burn."

Oh cripe! I thought, and got there just in time. After eating my share like a hungry bear, I put Stu's in the microwave for heating later. The ready room showed no threatening change, so I let him sleep his full four hours before wakening him.

"Your chow is hot on the table," I told him, "and the pot of stew on the stove is for snacks when you want them."

I was asleep on the same bed before he left the room.

THIRTEEN

I dreamed I'd been wounded in a raid, and left to survive as best I could, or die; that was the custom of the mountain tribe I belonged to. I had crawled off the trail into a cleft behind a huge boulder, to hide and let my wound heal.

When I awoke, the sun was well up, and the bleeding from the arrow wound had stopped. I felt inside with my senses as Nana had taught me; the internal bleeding too had stopped. Then, looking around, I found I was not as well hidden as I'd thought, but when I tried to move, I realized that a safer location would have to wait.

That's where she found me that afternoon, praying. Her hair was white, but she was about my age, sixteen, or maybe a little older. I held my knife where she could see it, but she was unafraid, and sat down just beyond my reach. Her black eyes were steady on mine; neither of us looked away.

Soon her eyes turned golden and grew larger and larger. I knew from this that she was a powerful shaman, and tried to look away but couldn't. Then there was a snap, and I was in them—in her eyes looking back at my body, which appeared to be frozen in some kind of spell.

And there, inside her eyes, I heard her voice. "Don't be afraid," she said. "*She* sent me. I am the magh of my people. She saw you here and knew that only I could help. She showed me a new power to heal you. Go to sleep now. You will stay with me until you are well."

As I was fading into sleep, I thought I saw my body lying flat, like a skin ready for the stretching frame. She was rolling it up.

When I awoke sometime later, we were in a cave,

and I was still in her eyes. I had been right: My skin
was in a stretching frame, and she was daubing something on the arrow hole in it.

"Go back to sleep," she told me. Her voice was
gentle. At least if I had to be her slave, I would have a
gentle owner. I went back to sleep wondering what an
eye slave did.

The next time I awoke, I saw her face rather than my
own. I was back in my body, which was no longer flat.

"Can I go now?" I asked, for my body was indeed
healed. It felt stronger than ever.

"Yes. You are not to be my slave," she said. "The She
who came to me said to save your life in the way I have
done. I am in my time, and She said you would repay
me with your seed. I will bear a boy child that will be
both you and I.

"He will grow tall and have long white hair, and be
both a great magh and a great warrior. His greatness
will unite our people. We must be united, She said,
because in twenty summers a strange foe will come to
conquer this land. Only our son can stop them."

I had heard such legends, of great spirits coming to
prepare the way for births, but had never thought to
be a part of such things.

"Will you do that for me?" she asked, and putting her
hand between her thighs, she patted her groin. Her
eyes were gold again, and as they started to eat me in
their hugeness, I took her hand and pulled her toward
me.

After I had given her my seed, she pulled on her
dress of fawn skin and looked at me, her eyes dark
again. "One more thing you must promise," she said,
and waited for my nod. "You must never tell anyone
that your seed made this child. I am the magh and can
have no man. Only spirits can make me with child, and
no one but me saw your body turn into a spirit with
only one side."

She seemed very pleased.

"One more thing," she went on, "and then I will lead
you back to your own people. If you should die before
the child is born, you are to look for my eyes. Their

goldness will keep you and both our peoples until She comes for you."

After a time we went outside and there, a half dozen arrows found my chest. I twisted as I fell, and saw that the white-haired magh did indeed have golden eyes again. For a moment I felt betrayed, and wanted to pull away and not enter their hugeness, but a realization came to me: I must enter. I had to be reborn again in time to meet the evil warlord who would come among us.

I woke up a second before Stu's hand reached the doorknob. He turned it and looked in. "Rise and shine," he said. "It'll be getting dark pretty soon."

"Right." I swung my feet out of bed. "I'm ready."

On the way downstairs I checked the ready room. On the face of it we were still in the clear; there were no bogeys. That didn't feel right. Buc wouldn't be that slow to twig that we'd somehow taken over the chopper, and he'd have a pretty good idea that we'd come north with it, toward D.C.

Stu had coffee ready, and a tin of crackers open to go with the stew. I'd been right: Even out of a can it was good.

"Where do we go from here?" he asked.

He'd done something to the stew—added a touch of powdered garlic, apparently. "This might be a good time for you to head south for Bermuda," I suggested.

He looked sharply at me, then grinned. "No way. I'm in this till we get it settled. And don't ask me why; I haven't figured it out yet. Maybe I don't like the idea of a private army that might decide to come hunting for me."

"I thought you'd say something like that. But before we go any further with this, I need to tell you more about what you've gotten into, because up till now I've lied like a horse thief. You saved my life today, and that entitles you to some straight answers." I paused to sip coffee and let the scene sort out in my mind.

"First of all, I'm not with the Secret Service. The

people we work for aren't connected with the government. And there *is* a plot, but it's against the entire country, not just the President."

I had his attention now, all right. He'd stopped chewing, his eyes had narrowed, and his whole body had tightened a little. I continued.

"Ms. Anderson and Dak—who's actually her partner, not her secretary—discovered that General Decker, the air force chief of staff, was mixed up in a scheme to make secret weapons for an enemy. And we don't even know what enemy! There's no indication that it's the Soviets or any other country. Anyway, this weapons development is apparently being coordinated through NORTEC."

I gave him a few seconds to let that sink in, while I added some tinned butter to a brown-and-serve roll. Then I told him about the registration papers for the launch.

"You think General Decker is behind NORTEC, and you don't think they're working for the Soviets?" he asked.

"I don't have any proof yet, but I don't think it's the Soviets. I was the head of an air force research team until about seven weeks ago, and I personally took the research one step further than the contract called for. I made a discovery that's centuries ahead of our science—a discovery too damned dangerous to exist in today's world. So I trashed it: models, files, computer files, everything. Then Decker or someone connected to him sent three men to kill me.

"I was on my way to neutralize Decker, but now I've got a hunch that someone else controls him, and that Ms. Anderson and Dak knew it all along. And whoever controls him has a science way in advance of ours."

Stu chewed thoughtfully, his attention inward; what I'd just told him would be awfully easy to reject as paranoid raving. But his mind was less fixed than most. "From what I've seen," he said slowly, "our Ms. Anderson just might have a science way in advance of ours; a mental science anyway. I'm thinking of the wide-awake dream I had this morning, while you were having yours asleep, and of a few things in the past that I just passed off as observational errors."

Briefly he pursed his lips before going on. "Like Dak driving away in their car, and an hour later being there again without me ever seeing her drive back. And an hour after that, she drives back." He paused, looking hard at me now. "And I glanced back at you this morning while I was bringing the Cub in to land. You weren't you in the back seat; you were someone else: an old guy in different clothes. I knew I wasn't seeing things that time, but somehow I just put it aside and covered it up for then."

He stopped again to eat some more, while he examined the idea long and hard. I just nodded acknowledgement and waited. Finally, he went on. "Not the Soviets," he mused, "and not any other country as far as you know. Advanced science. Sounds like you're talking alien invaders." His eyes found mine. "Then why wouldn't they just take over the world?"

"What I'm really talking is hunches," I replied. "But if I'm right, then apparently they're restricted in some way to using only technology developed on this planet. Now that's pure speculation, but with only the data I have, speculate's about all I can do. I don't think we'll know anything about them for sure until we get to NORTEC and take a peek."

"Get to NORTEC and take a peek?" Stu looked quizzically at me. "Two days ago I'd have said 'thank you, goodbye.' But I'll tell you what: I've never been involved with anything this intriguing before in my whole life. So let's go find out."

"Right," I said. "And we'd better get started before we have callers here. Pour the coffee in a thermos and put out the lights. I'll put the stew in a jar and grab the crackers in case we get hungry later. It may be a long night."

Although it would slow our getaway, I decided maybe we should take the two bodies with us. But when I went to check them out, I had second thoughts. For one thing, they were swelling and getting aromatic, and the flies were interested in them. I might have left them then, except that Stu came jogging up from the dock with another wild example of Dak's foresight, or maybe El's—the most uncanny yet. *He was carrying two body bags,* and the expression on his face qualified as both sober and thoughtful. Mine must have been about the same.

So we shooed the flies off, bagged the carcasses, and carried them to the boat. It was getting dark enough that the flies didn't follow. Then we grabbed a mushroom anchor and an old outboard motor from the boathouse for weights, and a coil of wire to tie them on with. After that we cranked up the launch and left. As I was steering her out of the inlet, Stu came back to the bridge after tying the weights on. For a little while he didn't say anything, which was fine with me; I had some sorting out to do myself. What with the camouflage cover for the chopper and the two body bags, it seemed to me that the script might be more complete than I'd been led to believe. There were a lot of things I could write off as educated foresight and even coincidence, but two body bags?!

Not that it made any difference in what I had to do. I'd just keep doing what seemed appropriate and see what happened next.

"Lee?" Stu said, then didn't follow it up right away.

After a minute I pushed it. "Yeah?"

"Last night you asked me what I thought about Ms. Anderson and Dak. What do *you* think of them?"

"Right now I'm not sure. But I got to know them pretty well recently. Very well. I won't tell you yet some of the things they showed me, but I will say they've got abilities and resources that are—the term 'out of this world' comes to mind. Maybe even more important, though, everything they did and said demonstrated to me that they wish the people on this planet nothing but good. In fact, they're working their tails off for us. It's their job."

I turned to him and our eyes met, holding. "That may be a dated, hokey-sounding concept in this cynical world," I added, "but that's how it looks to me, seeing as how you asked."

He nodded. "You don't have to defend that to me," he said, then paused. "Though I can see why you might." Changing the subject, he gestured with a thumb at the body bags on the stern deck. "Is it time?" he asked.

"Yep." We were out of the inlet now, on the bay. Using a chart mounted on the bridge, I locked the helm on a heading toward the mouth of the Potomac and went aft to help dump the bodies. As we slid the first one overboard, I found myself remembering: We'd come out of Norway in forty longships to conquer the Orkneys, and our own ship had diverged to loot a Pictish ship out from the mainland. There was no one who fought more savagely than Picts, but after heavy hewing we'd over-run them. The only ones we'd taken prisoner were a few helpless wounded; the rest had died fighting, and we'd given them to the sea, along with our own dead.

Stu's questioning glance brought to my attention that I was humming. "It's an old Norse funeral dirge," I told him. "From a time when you honored the enemy dead."

He nodded, and didn't ask how I knew. I sent him to sack out for a few hours, and went to the bridge before remembering I hadn't told him about the arms locker. So I went below and showed him where and how to open it in case we fell in with bad company. Back on the bridge again, I started watching for the Potomac light; there had to be one. It was getting pretty dark.

I mused over the dream I'd had earlier. In or around battles, a warrior will dream about old unbalanced equations that relate to the present situation. The evil warlord in the dream and the alien warlord behind this action might well be the same person, and now, somehow, he'd gotten control of Bucky.

Damn! That's why it had felt all right earlier to be going up against an old friend. I must have known at some level that it was really a—a something else I was fighting. My memory of this actual enemy was very vague, but I could recall the feeling of having lost, no matter which way the war ended.

And I recalled very clearly the magh teaching me to tune my body with dreams.

The Potomac light came into view, and I changed headings for the center of the channel. According to the map I'd found with the papers, the NORTEC dock was about ten miles downstream from the Pentagon and on the Virginia side of the river; we should get there sometime before dawn.

I turned my attention to Stu then; I needed to help a warrior sleep. He was already dreaming of dying, and resisting it. I shifted my attention to the other side of time and found "the girl of his dreams," then had her help me create a script for a body-tuning dream—one that would make him more debonair. We wrote it in two acts, with the fallen warrior bedding her as a seductive Indian maiden on both the side of life and the side of death.

Then I opened my eyes to give my attention to the boat, but almost at once I began to suffer the ailment which afflicts most script writers, and popped back for a quick rewrite. I also added a short third act and gave it to both Stu and his dream girl.

ACT III: House lights out; two golden orbs hang in the air above center stage, each lit with a dim spot.

FIRST ORB: "Well kid, how d'you like them apples? Didn't I tell you that being a warrior was great stuff?"

SECOND ORB: "I liked it just fine, especially the dream girl. She is my kind of Pocahontas. A warrior really does always win and lose at the same time, and she was great on both sides—life and death."

FIRST ORB: "Okay, soldier, now get your buns out of that sack and take some coffee to the bridge."

Curtain falls and stage vanishes.

Some time later, Stu arrived on the bridge carrying two cups of steaming coffee. He looked preoccupied.

"Was two hours' sleep enough?" I asked.

"Must have been. I feel rested and ready for action." He paused. "Funny thing, though. Before when I've dreamed of dying, I woke up tired, but not this time. At the last, I was talking to a PAC-MAN character, and it was you. You told me to get up and bring you some coffee." He grinned then and handed me one of the cups. "So here you are."

I grinned back at him. "What else was in the dream?"

"Before I met you as PAC-MAN, I was in two battles and got the same wound in both. In the first we beat the white-eyes, and this beautiful maiden nursed me back to health. In the second, we lost and I died. But the same maiden consoled me afterward." He shook his head. "I've dreamed about that gal before; I'd like to meet her in the flesh."

"Sounds like a good dream. And a good idea. Do you play video games?"

"No. Do you?"

"No, but I used to make them. That part of my past seems pretty far away now."

His expression changed, and I could see that he'd realized something. "More on the dream?" I asked.

"Not exactly. But I not only got enough rest; I feel super." He laughed then. "I feel a little horny, too. PAC-MAN has bad timing."

We drank some of the coffee and he went below. I checked the ready room and there were even fewer bogeys. Most of the ring around D.C. was gone, and the Potomac approach was clear. "Bucky baby," I said softly to the breeze, "don't try to blow smoke up an old magh's ass."

The son of a bitch was up to something.

Then Stu was back with a tin of cigarettes.

"I know you don't smoke," he said, "and I don't either, but here's one tin flat pack put on board by those two witches—with two cigarettes in it. They knew we'd need one each to satisfy an urge I got in that dream."

I hadn't written cigarettes into the dream! "Tell me about it," I said.

"I woke up knowing that smoke is a thing for close-ness. It can be for a closeness within one's self or between warriors before a battle. In the dream, an old medicine man passed me the pipe and said, 'Let your spirit be as free as this smoke, and you will win against the white-eyes. You will win in the battle of the Po-to-mac because you are *human* and you will have the smoke with you.' "

He had already opened the tin; now he held it out to me. "Join me in a smoke for closeness in the coming battle," he said.

"Right," I answered, and took one. He lit us up, and I asked if he had a toast to go with the ritual of smoke.

He looked thoughtful for a moment. "A good idea, and I do." He cleared his throat and held out his cigarette. I crossed mine with his, and the twin plumes spiraled in the eddies of the partly open bridge.

He grinned again. "Here's to the warrior who, though he may die, lives on to fight and win another day."

"Bravo," I told him. "And right on." Jesus, I thought, he's *really* got it together.

We each took a drag and blew the smoke away into the cool night air. The space of the bridge was filled with the sharp keenness that comes with a debonair approach to battle. Now it was all right with him to win or lose, to live or die. We were ready for a new battle of the Po-to-mac.

I wondered who had rescripted his dream after I'd finished with it. Probably El. With the thought, I heard female laughter in my mind: It sounded like three voices instead of two.

And then it hit me out of nowhere. I knew it had to be from my own knowingness, because it was the kind of thing that the girls couldn't tell me. "Stu," I said, "don't ask me how I know, just trust me. The air force search has been called off, not because they think we're dead, but because Buc—General Decker—wants them to think we're dead.

"He knows we're close, and he feels confident that his NORTEC mercenaries can handle us now. He'll have crews out stopping every boat on the river. I'd go ashore and pick up a car, but with these fake NORTEC registry papers, we should be able to go through them. Or better yet, maybe they'll give us an escort straight to the general himself.

"We'll neutralize him if we can. If not, we'll kill him. After that, we'll look for some proof that an alien warlord is behind this whole scene—someone not human. That'll satisfy our dream makers."

We continued up the river then, Stu at the helm, while I went to find out what was wrong with my ready room. I knew they were laying for us, but the battle board didn't show it.

FOURTEEN

Ready rooms are covered by an inflexible set of rules, knowledge of which goes with the war bonnet. And battle boards are usually free to show all actions in progress, the exception being in cultures with the technology for building cloaking devices. My board wasn't showing anything on the river ahead, so I assumed someone was using a cloak.

As far as I knew, cloaks were beyond Earth technology, so as the warlord I put in a psychic line to the DUO-HEX and demanded a ruling on the freedom of ready-room screening. Now came the waiting.

Well, not waiting exactly. A glance at the map showed the Potomac about five miles wide along there. According to the chart, the first good place to set up a blockade would be around a bridge near Pope's Creek, where the river narrowed to about two miles. We still had about ten miles to go.

Stu came back to the bridge wearing a grin I could see in the dark. "I was in the cabin," he said, "looking at the pictures on the license and the NORTEC I.D., and then I went into the head, and what do you think I found?" He paused, setting me up, then turned on the overhead light. "A *damn makeup kit!* How do I look?"

He was dressed in navy denims that looked as if they'd been washed with sweat, salt water, and diesel fuel. By darkening and thickening his eyebrows and shadowing his cheeks, he'd become a surprisingly good likeness of the photographs on the master's papers and the NORTEC I.D. card, the same ones I'd planned to pass for. This took some of the risk out of it.

"You'll do just fine," I told him. "At least till daylight."

He handed me a pair of wrist and leg irons. "These were down in our floating prop room. This time I wasn't even surprised."

I examined them.

"Are you thinking what I'm thinking?" he asked.

"Congratulations," I told him, "on capturing Jan Ambers. There ought to be a bonus in this for you. Do you have the keys?"

"One key opens both of them." He showed it to me, with a duplicate on a ring. I was sure there was more to them than it seemed, and examined them closely. On each, what looked like a rivet head was actually a release button; they were probably the sort of thing escape artists use in their acts.

"I'll have to thank the prop ladies for getting a trick pair," I said, "but I'd better practice with them before any visitors show up. You take the wheel, and I'll bring you some coffee and stew."

While Stu was eating, I worked with the cuffs till I was satisfied I could open them with my wrists chained to a bunk post. Then I snooped through the arms locker more carefully and took out six 3-mm handguns. These were machine pistols, longer and heavier, with larger clips. Two of them had silencers—mufflers would be a better word. By secreting them around the boat, along with the six smaller versions we already had, we'd be pretty well prepared for company.

Between two ammo boxes was a smaller box labeled "gas." It contained four sets of ten-minute nose plugs, and twenty gas pellets that looked like ball bearings. These must be CIA-made, I decided, or KGB, or maybe the British MI-6. I could see us taking out the entire NORTEC HQ with those nonlethal marbles. I left them in the locker and took the guns topside.

"Take three of each type," I told Stu, "and hide them where you can get at them quickly without causing suspicion. I'll do the same below with my six, just in case they decide to relieve you of your prisoner."

"What if they decide to shoot you and take you in in a body bag?"

"The moment anyone on the boat gets the idea of shooting either of us, I'll know it. If you hear any shooting—these won't make much noise with silencers— or see any of them fall or anything like that, act fast." Then I told him about the gas pellets.

I paused to reflect on our plan. "Having a mercenary force inside the U.S. is tricky business," I said, "even for a general. I don't think he'd trust more than a small core group with orders to murder me. While I was loose in a plane, he could more easily justify shoot orders. But here, where they can take me prisoner—that's something else. I think they'll have orders to bring me in alive, and that way he can see me shot."

Unless, it occurred to me, *unless Buc was still in the psychotic break of the night before, when he'd targeted the airport at Jefferson, Missouri for a nuclear bomb. I'd just have to play it by ear.*

I took the helm while Stu went to stash his guns. He was back in no more than three or four minutes.

"So," Stu said, "what now? Looks like all we need to do is keep paddling up that well known creek: the ole Po-to-mac."

His voice had the lightness of smoke.

"You've got it," I said. "Hell, we may even have some fun tonight. I'll go below and get ready for the party. Have a good one." I started to leave, then paused.

"You fished me out of the bay," I said. "So I'd better be wet for them when they check me out."

The first thing I did was hide my guns. The one under the pillow had a silencer. After that I stood in the little shower for a few seconds with my clothes on. Then, after chaining my ankles and wrists to the bunk posts, I closed my eyes and saw El's face coming close. She kissed me. Dak gave me a peck on the cheek and a slap on the stomach. "Keep this in," she thought to me, "and don't get the other side shot off."

They withdrew and I checked the ready room again. Old DUO-HEX had decided in our favor: The battle board showed plenty of bogeys along the Potomac, and there were others along the roads leading to NORTEC. We were almost to the first bogey now, just downstream of the bridge, and I lay there watching the two symbols, bogey and us, get closer and closer. My wet clothes weren't uncomfortable yet; the June evening was warm.

Then the engine speed dropped; we'd been challenged. After we hove to, the engine idling, I heard the anchor cable running out. There was a slight bump as two boats came together, and obviously we were boarded because over the idling diesels I could hear Stu, just outside the companionway, identify himself, saying he was returning from a sea test.

"And I fished a guy out of the bay," he added, "just before dark. He was unconscious, floating in his life jacket. His I.D. says he's with the Secret Service, but he fits the description of the guy everyone was looking for this morning.

"I've got him in irons down below, just in case."

"Shit, man!" said the other voice. "Why didn't you call in? We been working our asses off, searching boats!"

Stu laughed. "You gotta be kidding! With a big search like that going on, there's gotta be a reward. If I'd called in, I'd have been up to my ass in bounty hunters."

His interrogator grunted. "Let's have a look at this fish you caught."

Stu led him down to the cabin, where I pretended to be unconscious. The guy pressed something against my right hand for a few seconds, then removed it and waited.

"Yep, that's Ambers all right. The bastard killed a buddy of mine down in North Carolina this morning. I'd like to finish his ass right here, but we got orders to bring him in as undamaged as possible."

They went back up and named off someone to guard me, along with three other men to stay aboard with him; I heard the guard's feet come down the ladder and stop. After half a minute more I heard the anchor cable again, then the twin diesels speeded up and we were underway. Briefly I heard the engine of the other launch as it swung in behind us; we had an escort. About now, I assumed, the leader would be radioing in that I'd been captured.

I checked the ready room again. The other bogeys were moving upriver well ahead of us. Our escort was following us at about a hundred or a hundred and fifty feet. The chopper was still secure, but the jet had been discovered in the Ozarks; I hoped Jim wasn't having a hard time of it.

Pretending to wake up, I looked around. My guard, holding an automatic rifle, had stationed himself with his back to the hatchway. I tried engaging him in conversation, to relax him in case I had to make a move, but he told me to shut up or be gagged. So I feigned resignation and waited, my attention on the ready room but my senses alert. It was beginning to look like we were home free—until a bogey, a chopper, moved off the river and headed toward the mansion. It made one pass over the place, then returned to it and stopped.

Shit! I thought. *That shoots Stu's story all to hell.* We had minutes at most before the NORTEC team leader topside got the word, and Stu didn't know. Faking a cough to cover my motion, I jerked my head up while I released the wrist cuffs, then snatched the 3-mm from under the pillow. Before my guard could complete his reaction, the magnum-charged bullet was on its way to his breastbone; the discharge was hardly audible above the quiet throb of the boat's engines. He fell against the bulkhead and slid to the deck. One down and four to go.

It took me about four seconds to get the leg irons off. The now-empty bunk would be visible to anyone who came to the foot of the companionway, before he came into the cabin, so I dragged the dead guard over and arranged him in my place, shackling him as I had been. Then over him I threw the blanket from the foot of the bunk and turned the throw rug over so the blood trail wouldn't be so damned conspicuous. That done, I stepped over to the hatchway and, imitating the guard's voice, hollered up toward the bridge.

"How about some coffee down here?"

I could hear the leader's voice, but not what he said. Assuming that someone would be down, I stood beside the hatchway, my back to the bulkhead.

As the man entered the cabin, I broke his neck, wasting a perfectly good cup of coffee. Then I put on his watch cap. There was no time to switch clothes, so I faked the guy's denims with the technique I'd used in the plane. As I exited onto the deck, I could see two guys at the bow rail. If their leader was on the bridge with Stu, he'd see his men fall if I shot them, so I needed to take him out first. I walked briskly forward to the wheelhouse door and shot him from an angle that wouldn't endanger Stu, then turned and shot both men in the bow before they could look around.

As their bodies fell, the radio announced one word, "blackjack," repeating it three times. The excitement in the caller's voice was obvious. Our escort was astern on our starboard side, so they couldn't see me as I hustled aft and down the companionway again. Twenty seconds later I was back on deck with the rocket launcher. Our escort had revved its engines and was overtaking us when my rocket struck her bow almost at the waterline; she went down in seconds.

Stu was slowing to go back for survivors when I

reached the bridge. "Good," I said. "We can't leave any survivors in the water to be picked up by the chopper. Now let's see if we can still pull this off. How did he report?"

"As Potan Leader to Blue HQ."

I looked at the dead leader on the deck, remembering his vocal pattern, and picked up the mike.

"Potan Leader to Blue HQ. Potan Leader to Blue HQ. Do you read me? Over."

"This is Blue HQ; I read you. Over."

"We copied your blackjack. We had a fire on board but we put it out. The catch is still on ice. Do you copy? Over."

"We copy you, Potan Leader: catch still on ice. Bring it in for weighing. Over."

"We copy, Blue HQ. Potan Leader over and out."

While I'd been talking, Stu had swung around and was sweeping the floating debris with a floodlight; we could see no sign of anyone. "How many were there?" I asked.

"Only two that I know of. One who stayed with her and one who went back aboard." He grinned again and moved one hand to a console. "I explored the control panel while you were below," he said. "This rig has quite a security system." From a speaker there came suddenly a sound I recognized from somewhere back down the time track—a sonar of what was, for present-day Earth, an advanced design. Then Stu shut off the engines, and things were abruptly quiet. The only sounds from the sonar were faint and irregular, as if of fish.

"Do you think it would pick up the sound of a swimmer?" he asked. "If this boat is supposed to be equipped to test advanced systems, it seems as if the sonar should be able to detect frogmen."

"Hell," I said, "let's make that our working assumption and keep heading for NORTEC. We'll have to abort before we get there, of course; all we've got for them now are the wrong bodies. But we might as well keep going upstream; it's the right direction."

I took the wheel and turned us back west again, turning off the sonar as I did so. Stu dragged the bodies into the cabin. It occurred to me that I no longer had a known objective, but that didn't bother me the way it would have a day earlier. One would come to us, I felt sure.

Then a voice sounded from the radio. "Blue HQ calling Potan Leader. Blue HQ calling Potan Leader. Do you read me? Over."

There was something not right in the voice.

"This is Potan Leader. Over."

"Potan Leader, take your catch to dock five for catch verification. Over."

"Dock five?"

There was a brief pause, long enough that he could have been questioning someone with his hand over the mike. Then, "Dock five," he repeated.

"I copy, Blue HQ. We're on our way to dock five. Over and out."

Stu was back, listening. "They're on to us," I told him. "Chances are there isn't a dock five; my guts tell me that was a test. It's time to bail out. Angle her over close to the north shore, close enough to swim for it. I'll get the satchel charge to blow this baby up, and we'll go over the side."

I went to the arms locker and grabbed the satchel charge. I'd thought I'd find out what it was for. Then I went back to the wheelhouse with it. Within two or three minutes we were only about a hundred yards from shore. "Can you swim there from here?" I asked. "With your clothes on?"

"No sweat," he said.

"Have you got one of the smaller 3-mms?"

He nodded. "Yep."

The Potomac had stayed relatively narrow since the bridge. In the light of the half moon it looked maybe two miles wide. We were slanting still nearer to the shore. "Okay," I said, "I'm setting the charge for five minutes. Head the boat so she'll be near midriver when she blows."

I did and he did. Then we went over the side and swam for the Maryland shore. Swimming was slow with our clothes on; I was glad it wasn't any farther. By the

time we crawled out of the water, a chopper was over
the boat, hailing it with a bullhorn. We sat on the shore
and watched. When it got no response it flew lower, as
if to land men. That's when the twenty-pound charge
went off, and the chopper was enveloped by the explosion, contributing to it. Because the satchel charge had
been in the wheelhouse instead of down below, the
boat didn't sink at once, and the chopper's fireball
made an instant torch of her.

I looked at Stu, his hair plastered to his head. "This,"
I said, "is turning out as messy as a James Bond movie."
Then we got up and started up the bank.

FIFTEEN

There was a party going on at the house just upstream, and the party-goers had gone down to the bank
to watch the fire. We slipped around to the front to
check out their cars.

"Find one with keys," I whispered.

"Just find one unlocked," Stu replied. "I'll take care
of it from there."

The third one we checked out was unlocked and had
the keys in the ignition. There was a road map of
Maryland and Delaware in the glove compartment, and
while Stu drove, I got us located and oriented; I'd
become a navigator who knew where he was but not
where he was supposed to go.

After a little we hit US 301 and headed north to get
off the peninsula. While Stu drove, I reviewed the day
in my mind, especially the parts that had left me with
unanswered questions. Bogeys in the air had decreased
markedly soon after we'd taken over the chopper and,
except along the river, they'd been absent while we
were cruising upstream. I thought I knew the reason,
and while there was a limit to what I was ready to tell

Stu yet about myself and things like the ready room, I didn't like to keep him in the dark either. His ass was on the line as much as mine now.

"Stu," I said, "try this out for size and tell me what you think of it. It's interesting that they knew we were on the river, or at least suspected we were. I think they knew right where we were as soon as we blew the Cub and left in the chopper. We threw them off when we left our prisoners, but they probably checked out the cabin and realized then what we'd done."

He threw me a questioning glance.

"I think the badges those guys wore were medical transponders: They not only knew where each of the badges was; they knew when one of their men died and how, and they didn't much care how many we killed, as long as they knew where we were. They could pick us up at their leisure."

"Then why didn't they pick us up while we were at the lodge? We were there long enough."

I grunted; he had me there. Maybe they'd made a move on us and it was canceled by the DUO-HEX for some reason. But that I kept to myself; I didn't think Stu was ready to hear about It yet. "Maybe they figured if they were patient enough they could pick us up somewhere without a shootout," I suggested.

"Hmm. If the badges were transponders, then it looks even more like we're up against an alien," Stu said. "*Our* military sure as hell doesn't have anything like that. Our vital signs transducers weigh half a pound and need a good-sized radio to transmit any distance. Or they did when I got out three years ago." He glanced at me again, this time smiling. "If we're up against an alien, I think we're doing pretty damn good. A couple of real hotshots."

As he continued driving north, I put in a line with El. "Have you been listening in here?" I asked silently.

"Yes," she answered.

"How about it? Were the badges medical transponders?"

"Right. Well done on coming up with that."

"Why didn't I know earlier?"

"I couldn't tell you, dear. That would have been a breach of the rules, and we couldn't have handled the penalty."

I felt a surge of anger. "And the DUO-HEX knew about it and let it go? He let them use a cloaking device too, until I challenged it."

"That's right, dear," El said calmly. "He couldn't make a ruling on it until it was challenged."

"Why, hell!" I flared. "Earth doesn't stand a chance against technology like that. I can't petition something until I know about it, and I can't know about it until they use it! To hell with it; that's bullshit! Pull us in and concede the damn planet. Let the DUO-HEX sort it out."

"No, dear," she thought firmly to me. "Believe me, I know how you feel, but we've worked for a long time to arrive at this nexus, and we *can* pull it off." I could feel the calm confidence in her silent communication. "Stu was right, you know," she went on. "You've both been splendid today. Now we need you to stay with it.

"And besides," she went on, "the resources they can *get away with using* are strictly limited. The transducers were legal; they were developed here through NORTEC. But the cloaking device—I'm surprised they tried it. It shows how worried Buc is, and how far gone, because if you'd been picked up and the cloaking device had been a part of it, the DUO-HEX would have canceled the pickup, penalized Buc, and put you back out for a retake. But only *after* the fact."

"Got it," I told her mentally. "Okay, we'll play out the hand. And sorry about the snit."

My anger had disappeared when she'd said that about "we've worked a long time to arrive at this nexus." She hadn't been talking just about Dak and herself; I'd worked a long time, too—a *long* time.

And something else occurred to me: Earlier I'd gotten the feeling that even when I'd won against our enemy, I'd lost. Now it seemed that maybe it had been the opposite of that. Even in losing, I'd built toward the nexus where we'd win.

"Thanks, darling," El said, knowing my thoughts.

"And it's really not that bad a hand to play. Oh! And tell Stu that the girl in his dream is expecting you two tonight, at her house in Dover, Delaware. Her name is Marcy Anderson, and she's a professor at the college there. Dak and I will join you later."

My morale went up the pole. "Both of you?!" I said aloud. "That's great! Okay, babe, we'll be there."

Stu's face jerked toward me, startled, almost shocked. "Who are you talking to?" he asked.

"Sorry. I've got an implanted headphone and got carried away." It wouldn't do to let him have a good look at that statement, so I moved quickly on. "I got some good news."

"What?"

"You remember that Indian maiden in your dream?"

"You know I do."

Right now he was leery of a partner who talked out loud to someone who wasn't there. He was wondering whether a lot of the weirdness and violence of the last twenty-four hours might not be due to a crazy companion.

"She's invited us to spend the night at her house." I looked at the map again. "Drive on north another twenty-five miles or so; then we turn right through Annapolis to Dover, Delaware. I'll let you know the turns."

After a minute he looked at me again. "You said something about 'both of you' just now. What was that about?"

"Ms. Anderson and Dak will be there later."

"You're serious, aren't you?"

"Of course I'm serious."

"You don't have any implanted headphone."

"What makes you say that?"

"It's too damned pat. And how would they hear you back?"

"Sorry. Headphone isn't all there is to it: It's a miniaturized two-way communicator. My words are conducted to the microphone through the skull; all I've got to do is murmur. What else don't you believe?"

"I don't believe in that degree of miniaturization. Equipment, power source . . . Goddamn it! if you're telepathic, say so."

"There you are," I answered. "Actually, I'm not generally telepathic, but El and Dak are. Ms. Anderson and Dak, that is."

He didn't say anything for a while, and I left it at that, watching the night-shadowed Maryland countryside flow by. "Well," he said at last, "considering what I've seen in the last twenty-four hours, I ought to be ready to accept almost anything, provisionally—especially where Ms. Anderson's concerned." He chuckled. "And if my dream girl is actually there . . ." He grinned at me! I was awed; now that's what I'd call resiliency.

"Trust me," I said, and grinned back. He laughed out loud.

Before we got to Dover, El gave me directions to Marcy's house. Stu wanted to phone ahead, but I insisted that we were not only expected but that our time of arrival was known. He decided that in light of everything else that had happened, he'd ride with it and see.

Her house, when we got there, was small and within easy walking distance of the Delaware State College campus. Stu pulled up to the curb and parked, and I got out. It was a beautiful early summer night, late and quiet, still shirt-sleeve warm and smelling like freshly mowed grass. Trees shadowed the street, and there was cricket music.

Stu hadn't moved; when I looked in the car, he hadn't even unbuckled his seat belt.

"Uh, you going to sleep out here tonight?"

He muttered something uncomplimentary, then released the belt and got out. We closed our doors quietly, and I led the way to the house and rang the doorbell. Then we waited in the glow of the entry light, like two large, bedraggled water rats, looking at each other, suddenly self-conscious. The wind through the open car windows had dried our hair stiff, and as if combed with an egg beater.

It was Marcy who opened the door, and she was absolutely lovely. I mean—just marvelous. She looked like El's younger sister, and her name was Anderson, too. She knew who we were as soon as she saw us, or maybe when she heard the door chimes. She greeted us by name and ushered us in like old friends.

If I was entranced, Stu was more like stunned at first. And while she was sweet and friendly to me, it was perfectly obvious who her dream boy was. She had a hoot owl special ready for us, the bacon still hot, the eggs sunnyside up but firm, the toast buttered to perfection. There was even strawberry jam for Stu—his favorite, he insisted—and orange marmalade for me. I wondered if this was on her own knowingness or if El or Dak had clued her in. They must have, I decided—either that or she was another one like them, and it didn't really feel that way.

While we ate, she extracted from Stu a summary of our trip from California. Then, while we finished with Irish coffee, she phoned a friend and arranged to have our stolen car driven to New York and left in a parking garage. She also said to be sure to wear gloves.

"Dak will have it returned to the owner after it's washed and waxed," she told us. "When they see the rental payment, they'll pray for you guys to take it again."

"Thanks, Marcy," I said, "for taking care of that, and for the food. Do you have a bed I can borrow? I'll hit it as soon as I've wiped the prints off the car-door handles and stuff."

"The bedroom on the left," she told me, pointing, then turned to Stu. "I only have two bedrooms; you'll just have to share mine." While he stared with his mouth a little open, she turned to me. "Thanks for bringing him. It's been a long wait."

The goosebumps flowed. So that's why he'd been selected for this, and why he'd adjusted so well: *They're gathering the clan*, I thought.

I showered before I hit the hay, to wash off the dried Potomac River sludge. The hot water and soap did their magic, and afterward I lay between clean sheets, wondering how I was supposed to defeat the alien. I knew, without knowing how I knew, that what he had in mind for this planet was lower than any level in the history books. And I knew zilch about how to handle the situation. In fact, I knew zilch about the situation—not even enough to plan, for crying out loud! All that I did have a good feel for was how badly I'd fared when we'd met before, and I couldn't see why the hell I should expect to do any better this time.

I was sitting on the edge of the slide into self-pity, ready to push off, but something kept distracting me— a voice. I concentrated, and it was El's. "Poor, poor little poopsy warrior," she was saying. "Him gotta go fight a galactic-class war wagon with three rocks and a brittle stick."

I hissed angry steam in her direction.

"Shall Dak and I bring party favors and have a pity party for poor little you?" she asked.

I got a picture then of a vast crowd of people wearing party hats, all blowing noisemakers at me, led by the DUO-HEX. And it seemed to me that they were real, honest to god, that there really was a multitude of people with some little degree of subliminal attention on me, rooting for me. *Damn!* I thought. *If I don't have anything else here, I've got the home court advantage.*

"El!" I said. "When I get my hands on you . . ."

"You'll what?" she asked, and there she was standing by the head of my bed.

"I'll think of something," I said, grinning.

Dak had come through behind her and now went to the bedroom door and left.

"Can't the alien detect your gate?" I asked.

She'd already pulled her dress off over her head; now she was slipping out of her underthings. "Not on Dak's band," she said, and slid in next to me.

Afterward we slept for a while, and it must have been in the altered time mode because I awoke completely refreshed.

"You're looking alert and chipper this morning," came El's voice by my shoulder.

I looked at her. "Yes, and I'm starving. I wonder if Marcy's kitchen is stocked for an army?"

"Let's go find out."

She found matching robes in the closet and we went to the dinette. Dak had just finished slicing a freshly baked ham. Beside it was a platter of deviled eggs and a tray of hot croissants. I gawped for a moment, then stared at Dak in awe.

"Madam Lazonga reads in da crystal ball dat hongry warrior want . . . *Ho! Dat moch, eh!*" Dak's gypsy mindreader dialect was helped by the brief appearance of a head kerchief, long print dress, and colorful shawl.

I gestured at the feast; it looked like at least an hour's work. "What do you do in your *spare* time?" I asked.

She grinned. "Never ask a witch or a master chef for their secrets." Then she laughed. "It's all real; I just have certain—procedures available to me."

I walked across the room and gave her a hug and a salvo of kisses. "Thanks for all the logistical support, and for saving our bacon yesterday, and for"—I waved my hand at the table—"all this this morning."

Briefly she purred, a purr too truly feline, I thought, to come from any other human throat. "You're welcome," she answered. "Now sit down and eat while it's hot. I'll be with you in a jiffy." She went back into the kitchen seeming noticeably younger than I'd seen her before. And more playful, or differently playful.

The food tasted every bit as good as it looked, and I gave it my nearly undivided attention. After a while I felt full, and stopped eating. It occurred to me, as I got up for a refill of coffee, that I should actually feel grossly stuffed.

"You only ate half a ham," Dak said, "and not more than a dozen eggs. Is that enough to take on eleven galactic-class wagons?"

I looked at El, wondering how the fleet had grown to eleven so fast.

"All right," El said, "so I left out ten of them. I didn't want you to fret."

"Hell," I said, "one or eleven, it's about the same—impossible." The futility I'd felt the night before welled up again from some still-buried memory.

"Well, let's see," El said. "Round one in this rematch was the assassination attempt at your house. Round two was shoot him out of the air. Round three was capture him on the river. How's our alien done so far?"

She was running her bare foot up and down my leg as she said it. I sensed that the war was still in the feeling-out stage, but I couldn't argue with how things had gone so far.

"Cut it out!" I said. The foot stopped. "Not that! Keep doing that, but stop undercutting my poor, poor thing act." I turned off my mock glare then. "How the hell did Bucky get mixed up with the alien?"

"He didn't," El said, "not in the usual sense. They're using him in a way we can't explain to you now. This war is a special situation—wilder, with its own special set of rules. The DUO-HEX gave it his stamp of approval. Dak can answer that another way."

"It's like this," Dak said. "These eleven visiting warlords are *really* alien. They have a different flavor of consciousness, and they've been helping Buc and others accelerate their destruct phase. They even threw some monkey wrenches into Puk's Mentie game to cut short its phase-one rise. These guys *love* chaos, in a way that makes it infectious across the whole field of play. It's their specialty. And if they win, that's what we'll have here—chaos, utter and complete."

"God!" I said. "Why would the DUO-HEX approve something like that?"

"We can't go into details," El replied. "But take my word for it, this is well planned and for a good cause. And it's leading to a very interesting climax."

"Interesting climax," I echoed. "Okay, so let's look at it operationally. I have no line on the alien at all. The only target I can locate is Buc. So let's say I neutralize Buc. What will that accomplish? The alien is bound to have resources a lot bigger than Bucky. Doesn't he?"

I looked from one to the other; neither was going to tell me anything useful, I could feel it.

"You're right," El said, "we're not. The answer to that is part of the mission script, and has to remain hidden. But all the special rules aren't in the enemy's favor. They included allowing us to rehab your warrior pattern and give you so much on-site support."

"Two things looked very positive yesterday," Dak put in, "besides the way you and Stu performed. First,

Bucky went temporarily psychotic. That H-bomb strike he ordered on you, even though it was a small one, would have blown their whole plan to hell."

"Not to mention what it would have done to Jefferson, Missouri, and to Stu and me."

"Right. But I'm looking at it from the aliens' point of view, and it shook them. I could almost smell the panic. I had the distinct feeling they were thinking of pulling him out with a teleport beam. And if they had, we'd be in the DUO-HEX's court right now, watching them squirm. It would be all over except the formalities, and those wouldn't take long."

We heard bare feet and murmuring, and cut short our discussion. Stu and Marcy joined us, and they, Stu mainly, finished up the food while we sat around the table drinking coffee. We didn't talk about anything in particular, but with them there, there was a genuine sense of reunion.

SIXTEEN

After we'd sat there a while, Dak twinned, or cloned. Whatever. One moment she was sitting at one end of the table with the rest of us along the sides, and the next moment she was at both ends. No one said anything. I glanced at Stu to see how he was reacting. Very briefly he froze; otherwise, for the moment, we all simply continued whatever we were doing, whether sipping coffee, eating one more deviled egg, or just relaxing.

Then the space in the room brightened and shimmered, and the six of us seemed to pulse toward a common center, to nearly become one and pulse outward again. The physical presence of a table was no barrier; it could have been air. We were doing something like attuning to each other's personal realities, lending one another power as individuals, gaining power as a team. I could feel Stu and I becoming more the warriors, and El and Marcy more the masters of play. The two Daks were more at holding us apart, guiding and balancing.

Finally, after some unknowable span, the sense of timelessness vanished and the room returned to normal, or our perception of it did. An even younger Dak broke the silence.

"Well, kids, that takes care of about a thousand years' worth of communication. You'll find yourselves knowing things about one another now—not everything, by any means, but everything you're ready for and need now."

She gestured at her duplicate. "Now let's welcome sister Kad. We'll need her for this mission."

We all got up and gave the identical twin hugs and kisses, and in general made her welcome. The remarkable sameness of her appearance was outweighed by an unquestionable sense of her individuality; Kad was a separate person.

"I'll keep Dak from pushing us into things too far," Kad said.

We moved into the large living room, just right for a professor entertaining students, and sat down. The way these people seemed to me now had certainly changed, and I felt the need to sort some of it out.

I looked at Marcy. "Last night it was as if you'd known Stu before in this lifetime. What's the story there?"

"El told me about you and Stu a long time ago, when I was about five. She told me that someday you two would be our mates." She looked at El, as if for an okay on something, then back to me. "I've always known where each of you was, all along, and basically what you were doing. And I knew just about when we'd meet. Waiting is hard when you're a little girl, but Dak helped me keep scrapbooks on each of you, throughout your careers.

"And Dak always let me be aware when she arranged for me to dream with Stu. I wanted to contact both of you, but mom—El, that is—said it was too early yet. When I was eight, and it was Christmas time, I got each of you a present, and wrapped them myself. Dak promised to deliver them, but without a card."

"We're a team," Dak put in. "All of us. We have been all along, as you know now. Mar was raised to know that, and to know what her position on the team would be.

"Now, about the team's mission: We have eleven very alien aliens who've been working toward this same nexus, in something like high glee at the prospect of destroying civilization without a war, of plunging nearly five billion people into a primitivism that can't support ten percent of them."

She paused to fix Stu and me with sober eyes. "They have no interest in ruling or exploiting the planet. None. They couldn't care less for anything like that. Utter chaos is their goal; they love it."

Dak paused to let the grimness drop away, and continued in a softer voice.

"It's time now to take dear old Bucky out of the picture before he does something overly rash. And we can do it now in a way that wouldn't have worked last night. I'd like to just gate him to a good psycho ward, but that would be an act of play, and this scenario is for warriors and warlords only.

"One of his alien puppet masters is with him now, to make sure he doesn't crack too much and hit the daisy button for World War Last. The alien will have him calm enough by tomorrow to make his scheduled address at the Naval Academy. Wouldn't you know that Buc would be the only air force general to insist on speaking to the naval cadets every year? Our warriors can be his escort, dressed as Naval Security. Kad and I will be the prop girls. How does that sound?"

Something had changed: Now Dak was helping us plan.

"Be easy to get him out with a navy chopper," Stu said.

"Let's make it a marine chopper," I suggested. "The same model that hauls the President. Then we'll take

him to the White House for confession time." I listened
to myself saying it; it felt as natural, and as doable, as
anything. Turning to El I asked: "Can someone arrange
for the chopper, and for the President to be available
and willing to listen?"

She laughed, her eyes delighted. "Mar and I can
handle that. As Ms. Dorothy Anderson, I was his
number-one campaign contributor four years ago and
never asked for anything in return. Now election time
is coming again."

Dak and Kad laughed, too, then spoke in stereo-like
unison. "He's been praying to his tooth fairy every
night lately for Ms. Anderson to return his calls. Needing money is the excuse he uses with himself, but the
key reason he likes to see El is that she makes him feel
good—takes a load off his mind. So he'll listen to her,
and do favors that he'd never do for other big contri-
butors."

"Good," I said. "El, set it up to be there when we
deliver Buc. Tell the President you've always wanted to
meet the general, that you're a great admirer of the way
he's reduced interservice rivalry or something. Whatever comes to you; you guys are the pros at these
things."

I paused, and Kad cut in. "Here's the real beauty of
having Bucky spill his guts to the President. After the
President hears Buc's story about NORTEC, he'll be
afraid to go public with it, because the money used to
start NORTEC was funneled from several air force slush
funds and supplemented by kickbacks on defense contracts. The alien warlord won't have grounds for a beef
to the DUO-HEX, and the President's best course will
be to sell NORTEC to El."

"If we buy NORTEC," Mar put in, "what do we do
about its mercenary army?"

"Maybe we should keep it," Stu suggested. "We
might need it for something."

Dak and Kad agreed. Then I told about my ready
room, and about Buc calling out the nuclear strike to
stop us from reaching D.C. That, of course, was no
news to El and Dak/Kad, and Mar already knew, too.

Stu was only mildly surprised and not shocked at all. His acceptance level for wild data had expanded during the team reunion ritual, and it had been pretty darned high before.

"Now, what I want to know," I said, "is why Buc was that afraid of me. What is there about SWAC that scared him psychotic? Or wasn't it SWAC?"

It was El who answered, or partly answered. Actually, it was a no-answer response. "He put two and two together and came up with four," she said, "but the twos were erroneous data. And when someone is working on covert destruction, the way Bucky is now, they get very touchy about their privacy. That's all I can tell you about it."

I was intrigued, but knew better than to try for more. "Hell," I said, "I designed and built SWAC, and I don't have the foggiest idea what the aliens intended for it."

"Neither does Bucky," El answered, "but you'll be able to sort it out if we can get NORTEC."

Dak stood up then. "Enough," she said. "Too much preliminary talk spoils the warrior for battle. Go walk around some. Reconnect to physical reality."

Then she and Kad left on business while Mar went to get ready for her afternoon class. The college had installed a master's program in math, and this lovely young professor was in charge of graduate seminars. Stu and I offered to handle the breakfast debris, but El told us to go shave and make ourselves presentable—that we'd find clothes to fit us in the closets.

When we'd done that, he and I went outdoors and walked around the neighborhood, talking. Before long, the conversation turned to the next day's operation. We decided that what we really needed was a chopper with the presidential seal. It would make a lot of things easier, and Buc couldn't refuse a ride in a presidential chopper to a command appearance at the White House. Stu also said we needed to locate a store where we could buy the necessary uniforms, but I said we ought to leave that to our twin supply officers.

When we got back, the car we'd stolen the night before was gone, and Mar was just leaving for class. She was walking, and Stu went with her. El came out of the house as I started up the walk. She took my hand and we walked together to a gazebo in the redwood-fenced back yard. Its interior was dark and cool beneath a thick covering of pink honeysuckle, and we sat down inside together on its padded bench.

"This place smells as sweet as you feel," I murmured in her ear.

She kissed me, a soft lingering kiss. "Once, long ago," she told me, "when you first became a warrior, I met you in a place very much like this. There was already a lot you weren't allowed to remember; you didn't remember who I was, or what we'd been, but you sensed it at a deeper level. It was not a happy time. Close your eyes and look with me."

I did, and remembered. I may have had my memory unblocked, but there was an incredible lot of it, most of which I would never get around to looking at. It was background, very little of which needed to be revisited. But this did. Seeing it again tapped an area of grief that, unlooked at, would have continued to lie there, tainting our happiness with ancient loss.

"You do remember," she whispered.

I nodded. Till then the span of our separation had been an abstract concept to me. Now I felt the extent of it, the *immensity*. I saw myself reaching out to her in a myriad of mystical moments of loneliness, leaving a trail of tears that spanned the sky. And I'd never truly forgotten her, even though all memory of before was locked away, had had to be. This war, and our separate roles in it, were far, far older than Earth.

She was crying softly. We lay down close on the bench and journeyed quietly with each other to clear twin trails of tears, trails that sometimes crossed, but all too seldom and all too briefly. After we'd done that, a bubbly laughter replaced the sobs, and we kissed each other's faces in a fuller reunion.

Two panther-sized black cats jumped over the gate then and mauled us softly, joyously, as if to say, "Now that your grief is gone, we'll join you." Their wrestling was strong, energetic, despite sheathed claws, and when it was over, El and I were pink and sweaty.

Then the twins, in their feline mode, nudged us toward the gate. "We're commanded to the showers," El said, and taking my hand, drew me after her.

I looked back, ready to see two panthers crouching to pounce again. Instead I saw two youthful, nude, and nubile human twins putting down air mattresses for sun bathing. With cheshire cat grins they watched us depart.

After showering and drying, I led El into the bedroom. "Now, if the twins will leave us alone," I said suggestively.

"Hmm. Don't depend on it."

My face took on a look of concern.

"They will come to bed with us," she said, "now and then, but not to interfere. Dak/Kad is our third terminal, remember. She/they are always and everywhere with us, but until we cleared our trail of grief, they couldn't fully enjoy our reunion, so they kept a certain distance."

We got into bed then, and out of regard for my relict self-consciousness, the twins didn't appear physically, but in a sense they were there. Sex without a background of grief, and with happy third terminals in the wings, had a sweetness I hadn't suspected. Then, as we lay quietly side by side, the door burst open and the air was full of bodies and squeals. The twins landed giggling on top of us, hugging and kissing us like playful children, laughing and jabbering in unison. It was hard to realize that they had been one middled-aged marine sergeant type just a few days earlier.

"You guys are delicious," they said in unison, "and we love having you really together again." After more hugging and kissing, they pulled us off the bed.

"Time for tea, kids, time for tea." They sang it like a TV gum commercial. I was surprised at how comfortable I was with them in the nude like that. When Stu and Mar returned, the twins danced around, undressing them, too, throwing their clothes into corners. Stu survived with no real trauma. Then we continued our meeting around the table.

Afterward all four girls left us to arrange a formal, catered dinner party for that night, our first together as a team.

SEVENTEEN

Stu and I had been dressed in tuxedos for an hour. Neither of us was used to wearing one, but we agreed (1) that it was surprising how comfortable we felt in them, and (2) that we looked pretty darned good. Then El and Mar entered, which gave us a lesson in what looking good was all about: they were gorgeous. Their gowns, strapless and backless, had to have been molded by a master anti-gravity engineer; they showed no sign of artificial supports. Their hair looked like they'd spent the day in an ancient Greek salon. El's dress was a sheer light green silk with a plain underlining. Mar's blue silk was in the same design, with a low-key overprint.

Each wore an aura that enhanced their physical beauty, and I applauded as they took turns doing spins for us.

Hearing nothing from Stu, I turned to look at him. He was standing there transfixed, staring at Mar. After a moment he spoke: "It was you," he said simply.

He moved to her and took her hands.

"Yes," she said, looking up at him. "El and Dak arranged that one meeting. Perhaps you'd better tell Le, so he'll know what we're talking about."

It took him a minute to start; it was hard for him to take his eyes off her. "When I graduated from the Air Force Academy, I didn't have a date, so a friend fixed me up with his cousin. She was really good-looking, and I got the distinct impression that she had plans for me. Then, still early, she went to the powder room. I was waiting for her at the edge of the dance floor when someone touched me on the shoulder. I turned and there was Mar in what might have been this exact dress."

Stu's eyes had gone back to her as he talked. "She smiled, and said, 'This is our dance.' We stepped onto the floor together, and, as if on cue, the band changed to a slower tune. We danced just that one dance, close. I couldn't even talk to her, but I recognized her from my dreams. Then, after the dance, we got separated, and she seemed to vanish. I was distracted all the rest of the evening, watching for her, and my date got upset and changed her plans."

He looked at El, as if seeking an explanation. "I thought about my disappearing dream girl until I went to sleep. Then somehow I never remembered it again until now. Not once. It was as if it never happened."

El smacked Mar on the backside. "I had to give her that one dance or she would have fried the air academy that night. She almost rained Missouri off the map when Dak showed her a picture of you and your high school prom date."

"Oh, Mom! I was going to tell him that later when we looked at the scrapbook."

"Sorry, dear."

Our attention was diverted then by two female marine officers storming through the front door. One twin was a burly full eagle colonel, the other a compact major. The colonel patted her briefcase and rapped out, "All right, you jarheaded chopper jockeys, we've got your goodies. Your chopper will be ready tomorrow at ten hundred hours, sharp. The major here has hung your dress blues in your closets."

"I wanted to be the colonel," Dak pouted. She said it in the voice of a nine-year-old.

Our laughter was interrupted by the arrival of the caterers: some students who did small-scale catering as a sideline. They were quick, setting up a buffet as if they'd drilled it, which they probably had, then departing without leaving anyone to serve. Apparently Mar had specified that this was a family affair, with privacy required.

While the buffet and dining table were being set, the twins had gone to the bedroom to change for dinner. They returned as the last student closed the door behind him. And when they changed for dinner, they changed! They were back to their younger versions, and wore costumes barely legal even on rim worlds.

It was obvious that someone had done something to the food again—either the food or our bodies—because we ate and ate, but no one seemed to suffer for it. We ate slowly though, visiting and listening to music. Gradually, eating graded into looking at scrapbooks. Then we danced to Mar's special record, an LP with six repeats of her and Stu's song, "Moonlight Serenade."

And finally, El and the twins must have done something with time again because we stayed up fairly late, yet awoke bright and rested when the twins banged on the door at 5:30 A.M. Breakfast was scrambled eggs, along with chipped beef gravy on toast, a fitting sendoff for marines. As we ate, Dak briefed us on the arrangements they'd made for the day's plan. We'd have a lot of ad-libbing to do.

"You guys will have a presidential chopper waiting for you in Baltimore. It'll be there by ten hundred hours, and you can pick up Buc at the Naval Academy at ten-thirty, after he's finished his address. El and Mar will meet you at the White House."

"If there's any hitch in getting Buc there," El put in, "I'll tell the President about NORTEC and insist he raid the place at once with a company of marines. It won't be easy without Bucky's confession, but we'll have to try."

"Right," Kad said. "It's important that you guys get Buc, because we *need* to take over NORTEC, and El isn't allowed to exert any influence beyond friendship, strength of personality, and drawing on old favors—what any personal friend and major financial supporter might use on the President."

Dak took over again. "The White House is sending a limo to fetch El and Mar to a ten-thirty meeting with the President." She turned to them. "It's on his calendar, although if he asked, no one would remember putting it there. The limo will meet you two in front of the Maryland state house in Annapolis at nine-thirty. Kad and I will hang loose and monitor the aliens."

After they'd finished briefing us, we went to dress for our roles. El and Mar looked very chic, but also very competent and professional, as the exorbitantly wealthy Dorothy and Marcy Anderson. They gave us pecks and left in Mar's Porsche to meet the limo. The twins were still a marine major and full colonel. They looked a little on the young side now, but had an aura of military toughness and efficiency about them.

I wore a lieutenant colonel's oak leaves. Stu was my pilot and wore captain's bars. We walked the six blocks to the local recruiting office, where the sergeant in charge had orders to drive us to Baltimore. It wouldn't do to draw attention to Mar's home base by having a presidential chopper pick us up in Dover.

Before I'd recovered my warrior pattern, I doubt if I could have fooled a marine sergeant first class for more than a minute. Now Sergeant Jerry Marston accepted me as an officer without hesitation. When we went out to his big G.S.A. station wagon, there were a pair of briefcases on the floor in the back seat. We examined their contents as the sergeant pulled out of the parking lot. Each contained a pair of 3-mm's—one standard mini and one rapid-fire. A note said, "For other stuff you might need, see under the deck in back." The Dak/Kad prop crew had struck again.

I checked the ready-room battle board. We were already a target, with bogeys fore and aft. The two bogeys ahead, about nine miles west of town, were standing still; the other two were a few blocks behind us and holding their distance. I didn't know whether they knew our exact location, but at least they seemed confident of the route we planned to take.

It struck me then how they'd known where to find us: Someone, almost certainly the alien, had access to his ready room. I was reasonably sure that Buc was in no shape to have access to his. As soon as we started a hostile move, we read on the alien's board. When the sergeant had been ordered to chauffeur us, he'd read on it, too. Marcy's place could be a "safe house" in the fullest sense—somehow untouchable.

The alien probably operated by informing Buc of developments, and Buc would instruct his people by radio. I doubted that any of Buc's people had been rehabilitated to the point of receiving explicit telepathic instructions, because the alien had a psychotic compulsion to *de*habilitate. People around him would go downhill.

All of this was speculation, of course, except what I felt about the alien. Briefly, I wondered why I felt so positive about what he was like, then realized I knew him well, from long experience. What was missing was any explicit recalls of him or of my encounters with him. Part of the conditions of the game, I supposed, or maybe I simply wasn't up to remembering him yet.

But then . . . If the alien could relay our positions to Buc, why hadn't Buc had us picked up or killed at the lodge? Or while we were driving to Dover? And why the big location uncertainty when we were flying cross-country? It began to sort itself out for me, and the answer seemed to lie in the DUO-HEX's office. The alien had probably petitioned It last night for authorization to give Buc that kind of direction. And El and Dak/Kad had agreed to a trade-off: They'd go along with that if they could give me planning advice. That would explain the help they'd given me this morning.

Anyway, if I was right, then the use of radio, and relaying messages through Buc, would keep their response time slow. If I was right. It felt right somehow, but I wasn't going to rely on it.

We were out of Dover's small downtown district, heading west. I leaned forward, toward the driver. "Sergeant Marston," I said, "we're on a top-secret mission for the President, as I presume you've been told. That's not for the President's office, or for the Secret Service, but for the President himself.

"Well, something just went wrong. The Secret Service people covering us left us a present in your vehicle: a radio and some small arms. Apparently our secrecy has been blown, and we can expect to need these."

The sergeant nodded. "Yes, sir. Colonel Felin told me to come armed, and to offer any assistance needed. That includes taking the flight with you if you request it."

I sat back and, cupping my hand over my ear, pretended to use the radio in the briefcase, then checked the ready room again. The two cars ahead were standing still. We were holding our distance on the two behind; we'd open it up a bit by getting out of the city speed zone before they did.

"Right!" I said aloud to the open top of the briefcase. "We'll take care of them. We're on our own and on our way. Over and out."

I looked up. "Sergeant, as soon as we're out of town, accelerate this sonofabitch and don't worry about the speed limit. We need a gap between us and the guys following us. Captain, we're in the soup. The Secret Service people are pinned down, and there are bogeys behind us, pushing us toward an ambush about eight miles ahead.

"Sergeant, once we're out of town, find us a side road—one with some cover near the highway."

"Yes sir."

As soon as the housing developments began to thin out, the sergeant hit the gas hard. The battle board showed our followers dropping behind. I was surprised that a G.S.A. vehicle could respond that well, and wondered if Dak had anything to do with it. Shortly a row of maples, rich green, appeared along the sides of the right of way, and the sergeant slowed.

"Turnoff just ahead, colonel."

"Take it."

I could see where a narrow dirt lane opened through a gap in the maples. The sergeant braked sharply and turned onto it, taking us between two fields of clover. Ahead, the lane went past a barn and ended about a quarter-mile beyond it at a country road screened by another tall hedge.

"Captain," I snapped, "leave your white cap on the

seat. You'll take cover behind the barn. I'll be behind
that hedgerow across from it. Sergeant, come to a full
stop at the barn when we get there, so we can close the
car doors behind us. Then make dust to that road up
ahead, turn east, and stop as soon as you're out of
sight."

We had the doors open before he stopped, then
bailed out with our miniature armories, slamming the
doors behind us. The sergeant hit the gas pedal again
and sped away as we headed for cover. There was only
about a hundred feet of hedge, leggy and open from age
and lack of care. I ducked behind it and doubled back
to near its south end, hitting the dirt at a little opening
in it. I'd be able to see the road in both directions from
there, and move out into it quickly if I needed to. Stu
was out of sight behind the barn about a hundred feet
away. In the still morning air, a train of tan dust still
hung over the lane to verify that we'd left the highway,
but our pursuers hadn't come to the turnoff yet.

The ready room showed they were about a hundred
yards from it, and speeding. The road block ahead
wasn't a road block any more, because those two cars
had started eastward on the highway toward us. The
sergeant was approaching the end of the lane.

I hoped Buc considered this four-car task force enough
to stop us.

The two cars trailing us reached our lane and turned
in. Now, if they just hadn't gotten word that we'd
bailed out . . . They slowed, and for a moment I thought
they were going to wait for the roadblock crew to join
them. They didn't, though; they came on down the lane
when they saw the sergeant turn back east at the junction ahead. They weren't the greatest warriors; they'd
bunched up, the two cars less than a hundred feet
apart.

I checked my warrior pattern, feeling at least two
hundred percent alive. The adrenalin was pumping.

There were three men in each car. The first drove
past me and on toward the barn. Stu fired a dozen
rounds in a three-second burst, apparently killing all
three men in the first car. The second car closed half

the intervening distance before it stopped, and its men piled out on my side of the road, as I'd expected, to keep their car between Stu and themselves. I squeezed off a long burst, and they were dead before they hit the ground.

Stu had started out of the barn, and I jumped out yelling and waving for him to get behind it. Then I hit the ditch. We'd just made it when both cars exploded, sending up twin balls of flame and columns of black smoke. It was a hell of a bang; it made the ground jump beneath me. I was surprised the barn didn't collapse; there wasn't much left of the cars but engine blocks and twisted frames. I jumped up again and ran toward the barn. Stu saw me coming and came out from behind it.

"Wow!" he said. "You guessed that one right, and just in time. How did you know those suckers were going to blow up?"

"Good question," I told him.

The sergeant had turned around and was coming back down the lane. He pulled up in a fresh cloud of dust.

"Judas priest, sir!" he said. "What blew their cars?"

"They were rigged to self-destruct. Their bosses didn't want any useful evidence left around."

There still were two more cars after us. I checked again; they were about three miles away. Even as I watched, one turned north on a side road. I knew what they had in mind. They knew where we were, or more likely they knew where their other cars had been. They planned to turn into the lane from both directions.

It was time to see what our prop girls had put in the back. "Drive into the barn, sergeant," I said. When he had, I opened the tailgate and found a rocket launcher stowed beneath the deck; now I knew why the sergeant had been signed out with a full-sized station wagon. There was also a six-pack of rounds for it. I looked back at Marston. "Are you any good with these things?" I asked.

"Damn good, sir; I used to instruct in those babies. And hitting what I shoot at comes natural to me. Always has."

"Fine. I'm expecting two more cars of hostiles to arrive, one from each end of the lane. They'll probably stop a hundred yards away; farther, if they're smart. Can you hit a car with that at two hundred yards?"

"Piece of cake, sir."

"All right. You stay here in the barn. We'll be behind the hedge to gun down anyone who comes up to investigate the wreckage. When we fire, or when I yell to you, you pop out and hit the cars."

Then Stu and I ran to the hedge. I left him at the north end while I ran to the south. The ready-room battle board showed that the bogey on the highway had slowed a little, to let the other car pull more or less even. They were probably in radio contact, and both were within a mile of the lane. It would be about another minute. I couldn't see Stu, but the sergeant was visible through the barn door. I felt pretty sure he was as good as the impression he gave. Our casting director wouldn't have it any other way.

The first car turned in from the south and stopped. A few seconds later the other turned in from the north. Then both proceeded slowly toward us. They could see the shattered remains of the first car; these guys were going to be very wary, very professional.

They stopped about a hundred and fifty yards from the barn. There were four men in each; the battle board had told me that. One man stayed at the wheel of each car; two, with rifles, took cover in opposite ditches, prone, very low; then one from each started up the road, also with rifles, walking bent-kneed, ready. I flattened for better concealment and couldn't see the man from the north any more.

The man from my end stopped right in front of me and knelt, as if to cover the other guy. His eyes were on the barn, his rifle ready at chest height, his aura thick with tension. I had no idea what the other was doing. Half a minute later I heard Stu's pistol rip a short burst, and I let the man in front of me have four rounds in the upper torso. Almost instantly there were long bursts of automatic rifle fire from the north, bullets snapping and singing low down through the hedge, followed quickly by similar bursts from the south. Twigs, branches, and splinters flew. A powerful explosion slammed the morning air from the north, and for just a moment the shooting stopped. Then a single burst of rifle fire repeated from the south, to be extinguished by another powerful explosion—the second car.

I gave it three or four seconds before crawling out where I could see more. The sergeant was peering low around the corner of the barn door. Both cars had been shredded by the combination of rocket rounds, the charges they'd been rigged with, and gasoline. I could see no sign of men near them, and wasn't a bit surprised. Crouching, I ran out and grabbed the rifle of the dead man in front of me, then spun, and hit the shallow ditch again. Nothing happened. I looked back and saw Stu crouched with the other rifle, peering in my direction. The sergeant was still looking around the edge of the barn door. After scanning all about with my warrior senses, I peeked in the ready room, then got up; there were no more bogeys around, but we were likely to be receiving visitors from the sheriff's department pretty damn soon, or maybe the highway patrol.

In another minute we were back in the station wagon. The sergeant skirted around the twisted chassis in our way, and we were quickly on the highway.

"Great shooting, sergeant," I said. "We're a team. Suppose I call you Jerry and you call me Le? The captain is Stu. That's the way I prefer it when it's just the three of us together."

"If you say so, sir—Lee. But I may forget sometimes."

"That's all right, too; feel free. I'm comfortable either way."

"Jerry," Stu said, "what's a rocket expert doing in a recruiting office?"

"Don't know, sir. Just got transferred a week ago. Maybe it was for this."

Another one of us, I was willing to bet, and wondered when and where we'd served together.

"Well, welcome to the best damn fighting team on the planet, Jerry."

"Thanks, uh, Lee. Glad to be part of it."

The ready room still showed no bogeys, which seemed to mean that whatever new decisions might have been made with regard to us, nothing had been started yet. I pretty much kept quiet the rest of the way to Baltimore, monitoring. We arrived less than ten minutes behind schedule, to pick up the chopper from the ferry pilots. They eyed our mussed and dirty dress blues while I signed the receipt.

"What happened to you guys?" asked the major in charge.

"Had a fire-fight getting here."

"No shit!" His face lit up, and his eyes went to Jerry, who was carrying our two rifles and the rocket launcher. "Colonel Felin told us you were out to handle a terrorist threat. Is there anything you want us to do?"

"Any rockets in this flying office?"

"No, but I have a buddy who can have a flight of gun platforms here in under thirty minutes."

"Good. Climb on board and call him to meet us at the Naval Academy. We're picking up General Decker there, the air force chief of staff, to take him to the White House. But we can expect to be jumped along the way."

The major looked pleased as hell, and went forward to help Stu with any defensive gadgets this bird had. I checked the ready room and saw two fast-flying bogeys, presumably with our chopper as their target. Hopefully the presidential air taxi would have good ECM equipment—electronic counter-measures: I could sense missiles in our future.

There were, and they were almost good enough. As we swung around at 500 feet, the bogeys approached from both sides forward—small, nimble, private jets. Jerry, using his rocket launcher, got the one on his side before it fired, which impressed hell out of me. The other one launched two missiles before it disengaged.

The ECM turned one of the missiles away, but the other ripped through the cabin, tearing a gash through the airframe. It shook me for a moment. We should have been hearing the DUO-HEX's harps, but the damn thing hadn't exploded.

The pilot of the jet swept by to inspect the damage, and Jerry got him with another rocket. Twice was no accident. I wondered if infantry rocket launchers were that advanced or if Jerry's warrior pattern was that good.

There were headsets for communicating with the pilots, and I'd put one on when I'd sat down. Now I spoke through my throat mike. "Gentlemen, you can thank your lucky cats that that sucker was a dud."

The major in the cockpit with Stu described the air battle to his friend warming up his flight of gun platforms, and told him to tilt his ass and cover our landing in Annapolis.

Our other ferry pilot, a first lieutenant, had donned a headset, too, and used it now. With the door open and the sound-insulated airframe breached, the cabin was almost as loud as the chopper we'd flown in to the bay. "Colonel," he said to me, "the CO of the marine honor guard at the Academy is my cousin. Shall I get him to arm up and cover us on the ground?"

"Right, and well done on thinking of it. We're picking up the air force chief of staff, General Decker, for a meeting with the President. But the general mustn't be told about the trouble. We think that an aide with him is connected to the plot, and the general could be endangered if he's told."

The lieutenant disappeared into the cockpit to make the call. The marines would be covering our pickup on the ground and in the air now, and I could see Dak's hand in the selection of three key pieces: Jerry and the two ferry pilots. The ready room showed no more bogeys around Annapolis, but I couldn't see the alien letting us get to Buc without his activating some backup plans. How would I handle it, I thought, if I were the alien?

Of course! Have someone on hand to kill the general as a last resort. I'd been faking when I'd said that about Bucky's aide, but something like that was just what I'd do. I went forward to the cockpit and tapped the second ferry pilot on the shoulder.

"Call your cousin quick, and tell him . . ."

He handed me the mike. "You tell him," he said. "He's on now."

"This is Colonel Le Sal," I said, "with a special anti-terrorist team protecting the President. Surround the general at once and don't let any of his aides near him. Shoot anyone who tries to get to him except your own people. And get this; it's important! Disrobe General Decker *completely;* strip off everything—socks, shorts, dental appliances, hearing aid, hernia truss, whatever he's got on. This is *vitally* important. If he has a toupee or bandage, rip it off, too. They are all considered minibombs. Do it *now!*"

The honor guard CO left the battle phone open and I could hear him snapping orders. A long minute later I heard an explosion. After that there was virtual silence for a minute, with only some rapid talk that I couldn't make out. Then the CO was back, his voice vivid with excitement. "My God!" he said. "His false teeth, shoes, and coat buttons just blew up! I had to choke him to get his teeth out, and almost lost a hand throwing the damn things away!"

"Great show, man!" I said. "Get a blanket or something on the general and put his aides in front of a firing squad. One of them has a detonator. Don't shoot them, though; save them for me. Did you have the general on the ground when you undressed him?"

"Yes, sir. Surrounded by a squad of men."

"That's what saved the day. The aide didn't realize you were taking the bombs off until it was too late."

Coming in over the Academy, I could see the honor guard in a circle on a broad lawn. Other than that, the area was pretty well cleared of people. To one side of them stood a squad of marines with rifles leveled, facing two men in air force uniforms.

Stu came back from the cockpit as soon as we'd landed. "Anybody here have a pocket calculator?" I asked.

Jerry handed me his.

"A little joke on a traitor," I told him, and jumped out. I walked over with all the authority of a lieutenant colonel on special orders, and told the marines to put the general aboard. Then I walked to the firing squad with the CO. The two aides looked nervous; they had their eyes on me, not knowing what to expect. I held the pocket calculator up for their attention—a small black object that looked electronic.

"I got this off the boss of one of you a little while ago; he told me how to use it before I killed him. How about you? Shall I push it?"

The traitor, a major, had stopped being a warrior long before, and his body reaction gave him away—he flinched. I told the CO to take the other aside and keep him covered. Then, staying well back, I made the major an offer. "Take all your clothes off," I told him, "and come with us to see the President, or you die right here."

He started to undress, then the fear dropped from his face and was replaced by a blank stare. He began to move toward me. The CO and I shot him at the same instant. Before he hit the ground, several mini-bombs went off. Talk about an instant mess!

I scanned the other aide, a first lieutenant. He was clean of bug bombs, and staring in shock at the major's tattered remains. "Okay," I said to him, "you seem to be clean. If you know of anyone else in the military who's undergone a personality change the way that poor bastard must have, get his name to the President's office within the hour."

I turned to the CO. "Thanks," I said. "You and your men saved the country today. But we need to keep this whole affair absolutely confidential; let the President decide what to release and when." Then I trotted back to the chopper and went forward to the cockpit. In seconds we were off the ground.

Overhead we were met by two circling gun ships as we headed for the White House. A glance at the ready-room battle board revealed no bogeys in the air, but I knew we still had to be a target, and so was the White House.

The White House! "El!" I shouted nonverbally, "get out of there quick."

"Don't worry, Le, we'll be okay here. Dak and Kad

got the DUO-HEX to issue a special order. Nothing can touch the White House until confession time is over—not even a G-class wagon. That is, if you can get Bucky here in one piece."

Jerry asked us to be on the lookout for bogeys—said he could feel them coming. He was right; there were four of them on the battle board—missiles. Judging by their speed, apparently surface-to-air missiles—approaching in a cluster from the southeast. Someone was really throwing caution to the winds. Stu spotted them before I could say anything, and changed headings toward them.

Then our gun ships did the miraculous. When the missiles were three seconds away, they laid down a curtain of bullets. One of the missiles exploded, detonated by a .50 caliber slug, and that took out the other three.

At least that was one possible interpretation, and the marines sure as hell believed it. I could hear our escorts cheering on the radio, along with Stu and the three with us. Maybe the DUO-HEX would buy it, too.

EIGHTEEN

El filled me in as we flew to meet her. An elite platoon of marines—one shift of the presidential SWAT team—was already on its way to NORTEC with a bomb squad. The CO of the Naval Academy honor guard had given them the procedure for defusing the top men.

As we swung in for a landing, there was no sign of tourists, but I could see a group of men and one woman near an entrance to the White House. That had to be the President and El, I decided, with Secret Service personnel. From above, I could also see inconspicuous armed marines at vantage points around. Thirty yards from the President and El, and near the helipad, two female marines waited in dress blues, obviously Dak and Kad.

Both twins came over as soon as we'd set down, even before the rotor was stopped. Meanwhile, the gunships were waiting above to escort our chopper to NORTEC when Stu and I deplaned with Buc.

But there was something that had to be done first, El had told us: They needed both Stu and me, in two places at the same time—at NORTEC and the White House—so Dak was going to twin us. We waited for her and Kad to come aboard. Stu had already traded places with the ferry copilot and come aft. All we needed to do was get Jerry out of the way so he wouldn't see what was going on.

That was easy enough. While the twins were boarding, I sent Jerry forward to monitor the radio—told him to keep track of the raid on NORTEC for me.

"Well, warriors," Dak said cheerfully as she stepped aboard, "how'd you like those near-misses?" She wasn't looking for an answer; the question was filler. While Kad went forward toward the cockpit, Dak helped Stu and me pretty much carry Buc down the ramp. Once on the ground, Dak just kept walking. I hadn't felt any splitting or anything else—hadn't realized it had happened—and thought the question after her: "When?"

"It's done," she told me in the same mode, and chuckled. "You're twice the man you were." Stu and I were still supporting the sagging, blanket-wrapped Buc toward the President and El when the chopper lifted, clattering off above the mall toward Virginia with another me aboard, and another Stu.

The President and El came to meet us. "Mr. President," El said, "meet our heroes of the last three days: Jan Ambers and Stu Rogers." There was a trace of self-vindication in her tone. It couldn't have been easy, selling him her explanation of the recent strange events—air force alerts, reports of aerial gunnery and explosions, plane crashes, explosions on the Potomac . . . I mean—*aliens!* It must have sounded like classic paranoia. It had probably taken the marine reports from Annapolis to get his agreement to meet us.

President John Roubideaux Fuller ignored Stu and me for the moment, peering intently into Bucky's vacant eyes. "Gawd! He looks terrible!" he said, sounding even more country southern in person than on television. He turned to me then. "I'll want to hear your stories later, colonel, but right now let's get General Decker inside and have my doctor look at him."

He led the way and we followed, surrounded by a moving ring of stony-faced Secret Service men. It wasn't easy; Bucky was heavy. Inside, we lowered him into an upholstered, wing-backed chair that would keep him from falling sideways, and in moments the White House physician arrived and examined him.

"This man should be in a hospital," he said.

"Not yet," the President answered. "We've got a dangerous situation, and General Decker's our main source of information on it." He pinned the doctor with his eyes. "Someone just tried very hard to kill him. We need him to tell us what the hell's goin' on. As soon as possible. I want you to give him somethin' so he can talk."

"All right, Mr. President," the doctor said unhappily. He prepared a hypodermic and injected Buc, then even more unhappily left when the President indicated he didn't want him there during the interrogation.

I'd expected Buc to respond right away, but he didn't. He sat there with his mouth slightly open, his eyes still vacant. Apparently the doctor had given him something not designed to kick the system into gear too abruptly. The President looked at Buc, waiting for a long moment before turning to El.

"Dorothy," he said, "I've got decisions to make, and I need all the information I can get. One thing that's not clear to me is how you stumbled onto this plot." He turned to Stu and me then, his eyes examining. "Miz Anderson tells me that you men aren't really marine officers."

El picked up the question. "Mr. Ambers here is the one who discovered the connection to NORTEC in his

DOD contract, in an obscure and unusual security clause. He did some checking and found that the local security people had set up a direct access line from his computer to NORTEC, bypassing the Pentagon."

For the moment his eyes remained on me; I was the one he'd asked a specific question of. But I couldn't risk saying something not consistent with what she might have told him earlier, so I let her continue to talk.

"And Jan felt that if something like that was going on, there might easily be something deeper beneath it, possibly something sinister. He knew I had a lot of connections; we'd become—very well acquainted when I tried to buy his company after his first big breakthrough in holographic imagery."

She knew the President better than he knew himself. She'd paused slightly between "become" and "very well acquainted," and the President interpreted it as indicating a love affair. Beneath the tough hide of that pragmatic and sometimes ruthless product of Louisiana politics, there dwelt what was left of a romantic. And somehow this new datum made the story more credible to him than it had been; he lightened.

She didn't leave it at that, though; it was time to handle his remaining skepticism as thoroughly as possible. We could expect to need his agreement on future actions. Now I felt her nudge me mentally to take it from there, with a nonverbal sense of the direction to go with it.

"How I got involved so deeply, Mr. President"—I gestured at the uniform I wore—"was partly because of my breakthrough in holography and partly because Dorothy's probing had to have worried certain people.

"Anyway, our security suddenly got very tight. A computer specialist, presumably from the DOD, was assigned to us full-time. Now that was *really* fishy. The contract had no provision in it for that, and from a DOD point of view, it made no sense. So it seemed to me that he had to be from NORTEC. I asked Dorothy if she could find out anything for me, and I told my staff not to give him any privileges at all. They were not to give him access to anything or let him do anything without his written request and my signed concurrence, and he was to surrender the original to them."

"Right after that," El put in, "we both became aware that we were being followed." She looked at me then, telling me mentally to continue.

"That confirmed my suspicions," I went on. "I pulled all the work on the DOD contract into my private lab and disconnected it from the reporting system. Not long after that they tried to kill me, and the . . ."

It was Bucky who interrupted; he'd come out of whatever he'd been in. "What happened?" he mumbled, then his eyes widened. "Mr. President!" He looked around. "How did I get here?" He was pale and dazed, and his speech a bit slurred, perhaps partly because he wasn't used to talking without his dentures. Then he looked down at himself. "My God!" he said, suddenly wide awake. "Where are my clothes?"

"You're all right, Ben," said the President. "You're just fine now. And these folks are friends; they just saved your life. Now I need some information from you. I need to know all about NORTEC, right now, off the record, no tapes."

Fear flickered through Buc, passed. He gave a small shudder, sighed, and looked around the room, visibly relaxing. His eyes settled on me. "I know you from someplace," he said calmly.

"He was on the cover of *Time*, Ben," the President answered.

Buc nodded as he turned his pale face to the President. "All about NORTEC?" he said after a moment. "You'd better brace yourself then, Mr. President; it's a wild story." He actually smiled slightly. His recovery seemed too complete to be explained by an injection. It was emotional as well as physical. I wondered if El had done something to help him.

"About five years ago," Buc said, "Captain Pat Quinn, my aide—Major Quinn now—hired a bright young computer whiz to do a system security study. The kid was fantastic—quick, likable, and very, very competent. Within a week he uncovered two active Soviet spies in the Air Force Technical Information Branch, and a mole on my own staff. All three suicided when confronted."

The President looked thunderstruck. "I never heard about that!"

"We never let it out. Remember, we were fighting for our lives before you took office. A scandal of that caliber would have cut our R&D budget to nothing, and crippled national defense. Anyway, the damn NSA should have caught those guys." Buc paused to regain his thought train. "So Pat and this whiz kid, Charles Larson's his name, came to me with a plan to not only protect ourselves from any future NSA foulups, but to ferret out the leaks in the other services. It sounded to me like a stroke of genius. The new breed of spies are technologically oriented; the old cloak and dagger have been replaced by electronics, so we'd use computers to catch them.

"That was the effort that grew into NORTEC."

He paused for a moment to clear his throat. "Could I have something to drink? This is dry work."

The President called for Cokes to be sent in.

"General Decker," El said, "is Charles Larson the actual head of NORTEC?"

He looked at her, surprised. "Yes, and we never knew it until about six months ago. The kid hoodwinked us all. Hell, he wouldn't even take a promotion; said he just wanted to do what he was good at." Buc grunted. "That sounded fine to me. I didn't know then what it was he was so good at."

I felt an urgency to get through to the other me, arriving at NORTEC about now, to give him/me the data about Charles Larson. I put the thought to El. Her nonverbal response was, "All handled."

Buc sipped his Coke and regathered his strength. "In the first year he found fifty more computer leaks, but they all evaporated when Air Force Special Intelligence started to examine them. So he suggested a new approach for the second year: He brought me a list of 1,005 contracts the Soviets might be interested in tapping. He'd studied every damn one of them, and said he could expose the whole Soviet network by setting up a computer security system he had in mind.

"He believed—he said he believed—that the Soviets had set it up so our people would do a major piece of Soviet research for them. And he made a strong case to back up his thesis. The Soviets had broken up their project, he said, so it would be totally unrecognizable. The pieces could only be fitted together by the project's central program in the Soviet Union. And the pieces would seem . . ."

Abruptly Buc became rigid and stopped talking. His face grew red, his eyes wide and staring, as if an implanted command had been activated to stop his talking, and he was fighting it. El leaned over and patted his arm. "You're doing fine, Bucky," she said softly. "It'll be over soon."

The President didn't seem to notice the new name she'd used, but it snapped Buc out of his rigidity, and after a moment he continued almost as if it hadn't happened.

"The pieces would seem to fit into our own projects, and never be questioned. About midway through the second year, Pat rushed in to tell me that Charles had located a whole nest of agents. He took me to the office he'd rented for Charles and his computer, and showed me a map with all 1,005 contractor locations. It showed the telephone routes the DOD used to access the computers at those companies, both for billing and for technical progress reports. Most of the latter took a different routing, not the ones assigned to the Pentagon. The technical stuff was being routed through a substation in West Baltimore."

Buc paused for another swig of Coke. The President looked a little green, presumably at hearing about a large spy operation during his administration.

"Incidentally, Mr. President," Bucky added, interpreting the President's expression, "NORTEC has no official connection to the Pentagon except as an on-call consulting firm for computer system security.

"Anyway, Charles had a new device he said would detect a CPU—a central processing unit—in operation from two hundred yards away. From the size of the read, Pat said, Charles could tell that this Baltimore computer was large enough to handle all the data from those 1,005 contracts. So he asked for a truck and a squad of men to raid the place.

"They found the computer all right, a big one. *But all input and no output!* Not for a week. Then the first access-for-information request came in from a bakery near the Soviet Embassy; they pulled out a digest in five parts of all the week's input."

"What did you do about the spies runnin' those places?" the President asked. "I didn't hear about any arrests."

"That's the funny part. There were no spies. *The people in Baltimore believed they worked for the National Security Agency,* even had the papers, but the NSA denied them. No one in either facility knew what was going on, except probably one man who suicided in his home while the raid was in progress. And the people at the bake shop didn't know anything about anything except baking. They didn't even know their computer had any access to the one in Baltimore. The output from the Baltimore machine didn't print out at their end; it went onto a program disk in a code that wouldn't even read to their unit!"

"Why didn't I *hear* about any of that?"

"Well, Mr. President, you were new in office, and we didn't want to distract you from the push you had going for the military budget. And besides, we really had no evidence we could do anything with. Everyone checked out clean.

"But here's how it seemed to work. The bakery's computer was just a small business model, and it'd been breaking down two or three times a month. The people who sold and serviced it couldn't be found. Their business phone was in a tenement room, and no one ever turned up there after we got onto it. So they were obviously the connection. All they'd had to do was replace the message disk with a new program disk and leave.

"So all we'd accomplished was to satisfy ourselves

that our suspicions had been correct. What we'd uncovered didn't lead anywhere."

The President whistled silently, worried. Buc continued.

"Toward the end of that year we made another raid and found a group of people who thought they worked for the navy! They were monitoring the same group of contracts, and the data were being put out in a weekly digest through the satellite TV network, hidden in old movies. Anyone in the world could have access to top secret data if they knew where to look and had a decoder."

The President interrupted. "My gawd! That's terrible! And I never heard about that fiasco either! Was the navy involved, or wasn't it?"

"They insisted the facility wasn't theirs but that they'd been looking for it. They'd caught a Soviet courier en route to a sub with a suitcase of microtapes on all 1,005 contracts. He'd suicided, too, the same way as the guy in Baltimore: bit down on a cyanide capsule.

"But the key factor is that someone was telling every security team in the world that everyone else was vitally interested in that group of contracts."

A light dawned, and I almost laughed out loud. The damn alien was playing a joke on everyone!

Bucky had paused to finish his Coke. He looked tired but rational, and thoughtful, as if a realization was growing on him. "In fact," he said, "I'm beginning to think—hell, it's the only way it could be . . . Those 1,005 contracts were a sham to set us up, to get us to establish NORTEC to find a nonexistent mystery hidden in them. I mean, the contracts were all right, but setting them up as special was a sham. Hell, yes! And we fell for it, and so did every security agency in the world! We've been had!

"Larson controlled everything! I can see that now!"

Abruptly Buc's eyes seemed to bulge and his mouth fell open; for a moment I thought he was having a stroke. El stepped over to him and put her hands on his shoulders as if to massage them. After a moment he blinked, looked up at her and then at the President.

"Could I have something a little stronger to drink?" he asked weakly. "I'll need it to tell you what I just remembered. Maybe you better have one, too."

The President ordered only one, for Buc, a double bourbon on the rocks, and we waited silently through the long minute until it arrived. Buc took a big sip and shuddered, then looked down at his neatly manicured hands resting on his blanketed lap.

"I don't know how to tell you this, Mr. President. You may think I've gone over the edge, and I'm not sure it's real myself. But I seem to remember being taken on a spaceship, a huge thing. Charles drove me to a lab on it, down long corridors in a little electric cart, and did something to my mind."

Buc took a deep breath, shivered, and closed his eyes. We waited.

"I'm all right, sir," he said when he opened them, and looked up at the President. "I'm just feeling—used up. What NORTEC really produces is inventions—inventions way ahead of their time. Ask this guy," he said, thumbing at me. "I remember him now; he was one of the contractors. Charles showed me a prototype for a TV set that looks just like that one over there but doesn't require a broadcasting station. It doesn't even require a camera! When a few components have been debugged, it can be tuned in on any spatial coordinates on the planet, and show what's going on there in full-color video with sound. The ultimate in spy equipment."

The President was staring at him, wondering if the general had gone crazy—hoping he had. Then he turned to look at El and me.

"Such a device is possible, Mr. President," I said. "It wouldn't be such a large advance over what I developed on my project."

Bucky continued in a subdued tone. "When Pat protested NORTEC's growth last year, they took him over, all the way. I didn't realize it at the time, but that's what happened. All I knew was that Pat had a sudden personality change. I suppose I did too, a few weeks later when I was taken to the spaceship—if that's what really happened. It was after that that Charles showed me the TV device. He painted a great picture of how we could use it to control the Soviets or any outside threat, and prevent World War Three. I bought it without question; ate it up."

El interrupted. "Where was the device being built?"

"In a complex beneath the NORTEC building; ten secret labs. The technicians in them don't even know what they're working on. Charles and the NORTEC president, Simpson, took me into it through what appeared to be a data storage vault off the computer room. The vault is also an elevator, when you know how to operate it, that takes you to the secret lower level."

He paused for another sip of bourbon. "About six months ago, I found that Charles was pumping large sums of money from somewhere into NORTEC for a private paramilitary outfit, a mercenary army. They were paying $10,000 sign-up bonuses and double military pay, plus expenses. I put my foot down and called a halt to it. Charles said he'd show me why the unit was needed, and took me for a ride. That's when we went to the spaceship." This time Buc didn't shudder, but he was bushed—starting to sag again. "One minute we were driving along just past Mount Vernon, and the next minute we were in the ship."

He finished his bourbon. "Those people—Charles and whoever else operates from that ship or on that ship—they don't control someone directly. What they do is find something in them, something clean and good—patriotism or whatever—and corrupt it somehow, turn it rotten and ugly."

Buc seemed to be deflating, shrinking before our eyes. His voice dropped almost to a whisper. "Listen to these folks, John. I don't know how, but . . ." He looked around at us, his neck seeming barely strong enough to hold his head up. "If anyone can deal with the aliens, it's them."

His chin flopped to his chest then, and El felt his pulse.

"He's just asleep, Mr. President. Can you check with

your SWAT team at NORTEC and see if they have
Charles Larson in custody?"

The President picked up the phone. "Connect me to
Captain Johnson of my SWAT team." He waited, then
spoke again. "Johnson, this is the President. Have you
got the NORTEC people in custody?

"About four hundred of them, you say . . . but five of
'em *exploded?!* I'm especially interested in a Charles
Larson. Have you got him? . . . He *what?!* He *vanished?!*
With the female marine officer I sent with you? What
do you mean by 'vanish,' Johnson? Folks don't just
vanish! . . . These did. All right, thank you, Johnson. I
want a full debrief when you've been relieved out there."
He hung up the phone and tried to compose himself
before turning to a stunned-looking Dak.

"I'm sorry, major, but it looks like your sister has
vanished, whatever that means."

She nodded. "Mr. President," she said huskily, "with
your permission, I'd like to leave now. I want to go
over to NORTEC and see what I can find out."

"By all means," he said. His concern was genuine; I
could feel it.

She saluted and left. The President turned back to
us.

"Dorothy, you're the only one who seems to have
any handle on this at all. What do you think of Decker's
story?"

"Mr. President, it fits what I've been able to learn of
NORTEC's activities. They didn't seem to follow any
visibly logical sequence. What the general told us gives
us a rational framework for it, if we're willing to swallow
the idea of aliens from outer space. And we both know
that the air force has been sitting on firm evidence of
aliens for years.

"So in a word, yes, I believe General Decker, at least
as a provisional, operating assumption. NORTEC was
established by an alien, it's been operating with alien
direction, and Charles Larson is apparently the alien."

The President pursed his wide mouth, his chin in his
hand, then turned to me. "What do you think, Mr.
Ambers?"

"It's the only explanation, Mr. President. For some reason, perhaps some cultural restriction of theirs, the aliens can't use their technology actively and directly against us. The general was right: It looks as if they want us to reinvent their technology under their guidance. And the only reason for them to be so covert about it would seem to be that they have plans for us we wouldn't like. I suspect they'd make Orwell's 1984 look like utopia."

The President nodded. "Thank you, Mr. Ambers." He turned to El. "Dorothy, I'm goin' to be under the gun to go public this evenin' about this mornin's air battles and the rescue of Ben from Annapolis. Obviously I can't holler alien, and if I bring NORTEC into it, the shit will surely hit the fan. Do you see a way to handle this?"

"I believe so, Mr. President. Let me lay it all out. Entirely aside from anything else, NORTEC is definitely a potential threat to your reelection. Beyond that, it appears to be a direct threat to the United States, and probably the entire world.

"Now, I'm in the business of buying and trading companies, and NORTEC is owned by a Bahamian corporation which seems to be owned nominally by General Decker under a pseudonym. I'll buy it and pay the amount the government's already put into it. And since Jan is probably the person best qualified to sort out what they've got over there, I'll let him run it." She turned to me. "If you're willing?"

I nodded; she probably had the transaction set up already. "I'd be angry if you gave it to anyone else to handle," I said. "I'd love to dig into that."

"I knew you would." She turned back to the President. "From my investigation, Jan was the most independent, and independently innovative, of all NORTEC's contractors. And he's tough and adaptable or he wouldn't be alive now.

"There's something else—something positive. This whole thing could turn out to be a blessing in disguise, if it's handled correctly, *because NORTEC can be the solution to the balance of payments problem!* Consider the position of dominance that NORTEC inventions can give to American industry!"

The President had been staring at her; now he slowly smiled. "All right, Dorothy, NORTEC is yours. I don't know what legal stumblin' blocks we may run into, but we'll handle 'em some way. I may have to scald a few asses and kick a few others, but consider it yours.

"Just don't ever let it be known that it's the air force you paid for it. We'll provide some creative accountin' on our side, and you owe me a tour after you open those labs and discover what's in 'em."

He was sounding and looking remarkably more cheerful.

"Now, what kind of a cover story can you give me for today's aerial shoot-out and rescue mission?"

"I was just coming to that, Mr. President. But you see, that was no rescue mission, though most of the participants thought it was. The pyrotechnics were necessary to make it real for them. Terrorism has become a very real threat today, and this whole affair was a drill, as realistic as possible short of the real thing. It did get a little out of hand, and some accidents resulted, because most of the system had to think it was for real. But that just helped prove how swift and decisive your anti-terrorist system is. And of course you can't release details; that would threaten its integrity."

She smiled at him. "You mentioned creative accounting. There is also such a thing as creative journalism. I'm sure your press office can take it from there."

The President grinned; it got wider and wider.

"Thank you, Dorothy," he said. "You're the kind of person I need around here—a source of solutions, not problems."

We left President John R. Fuller a less worried man, and Bucky a saner one. Now if only Kad was all right. . . .

NINETEEN

While I was busy with El and the President, my other self was independently busy. As soon as the general had been gotten well clear of the chopper, we'd lifted off to meet our waiting gunship escort.

"Stu," I said, "we'll send the gunships home after we land at NORTEC. No point in drawing any more public attention to the place than we need to. Kad, how is the scene ahead?"

"I don't like it. Just ahead is a critical moment of truth for you, and I can't be with you when you run into it. When we arrive, I'll stay outside and sort out the human bombs."

I'd hoped she could help us locate bombs inside the facility; if people were being wired with charges, the building probably was, too.

From above, the spacious front grounds resembled a picnic area on overload. We landed fast on the side lawn, and the chopper left at once. Up close, the picnic impression, such as it had been, was gone. It would have been a madhouse if the marines, armed to the teeth, hadn't been controlling movement, hustling people into clusters. Most of the employees seemed in shock; some of the women were crying, frightened by the weapons and the marines' forceful herding. A small heap of I.D. badges was growing as marines filed people past it at a little distance to toss theirs on the pile. I was glad the place was isolated from view by distance and landscaping.

Kad left to check with the SWAT commander.

"Jerry," I said, "go around back and unplug this place. Shoot out the transformer if you have to. I need the computer down, so no one can erase the disks and

161

tapes. Meet me in the computer room when the power is off."

"Right, sir." He ran for the rear of the building. I noticed he was still calling me sir; you don't usually change trained-in responses in a day.

Stu and I ran around the corner to the main entrance. The building was one of those security-conscious affairs: a long low box with no windows to the outside except at reception. In the foyer we found a map of the layout, and after a quick look, started trotting past more people being hustled out by marines. They'd begun in the front and were quietly clearing out offices one after another. Apparently they'd disconnected the security alarm at the start, because there was virtually no confusion or noise inside. Anyone appearing in a hall being evacuated was quickly under marine escort.

The computer room was located in the back of the building. About halfway there, we entered an unevacuated section and slowed to a brisk walk. The building had inner garden areas with glass walls facing them. The third garden was also an outdoor dining area full of people on their morning break. It was almost spooky: They appeared serenely unaware of the roundup taking place up front.

The computer section had its own guard station. As we approached, the guard on duty looked for our visitor badges. His courteous smile, which vanished when he saw we didn't have any, was replaced by chagrin when we drew our 3-mms. After Stu had removed the guy's gun, I took the handcuffs from his belt and shackled his wrists in front of him, then told him to take us into the computer section, which he did. He had to unlock the door, but his keys were accessible to him on a belt lanyard.

Inside was a sort of small check-in room. No one was on duty at the control clerk's desk; she was on break in the garden we'd just passed.

"Stu," I said, "hold him here quietly while I check the other rooms in this section. Something doesn't feel right."

The main computer room was empty, but the door to

the data storage vault was ajar. There was a detonator on a table just outside it, so I stepped quietly over and put it out of sight on a high shelf. Through the open door, I peered inside the vault; two guys were in there, setting plastic explosives. I was about to hail them when my warrior senses told me they were programmed to self-destruct. If one of their badges exploded, it might be detonator enough that the explosives they were setting would destroy the whole contents of the room—including me.

So I shot both of them in the leg, just below the knee. Neither of them even had time to begin turning. The shock of the 3-mms smashing bone knocked them out, and at top speed I dragged both limp forms back into the computer room, away from the explosives. Then I headed for the exit, but before I got there the lights went out; Jerry had turned off the power. I was groping in utter darkness for the door when there were two small explosions behind me, almost simultaneous.

A moment later, Stu opened the door. The check-in room was somewhat lit by the sunny corridor outside it. The guard was standing next to a wall, and I strode over to him.

"Who else was back here besides the two I just shot?" I asked evenly, pressing the 3-mm against his breastbone.

He turned pale. "Only the two, sir: Mr. Simpson, the president of the corporation, and Mr. Walters, the vice-president. They sent everyone else out on break except me."

"Thank you." I lowered the gun a bit. "Why did their bodies explode when I shot them?" I asked it to watch his reaction.

"Explode! I never heard of such a thing!" He looked more shocked than scared now.

"Okay, I believe you." I shoved the pistol back into my waistband. "Where do you keep the key to your cuffs?"

It was on the belt lanyard; he could have freed himself if we'd left him alone. I did it for him. "Do you know where there's a flashlight around here?" I asked.

"Only the one in my glove compartment, outside in the parking lot."

"All right," I told him, and clapped his shoulder. "Here's what I want you to do. There's a platoon of marines in front of the building, holding a crowd of people under guard. The people here know you, so I want you to go out there and help keep them calm. Tell them no one's in any danger from us here except the traitors."

The traitors. His whole demeanor changed; that made us the good guys. He saluted and hurried off down the hall. "Something's damned fishy," I said to Stu. "They were just now setting charges, as if they didn't know we were coming. Why would they react that slowly?"

"Damned if I know. You don't wire a guy's dentures and buttons and forget the data bank."

I felt absolutely crawly. If they didn't care enough about the data to preset explosives, why do it now? "Go out front and check with Kad," I told him. "Maybe with these two dead she can say more now. Then see if you can locate an operator to help me with this computer. I'll see if I can find a light and unwire the charges in there."

As he left, Jerry trotted in. He'd known we'd probably need a light, and had brought a battle lamp from a marine chopper; a guy like that is worth a lot. Together we went into the computer room.

"Good work on getting the power off," I told him. "We've got two bodies in here," I added, pointing with the electric beam. "They were trying to blow up the data vault." I got down the detonator and handed it to him. "Are you familiar with these?"

"Standard military detonator, sir. Where are the charges?"

I showed him the vault and held the lamp for him while he pulled fuses. He finished quickly. There were a number of charges, all small, but in combination, a lot of potential destruction. And they'd been packing them into corners rather than distributing them among the cabinets. Something felt definitely peculiar about this.

"What do you think, Jerry?"

"This is not the way to take out a magnetic data vault," he said. "With the door open you can burn it with jellied gasoline. With the door closed, a small magneto would destroy all the data. Either one would be simpler and safer."

"Thanks," I told him. "I'm not going to let my attention get stuck on it; something will turn up. What I'd like you to do now is go outside. As soon as the building is secured, turn the power back on. Then snoop around a while—just look into anything that strikes your curiosity—and check back with me here when you've got anything to report."

That's what I was going to do too—snoop around—but right where I was, in the computer room. The computer files were our major data source. While I waited for power, I set the battle lamp on a table and dragged Simpson's and Walters' bodies back into the vault—by the feet; their upper torsos were a mess.

In five or six minutes the power came back on. I sat down at the console, called up the SWAC file, and checked its update frequency. Toward the last it had been updated every day. No one at HOLEX could have done that without my knowledge: I'd kept tabs on the access register. I searched the update program and found this:

UPDATE FILE VIA AUTO-ACCESS DOD PERM BP

If that meant what it seemed to, these bastards had a way to bypass the access register!

"Hey, Le." Stu had come into the computer room. "Here's someone I want you to meet."

I swiveled around in my chair to see him with a young man in a white lab coat. "This is Charles Larson," Stu said, "the guy who designed this system."

"Charles," I said, "I'm glad to know you. My name is Le." I shook his firm hand, liking him at once. He came across genuinely friendly and not at all freaked out, which I considered pretty damn good, considering what had been going on.

"Le, what can I do to help you?" he asked. "And excuse me if I haven't gotten my equilibrium back yet;

I'm not used to weapons. I was on coffee break when some of your men came storming in."

"I need to know how your files are set up," I told him.

Stu interrupted. "I'm going back out front. When Charles and I passed Kad, she was looking—kind of sick, actually."

"Okay, see you later." *Kad looking sick? That's odd,* I thought, then dismissed it and turned back to Charles.

"What do you want first?" Charles asked. "Anything in particular?"

"Yeah. How does SWAC fit into your file structure?"

"SWAC is one of twenty-five projects with primary monitor status. There are five groups; SWAC is number one of group two."

"Exactly what does 'auto-access DOD perm bp' mean?"

"For those twenty-five projects, NORTEC has a think-tank overseer status, and an access to contractor data banks in three modes: Summary Request, Manual Request, and Auto. The Auto can be monthly, weekly, or daily, or any other interval you specify, all bypassing DOD."

"How can that get around a contractor's access register?"

"It can't. The NORTEC telephone number and access code has to be in the register, and its use would be logged."

"But it did happen, and it wasn't logged."

"Then there'd have to be either a faulty register, or an asshole DOD security man who overrode the system because he couldn't understand how to repair it."

We both laughed, recalling the type: know-it-all stumblebums.

"How did you come to be here?" I asked.

"Major Quinn saw my doctoral thesis on computer system security and hired me to help design NORTEC's system. Mr. Simpson, the president of NORTEC, was given a contract to design and operate the system to enhance scientific and technical manpower utilization. I did the actual design to give maximum security and optimum utility for the think-tank teams."

I noticed that I'd almost dozed off during his explanation. Vaguely I recalled reading something about misunderstood words making one sleepy, but that didn't seem to be what was going on with me.

"Is it warm in here?" I asked.

Charles walked to the thermostat. "Nope. Seventy-five degrees on the nose. This mission's been a big strain on you, hasn't it?"

I ignored his comment on strain. I'd hang in there until we had a handle on things; then I'd really sleep. "Charles," I said, "I need to understand how these five groups of projects tie together with SWAC." I fought the grogginess to arm's length. Charles reached past my shoulder and called up a subject list for each of the five groups.

Mission . . . Had he said something about my mission? I asked myself. I began reading and cross-checking between SWAC and the various subjects listed. A mental circuit seemed to take over and continue the process automatically. My consciousness was fading, but not into unconsciousness. It was more like locking into a fixed pattern that would not shift. I felt as if my body were encased in a block of Jello, and then the thought formed: Charles Larson knows about the mission! Charles Larson is the *alien*. Hell, that couldn't be right. Charles is a great guy—personable, helpful. . . .

An image of a very angry warlord appeared somewhere in the Jello: The warlord was me.

"Call yourself a soldier, Le Sal? You're in big trouble, Mister! Look at the goddamn battle board! You're the target, and the bogey is at five o'clock, range six frigging inches."

I couldn't see or hear the computer-room reality, just my warlord chewing me out and pointing to the board. A klaxon horn was blaring raucously.

The scene snapped off. I was in an arena surrounded by the planet's six best warriors, all skilled in an art that combined the fluid ritual of *aikido* with the abrupt attack violence of *choy li fut*. They were supposed to kill me slowly, to entertain the emperor and his extended family. I'd been caught in the bed of an assigned daughter—assigned to someone else, who had then hired these six to kill me. That damn Bucket Bottom! Sending me solo to a Kushet world! He should have known something like this would happen.

They were about ready to start, so I pulled it together and took a deep breath. I considered myself as talented and skilled as any of them, and I had, I hoped, a technique or two they didn't know about. If I lost, my body would be sent back to the fleet, but if I disabled or killed even one of these top assassins, the Kushet would complete negotiations with me.

The warrior at five o'clock moved toward me and I reversed the vector of his stiff-fingered jab.

Stu's voice snapped me back into the reality of the computer room. "How in the *hell* did you do that? He hit you, and it was him that fell unconscious!"

I finished shaking off whatever state I'd been in. "It's not something I know how to show you. Ask Dak to teach you, or Kad."

Stu still couldn't get over it. "I was standing in the door," he said. "Right over there. Your head had flopped down like you were asleep, and he was just about to sucker-punch you. I was going to blow him away. I'm glad I didn't; that was something to see."

I remembered the price I'd paid that time to get Buc and the confederation a trade agreement. It ended up that he got the fleet while I got transferred to the Embassy Corps and became part of the Kushet Emperor's extended family. I pulled myself away from the memory as Kad ran through the door. "You got him!" she whooped. "I knew you would."

The marine captain had come in behind her with four men. "Is this guy going to explode?" he asked, indicating the prostrate Charles.

"No, Captain," she said. "This is the chief honcho, and he wants to keep his skin. But don't let your men close to him. If they're within ten feet when he wakes up, they'll shoot each other."

The captain looked at her uncertainly. "That's an order," she said. "And I wasn't exaggerating. Within ten feet of him they'll shoot each other or do anything else he wants them to."

She turned to Stu. "You, too, Captain Rogers. Stay back. I'll explain later. Le and I will handle him." Stu moved back toward the door.

Kad started to lift the unconscious Charles and then slowed to let me help. "Yeah," I thought to her, "it wouldn't do for a gal like you to be too fast or strong. You might bruise some of these male egos."

We supported Charles between us—he wasn't very big—and started toward the door as the others moved back. In almost the first step he vanished from the room, and we vanished with him.

"Thank you for joining me in my humble home."

The voice came from a person to our right. It was Charles, about twenty feet away behind a very impressive black desk. The top resembled a bowling alley—an obsidian bowling alley. "Would you care for refreshments before we begin our discussion of terms?" The friendly, alert, "I'm a neat bright kid" quality was gone, but he was recognizable.

"Why thank you, Admiral Cha," Kad said, "we'd love to." Her voice matched and countered his, its playfulness underlain with sadism. A black table and chairs moved to us. They too looked like obsidian, and should have weighed hundreds of pounds each, but they glided silently, light as air, and somehow menacingly. Charles stayed behind his desk. His uniform was a shiny black material resembling leather, with ovals of dull copper about the neck and chest. His black desk too had copper trim.

"Please, Kad!" he protested. "Not admiral! Titles are so formal! Call me simply Cha, and let's celebrate the recrossing of our destinies. Surely that alone is enough to evoke a mood of friendliness. Any moment so long in preparation deserves mutual respect among its co-creators."

"Cha it will be then," she said, and we sat down. "But you'll gain no concessions by invoking friendly ritual."

Two very beautiful young ladies appeared with trays, their costumes in the same color motif as Cha's uniform.

"First a toast to Le," Cha said, and raised his glass. "To the great and sly warrior who won the day and foiled my coup."

We drank.

"Now another toast," Kad said, lifting her glass again. "To the great Cha and his decacts, who have warred with us so long and skillfully. May the scene just ended be the penultimate in your quest."

His quest? Her closing words had almost slipped by me.

Cha drank, then laughed loudly and joyfully. "Ah, Kad! Beautifully done! Getting me to drink to my own final curtain! How delicious! But let us say, in joining your toast, that I was celebrating your good wish. Because, alas, I cannot agree to make this retreat more than a brief intermission for adjusting the scenario and shifting a prop or two."

Allusions were being made that were beyond me, and I was also getting ticked with his pretense that there was no war underway. Cha interrupted my mood with an outburst of merry laughter.

"Le," he said, his eyes on me now, "you are a perfect foe." He began laughing again.

Kad smiled and spoke into my mind. "We've done a lot of things to arrange this moment," she thought, "so enjoy it, even if you don't see the reason to. You will later."

Cha's laughter tapered off and stopped, as if he too had heard her thought. He waved the girls to refill our glasses.

"Le," he said more soberly, "you give us great pleasure with your anger. My decacts and I thank you for agreeing to play with us, that time so long ago, when we arrived here stultified by boredom."

"The game is over now," I snapped. "It's time to round up your troupe and go home, lost brother and all."

Lost brother? I wondered where that came from. An

intense silence fell over the room, and even molecular motion seemed slowed to a crawl.

"*Le! Do you know our brother?*" Cha's voice had changed; there was an echo chamber effect, like many voices not quite in unison. Then eleven versions of Cha were crossing the room toward us, each with a friendly but earnest expression on its face. But they weren't all Cha, or even all male. They were eleven different people, six female and five male, all with the same uniform.

"Le, Kad," Cha said, "please excuse my brothers and sisters their sudden appearance, and their intrusion into your assigned space. But we are very excited by your mention of our brother. For word of his whereabouts, we would gladly forfeit whatever play time remains to us here. Indeed! We will do more than that! For such news we will stay and serve you in any way you wish, all twelve of us, for a time selected."

For some reason my anger was gone. "I don't know why I said that about your brother," I answered. "If I know who or where he is, the data is hidden from me."

"Excuse us, Le. In my eagerness, I overlooked the fact that you must remain cloaked from yourself to stay in the warrior mode. You are not free to go in and out as we do. But the tone of your thought, a moment ago, indicates that you do have the data we have wanted so badly for so long."

He turned to Kad. "Will you agree to a temporary recess in the game until Le can sort this out? Say, four weeks?"

"Six weeks," she replied calmly, "and only on the condition that all of you stay off the planet during that time, while we are free to stay on it. We'll have NORTEC under our control within six weeks."

"Very good then. But of course, NORTEC is yours now in any case. We will await your call."

With that the room went two-dimensional and vanished in rotation.

TWENTY

There seemed to have been a brief hiatus of awareness, as if I'd dozed, but shallowly. El and Kad were smiling at me. Then I realized I had two memory tracks of the last three hours. El stepped up and hugged me. "You guys were great on both fronts," she said, "you and Stu both. All four of you."

"Where are we?" I asked. Having a split memory was disorienting, and for a moment I felt a tinge of panic.

"You'll have it back together in a minute or two," El assured me, then stepped back, gestured around her. "This is our new board room. We six are the new NORTEC board of directors."

"Six?" I said, still confused.

"You and I, the twins, Marcy, and Stu." Then, laughing, she pirouetted to show her delight.

For a long moment I looked back down the twin memory tracks, sorting things out. "There's one point I'm stuck on," I told her. "In the White House, when I wanted to contact myself with the data about Charles Larson, you said it was handled. Hell, he almost killed me—one of me, anyway."

"It was your moment of truth," El said. "Which, I might add, you handled very well. And the you in the White House needed your full attention right there."

Then Dak came in. "Well," she said briskly, "I just dismissed the White House SWAT team, and promised them a party on Saturday night. Then I told the NORTEC employees that this whole thing was a realistic security drill, and sent most of them home." She grinned. "The marines who saw you two disappear have been told it was a holographic illusion. That's not totally real to them, but they're glad to have some kind of explanation." She paused and looked at me. "And I used a little magic to clean up the mess you made of Simpson and Walters."

Stu came in then. "I asked the security chief to call NORTEC's paramilitary officers for a meeting tomorrow morning. That looks like the area for me to handle while you guys work on the technical end. I'll need Dak and Kad to help me develop a good martial arts training unit, and give me some training, too."

The twins laughed in unison. "Train you?" said Dak. "We'll do a lot better than that. Tonight we'll help you reclaim your old expertise. You need training in martial arts like Cha needs training in generating confusion."

Just then a buffet cart was wheeled into the board room; the place was turning into Grand Central Station. "Why is the kitchen staff still here?" I asked.

"So we can eat Cha's lunch," El said. "I hope you like it. Charles preferred his food French, and hired from the best school in Paris. The staff doesn't speak much English yet, but in case you've overlooked it, we all speak French, even if some of it's a bit archaic."

"We do?" I picked up a plate and selected some items from the cart. "Did anyone check the labs in the basement?"

"Yes," Stu said, "Jerry did. He found out how to operate the data vault/elevator. I had him bring up the lab technicians; there were only ten of them. And incidentally, Buc was right: none of them knows anything about what the others are doing. They'll return to work tomorrow like the rest of the staff."

That, I thought, was screwy. How in hell could people develop new technology without exchanging ideas and data?

"Good," I said. "Let's go down after lunch and look the place over." Then something occurred to me. "Where's Jerry, Stu?"

"Dak had him driven back to Dover; he just left. He's still in charge of the recruiting office there. But I want him back to help me clean up and shape up our paramilitary force."

"He will be," said Kad, grinning. "The President will hear about his work with the rocket launcher today, and how impressed we were. He's already decided it's not safe to let us have NORTEC without a few spies among us, and Dak and I will help him select them in a very sweet little dream. He's sure to pick Jerry, though it may take a few days for it to happen."

"Anyone else special you guys want him to pick?" Dak asked.

"Maybe we ought to have someone from the office of the Joint Chiefs," I said. "That'll satisfy the new chief of staff that he has a finger on what we're up to."

We all got into eating then, and the shoptalk died. Afterward, over coffee, I turned to Stu. "You know," I said, "we killed quite a few of NORTEC's private army the last couple of days. Some of those guys must have had families; we need to get that taken care of."

"No families," Stu said, "or not officially, anyway. One of the guards I talked to said he'd been turned down for the paramilitary force because he's married. He said they wouldn't even take divorced men with children."

"Kad and I will find out if any of the casualties were secretly married or living with girl friends," Dak said. "We'll visit them as intelligence officers. They'll get a cash payment and be sworn to secrecy."

"Okay," I said, "and something else: How is the President going to explain away the crashed airplanes, burned out cars, and bodies? That's a little much for a drill."

"What bodies, dear?" El said innocently. "The planes and cars were all remote controlled. NBC already has the whole story ready for a special on terrorism tonight, right after their salute to the President and the Secret Service for their foresight and planning."

"How about the bodies on that country lane near Dover? Surely the sheriff's department must have investigated the explosions there."

"They didn't find any bodies," El assured me. "They could testify to that on a lie detector."

"And the honor guard at Annapolis? Those who saw Major Quinn get shredded?"

El shook her head. "We got the DUO-HEX's approval. As I said, this is not an ordinary war; some extraordinary rules have been invoked."

It occurred to me to wonder how much history—maybe even archaeology—on Earth had been colored or bleached or whatever by extraordinary rules invoked at special points. I'd have to sort that out sometime and see what I could remember.

"Mar," I asked, turning to her, "when will you be free to stay close at hand and help me here at NORTEC? I'm going to want help with the math I expect to run into, and it'll save Stu a lot of travel time, too."

"I can start anytime," said Mar. "Right now, if need be. I'll need to fly to Dover two afternoons next week for meetings, and a little later to sit in on a couple of graduate exam committees, but I couldn't ask for a better time to phase out of there. Do we have a company helicopter?"

El laughed. "We bought the one our warriors took over in North Carolina, and the pilot/owner asked to stay with the machine; he's ex-First Air Cavalry." She turned to me. "You guys must have really impressed him."

I stood up. "We didn't shoot him. Let's go below and see those labs."

The same guard had returned to his duty post outside the computer area, and grinned broadly as we walked up. "That was some drill," he said. "You guys scared me half to death! Everybody else back here but me has gone home. Can you folks find your way around?"

"No problem," I assured him.

"See?" Dak said after we'd gone by. "He didn't see any exploded bodies, so there couldn't have been any. By morning, everyone will know that Simpson and Walters were embezzlers who got spooked by the drill and fled the country. A week from now no one will think of them anymore."

We entered the elevator/data vault and started down. "Mar and I won't want a lot of traffic through here while we're working," I told Dak. "We'll need a regular elevator installed, up near the front of the building."

"I forgot to tell you," Stu said, "there's a stairway

sealed off up there. We can open it easily. Jerry found that, too; I think he's got x-ray eyes."

The elevator door opened onto a foyer which was light and roomy. It had an outdoors feeling created by a glass-enclosed space that suggested a small atrium, complete with grass, flowers, and fish pool. Two broad corridors led from the foyer in opposite directions, presumably to the labs and storerooms.

To the left of the atrium, a door led to an unfinished area like a parking garage where the four tunnels met. Electric golf carts were lined up at a charging terminal.

"Jerry checked out the tunnels," Stu said. "They lead to different buildings. One, almost a mile away, we found out is an electronics parts house; very security conscious. The others are vacant except for the guard stations."

"Do we get those in the NORTEC deal?" I asked El.

"Yes, dear. You'll have space to grow." She took my arm. "And all the little parts you want are close at hand," she added teasingly. "But right now it's time to go home. We've been through enough today. You guys can work here tomorrow and every day, *after* Mar and I give you permission to leave the house."

I'd intended to look over the labs, but there wasn't anyone in them to explain anything, and besides, how could I overrule El? She turned to the girls.

"We have a victory to celebrate, our warriors have a whole six weeks to save the world, and we haven't had a party since last night."

Everyone else applauded, so I joined in. "By the way," I asked as we started back to the elevator, "where do we live?"

"About five miles down the Potomac. We took a house there last year, just in case. We can use the bay house on weekends."

"Stu," I said, "we've got it made. These gals take care of everything." But I found myself wondering if her optimism about tomorrow, much less weekends, would pan out, with Cha doing whatever it was he'd be up to.

"We take care of the little things so you guys can take care of Cha and company," Dak said.

As El drove us home in a NORTEC station wagon, I found my mind feeding me a recap of the weeks since my discovery of Icon, and I began to feel nervous—anxious. Icons, the Great Cursor, heaven . . . It seemed as if some of it couldn't possibly have happened, and if it hadn't, then . . . El picked up on my line of thought and laughed softly.

"You don't *edit* reality to fit concepts," she whispered in my mind. "You experience it and then leave it alone. Start running on that circuit again and I'll send your mind out for a lube job. Or better yet, I'll take care of it at home."

There were promises and laughter in her silent words.

The house was rather new, but designed like an old colonial. We toured the outside first. A very well kept garden with gazebo and arbor dominated one side yard. In back was an oversized swimming pool, and behind the pool a wide, balustraded terrace overlooking the Potomac. We entered the house in back through wide French doors that opened into a foyer next to the living room. A window wall offered a clear view of the back yard. All in all, just a shanty.

"And that," said El when we'd finished our tour, "is where we live, at least for now. And now you guys and gals need to get drummed out of the Marine Corps. Don't they, Mar?"

"That's right. And we have a drumming-out party all planned, right after showers. Very informal and intimate."

"Drummed out?" I said. "I thought we did good. Are you sure you don't mean a medal ceremony?"

"Don't quibble, dear," El said.

I pretended to grumble as she led me to our bedroom, then suddenly felt very tired. An awful lot had happened in an awfully short time. Had I been alone, I would have stretched out on top of that smooth inviting bed fully clothed, and sluiced off later, whenever I woke up. But El pulled me to the shower, peeled the uniform off me, and pushed me in.

Afterwards I learned how great a return to civilian

life can be, if you've got the right drummer, and when I fell asleep, it was with satisfaction, not exhaustion.

The lecture had just begun as I entered the clearing. I'd run all the way from town. Pythagoras laughed. "We'll wait just a moment to let our warrior-turned-seeker get his panting under control."

The other students laughed too, which embarrassed me. They were sons of Crotonian aristocrats, and I a hoplite, the son of a farmer, the only real fighting man among them all. Thus they tended to shun me, wondering why Pythagoras had taken such a student.

I wondered too, for his politics favored the aristocracy, and certainly I was not among his better students. On the contrary: I understood little of what he said.

But I could feel the truth in it. And I could feel that beneath my ignorance I had a purpose in being there, whatever it might be. That seemed to be enough for us both, though not for the others.

Now he looked about at us. "Since the rest of you have changed the vector of your attention to Janus," he said, "I have become a little jealous of him. But also I wish to free him of the onus of bearing that attention; and to free you of something as well. You see, you have an unanswered question about our hoplite friend, and it is doing none of us any good. To entertain such a question is human, but to keep it is foolish."

His mild gaze included us all. "And to *act*, in any way, in the presence of such a question, is to make the person, place, time, and thing related to the question an adjunct of the action. Further, to let this continue is to condemn him, and here, and now, to go with each of you from life to life throughout eternity. Thus Janus, and this place and moment, become a necessary part of scholarship, of talking, and of listening."

His statement seemed simple enough, yet not simple, for what could be the possible mechanism of such a strange thing? And looking about me, I saw no sign that any of the others found his statement more manageable than I.

Pythagoras continued nonetheless. "I am sure that none of you wish to burden yourselves thusly. Now, the question you hold unspoken is, why is Janus here? The answer of course is that he is here because he is here. No other answer is necessary. No other is acceptable! There are no reasons why, for this or *any* thing; do not accept inner urges that demand them. Janus is here."

He went on like that at length, remaking the same point with different approaches, and at last dismissed us. I started forward to speak with him, but others reached him first, so I started back to town by a different, longer path than the others took. Maybe she would be by the pool again.

She wasn't, and I felt my spirit ebb. But before I could move on, she flew at me from someplace, taking me by surprise, threw me to the grass with a single smooth motion, and sat astride my waist with her hands on my arms.

"Surrender or die," she said hoarsely in a false bass.

"I surrender, fair El," I said, "for now and always."

I awoke to find El on top of me, gazing intently at my face as if trying to decide something.

"Yes. I think so," she said as if to herself. "Um-hm, yes. Definitely."

"What?" I said. "What did you decide? To keep me or throw me away?"

"I decided you were more handsome as Janus."

She jumped off me in midsentence, trying to get away, but I caught her. Later a knock on the door was followed by Mar's voice. "Dinner is ready, informal, in the kitchen. But do wear something."

It wasn't fully dark yet; probably about nine, I decided. Going downstairs, we heard giggling in the living room, where we found the twins in a preadolescent mode, dressed in outlandish jester costumes, rolling around on the floor like kittens. They jumped up and grabbed us.

"Oh! You guys are super. We love you oodles." And with that in bivocal, they kissed us. I wondered what had become of the hardboiled female marines.

In the kitchen, Stu and Mar were still preparing dinner, both wearing very feminine aprons. Stu turned to me. "Don't laugh," he warned. "You should see the one you get to wear tomorrow night."

"Hmph!" I replied, and turned to El. "Is that any way to treat a great warrior?"

Four female voices and Stu said yes, unequivocally. "I stand corrected," I told them. "This is great treatment for warriors, and I thank all of you."

Over soup I told them all about the dream, or nearly all.

"I always thought Pythagoras was into math rather than psychology," Stu said. "And as far as cause and effect is concerned, all science is based on it."

"Not the science of the eleven up there," said Dak and Kad, pointing upward. Just now they looked twenty-ish.

"We really don't have a category," El said, "that fits what Pythagoras was doing outside math and politics. Psychology doesn't fit it. Psychology isn't a science of consciousness; it's the study of stimulus and response." She paused for another taste of soup and continued. "And all he was really saying in that lecture was 'don't second-guess yourself.' Let reality be what it is or create it differently."

"He should have said it that way then," Stu grumped, "instead of being obtuse about it." He looked away from his soup, eyeing me. "I'll blame him instead of you; I've never heard you talk that way on your own, although I've never heard you in your dreams, either."

I didn't answer; I was examining two of El's statements together. "Don't edit reality," she'd said once, and now, "let reality be what it is or create it differently." I repeated the last aloud. "We'll have to remember that when we're trying to figure out what Cha's been building at NORTEC.

"Which reminds me: I'm supposed to know a long-lost brother of Cha's. Is there any way I can call up that datum and get them to move out of here?"

"Yes," El said, "we could take you back to the play mode of consciousness, but then you couldn't be a warrior. And the whole thing could be a ploy of Cha's to regain the position he lost. Then we'd have to go back to square one and start the mission all over again."

"Oh no," I said. "No way. Nope. Not that again."

"What about the DUO-HEX?" Stu asked. "Can he help us on that?"

"I'll check with him tomorrow," El said, "and see if I can get a lead of some kind. He's getting tired of our war game too, after all these trilennia, and maybe, just maybe, I can get a straight answer."

"Well, you could start by inviting me to dinner."

There was no question of whose voice it was. It belonged to the Great Cursor, the It, the DUO-HEX. He appeared a moment later in His rumpled white suit. His cigar could have come from the Three Stooges' prop room. George Burns had presented a more exalted God wearing sun visor and sneakers.

El laughed. "We might, if it wasn't for the suit. *And* the cigar. What's a Great Cursor like you doing in a video game like this, anyway? Slumming?"

"No, my dear. I heard my name taken in vain, and decided just this once to *be* vain and defend myself." He shivered, not as if cold but like someone sensing something unpleasant. "My, but this reality grid feels strange. Or have I been away too long?"

"Both," El answered. "See what Cha et al hath wrought. That's why we're anxious about a certain answer." She copied his shivering, and we all laughed.

"Coming belatedly to your question," the DUO-HEX went on, "you don't need to ask me who Cha's brother is, because I'm sure Le knows. But as you pointed out, he apparently knows it only at some level above the game. And I don't recommend jeopardizing the mission by going after it that way. I have a feeling that this round will be decisive enough that either they will want to move on, or I can invoke 'due cause.' "

He actually looked soberly at me for a moment, then grew a slow grin, winked broadly, and vanished without rotation.

"Well, gang," said El, "this is a red-letter day. Old DUO-HEX hasn't been in this reality since long before

Cha and his decacts arrived. But I knew he was feeling the need to end the war game." She laughed. "Otherwise, he would have called for a retake today, when Dak/Kad played fast and loose with rockets."

"Oh, El," the twins said as one, "you weren't suppose to notice that. We only used a feather." Their tone was comic, and we laughed again.

Then Stu got up and served coffee. As we neared the end of a pleasant after-dinner conversation, Dak stood up.

"My compliments to the chefs, and since Kad and I want all of you in the living room soonest, I suggest we all pitch in and clear away the debris."

We did. In five minutes the dining room had been cleared and tidied, the king-sized dishwasher loaded, and we were all seated in the living room with brandy, El and I on one couch and Mar and Stu on one opposite. Kad and Dak had removed both coffee tables earlier to have rolling room. Now they knelt in the middle with their backs together, Dak facing us and Kad facing Mar and Stu. They had exchanged their jester costumes for something brief and exotic, revealing forms like ripely beautiful sixteen-year-olds, with faces to match. Dak's eyes, at least, were golden and slightly slanted, with vertical slitted pupils, giving a clear sense of otherness that was not felinity. Beneath it all was a striking sense of vivid life.

Their voices and speech, sounding oriental, were like those of little girls as they recited verse to us, speaking mostly in unison but lapsing at times into alternating solos.

> You know that we
> are between you,
> and see in a different way.
> Now we will en'tain you;
> we need 'tention, too.
>
> Now we will be
> your NaJas,
> your CoBras,
> and show what we see
> to each of you.

Cobras; Najas. Now I knew what the eyes reminded me of.

With the last word we began a visual tour of the energy spectrums, beginning with visible light and going to lower and lower wavelengths, through the ultraviolet to the bottom of the electromagnetic spectrum, our visual "realities" shifting as we went. After a brief pause, they shifted our vision up the spectrum, through the visible into the infrared and beyond.

Dak's eyes turned human again, and we toured upward through another spectrum, totally different, which somehow I realized was the life force spectrum, with auras and silver cords. At the top of that spectrum her eyes turned gold without pupils, and we viewed still another spectrum, where matter appeared thinner and thinner and then vanished altogether. The space became golden, and I could see Dak only as a sphere of luminous golden light. Mostly, though, I perceived wave fronts, and at one point I was sure, without knowing why, that I was seeing gravity waves moving gracefully slantwise across the room.

Then the room returned to normal, and the twins spoke again in little-girl voices.

> Now you have seen
> what we see for you.
> Feel and remember
> what you saw,
> but never ask what or why.

Stu, Mar, and I were in wonder at what we'd seen, in awe of our twins, abstracted by the expansion of our world.

"Keep your seats," said Dak and Kad, still speaking in the little-girl mode. "Next we will show you some Cha-OS girls."

They vanished in twin streaks.

"Hold on to your hats," El warned. "This is going to be a whirlwind fashion show."

Amid blurred motion and giggles, they were back

before us as conspicuously female versions of Cha, dressed in the apparently standard black and copper.

The little-girl tones were gone. "We left out the vibes that Cha loves so much," they said. "Now we add them, but converted for this reality."

The effect was more than a little dramatic. These OS twins could have made any man a sex slave on contact. El caught my thought.

"Yes, dear, Cha's sisters have done that to more than a few Earth men. You weren't the only one."

The show was a smash, with bodies as well as costumes winking from one mode to another: I had forgotten how varied the galaxy is and how many versions of "human" there are. At the last the room became very quiet, and a voice came from somewhere near the center.

"You are now invited to select your partner for the evening from the parade of the finest Cat Girls on Delbaka-3." The parade started with soft music, and these were truly cat girls—humanoid cats, about twenty in all, with every imaginable color of fur.

As the last one left, there was a round of giggles and jabber from the foyer, and another streak into the room ended with the twins dressed in beautiful Grecian-style gowns slit up the sides and leaving one breast bare. Their hair was piled high on very lovely heads, and they knelt, somehow demure again, back to back.

> And that was our show.
> We thank you.

Then they jumped up and hugged and kissed us.

On the way to bed, vague memories of other parts of the galaxy crowded in around me. I set them aside until later.

TWENTY-ONE

When I awoke at 0600, El was sitting up looking down at me. "Good morning," she said. "Remind me never to let you trek off to Delbaka-3 again without a guard cat."

The twins burst in and jumped on the bed in their preadolescent versions. Amid giggles and bouncing they said, "El, we're going to show him Delbaka girls every night! They made him feel funny."

"Get, you scamps!" El responded. "Let us wake up properly without naked cat girls in our way."

"Only if you promise to squeeze him good for liking cat girls so much." Then, squealing, they jumped off the bed, pausing at the door. "Breakfast is ready when you are," they called back, "and it's no clothes only."

I was flabbergasted at such unabashed eagerness to begin the day. I usually needed a little time to get fully awake and ready for harness.

"They don't get kittenish very often," El said, "and when it's gone we'll miss it. Dak was all too serious for all too long."

"Right," I said. If we beat Cha, I told myself, maybe she wouldn't have to be so serious again. Maybe a little now and then for change of pace.

I swung my feet out of bed and started barefoot for the bathroom. "Let me jump in the shower for a minute," I said, "and I'll be ready to eat. I'm as hungry as if I'd climbed Mount Everest or something."

It seemed as if I was ready to eat at any opportunity lately. Mar and Stu were already eating when we got to the dinette, and the twins in their new ten-year-old beingnesses were fussing over serving them. Dak/Kad was amazing. No, I told myself, not Dak/Kad, Dak *and* Kad. Plural. They were two separate individuals, two individual consciousnesses. After my experience of the day before, I should realize that.

And they could be so many things, without acting. When Dak was Monitor Cursor, she hadn't been acting; she'd been Monitor Cursor. When she'd been the black jaguar, she'd been a black jaguar, albeit with human intelligence plus. And now that they were being kitten girls, kitten girls was exactly what they were. Yet I knew that, in a way, those all were roles. But there was no imitation involved, no simulation of something they weren't. In each role, they were the thing they were being then, without losing their individuality in any way; they were always themselves, too.

And whether they were manipulating an international banker or being children running around nude with a coffee pot, it seemed all the same to them, because whatever they were doing, they did it unself-consciously.

I grabbed the twins one at a time as they flitted past, sat them on my lap and squeezed them, and thanked them for being, and for sharing their realities. El, in turn, thanked me with her smile for appreciating them.

After breakfast, Stu and I started for NORTEC. El and Dak would soon be off to pay for the company and handle the legal formalities. Mar and Kad stayed to await our newly acquired chopper for a trip to Dover. It would land on our spacious lawn here.

As I drove, Stu stared reflectively out the window for a while. "Tomorrow is Saturday," he said, "and we'll be busy most of the day with the marine party, but in the morning I plan to have a meeting with our paramilitary unit at its base. Kad and Dak agreed to help me sort out who to keep: We don't want anyone around who's really in Cha's pocket."

He turned to me. "I'm meeting with their officers this morning, to feel out what they're like before I meet the troops. I've got the feeling we're going to need a crack unit to handle something. Or someone."

"You're right," I agreed. "You can bank on it; I can feel it, too. And if we weren't, El and the twins would probably have told us to drop the paramilitary."

We arrived at NORTEC and parked in the company

president's slot. The place still had an aura of ugliness about it, but hopefully after today it would be gone. The guard from the computer area met us at the front door. "Mr. Ambers, I'm glad you and Mr. Rogers are okay today. I worried last night after I recalled what happened."

"What's that, Steve?" I asked. I'd sneaked a look at his name tag while he spoke. Very handy items, name tags.

"In the excitement, I forgot to warn you about the radiation. All people entering the computer area are supposed to wear special cloaks. Otherwise, the radiation can make them awfully sick."

"What kind of radiation?"

"Something invented here. I understand it protects the computer from magnetic damage, but that's all I know. Anyway, I'm glad you're both okay." He saluted then, and Stu and I started to my office. It didn't seem to bother Steve a bit that we were now company executives, where we'd been marine officers the day before; I suppose where rank was concerned, he didn't question. Or maybe El or the twins had something to do with it.

"Le," Stu said, "that doesn't make sense, to protect against magnetic damage with radiation! But it might explain why you got so sleepy."

"More likely one of Cha's little jokes, to protect the computer against snoopers," I answered. "Or the cloaks could be protection against something else he was doing."

Our office staff met us in the executive reception area with visible apprehension. Stu's secretary said that the field reps were waiting in the board room, just next to the executive reception area.

Field reps? I'd thought he was meeting the NORTEC paramilitary officers. Maybe "field reps" was a euphemism for the company's mercenaries.

"Is it usual for them to take over the board room without the president or vice-president on hand?" Stu asked.

"Yes, sir. They have—a rather free hand when they come in, sir."

Pretty damned arrogant, I thought, considering that

a new regime had moved in. As if they were trying to tell us something.

Stu was nodding thoughtfully. "Could you have some coffee sent in please, Alice?"

"They are already having coffee and rolls, sir." The tension was growing around her mouth.

He nodded again, curtly this time, and crossed the reception area, disappearing into the door marked "Board Room." I'd thought very briefly of going in with him, but it occurred to me that he'd prefer to handle them himself; there was a definite hint of steam coming from his ears. So I stayed to get acquainted with the secretaries.

"What's all the tension in the air this morning?" I asked.

My secretary, Norma, seemed to be the leader; she spoke first. "Mr. Ambers, we were all upset by the things that happened yesterday. And those field reps always make us nervous when they're around. They're not like any other technical people I've ever seen."

Alice spoke then, her voice thin with tension. "We didn't want to come back here today, but we were afraid not to, with a security investigation going on."

I grinned at them. "I promise we won't burn any witches," I said, crossing my heart. "In fact, if you know of any, send them to personnel; we'll put them to work in research."

They laughed, some of their nervousness blowing off. I chatted with them until the board room door opened. Then Stu ushered the "field reps" out through the executive reception area and into the hall. One of them, a large burly guy, looked a little mussed up and stunned. In fact, his face was gray, and he'd staggered a bit coming out the door.

Stu didn't offer to introduce them.

We watched them walk down the hall to the front door, where Stu scowled them out, while our office staff watched big-eyed. When the last mercenary was out, I grinned at the women. "Come on," I said, "what do you think those guys really do for the company? Honest now."

"The rumor is that we have a contract with the CIA to train agents," Norma said seriously, "and that our so-called field reps are the trainers. They usually act as if they'd like to kill someone; they seem kind of crazy."

Stu had returned while Norma was speaking. "Ladies," he said cheerfully, "I don't think you need to worry about our field reps any more. They're going to be much better behaved in the future."

I wondered what had gone on behind the board room door. "Norma," I said, "call a meeting of all department heads for nine o'clock. Do we have a meeting place other than the board room?"

"Yes, sir. There's the contract briefing room."

"Is it big enough?"

"Yes, sir. It's where such meetings are usually held."

"Good," I said. "That's where we'll have it. At nine." Norma went to make the calls. I went into Stu's office with him and closed the door.

"So those were our paramilitary officers?" I said.

"Right. One of them was the EO, the executive officer, and the others were deputy platoon leaders. Their table of organization has two officers per platoon and no platoon sergeant. All the original platoon leaders were either killed trying to nail us, or they self-destructed when the missiles failed to get us yesterday. Seems like the platoon leaders took the manhunt jobs for themselves; didn't want someone else to get the bonuses. Or maybe they'd been processed to be 'reliable.'

"Incidentally, these guys didn't have a clue that we were Wednesday's targets, and I didn't tell them.

"I don't think any of these guys were under Cha's direct influence. Four of them are real pros and feel like good leaders; they just needed their arrogance trimmed. Two others are in the maybe category, and the other one—the EO—I canned. I gave him till ten o'clock to pack up his gear and get his ass off the premises, and assigned two others to walk him through it and see that he doesn't make any trouble.

"Incidentally, I noticed a couple of smiles when I canned him. I suspect the others will be glad to see him go."

I grinned; I found myself admiring Stu more and more. "Uh, what else did you do to him? He didn't look too good, coming out."

"It was kind of interesting; the twins really came through last night on tuning my warrior patterns. The first thing he did was stand up and question my authority, so I told him to sit down and shut up. He came for me then with a move I don't even have a name for, and I just seemed to do something without even thinking about it. He ended up sitting semi-conscious on the floor against the wall."

He grinned ruefully, but I could see he was pleased with himself. "Now," he said, "I need to get some training so I can say what I did."

"Did any of them seem to know the purpose for their outfit?"

"No. It was like you said it would be: Apparently only the top executives knew what was afoot. These guys had been invited here a few times for after-hours parties, but that's all. Walters had a stable of hookers he brought in 'to boost morale.'"

"Hmm. Stu," I said, "let's make your paramilitary unit legal and up front with a DOD contract for security research. I'll bet the girls could set that up. We could even get some contracts in the private sector for anti-terrorist training: Dak and Kad would have ideas on how to run something like that."

Norma rang to say that the meeting with the department heads was arranged and that Mr. Al Peters would fill in for Mr. Larson, who had been manager of the computer department. Then I went into my office to clear out what had belonged to Simpson, its previous occupant, starting with the desk. Besides the usual, there was a stash of personal entertainment items that had to have come from an adult books and novelties store. There were also some keys hidden under drawers and in secret compartments; I had Norma send them to building services for labeling.

I found a panel on one side that slid open to reveal a well-stocked bar. The other wall opened into a small rumpus room which had another panel leading into

Stu's office. I called Norma to come in and view the scene. She was aghast at some of the equipment used in rumpusing.

"Mr. Simpson told us that this was an ultra-top secret file room, and that no one but he and Mr. Walters were allowed in."

"Did Simpson or Walters have many lady callers?"

"A masseuse came three times a week, a barber once, and a manicurist on the other day."

"You know what, Norma?" I asked.

She looked worriedly at me. "What?"

"I want you to come up with a good use for this room. Maybe something aesthetic. We'll get this stuff cleared out next week."

She left feeling better about things.

Behind a shelf panel in the rumpus room was an unusual-looking TV set. I turned it on and saw Cha's grinning face. "Sorry!" he said. "This set is off limits. Please step back."

I did, and its innards melted down with very little heat or smoke.

Norma beeped me: It was time for my meeting with the department heads. She insisted on guiding me to the meeting place—"Until you get used to the building." She was positively cheerful now.

The building was designed so that every section except the executive and security sections up front and the computer and building services sections in the back had glass walls overlooking one of the several enclosed inner gardens. Contract briefing was on the right side, off the center garden, a very pleasant place. I was the last one in. After looking over the small group of managers in front of me, I began.

"I am Jan Ambers, recently of the HOLEX Corporation in California. We were the prime contractor on the SWAC project, which NORTEC is monitoring for the DOD. I'm the new president here, and I'll want to get to know each of you personally. But for right now, you all need to know me, and I want to exchange some information with you.

"How many here knew that Charles Larson was the actual head of NORTEC?"

I waited for a response without expecting one. No one spoke.

"I thought not. He was also an enemy agent—a new kind in the information cold war.

"How many here know that the data being extracted from the five contract groups was being used to construct devices in some basement labs under this building?"

A lot of dumbfounded faces glanced around at each other; only one hand went up. "I'm Al Peters," its owner said, "Computer Department, and I knew there was something mysterious down below the computer room. I'd noticed Mr. Larson and Mr. Simpson go into the data vault a lot and sometimes stay for long periods with the door shut. Three weeks ago they'd been in there for about an hour, and I needed a file for a scheduled update, so I pushed the buzzer to get them to open up. When they didn't, I put my ear to the door and rang again. The buzzer sounded very faint, hardly audible, and then I heard machinery running, and the buzzer getting louder as if it was moving toward me." He paused.

"I thought at the time that it sounded like an elevator. When it opened, Mr. Simpson was alone, and pretty angry that I'd disturbed him. Mr. Larson definitely wasn't there, so I decided that it had to be an elevator, and that he'd gotten out down below. Mr. Simpson had grease on his hands and some white metallic-looking powder on his suit. I got the disc I needed and he closed the door. That's all."

Peters sat down. Another of the managers rose.

"I'm Stevens, of Technical Documents," she said. "The white metal powder Peters saw fits with a report we got at about that time. One of the contractors claimed to have come up with some new developments in fluidized magnets, using powdered indium. I believe the report is still being evaluated, but Larson or Simpson may have seen something in it that others missed, and been working on it down there."

"Thank you, Stevens," I said, "and thank you, Peters. If any of you think of something that might indicate anything wrong, please let me know personally.

"Now I want to share just a bit of my philosophy on how a company can best operate. And I've proved it works; I was the sole owner of HOLEX.

"The trick to it is that, in fact, there is no such thing as 'The Group,' 'The Company,' 'The Organization.' There are only individuals, who may or may not act in association. A company is like a government; it's a legal and operational convenience, which can be useful to facilitate working together. But it's an artificial construct without life of its own. Someone sets up a company, and people fool themselves into thinking it has an independent existence. They expect 'The Company' to do something.

"The fact is, the only life, the only creativity, and the only responsibility in an association of individuals is the life and creativity and responsibility of the individuals who happen to be associated. *People* do all those things, only people. People do every single thing that a company supposedly does, and each and every one of us is totally responsible for his or her acts within it. The concept of the limited responsibility of corporate personnel is a legal dodge, an unethical fiction by those who want to avoid responsibility for their actions.

"Got that?"

I'd delivered my little lecture casually until I snapped out the "got that." Now I looked the group over for a moment, feeling for whatever their inner responses might be. Their expressions were noncommittal, for the most part, something to hide behind while they watched and evaluated. They all had more or less conditioned "corporate minds"—hopefully salvageable, most of them; I'd soon know.

"Companies are built by people," I went on, "and they are destroyed by the concept of the company as an entity senior to individuals. In a family, we are likely to admit to the value of each person, but somehow we take that good sense and set it aside in the work place, and say that the company is senior to the individual. That's a perversion, a perversion of the valid principle that individuals operating in association can accomplish things they couldn't accomplish in isolation. Each individual should value *other individuals*, and respect their needs and wants.

"The best people value themselves, and in the best families they value each other. And ethically, the officers of a company—that's 'company' with a small *c*—must value and respect its associated members.'"

There had hardly been a movement during most of my talk. But as they digested what I'd been saying, masks were beginning to drop away or at least thin a bit.

"So as managers," I went on—now I could see their attention sharpen; they were about to be given policy— "as managers," I repeated, "I expect you to treat each and every one of the people who work in your department as individuals to be valued. Your office is always to be open to them, and mine is always open to you.

"We will very soon have a profit-sharing and bonus plan that will reflect that philosophy. I want each of you to inform your staff of this today." I paused. "Not next week; today.

"Now I'd like to thank you all, and extend my warm regards to your people. And that's it. End of briefing."

I stood by the door and shook their hands as they filed out. When Al Peters came by, I asked him to wait. Afterward, we started toward the computer room together. "What's this I hear about a radiation system that requires you to wear special cloaks?" I asked as we walked.

"Mr. Larson invented it. He said it protects magnetic systems from damage. We had it put in three weeks ago, just after I discovered that the vault is also an elevator. But it doesn't involve hard radiation: I tested it on my pocket tape recorder. I sure as hell didn't mention that to Larson or Simpson, though. What it does do is make you tired as hell, and fairly quickly, if you take your cloak off."

"Show me where it is," I said when we got to the computer room.

"There are five in this room and four in the vault."

He walked over to the main console, knelt, and pointed to a flat, off-white plastic package under the counter top.

"How is it attached?" I asked, peering up at it.

"A stick-on." He pulled it off and handed it to me.

As soon as I took it, I heard Cha's voice coming from the device. "Off limits. This device and the others will self-destruct in five seconds."

I tossed it in the wastebasket and pulled Peters back. He didn't seem to have heard Cha's voice. All nine of the apparatuses went off simultaneously with gentle pops and sizzles, not emitting enough smoke to trigger the alarms or sprinklers.

"They were saps for life-force energy," I told him drily without wondering how I knew. "Something new and wonderful from the world of technology."

I'd lied in part; he wasn't ready for all the truth. They weren't new, just new to this civilization.

"Son of a bitch," he murmured. "That's just how they felt to me: like little plastic vampire boxes."

"You've got it. Now I want you to check the report given to Stevens on fluidized magnets. Compare it with the contractor's report and see if the one Stevens got was complete."

"I'll do it right now," Peters said, and sat down at the main console. "That file is on line." He called up an edit routine which compared the two reports. "Okay." He pointed to the screen. "This section here isn't in the report that Stevens got."

Which seemed to make no sense at all. But it would, I was sure of that.

"No wonder our people are still trying to evaluate this," I said. "They've been working with incomplete data. Print this up and send it to Stevens as an error correction in the earlier report.

"And now comes the big job; I leave it to you how best to handle it. I think you'll find a lot of stuff omitted like that. You can either redo the reports or make up errata sheets."

"It'll be errata sheets," he said. "This baby has the

best edit routine in town. They'll all be done by morning, with just one extra man on tonight."

"Good show. How did Larson delete the data from the incoming reports?"

"He always handled the report routine personally, after hours. He'd kick the night crew out for coffee while he set it up. Said it was super-confidential, which didn't make sense, but who was going to argue?"

"Okay," I told him. "Peters, I think we've got ourselves a winning team. If you remember any other flaws, let me hear about them."

Then, before I headed for the vault/lift, I phoned Norma. "Pull the personnel records and sick leave files for all the people connected with all five monitor teams," I told her. "I'll study them after lunch. Any messages?"

"A Dorothy Anderson called and said she'd see you for lunch. She said it as if there wasn't any question about your agreeing."

"She's right, there isn't. And Norma, it's not 'a Dorothy Anderson,' it's 'the Dorothy Anderson.' She owns this place, all by herself." I put on my version of a mafia accent then, learned from old movies. "And if we're good to her, she'll let us have a piece of da action. Keep dat under your hat."

Norma surprised me then. "Gotcha, boss," she said in a false baritone. We hung up. Norma was loosening up nicely.

"Al," I said to Peters, "I'm going to see where this elevator goes, but first let me apologize ahead of time for the traffic you'll have through here until we get some stairs opened up, up front."

Then I left him with his computer and, after sensing out the controls, rode the data vault down to the lab level. There I went to the first lab on the right down the left hall. A number "1" on the door was its only identification; there was no plate with the lab name. The door was locked, so I pushed the buzzer beside it and stood waiting. After a long wait, I could hear bolts being disengaged; then the door opened a crack. It was still secured by three heavy chains.

The technician peered furtively out at me. "What do

you want here? This is a *top secret* lab, and no one but
Mr. Larson or Mr. Simpson is allowed in."

"I'm Jan Ambers, the new president here," I answered stiffly, the way I assumed he'd expect of a
company president denied. "Mr. Larson and Mr. Simpson both absconded; I presume you were informed of
what happened. Let me in, please."

"Oh! Of course! I'm sorry, sir." He began to unchain
the door, still talking. "Security here is so strict, you
know."

"How strict is it?" I asked, pushing past him into the
lab.

"Well, sir . . ."

"Mr. Ambers," I said; he wasn't ready to call me Jan
yet. He stared as if he didn't know what I meant. "My
name is Mr. Ambers. I'd rather you not call me 'sir.'
How tight is security?"

He looked as if I'd caught him doing something he
shouldn't—something degrading. "Well, Mr. Ambers,
it's tight enough that I've never spoken to the other lab
guys here. Until yesterday I'd never even seen them
closer than a hundred feet. And I've never seen anyone
else here except Mr. Larson and Mr. Simpson."

That startled hell out of me. "How did you guys get
down here to work?"

"Guards brought us in separately through a tunnel,
in electric carts, and picked us up at the end of the day,
one at a time. The rest of the day we just—stayed in
our labs. We have our own washrooms." He gestured at
a small door in one wall. "We were strictly forbidden to
meet or talk at any time, here or anywhere, and ordered to report any approach. They even watched us
drive into the lot and park."

The worst part about all this insanity, I told myself,
was that it was deliberate. Cha wanted these guys to be
nuts, to feel degraded, just like he wanted the top
executives to be degenerates. I wasn't surprised, though.
He may or may not have had tactical reasons, but
basically that was his style, and too much contact with
him *was* degrading.

"How did the marines get you out of your labs yesterday?"

"The fire alarm went off, and they were in the foyer with machine guns."

"Good. Come with me." We walked into the foyer, where I hit the fire button by the elevator. Alarms jangled furiously for half a minute, till I pushed it again. The technicians exited their labs cautiously, seeming relieved that no machine gun was in view but uncomfortable about being together. They were experiencing the breech of a very firmly implanted taboo, and glanced nervously at the TV monitor high in one corner.

"Thank you for coming," I said, "and sorry for the alarm. I'm Jan Ambers, your new boss. What do you call the company you work for?"

No one answered. I pointed to one of them, the one who seemed the least hangdog. "What name do you know the company by?" I asked.

"I don't, sir. I'm paid in cash and have no badge. One of the guards where I enter checks my thumbprint when I come in and searches me when I leave. Mr. Larson and Mr. Simpson are the only names I know here."

"Thank you." I looked them over, but mildly. "All right, gentlemen, the management and policies here have changed. Drastically. You were and are working for the NORTEC Corporation. That's NORTEC: N-O-R-T-E-C. My office is in the building above, through which you will shortly start coming to work."

They still stood without even looking at each other, almost as if they were embarrassed at being together. There were definitely some barriers I needed to break.

"As of now," I went on, "I want all of you to ignore all you've been told about internal security. To start off with, I want each of you to introduce yourself to the rest of us, right now."

They gave their names, still addressing them to me instead of each other. I looked at the guy from Lab One, Charley Mahavlich. "Charley," I said, "I saw a coffee maker in your lab."

"Yes, sir. It was provided," he said defensively. "Each of us has one."

"Okay, so here's what I want you guys to do next. Brew enough coffee for all of you. Then you all get together in Mahavlich's lab and just get acquainted with each other. Tell where you live, your wives' names, your kids' . . . Like that. Drink coffee and shoot the bull for an hour or so. Then Mahavlich shows you what he's doing." I paused. *"Nothing any of you is doing on the job is a secret from the others. Got that? Nothing!"* I paused again to let that soak in. "It's just the opposite from that bullshit the previous management laid on you. And when Charley's done, you go to Lab Two and get the same kind of briefing, and then Lab Three, all the way to Lab Ten."

Their expressions were beginning to change: They were starting to realize that the oppression and insanity were really being lifted. Now it was time to handle the final symbol staring down at them.

I looked at the TV monitor. "You in Security!" I said, loud and hard. "Listen up! I'm Mr. Ambers, the new president of this shop. From now on, this monitor is only for the protection of this area from unauthorized intruders. These gentlemen assigned down here have complete freedom to circulate between labs and talk about their work." I lowered the intensity and volume of my voice then to conversational. "Your boss, Mr. Kruger, will be briefing you on other new policies, but this one you have from me here and now, and it cancels anything different that anyone told you. If you have any misgivings or uncertainty about this, talk with Mr. Kruger. You have access to him per my order to him of this morning. Thank you."

I turned back to the technicians. "Before I leave, let's go in Mahavlich's lab." I herded them in ahead of me. "I haven't had a chance to check out the guy on that monitor, and if there's anyone I *don't* trust around here yet, it's Security. I'll trust them after I get them sorted out. And unless someone shows me it's actually needed, we'll take that monitor out entirely.

"Whatever. What you guys need to know right now

is that we have a puzzle here which is also a national emergency and a national opportunity. And you're the ones with the smarts to help solve it.

"The devices you're working on are not what you've been led to believe." I surprised myself when I said it, but somehow I knew it was true, entirely apart from any rationale I could think of.

Plus it fit Cha's chief operating principle: *confuse*.

"And one of the things it's vital to know is what those devices really are. They'll probably be something like what you were told, but more.

"You guys had closer contact with Larson than anyone still around. He mentioned things to each of you individually, and now we need to put all the pieces together and find out what the hell we're making here. It may be just one thing, with each of you working on a separate component, or it may be several different things.

"Meanwhile, I don't know what they've been paying you, but all wages around here will be reviewed, and there's going to be a profit-sharing and bonus plan in the immediate future. It will probably mean a raise, and unless you're a dog, it will not mean a pay cut. Now go brew your coffee and start briefing each other!"

Except for Mahavlich, of course, all but one started for their labs to get coffee. DeMarco, the boldest-seeming of them, stayed, looking at me half apologetically. "Uh, Mr. Ambers," he said. The others paused then, in case this was something they should hear.

"Yes?"

"I haven't had a day off, even on weekends, for more than a year. I think probably the others haven't either."

I stared, probably with my mouth open. They were all nodding.

"That," I said, "is totally frigging crazy! Look, I need you guys to stick around for the rest of today, because I want to talk with you again later. But the weekend is yours. Weekends in general will be. Stay the rest of today and be back on Monday, and come in through the NORTEC building. Someone will get in touch with you later today and equip you with I.D.

"And leave your lab doors open when you're here, so I can visit you without fire alarms."

Then I left. Going up in the lift, I felt a certain admiration for Cha's ability to create a bucket of worms, and I had a better understanding of something Dak had said about Cha and company having "a different flavor of fun." Sadism is sadism, but to some it's enjoyable, and Cha at least had his own style.

I wondered how a brother of Cha's family could stay lost even for a week. Just follow the trail of chaos and insanity and you'd find him. Or maybe that's why he was lost. Maybe he'd gone sane and couldn't stand the rest of them.

Al Peters looked up as I passed through, and I waved. He was sitting at his computer, relaxed but intent, clearly enjoying himself. It seemed to me that he was going to be one of my main people; he'd stayed rational and thought for himself, even in close regular contact with Cha, which took a hell of a strong personality.

TWENTY-TWO

As I walked into the reception area, Norma looked meaningfully at me and murmured, "She's here!" I nodded and went in to find a very nifty-looking lady behind my desk, poking through a secret compartment I'd overlooked.

"You should see the playpen," I commented.

She gestured toward it with her head. "I felt it, but I hadn't gotten around to it yet." She got up and I gave her a peck on the nose.

"Is that all I get after buying you this 'play pretty' this morning?" she asked. "We own this place. Officially."

I brought my dispersed attentions together and gave her a longer, warmer kiss. "How's that?" I murmured.

"Considering the time and place . . ." She laughed, picked up a briefcase, and opened it.

"Look what we got for a measly $80 million." She handed me a thick sheaf of legal documents. "Some of these would never have been found without Dak and Kad doing their special kind of snooping. The trail of dummy corporations would seem to end, and then a whole 'nother branch would appear after they checked for hidden connections."

I hefted the bulk. "God! It would take me a week just to read this."

"I'll highlight them for you." She took the stack back and handed me a single page. "That one is NITOR, the wholesale electronics supply house next door. Through a set of dummies, it owns twenty electronic parts manufacturing firms. Two of those are in Japan, and they in turn own four mining and refining firms for copper and some exotic metals."

"Hey! It looks like you bought half the planet! How did you accomplish all this in one morning?"

"About half a morning, but don't be too impressed with the time. We started this project quite a while ago, and put our staffs on it, just in case today arrived." She said it grinning, and puckered for another kiss. It seemed like a good idea to me, so I cooperated. Then she continued.

"We took NORTEC in Dorothy Anderson's name and relocated the rest of Cha's holdings under a nest of dummies we had already set up for other purposes. NORTEC alone is worth $20 million tops, so the $80 million we're paying for it will make the Joint Chiefs and the President feel a little guilty, and help set them up for our next whammy."

"Them feel guilty over something like that? I'd expect high glee."

"That, too, but beneath it a functional dollop of guilt."

I hefted the stack of papers. "What is this really worth?" I asked.

"Everything included—well over a billion." El's smile qualified as smug with no trouble at all.

I set the stack on my desk. "I'll go through these

later for a clue to what we're making here," I told her. But while I said it, I was thinking: Sure, we bought it, but can we keep it, with Cha sitting upstairs in his G-class wagon?

"What are Dak and Kad doing now?" I asked.

"Partly their usual business, but mainly they're arranging the Marine Corps blowout for tomorrow night. Important PR, plus lots of fun. How's your day going?"

"El, I have never seen a place run at such a high level of confusion and disunity, both here and in the lab. The lab techs even have a nice case of paranoia and social deprivation."

"The place does feel yucky. I'd like to have Norma take me on a tour after lunch. I can scan off some of the psychic grundge Cha always leaves in his wake. And speaking of Norma, what did you tell her about me? She gave me the royal potentate treatment."

"I just told her the truth: That you're the top boss in the whole world—sort of like Santa Claus, Daddy Warbucks, and the captain of the Good Ship Lollipop all rolled into a delectable one."

El pushed me onto the couch where she penned me shamelessly. I was saved by Norma's voice on the intercom, announcing that our luncheon guests had arrived.

"Luncheon guests?" I asked El as I brushed back my hair. "Who's for lunch?"

"Sorry, dear. I snooped and read your stack of personnel folders. You were right; there has been a lot of illness, and more than a bit of neurosis going on among your contract monitor teams. Except for six people— the head man, Morrison, and his five team leaders. They've been steady as a rock and never missed a day. They're the ones I invited."

"Great! I was going to do that tomorrow and get you to do a marbles check on them. No sane scientist could work with filtered data for very long without blowing some fuses. Those guys are either in on the scam, or something's been done to their minds."

We went into the board room to meet them, and I introduced Dorothy Anderson as the new owner. She seated three on each side and took a seat at the far end.

"Mr. Ambers," she said, "would you please serve the aperitif? The occasion calls for a toast."

There was a bottle standing conveniently on the side table, and I poured some of the contents into eight of the small glasses there. The liquor was a creme, light blue in color, in a bottle that could easily have been hand blown, with a label I couldn't read that might have come out of a home press somewhere. I felt a bit like an old Barbary Coast bartender out to shanghai sailors.

When I'd set them out and taken a seat, El proposed the toast. "To the key brains of NORTEC," she said. "May you find the Key to Naldar, and to success."

They drank, after which Morrison asked, "What does the word 'Naldar' mean? I am not familiar with it."

"Oh, it's sort of a family joke we found in a very old diary. A sort of legend, and it went that every life had two sides to it. One side was Naldar, a kind of personal heaven where all went well and life was fun. The other side was Radlan, a personal hell where life was rough and rocky, and made one take pleasure in the suffering of other people.

"Now if one could find the Key to Naldar, he could lock the door between the two sides and stay out of Radlan. A nice legend, don't you think?"

"Yes, ma'am." Morrison said it nervously, with a little twisting of his torso.

"Oh, no! Not ma'am," said El. Her voice was changing, particularly its cadence; she was up to something. "*You*, all of *you*, must call me Dorothy. We are teammates, and must be *very* close friends to work together. All of *us* here are on our way to *Oz*, and *I* am the *Dorothy* who will take *you* there. You will each meet the *Great Wizard*, and learn all the great *secrets* of life!"

She had spoken slowly, with careful if peculiar emphasis, and an excitement in her voice, as if she were speaking to small children. You'd think that grown men would take offense at that kind of talk, or at least pretend amusement, but their reactions were shocking. Morrison was in stark terror! His body was shaking as if trying to move in every direction at once. Finally, he found one set of signals and bolted from the room screaming. He bounced off the glass wall in the reception area and fell to the floor unconscious.

Another of these top-flight think tankers had fallen face down on the conference table; three had gone into an apparent trance state and sat foaming at the mouth; the sixth was limp, crying softly. And it was starting to smell as if someone had messed his pants.

I stared at El. "What in *hell* did you do?" I asked in an undertone.

"I recited a formula to release them from their personal Radlan." She left the room and I followed, a bit overwhelmed by the effect. Norma was crouched beside Morrison, hunting for a pulse.

"He'll be all right," El told her. "Have the medivac team come in."

"Yes, Ms. Anderson." She looked both bewildered and considerably frightened.

El turned to me. "I had a medivac team on standby, and arranged transport to a clinic in New Zealand. It's the only one on the planet that can help these people, and they really need help. I'm afraid Cha got into them pretty deeply, deeper than he did with Buc." She spoke to Norma then. "Norma, call their wives and tell them that their husbands have been sent on a top secret trip—that they'll be hearing from them soon."

She turned back to me then. "Some people Puk trained run the place. They're not part of the Menties, though—help isn't work or a game to them. They just help."

We stayed to watch the paramedics assist or carry the six men to a waiting helicopter and still had ten minutes to get the board room tidied up before lunch arrived.

"I actually only ordered lunch for two," El said. "Let's eat in your office. The board room is angry with me for letting Radlan in. After the vibes dampen out, I'll sing it a song and make it feel better."

The board room angry? I decided that if El said so, it was.

We went to my office. "Did you know ahead of time

what would happen from your fairy tale?" I asked. "Or was it the blue stuff? No, it couldn't be; we drank some, too."

"That wasn't a fairy tale, Le, and that 'blue stuff' is simply a fantastic appetizer with an honorable and ancient heritage. It's called 'kruu' by its makers, and don't ask where they live.

"I was sure that poor Morrison and his crew would at least get too upset to eat. And in any case I'd have shipped them to New Zealand on some pretext or other."

"When I planned to have you check their marbles," I said, "I had no idea they'd lost them so thoroughly. Were these people a bit, uh, degenerate before Cha got his hands on them?"

"Right. It's a matter of attraction. Le, at HOLEX you didn't have people like those. They get uncomfortable around you and either never start or leave very quickly."

She could see that I still had some attention on what had just happened, so she went on.

"People like those are stuck rigidly in a past moment in time, and in another space, a moment when the level of confusion and danger far exceeded what they could cope with. They tried to handle the situation and failed, and it destroyed them. And they tied themselves to it with dread. It's in the past, but they're still trying to hold it off, suppressing that it ever happened, and that keeps it forever with them, just out of sight."

There was a knock at the door. "Ah, the food is here," El said. "I ordered something special."

It was bouillabaisse, our chef's specialty. The aroma had me salivating furiously while I filled my dish. Just as we finished eating, Dak walked in, through the door in the conventional manner. "Stu just dropped me off," she said, "and left for Dover to spend the night with Mar. He's all primed to work with his mercenaries next week. Kad and I are going to help him sort through them and separate the wheat from the chaff."

She sat down and rubbed her hands in anticipation. "I dropped everything to get what's left of your blue plate special; I could smell it from home, before it was even ready."

We watched an Epicurean version of Dak attack the fish stew with considerable zeal, giving us no further attention till she'd emptied the dish.

"Boy, are we going to have a party tomorrow!" she said when she'd finished. "Two marine units—the SWAT platoon that handled NORTEC, and the honor guard that saved Buc for us—plus the two gunship crews and the President's flyboys that flew for us. And lots of debutante types for partners. There'll be a big buffet and dance, all formal, of course. The band we wanted was doing a gig in Miami, so the club owner decided to close for remodeling. We're all set."

She turned her attention to me. "How did your inspection go here this morning?"

"We've got ten techs downstairs who've been living under enforced silence. I've got them yakking up a storm now—at least I hope they are. Can either of you think of something that would get them to tell what they don't realize they know about Cha's project?"

"I'm afraid El and I can't help in that direction. It's you against Cha's plan and secrets. All we can do, normally, is provide support for your self-determined actions. But it sounds as if you're doing fine. And if your techs can get light enough about it, make play out of it, they may get comfortable enough that their channels of consciousness will open up. Cha is great at getting people to close them down."

"Thanks, Dak. I haven't decided what to do with the think-tank teams. They've taken a mental beating, and when they discover how they've been duped with phony reports, they may give up altogether. Although they may have been just an unwitting cover anyway, for the real operation going on downstairs.

"I'll tell you," I added, "I'm feeling a little uneasy about taking time off for an all evening, public party. I'd like to have this ten-sided monster put together before the six weeks are up and Cha comes back at us. And I also have a vague something floating around in my mind about the way he told Kad and I that NORTEC was ours. He was too casual about it, at least from a warrior's point of view."

I stopped as it hit me: "Unless," I said slowly, "unless he set this place up"—I looked at El, the light dawning—"with the intention of letting us have it—giving it to us."

"What do you mean?" she asked casually.

That's it, I thought. *I've got it. She's excited, and covering it. Otherwise, she wouldn't be so cool. But there's more I need to see, to realize about it, or she wouldn't be covering.*

Now I needed to play my part accordingly, and so did she, even though she'd undoubtedly read my mind just now.

"Suppose that this entire operation was a sham," I said, "both upstairs and down. Just a place to hold our attention while the real lab goes on being undiscovered somewhere else. Or maybe the lab downstairs has a twin." I began to feel excited. "Yeah, that feels right! That would explain Cha's lack of concern about losing NORTEC!"

"How could you discover if you're right?" El asked.

"Well, look! The electronics wholesale house must be the main supplier to the labs downstairs, right? So comparing the shipping lists for here with other places ordering the same or similar parts might give us a lead, unless NITOR's got a duplicate somewhere, too."

I could sense El's pleasure, but she wasn't jumping on my neck yet. Apparently I'd have to nail it down first. "Sounds like a good place to start, dear," she said. "Now Dak and I have to run. Things to do and spells to cast, you know." They both kissed me goodbye and left, again conventionally.

I got Norma on the intercom. "Ask Peters to meet me in the computer room in five minutes. And I'll either be there or in the basement all afternoon."

Peters was at the computer, waiting for me. "Do you have a billing record in that thing that shows parts and supplies being bought from NITOR Electronics?" I asked.

"I think we have an access code for their computer, but I'm not sure whether we've ever ordered anything from them or not. We'd need an account number, along with the access code, to find out." His fingers moved on the keyboard. "Let me see what we've got on that."

[Write:]   NITOR

His fingers moved again. Words and numbers flashed
on the screen:

    [Read:]   ACCESS # 1753396481
    [Write:]   NITOR ACCT #
    [Read:]   NO NITOR ACCT

"Interesting," I said. "I'm sure we get our parts from
them."

His eyebrows raised fractionally. How could that be,
he was wondering, with no account number?

"We get them from somewhere," I continued, "and
they get to the labs downstairs. And they wouldn't
have gone through here to the vault/elevator; using it
for a freight elevator would have blown its secrecy.
Right?"

He nodded.

"So they must have come in through one of the
tunnels. There are electric carts down there, and at the
end of one of the tunnels is NITOR."

"At the end of a . . ." He jumped up. "Let me go
check something!" Hurrying to an office at one end of
the computer room, he came back thumbing through
an address book. "I found this in Larson's desk this
morning. Here, under *N*. There's a ten-character entry
that may be what we're looking for." Again his fingers
moved over the keyboard.

    [Write:]   1753396481
    [Read:]   ENTER ACCT #
    [Write:]   NOR2464963
    [Read:]   INDICATE FILE WANTED:
               ORDERS
               SHIPPING
               BILLING

Now we were getting somewhere!

"Which do you want?" Peters asked.

"Try orders." He moved the cursor to ORDERS and
touched RETURN.

[Read:] INDICATE TYPE:
NEW
DELIVERED
UNDELIVERED
BACK

"Try delivered," I said, "and copy the whole file for the year. We may need it later. Then see if you can get into their error routine and find out if any other customer has bought the same supplies. I need to find out if NITOR is serving more than one set of labs like we have downstairs."

Peters frowned thoughtfully. "Just a minute," he said. "If NITOR is just down the road aways, and it's connected to our labs by a tunnel . . . could NITOR have been run by Charles Larson, too?"

"Absolutely. We know it was."

"Then let me show you something about the way Larson programmed computers. If you or I use a routine, it works pretty standardly like the one we just saw. But one of our personnel clerks tried to cancel Larson's employment this morning, and . . . Let me show you. She accessed personnel and wrote in his name, like this:"

[Write:] CHARLES LARSON
[Read:] GOOD AFTERNOON CHARLES
HOW CAN I HELP YOU?

"And that's as far as we could get the routine to run. Larson must have put in a special code at that point, and without it, nothing more happens." He began checking through the address book for possibilities.

I had a hunch, a wild one. "Try ChaChaCha."

He looked up at me, then punched it. Stars appeared all over the screen for a moment and then . . .

[Read:] AT YOUR SERVICE CHARLES

"Yippee! We've got it!" Peters yelled.

"Ask for the auto-access directory."

He called it up.

[Read:] AUTO-ACCESS DIRECTORY
PAGE 1 OF 6

The first page of the directory appeared. These were the companies from which Charles received automatic reports, and there were a lot more than the twenty-five I'd expected.

"Get a printout of this file, Al. It may help us sort out what's going on downstairs."

[Write:]   PRINT THE DIRECTORY
[Read:]   FOR YOUR EYES ONLY

Al ran from the room and returned with a polaroid camera. "I borrowed this from Wocelka," he said.

[Write:]   RETURN TO PAGE 1

As the directory rolled by, Al made a copy of each page. "You keep these, Mr. Ambers," he said. "I don't want to know what I just saw."

"Al," I told him, "we just entered a battle zone, and I prefer that my fellow warriors call me by my real name. I'm Le and you're Al. Without your help, I'm afraid we'll all lose this battle to the people that Charles worked with."

"Do you think they'll be sending someone to protect their investment?" Al asked.

"We're safe for at least six weeks, and I expect us to have this mystery solved before then. Call up the manual access directory."

He did.

[Read:]   ACCESS DIRECTORY
           PAGE 1 OF 249

I was really starting to feel excited now. We did a quick scan of the long list of corporate, private, and government computers and their secret access codes. "Try for a printout," I said.

[Write:]   PRINT DIRECTORY
[Read:]   FOR YOUR EYES ONLY

I picked up the phone and dialed. "Norma, this is an urgent rush need. Have someone send a high-speed camera back to the computer room as quickly as possible. With lots of film, enough for 300 shots. Make that 500. And thanks."

I hung up and turned to Al. "When the camera arrives, get a record of that file, just in case Charles has a booby trap in there somewhere. I'm a little surprised we got this far. And while we're waiting for the camera, try for the error routine in the NITOR system."

A thought had occurred to me that had cooled me down. The most astonishing information we'd gotten might well be irrelevant to our problem. The ownership and location of some of the computers we had ready access to was enormously interesting, and enough to shake half the world's governments, but to give it much attention could be a waste of time.

He tried for the error routine and couldn't get into it. "Okay, print up the NITOR order file for this year and I'll try the direct approach."

While the printer was buzzing, I called security and requested two armed guards to escort me to NITOR. When they arrived, I took the printout and went down the lift with them.

"Has either of you been down here before?" I asked.

"No, sir," they both said. The one in charge added, "I didn't even know this was here, and we were supposed to be thoroughly familiar with the whole place."

I nodded. "Okay. We're going down this tunnel to a supply house. I don't think we'll have any trouble there, but be ready for whatever happens."

We took an electric cart each and headed down the sparsely lit tunnel toward NITOR. At the other end we came to a large, heavy steel door with a call-for-service button and a video monitor. I rang, and a somewhat bored voice answered from a grid near the camera.

"Please face the camera and identify yourself."

"I am Mr. Ambers, replacing Mr. Simpson. I need to check deliveries for a special inventory."

"Thank you. Please wait while I check."

After a moment the voice returned. "I have no authority to admit a Mr. Ambers."

"Then let's get someone here who does. Get whoever's in charge of shipping."

The voice changed from bored to faintly irritated. "Just a minute."

Actually, it took a couple of minutes. The new voice was polite but sounded like a refusal preparing for delivery. "Please reidentify yourself."

I went through my request again.

"Mr. Ambers, no one here is authorized to let any-one through unless Mr. Larson brings them through."

"Mr. Larson is tied up. If you don't want your ass in a sling, open up and help me."

"Sir, my orders are explicit . . ."

"Mister," I told him, "these are your orders now. You've got just thirty seconds to open up or we'll blow the door and deduct it from your fucking salary." I kept the volume down, but the tone was crisp and the intention very high.

After a short pause the door opened, and we walked through into a freight elevator. Before going up, I keyed open the opposite door. Beyond was an underground warehouse, its wide, well-lit aisles lined with bins and shelving for parts and other supplies, the whole thing built for automated retrieval. I knew damned well that the labs I'd seen didn't need anything approaching that kind of resource.

We rode the lift up and were greeted by a very nervous, thin-framed man who had to be the senior I'd just spoken harshly to. "What's your name?" I demanded.

"Kenley. Robert Kenley. I'm the shipping manager." Behind his rimless glasses, the slight vibratory motion of his eyes began to increase as he looked back and forth between me and the two armed guards; Cha had infected him. I needed to reduce the pressure he was feeling, or he might unravel on me.

"Okay, guys," I told my guards, "you can go back now. Leave me a cart but take the explosives with you."

They never blinked at my lie, just yes-sirred and went back into the elevator. Within a day or two I'd have a pretty good idea of how tight-lipped our security people were among themselves. If these guys told around how I'd handled getting in here, I'd be getting looks from other security personnel. It was the sort of story they'd enjoy.

Meanwhile, I'd reverse my tough line now.

"Sorry about the hard words, Kenley," I said, "but I'm in a bind and a hurry. Simpson and Walters both absconded yesterday, and Larson appointed me to take over. I have twenty-four hours to find out what those bastards stole or I'll have to pay for it." I grinned at him. "And I'm sure you wouldn't want that. *You* might get half the bill."

Kenley's eyes stopped their flickering, and a visible sigh of relief eased some of the tension in his thin frame. "No, sir! I definitely would not want that. Where do you wish to start? I'm sure everything is in order at this end."

"See this list?" I held it up. "We ordered stuff, and it looks like you people shipped at least two of everything: one to us and one someplace else."

"Yes, sir, but I'm sure it was exactly per order. As a matter of fact, everything Mr. Larson ordered was shipped and billed to four separate accounts, not just one or two. Come to my office."

He had a very tidy office, which sometimes indicates no work, but in this case meant he was a stickler for order. If this guy ever screwed anything up, he'd probably have a nervous breakdown.

"Let's do it this way," I said. "I'll pick an item off the list and you show me the order, shipping, and billing on it." I folded the list open and pretended to check items at random.

"Indium alloy 342. Powder. Fifty pounds."

He glanced at the list for the stock number and punched in the appropriate codes. Data appeared on the screen of his office console.

"Here is the order number and date," Kenley said. "This is the shipping date, and here is the billing. For one drum"

"What's that address code under shipping?"

"That's the freight elevator. We would put the orders on the elevator, and someone, usually Mr. Walters or Mr. Simpson, would take them." He paused and shook his head. "I really can't imagine that anyone working for Mr. Larson would try to steal anything from him. He seems to know just what is going on everywhere."

"Well, those two got away with plenty in transferred funds. Now we need to sort out what else they got, and how. Show me where you've sent other drums of indium powder."

He did, and all the other addresses were out of the country. "Weird," I muttered as if to myself, then looked at Kenley. "Okay, this will do for now. Give me a hard copy on the four shipments and the billings, just for that one item. I'll take it back and see what we can find out about these other three places." I reached out and shook his hand. "And thanks, Robert. I may be back and ask for some help again. Or Mr. Larson may want to give it to a professional investigator now."

Kenley was beaming as he walked with me to the elevator. He was happy; he'd helped replace some disorder with order. A good guy.

Riding back through the tunnel, I reviewed again that last scene with Cha. God! No wonder he'd seemed so content to lose NORTEC. He had duplicate labs all over the world, even behind the Iron Curtain. And I saw no chance whatever of getting them all under control in the six weeks we had.

TWENTY-THREE

While I was at it, I stopped in the lab area. The guys there had been doing very well familiarizing one another with their projects, and the place felt as if El had already been through on her psychic cleanup.

Back in the computer room I showed Al the printout.

"So the war just expanded again," he said.

"Sure looks like it. After you get the errata printed, you might play around with ChaChaCha and see what else is hidden in there. And for now, let's keep this between us."

"Right. No sense in spoiling anyone else's weekend."

"See you on Monday," I said, and went to my office. El was there.

"Hi," she said, and waved a glossy eight-by-ten enlargement at me, which I realized was of the computer screen—one of the directory pages. There was a whole box of them on my desk; apparently photo-processing had experienced advances I hadn't known about.

"I see you found Cha's secret telephone list," she said. "You'll be surprised when you find out what he had in store for all these happy little computers."

"But you can't tell me, I suppose."

"Exactly." She changed then to the coquette mode, and taking me by the hand led me to the couch. "Pleasure before business," she murmured in her best sultry voice, and lying down, pulled me on top of her. With a little snuggling, the heavy layers of plans, ideas, and problems vanished. I could reconjure them later if I wanted to, those that were worth it.

Neither one of us tried to go anywhere with the snuggling. Not the least of her abilities was to soothe me instead of getting me heated up: It was pleasant just to be there together and nuzzle, a form of sweet and relaxing communication, mostly wordless. After a bit, with unspoken mutuality, we got up and straightened our clothes.

"What news?" she asked.

"You already found my surprise pictures," I answered.

"Don't try to tease me," she said. "What did you find out at NITOR? Remember Norma? She told me about your armed guards."

I handed her the printout and she glanced at it. "Australia, Yugoslavia, and Hong Kong. No one can say Cha was geographically partial," she said cheerfully.

"El, the part of this that I can't buy is the easy trail he left to follow. Why would Cha do that if he doesn't have other hidden labs besides those?"

"There are two big flaws in your reasoning there," she replied. "First, the trail was *not* easy. Nine hundred and ninety-nine people out of a thousand wouldn't even have looked for it, and of those who would have, not one in a hundred would have found it. I won't tell you how many times in the past you missed far easier trails.

"Secondly, you're still misreading Cha's purpose: You

think of war as hell, a thing to be avoided or at least won. But Cha thinks of war as a delight, to be enjoyed from all positions: win, lose, or watch. Of course he plays to win, but he is perfectly willing to lose, and he never has lost—not in the sense you think of as losing.

"War for Cha is something to savor and enjoy for the sheer beautiful randomness and confusion of it. Cha loves chaos, so he wins even when he might be said to have lost."

I thought about that. "So . . . could I be said ever to have beaten him?"

She nodded, her gaze calm and steady.

"If we've won before," I said, "why does the war go on? What's it going to take to end it?"

"I can't tell you, beyond generalities, but it involves what you are doing—what you've been doing since you left our old home. You'll need to bring all the vectors into balance in relation to the hidden script."

"But"—this was exasperating as hell—"how will I ever do that? How can I balance vectors I can't even see? I probably don't even know about some of them— Most of them, probably!"

"Darling," she said, "you're *doing* it. And at one level you *do* know. But clear channels aren't available to you in the warrior mode, so you play it by hunch. Look how far you've come in the last week! How far you've come *today!* And you've still got six weeks left."

That stopped me. "Have we come close to ending it before?"

"Several times, but never as close as now. Cha doesn't know how close you are, because he can't know the script any more than you can."

"Hmm. So in a sense Cha can't lose, because he wins even when he loses, but we can end the war by winning in a certain way. Or maybe by losing in a certain way?"

"I really can't discuss it any further right now," she answered, "except to say that you're getting the sense of it. So let's lay that aside; let all your sense of question and mystery about it vanish. Mystery is much too sticky to keep around, and it attracts more than flies."

"Okay. So what have you been doing today?"

"After my housecleaning tour with Norma, I had a chat with President Fuller by phone. He's still afraid to admit there are aliens, even to himself, but he won't flatly deny them, either. Actually, he's pretty convinced that there are, but he doesn't want to be, so he gets nervous when they're mentioned.

"He's anxious to visit your labs, and when you've got something impressive to show him, a visit will make us more real to him. It will also keep him from getting too anxious about what we're doing. But don't show him anything too advanced. We don't want to spook him, or tempt him to do something greedy. He's basically a good man, but he still flip-flops between statesman and shortsighted Cajun wheeler-dealer. One major break-through would be about right, if it's not too big."

The way she characterized him, he sounded to me about par for a top-flight politician. A presidential visit had already been on the back burner of my mind; now I turned the heat up a little and dismissed it from my attention.

"You mentioned something earlier about your staffs and a set of dummy corporations," I said. "How many companies do you own, anyway? Have I got the richest gal in the world?"

"Us rich bitches never tell, but we are well off. Remember the money you gave me to buy hay for Hannibal's elephants? That, combined with what you gave me for, um, personal services, was more than enough to start the first Swiss bank. Of course, during some centuries the interest rate was very low, but even at one percent since, um, 200 B.C., it would be a tidy sum. And we did a lot better than that in the fourteenth and fifteenth centuries. We raked in some fantastic profits in France, for example, and got out just ahead of Philip IV's big inquisition and general rip-off."

I could feel something nudging me from some deeper level of memories. Something markedly unpleasant to do with "Philip IV's big inquisition and general rip-off." Her eyes sparkled with mischief. "Yes, we've done very nicely, even without the other Hannibal types who mistakenly trusted you to keep their money out of my hands."

She tried to dodge then, laughing, but I caught and kissed her. She grinned at me from a distance of inches. "You really would be rich," she said, "if all the girls you paid had started a bank for you like I did."

I pulled her closer. "What a wonderful mate," I murmured, "to have followed me into some of the places I've been."

"True, I am wonderful. And you have been too, sometimes. At others you've been a lousy bastard—it went with the script—and I've had to stay away and wait for a more favorable lifetime to get you in bed."

"Didn't I recognize you at any of those 'chance meetings?'"

"Oh, yes! You always did. Sometimes you even admitted it to yourself! Sometimes you even admitted it to *me!*"

Someday when I had time, I decided, I was going to look back and fish and fumble, sort through those times for myself . . . Or maybe I wouldn't; life was today, and tomorrow there'd be tomorrow to live. And right now things were going incredibly well.

I pulled her close and kissed her again. "Thirty minutes ago," I murmured, "I felt so loaded with work and worry that I wouldn't have imagined being so free of it so soon. Now all I have my mind on is play, with you know who."

"Steady, boy," she said. "That kind of play will have to wait. We're having dinner downtown. A Brazilian couple who run a consortium of ours—notice I said *ours*—in South America, are here in Washington, and I arranged for dinner and dancing, mixed with a little business. We'll take along a list of NORTEC's South American interests, mostly mining, and have them check it out for us. We might want to take those holdings under their wing."

My intercom interrupted; it was Norma calling in to ask if she could leave. I glanced at the clock. "Sure," I told her. "It's quitting time. Have a good weekend, Norma. And thank you."

"Dinner is at seven," El said as I switched off the intercom, "so we have just enough time to go home and dress." She smirked. "They're very good friends of ours," she added, "and the suite I reserved for them has two bedrooms. We can stay there tonight and save a whole hour of travel."

At five minutes to seven we rang their room from the lobby of the Mayflower Hotel and were invited up for a cocktail before dinner. Mr. and Mrs. Penta were a surprise; I'd expected an older couple. They were in their early thirties, very handsome, and looked more Indian than Caucasian. They greeted El as Dorothy, and kissed her. She introduced me simply as Jan—"And this is Jan!" They both hugged and kissed me, and insisted I call them Arno and Cleo.

Arno served the drinks and proposed a toast:

"To Dorothy, whom we owe our lives. And to Jan, whom we have waited so long to meet."

I looked at El, puzzled: *Have waited so long to meet*. I had no idea what that was about.

"Cleo," Arno said, "we have Jan in a mystery." He chuckled then. "Right where we have wanted him." He turned to me. "Let us all sit down together and we will tell you the story."

We sat in four chairs at a low round table, and it was Cleo who spoke next. "When we were little children," she began, "we were very, very poor, by civilized standards, and lived in a village of huts on stilts. One day a flood came and washed many of us into the river even before it destroyed the village. Arno, with whom I often played, saved me, and found a piece of wood to hold us up. We floated for two days in the middle of the wide river, very hungry and tired, before a big white boat came along beside us. In it was Dorothy, and she pulled us from the water."

She paused to smile at El. "Dorothy was young and beautiful, even as now. She took us back upriver and found the place where our village had been, but now it was gone. An old man, who was Arno's great-uncle, was there in a small boat, mourning. He said that everyone was dead or gone forever. Dorothy tried to get him on board but he would not come. His duty, he said, was to stay and weep for a while, and then to take the long journey." Cleo paused for a moment until the sense of loss had passed. Her throat had been tightening, and her eyes were moist.

"Then came the most exciting time in our lives. We went down the river and got on an airplane! We had seen planes before, but only high up. We were very frightened, and Dorothy teased us; she pretended to cry because she didn't have any fear. 'You two are meanies,' she told us in Portuguese, 'for taking all the fear and leaving none for me.' Then she made us give her some of ours. We laughed because she took it all. For a minute she was twice as frightened as we had been, and then she removed a small gold box from her pocket. 'This fear is too good to use up all at once,' she said. 'I am going to save the rest of it till later.'

"So she put the fear into the box and put it away, and gave us a candy mint for making such good fear. We laughed so hard that the plane rocked. Then we came to a very strange place, the first city we had ever seen, Rio de Janeiro. There we lived in a hotel until she found us a home. We were ten, and she told us that someday we would meet the man the town was named for, that he was a very special man that we would all love. She said you would tell us how Rio de Janeiro came to be named after you!"

"You better ask Dorothy about that," I said.

She shook her head firmly. "We have asked her a million times already. About that and about no men in her life. But she always said we would have to wait till we met you," Cleo finished. She stared hard at me then, feigning determination.

I felt myself flushing. "Dorothy," I pleaded, "you'd better cue me or we're going to miss dinner."

"Le, they know about us. And they made up this little tease when they were children, as a fun way to get acquainted with you. They were far too inquisitive for me to keep secrets from."

Then Cleo took El to show her the bedroom we'd be occupying.

Arno looked at me with eyes that were steady but friendly. The hand that held his glass was small but strong, and immaculately groomed. "We are sorry, Le, if we made you uncomfortable with our teasing," he said. "We imagined—and scripted—this meeting still as children, long ago, and overlooked that no one had ever given you your lines."

He paused and smiled at me with perfect teeth. "Although from your performances in many times and places, you have long been a master of improvising in the things that count. We have been told much of those lives, and have followed all your progress in this one for many years. To us, you have been both our brother and our uncle, who lived far away."

He took a gold cigarette case from his jacket and held it out to me, then took one for himself, passed me the flame, and sat back. "For closeness," he said, lighting up.

"We are not psychic, Cleo and I, not in the usual sense. But we have been feeling an urgency to do something without knowing exactly what. Maybe you can tell us."

"Maybe I can," I said. "We just acquired a company here called NORTEC, and found that it has some hidden subsidiaries in South America." I handed him the list.

After glancing at it, he looked back at me. "I have heard of them all," he said, "and have even checked into several with the idea of purchase or merger. This one, Indper, is of great interest. They are mining and refining indium, but are not selling any. Instead, they are also buying it from tin and zinc mines all over the world and having it shipped to their mine site in the Andes. One would think that, if they wished to stockpile it, they would do so in a port city, to reduce shipping costs."

"Has El, uh, Dorothy, filled you in on the past two weeks?"

"No. She has only told us that our time has arrived. We thought she meant our time to meet her Le—her Jan—the founder of Rio." He laughed. "When we go to dinner, I will have Cleo tell you of the fight she had about you in school."

The girls came out looking beautiful, and we went down to dinner. After we'd ordered, Arno looked across at Cleo. "Tell Jan how the beautiful daughter of Cleopatra could get into a fight."

She blushed a little, a slight darkening of her Indian brown, then smiled. "One day at school we were studying Latin, and the teacher said our city was named for the Roman god Janus. I got excited and said, 'No. Janus is much older than Rome or even Greece.' She asked me to explain, but all I knew to say was that Jan was my faraway brother, and that Rio was named after him because he founded it."

She smiled, remembering. "At recess a boy teased me and said I did not have a brother, that I was only an orphan who told lies. When I thought of no Jan for our Dorothy, I became a little wild and knocked him down. We were at that age where the girls are bigger than the boys. He told the other children to be careful of me. 'She will go crazy and try to kill you if you tease her,' he said, and I was never teased in school again."

Getting up, I went around the table and, kneeling, took Cleo's hand and kissed it. "No Jan anywhere," I said, "ever had a lovelier or more courageous champion."

"You do a maiden honor, brave knight," she answered demurely, then laughed.

I went back to my seat and my drink.

"We have heard many warrior stories from your past, Cleo and I," Arno said. "Perhaps now it is time to tell us the latest."

"Before you begin that, dear," El interrupted, "I want to tell you a story about Arno." She paused then, to glance at him as he looked questioningly at her. "When he was sixteen," she went on, "he wanted to join the army and become a warrior like you. I couldn't dissuade him with words, so I took him on a dream visit to a time when you and he were together as brothers.

He was the oldest, and the law required him to stay with the family business. But you were free to become a warrior in that country, a country endangered by powerful enemies. So you went off and won glory, though not decisive victory, while Arno stayed home and invented a new kind of envy to hold the two of you apart.

"He used that envy to become very astute at business, and became so successful that he conquered the enemies where the army could not: He bought them." She smiled across the table at Arno, who smiled back. "You and others recognized what he had done, and went to him with praise, which melted his wall of envy, and the two of you rejoined in a mission that brought love and life and joy to many torn peoples."

"After having that dream," Arno put in, "I returned to the path that Dorothy said was the best for Cleo and me."

"I suspect that you two may have to save the bacon for this world, too," I told him. "War is very seldom a real solution; it rarely does more than buy time."

During dinner, I told them the saga of the past two weeks, then went earlier and told of my "accidental discovery" of icons. Later, while we were dancing, El confided in me.

"When I was fishing those two hungry, half-drowned kids from the Rio Negro, it seemed to me that some higher management had brought me to them. When I asked the DUO-HEX, he said, 'Bosh!' of course, but as they grew, I became certain of it. They've become almost as much my children as Marcy."

I held her a little more closely then. What a woman, I thought—warm and loving, so strong, yet so tender. And beautiful. And sexy. A warm glow of satisfaction filled me.

"Psst," she whispered in my ear, "you left out a couple of adjectives. I'll remind you of them when we get upstairs."

When we did go upstairs, we found Dak waiting. She grabbed Cleo and Arno for hugging and kissing.

"Sorry I missed the party," she said, "but I was busy

catching up on business." Smiling, she looked around at all of us. "I can see from your faces that everyone got reacquainted at last."

Despite Dak's warmth, which was real, I could sense beneath it something wrong. I felt deeper; pain. No, worse: grief.

"Kids," El said to us, "we could sit around and talk all night, but it's my bedtime." We kissed all around and went to our rooms; Dak followed El and me.

"I need to be close for a while," Dak said soberly.

El nodded. "Come to bed," she said, "and we'll hold you between us."

Dak stood at the foot of the bed, shivering visibly now, while we got ready and lay down. Then she slipped out of her clothes and crawled between us. El pressed her close and indicated that I should stroke her. Bit by bit the grief abated, until at last it was gone and she began to purr.

"Thanks for that," she said, then kissed us both, turned into a panther, and moved to the other side of El on the king-sized bed. "You kids play as you'd planned," she thought to us. "If I'm too close, or in the way, I'll jump down."

We played, and she wasn't.

TWENTY-FOUR

We awoke in the morning to find Dak still in a panther version, curled on the foot of the bed. I kissed El awake. "What happened to Dak last night?" I whispered.

"Oh, Le, she had to fight a once-beautiful friend whom Cha had turned into a monster. It was very hard on her, and she still hasn't fully recovered. Can we bring her back under the covers?"

"Sure."

Dak had heard or sensed the invitation. She uncurled and stretched, pulled back the cover with her teeth, then laid down between us with her head on my shoulder, to purr loudly as El pulled up the cover and stroked her. Then slowly Dak inched her way on top of me and took my shoulder in her mouth.

"Shall I bite him now or later?" she asked mentally. I could actually *hear* her voice in my mind.

El pushed the hundred-pound Dak off me. "Let me have him first," she said, "but bite him if he doesn't behave."

Turning into a girl, Dak grabbed her clothes and ran laughing from the room. I behaved well and didn't need biting. Afterward we dressed in casual clothes and went with Cleo and Arno to one of the hotel dining rooms for breakfast.

While we ate, we discussed their area of expertise—business. They viewed business as a single complex system—production/exchange/consumption—with that as the infrastructure of a greater system: civilization. I felt some realizations begin to jell.

After breakfast, Arno and Cleo had a plane to catch—a business trip to Japan. We had a round of warm goodbyes and left them with promises to stay in frequent touch.

On the way home, the jelling completed.

"You know," I said, "I'd been omitting a whole spectrum of possibilities that Cha may have had in mind for NORTEC. I was thinking of war in the usual sense, and NORTEC being into weapons design. But business could be a new kind of weapon. Are there any real social scientists on this planet—ones who could model the impacts of some really 'way out' technology? Say, like antigravity motors that don't use hydrocarbon fuel and can be installed in existing cars, or anything like that that might have a large and immediate socioeconomic impact."

"You were just talking to them, dear," El said. "Arno and Cleo have Ph.D.'s in both business and sociology, and very good contacts in those areas. And both worked in systems research for their theses. Mar can write a program for the model."

"Can we get them to start on that next week?"

"I think so."

El was trying to cloak her excitement: I'd hit paydirt again.

When we arrived at the house, Mar, Kad, and Stu were just landing on the back terrace, so we walked around to greet them. They were unloading boxes of costumes for tonight's party, and wanted them toted into the living room immediately. The pilot was enlisted to help.

"Mr. Ambers," he said, "I'm Gene Phillips. I want to thank you for bringing me in with you, and for your treatment under what were hostile conditions."

"Glad to have you with us, Gene. How about grabbing some boxes?"

"Right. One of them is mine. I was with the First Air Cavalry, retired on twenty last winter, and Stu invited me to the ball tonight as an honorary gyrene." He hoisted a box on one shoulder. "Before it starts, I'll be ferrying some young ladies from a girls' school to serve as hostesses for the men without dates." He grinned. "Like me."

When we males had all the packages piled in the living room, Gene left while Stu and I retired to the kitchen to make coffee. "Kad filled me in on the discovery of the other three labs," Stu said. "If they each have a paramilitary force connected with them, we'll have quite a corporate army."

"How did your meeting go this morning? Were the mercenaries agreeable about changing bosses?"

"So far all but seven. Six self-destructed and the other I canned," Stu replied. "I guess when Cha gives someone confidential information, he rigs him for absolute silence if captured."

We spent the rest of the day getting ready for the grand ball, where we were introduced to the twins' version of love goddesses. We spent Sunday recovering, and so did a lot of other people. Needless to say, the party was a smashing success, and within a few days the report had spread practically throughout the Corps, even in remote areas. Over the next couple of days, the phone rang itself hoarse with thank you calls to the twins, and invitations to just about every forthcoming party in the D.C. area.

They both were beaming, and on Monday only reluctantly gave up their love goddess forms for martial arts training, going with Stu to the paramilitary encampment to crack some skulls. Mar and I went to the office to crack some riddles. El stayed home, saying nothing about her plans.

Norma helped Mar get settled into what had been the office of our ex-contract monitor chief, Morrison, the guy who went off his rocker at El's story of Naldar. Then Mar and I went to meet with Al in the computer room. After introducing them, I asked him if he'd run into anything interesting.

"I think so," he said. "Started out kind of strange, though. Sunday I got a rush of anger about Larson like nothing I ever had before—totally irrational—and went over to a private shooting range in Virginia to brush up on my handgun skill. On the way back I had a flash and came in here to check it out. I ended up working on it till after midnight and sleeping in the lounge."

"What was it?"

"I don't really know, but it *feels* important. I pulled the program we accessed with ChaChaCha and found some stuff that doesn't seem to be part of it. I couldn't make any sense out of it, so I pulled it apart." He unfolded a printout on the console table. "Either of you ever see programming like this?"

"No!" we both replied.

"What does it do if you feed it in alone?" Mar asked.

"I tried that, and it won't run even with the Cha code."

"Hmm." Mar frowned. "Have you tried a core dump after putting in the Cha code, to see what's activated?"

"Yeah, and it's these twenty-six bytes here. Then, with that in place, I called for a program edit and got this out." Al unfolded another sheet. "Doesn't look like a program at all—not one that would produce anything."

"Al!" Mar said excitedly. "That's a base-eleven system. I've seen theoretical studies on them but never a program done in one. Does the rest of it look okay?"

"No. That's what I'd started on when you came in. I was trying to extract the next twenty-six bytes and see if that was another subroutine, but it doesn't seem to lead anywhere. The next twenty-six aren't used by the Cha code."

Mar looked it over and compared it with the first printout. "Al," she said, "print it out as a base thirteen and see what we get."

He did and it worked. He printed up the three programs as base ten, eleven, and thirteen. "Judas Priest," he said, "no wonder Charles insisted on doing all program rework by himself. No one around here ever saw this."

"Not and stayed around, anyway," I said. "Have you had much turnover?"

The question jarred him; I knew from that what the answer had to be. "Yeah," he said thoughtfully, "we have. More than you'd expect, anyway, mostly unannounced. People who just didn't show up for work anymore."

"Okay," I said, "I'll have personnel track them down, if possible, to see if they're okay. Now, back to these three-in-one programs. Any ideas about what the base-thirteen routine does?"

"We won't know until we find the code that goes with it," Al replied. He laid the three printouts side by side and wrote ChaChaCha on the base eleven. "Do you see a key, Mar? If this accesses base eleven, what will access base thirteen?"

She shook her head. "Print me a copy of these three and your input/output program. I'll work on it in my office and get back to you later."

"You guys have fun," I told them. "I'll be downstairs if you need me."

In the basement, all the lab doors were open and people were talking. I made the rounds of the labs to get an overall feel for what was being worked on. These guys had totally blown their phobia on communication and were making up for lost time; they sounded like a convention. The only thing I recognized was a version of SWAC in Lab Three. The technician working on it was explaining it to Mahavlich from Lab One. I listened, and when he finished I asked, "Won't you need a magnetic plate and net to stabilize the images?"

"No, sir. We had that on an earlier model, but we rebuilt the standing wave generator with some new parts designed somewhere else, and achieved stability without the net. Let me demo it for you."

He stepped into a roped-in area for a moment and set a red lacquered box on a stand in front of the projector. Then, as he moved a large calibrated knob, the projected image, a very realistic looking holo-box, moved slowly across the room until it rested against a copper plate on the far wall. It stayed there for a moment, then flared and vanished. The system shut down.

"That's what I was working on last week," he said. "A way to make it stable at thirty feet."

I picked the box from the stand to feel its weight, then put it back. "Let's try something," I said. "Turn it on again with the distance calibration set at closest range."

He did, and the holo-box floated there in the air without a waver, three feet in front of the original. "That sure looks real, doesn't it?" I asked.

Both techs agreed.

"Okay, now turn the power off." He did; the box flared brighter yet, then vanished.

"What's the power surge for when you shut down?" I asked.

"That's to clear the standing wave generator and icon plate of images, to prevent double images when we restart."

"Let's try something else," I said. "Pull your shut-off surge circuit and try it again."

He was good. He pulled a panel and had it cut out in thirty seconds. When the holo-box was back in place, I told him to cut the power. He did, and the holo-box fell to the floor with a crash that startled hell out of all three of us. I'd half expected it, but still it shook me.

After a few seconds to let the shock settle, I picked up the holo-box and said, "Let's go up to the garden and have some coffee." They followed without a word.

The garden was empty except for us. After we'd drunk half a cup in silence, I said, "Okay, guys, this is top secret, but *not* among you guys downstairs. You have no secrets from each other. And when you demonstrate that routine to anyone, warn them first. We don't want any heart attacks."

I stared at the one chipped corner of our red holo-box sitting in the middle of the table. "This will probably vanish pretty quickly. We need to get a picture of that event, and an exact measurement of its life span. Got any ideas?"

"Johnson in Lab Eight has a constant surveillance camera," Mahavlich said. "With a timer, of course." He paused, studying the box. "If the persistence of these things could be controlled or even predicted, it could save opening and disposing of a lot of shipping containers."

"Right," I said. "And presumably we can copy other things besides boxes." I peeked at the new name tag on the guy from Lab Three. Joe Byra. "Joe," I said, "I want you to call all the lab boys into your lab, two at a time, and make a box for each of them. Maybe this will be the shock we need to see through the cloud Larson built around your work. There's almost sure to be another piece of hardware around here somewhere that goes with our little red-box maker. Hmm . . ." I got up. "I'll be back after lunch."

Picking up the red holo-box, I left, and found Mar already back in the computer room.

"You're just in time," Al said. "We're getting ready to crank up the base-thirteen program. You'd never have guessed the code; it doesn't make any sense at all. I don't see how she did it!" He turned to Mar. "You're the genius who found it; you do the honors."

She wrote in the code, "BUCLEPUK," and I felt a rush of goose bumps from scalp to feet as a sequence of long-forgotten memory images began to run, overpowering the existing, present scene. I saw three young ensigns on their first duty assignment, on a recon vessel on routine sector patrol. We were so inseparable that the captain called us BucLePuk, singly and collectively. The last we saw of the captain was as we three were being thrown into the brig of an enemy cruiser. He'd surrendered to it without a run or a fight, and stood there with the cruiser's captain, laughing at us. "I'll always remember you, BucLePuk," he said.

Looking at the image now, I could recognize Cha in that laughing face.

Mar had gotten up and had me by the shoulders. "Le? Le! What's happening?"

I shook off the picture. "I was just remembering where Cha had used BucLePuk before. How in the world did you come up with it?"

"I don't know; a hunch. I was just trying things. I knew the three roots of course—Buc, Le, and Puk—and I've heard how inseparable you three were."

Al was staring at us, totally mystified. "She called you Lee," he said to me, "and you've been calling yourself Jan. And 'Cha'—that's short for Charles, isn't it? What's this all about?"

I pulled myself together. "Le's a name I used to be called by, one that old friends and family use."

"And you knew Charles before?"

I nodded. It looked as if somehow I was going to have to tell Al some things—some things most people would have a hard time accepting—if he was going to work closely with us on this. "Mar can tell you about it when she has time. But first things first." I turned back to Mar. "What does the program do?"

She pointed to the screen.

[Read:]   HELLO CHA. WHAT SET TODAY?

"What shall we try here?" Al asked.

"I don't know what it means by 'set'; try for a list," I said.

[Write:]   SET LIST
[Read:]   BUC
           LE
           PUK

[Write:]	BUC
[Read:]	TRIBE?
[Write:]	TRIBE LIST
[Read:]	#1 to #13
[Write:]	#1
[Read:]	CLAN?
[Write:]	CLAN LIST
[Read:]	#1 to #26
[Write:]	SCAN

Mar scrolled the pages through to twenty-six. It was one solid equation, all mathematese to me.

"Let's try a different tack," I said, getting another hunch. "Pretend we're Cha, and we're talking to a kid named Puk. Go to the conversation mode and ask PUK what we've got so far in indium products." Mar typed that in.

[Read:] CHA, WE STILL HAVE ABOUT EV-
ERYTHING COVERED JUST LIKE
LAST WEEK. ANYTHING SPECIFIC
YOU NEED?

"Well, that's a different approach!" Mar said. "What next?"

"Tell him to have LE recheck his figures on automotive market disintegration. Let's see what happens."

Mar tapped that in, and the reply flashed on the screen.

[Read:] ALL OK CHA. THEY CHECK OUT
FINE.

"Wait a minute!" Al said agitatedly, "the program's calling Charles Larson 'Cha' too, and you indicated that you knew him in the past, along with two other guys named Buc and Puk. And your names are the . . . What's going on here?"

Mar turned and took his arm. "Bear with us, Al, and I'll explain it to you when we're finished here." She typed in a request for the equations.

[Read:] TRANSPORTATION IMPACT DAY #1 TO
#300 PAGE #1 OF 120

"That's too much to handle now," I said, "even if I knew base thirteen. Call for a summary."

She did, and the equations vanished, to be replaced by a graph plotting number of unemployed and percentage of industry affected against units released, for a 300-day period. The unit side began with 10 per day and stepped up to 10,000 per day. At the upper limit, the entire transportation industry was gone in 200 days.

"And that's just from one or two inventions," I said. "Guys, there's the kind of war Cha had in mind. He planned to plunge the whole damn world into economic chaos."

"Are there really 450 million people employed in transportation worldwide?" Al asked.

"There's a hell of a lot, whatever the right number is," I said absently. I was trying to visualize the overall effect.

Mar frowned. "I have a feeling Cha is laughing at us. If we release his inventions, he wins. But if we withhold them. . . . Earth's petroleum resources aren't good for more than about twenty more years, and meanwhile, the carbon dioxide levels in the atmosphere are supposed to be inching up, so he wins that way, too. It looks as if Cha has his chaos in the bag."

"Don't bet on it," I said. "Let's try one thing more and then I'll leave you two to sort it out. Ask for the list of inventions already in progress."

Mar wrote that in.

[Read:]   OH CHA WANTS TO GLOAT AGAIN
            TODAY. OK. GLOAT LIST
            TRANSPORTATION, PERSONS,
            PUBLIC:
               PORT-2
            TRANSPORTATION, PERSONS,
            PRIVATE:
               AUTO-CAR 1
               AUTO-CAR 2
            TRANSPORTATION, GOODS:
               PORT-1
            MARKETING GOODS:
               TELE-VEND

                    AUTO-MAT
            MARKETING PEOPLE:
                    HOLO-WORKER
                    HOLO-PLAYMATE
            ENTERTAINMENT:
                    HOLO-RAMA
            COMMUNICATIONS, PUBLIC:
                    SPY-EYE
            COMMUNICATIONS, PRIVATE:
                    HA HA HA!

RED-BOX wasn't on the list, which supported my hunch: The projects downstairs weren't what they appeared to be.

I tried to scan through the list again, to figure where SWAC might fit in. But every cotton-picking one of those inventions stimulated a wave of emotions, a seemingly endless sea of them, a clamor of memories seen and unseen. My attention stuck on MARKETING PEOPLE, and suddenly I began to steam. That bastard was going to sell holo-clones! I started to swear, calling Cha all the vilest names I could think of, until I realized that Mar and Al were looking at me in shock.

I stopped, shook myself mentally, and tried to rationalize my strange behavior, but I couldn't think of a damn thing. So I ignored it, as if I hadn't uttered so much as a "damn."

"Mar," I said, "see if you can get schematics on the holo-worker." She typed it in.

       [Read:]   NAUGHTY, NAUGHTY! EQUATIONS
                  ONLY.
       [Write:]   LIST
       [Read:]   HOLO-WORKER EQUATIONS
                  PAGE #1 OF 200

My hand reached for the reset button and the screen cleared, then showed an innocuous opening instruction. I didn't want to see anything more about holo-clones. "That's enough of that for now," I said, and showed them the red box. "We just had a breakthrough downstairs and made this holo-box."

Mar took it and turned it over, examining it. "You mean this isn't real?"

"Oh, it's real, all right. It just wasn't made in the usual way. And I suspect its reality is temporary, that it'll vanish in a few hours, although I'm not positive about that yet.

"If you can sort out those equations or get some straight answers, we ought to have a fuller picture. See you later."

I took the box and started for my office.

Later, after a little help from my friends, I realized that I'd rabbited—run from fright—after I saw the list, So what was there about a read on a computer screen that scared me? What was it I couldn't confront about it just then?

Simple: At a slightly deeper level I knew more than I wanted to about holo-workers, and being reminded of it scared the metaphysical tar out of me. Fear is an emotional energy, and like other energies, has a spectrum of frequencies. The frequency that I reactively generated when I saw HOLO-WORKER on that list was way above my tolerance level. The thing that marked that fear, when I look back at it now, was the way I attacked Cha for reminding me—for having HOLO-WORKER on that list. When someone attacks something as ferociously as I'd just attacked Cha, it's because they're scared—not necessarily of what they attack, but of something.

And what was *I* scared of? You've heard about the Barbary Coast of San Francisco, before the 1906 earthquake—a waterfront district full of saloons and brothels. Also a good place to get yourself shanghaied—drugged or blackjacked—and wind up spending a year or two in virtual slavery on some sailing ship. Well, I'd once been involved in something similar but much worse. There was a time when I'd trafficked in holo-workers—secretly made holo-clones of people, using a device not much different from a camera. I'd shoot through a window, and the clones would materialize in a narrow, locker-like box. Then I'd sell the clones to spaceship captains involved in illegal or highly dangerous haulage.

Criminal, sure, but why such heavy, long-persistent guilt? A clone is just a clone, right? First, for nine or ten years—the length of clone stability at that time unless death destabilized it first—the clone was a sentient and separate individual, as self-aware as you or me, *but with the memories and sense of identity of the original*. And those were years of slave labor, usually dangerous, commonly involving gradual radiation or chemical poisoning and often deliberately cruel and degrading treatment. Most captains who'd buy holo-workers were captains who'd abuse them without compunction, and frequently with pleasure—especially if the holo-clone was a woman.

Then, to top it off, when the clone disintegrated, the memories of those years of slavery and suffering *came home to the person cloned*, like "bang!"—no warning, all at once. Usually the unlucky recipient went temporarily psychotic, or sometimes not so temporarily. At any rate, the rest of his life was likely to be nightmare-ridden.

So the dealer in holo-workers was considered the bottom of the criminal scale, even by criminals. If caught—I wasn't—his fellow convicts would kill him, slowly if they could. El was right: I really had been a bastard at times.

Subconsciously I was scared spitless of remembering what I'd done—sure that I wasn't up to handling the guilt—so I lashed out and then rabbited.

When I arrived at my office, Norma had a message for me. "Mr. Ambers," she said, "four of the scientists have called for an appointment with you. They seemed very agitated about something."

"Call a meeting for all the think-tank crew for one-thirty in the board room, and I'll handle all their problems at once. Has Stu checked in?"

"No, sir, but Mr. Switzer, the personnel director, wants to meet with you or Mr. Rogers."

"Good. Tell him to come over now." I started into my office.

"Oh, yes," Norma said after me, "and Ms. Anderson called. She said she couldn't make it for lunch today."

"Thanks. Have lunch for six served in the board room, and invite her daughter, Mr. Peters, and three of the other managers. Any three, for twelve o'clock."

"How would personnel, documents, and admin do? That will make it three men and three ladies."

"Sounds fine. Thank you, Norma."

"And Mr. Ambers . . ."

"Yes?" I knew from the way she said it that she had a question she wasn't sure she should ask.

"Is Ms. Anderson—are they really mother and daughter? I can see a resemblance, but she doesn't look more than five years older."

That stopped me; I'd never really gotten my own question answered on that. Not definitely. "By golly, Norma," I said, "I'm not a hundred percent sure. I only know that Mar calls Dorothy 'Mom.' I can see why you'd wonder."

I went on in and closed the door behind me, Norma's final question still on my mind. But not for long; the personnel chief arrived about five minutes later. I recognized him from the first meeting.

"I'm Carl Switzer, your personnel manager, Mr. Ambers, and I have some questions about policy if you have a few minutes." His handshake was firm.

"Carl, call me Jan. We'll make the time. Have a seat."

"It seems that before you came, a segment of our people were considered outside my responsibility. But when Mr. Rogers gave me the key to the field agent cabinet, I took that to mean they were mine now. So I began checking records, and something is very wrong. One thousand fifty field agents were hired, but only 250 are carried on our payroll. Yet the other 800 records show no termination or transfer, so theoretically they are still on staff.

"And in the same cabinet, besides the field agents, we have files for fifty-six technicians, including the ten downstairs. The others are shown to be on staff someplace, too, but it doesn't say where. Altogether we have more people unaccounted for than we do on hand!"

"Have you tried to trace anyone?"

"Yes, sir. I called the next of kin of one missing field agent and they said he was in Peru. His file jacket has the notation *IP* in pencil; it looks like Mr. Walters' writing. All of the missing have one notation or another; the others are *HK, AU,* or *YU.*

I reached out and shook his hand. "Carl, you are on to something important. Get me a list of those men by notation. IP is Indper, a mining operation in Peru. The others are Hong Kong, Australia, and Yugoslavia. That's right: Yugoslavia. I'll get you the addresses, but *do not* make contact unless you clear it with me first. We'll let those guys go on thinking they're lost a while longer. Do the technicians have the same kind of notations?"

"Yes, they do."

"Good. Make me a list of them by skills and location notation. We'll find out which secrets are going to which places."

"Shouldn't we notify the DOD or the CIA about this?"

"Absolutely not! There is evidence of treason in top levels on this, and I'm reporting directly to the President. That was his chopper that brought me here on the day of the raid, and the marine unit was his special SWAT team. He'll be here later this week for an inspection, and I'll have you on the tour with us."

Switzer was properly impressed.

"I always felt there were some—unethical activities going on here," he said. "Simpson and Walters felt— actually, like a pair of large, gleeful delinquents to me. But I never imagined it was anything of this scope!"

"Right," I said. "Simpson and Walters were just tools. Come on, let's go to lunch."

The rest of us had begun to eat when Mar and Al arrived at the board room in a state of high excitement; they calmed down when they saw the other guests. Lunch was mostly a friendly visit, and I wrote if off as necessary morale boosting. Afterwards Mar and Al went to my office with me.

"Wow! Did we find a goody!" Mar said, releasing her suppressed excitement. "After you left, we went back to PUK and discovered an INVENT routine! Honestly!

To test it, we asked it for a light bulb. It gave us a schematic for a microgenerator of some sort that provides the power as well as emitting light. Then we asked for a printout of the schematic and got the 'FOR YOUR EYES ONLY' notation.

"And that's just the beginning! Then we found a search routine that gave us what it called 'roots' and a list of about twenty research reports, from all kinds of places, that could lead to the development of the light-plus-power unit in the diagram. In the development phase, the schematics vanish and get replaced by notations of progress."

I sat there without talking for a moment, letting it sink in. "You mean PUK is a routine to invent anything possible, using the equations in BUC? Where does LE come in?"

Mar yielded the floor to Al. "LE," he said, "is a routine to convert the math in BUC into technology for the INVENT subroutine in PUK. Evidently the LE program takes theory and compiles application in terms of known human technology. But—and here's the tricky part—LE invents, or rather designs, research programs *without access to a data base*. LE is a compiler with artificial *super*-intelligence. The data from LE is presented to PUK INVENT, along with a search request for the Library of Congress and several other large libraries with call-in access.

"Now here's where the 'roots' come into play. PUK takes the root list and generates an optimum research program based on existing human capability. That's *Earth*-human capability."

Obviously Mar had had her talk with Al, and he'd accepted what she'd told him: He knew now that Cha was an alien.

"If no roots exist," he continued, "the equation is scrubbed. That seems to definitely show that Cha and his people are restricted in some way to 'homegrown' developments."

"Let me get this straight," I said. "PUK invented a light bulb with the aid of BUC and LE, but without using outside data banks except for literature references—data roots. How the hell does that work?"

Al shrugged. "I don't know. One disc we use for temporary on-off loading came into play, but when we were done, it off-loaded back into core memory. PUK used all three of the programs, but no record was kept of the activity—it retained no memory of it."

Mar handed me a polaroid shot of the screen. "There's the schematic of the light bulb. Recognize anything?"

"No. Did you copy the root references for this?"

"Yes." She handed me another polaroid.

"Let me check these under a magnifier," I said, "and read the original reports. Maybe we've got a good flashlight in this."

"Or a way to put utility workers out on the street," Mar added.

We were all silent for a bit. "My red box and I have a meeting with some think-tank scientists," I said at last. "Do you want to come along, Mar?"

She shook her head.

"Okay," I said, "but don't let Cha's little surprises put a damper on your fun. We'll get him by the short and curlies yet, just wait and see."

They left, and I had time to do a few letters with Norma before going out to apply some band-aids. The thirty scientists in the think-tank crew arrived at our one-thirty conference room meeting with notebooks and stacks of errata pages. I could see the anger and frustration on their faces.

"Gentlemen," I said, "I see an angry group here. Angry with damn good cause. I also see a group with toughness. It took that to survive what Charles Larson and friends ran you through.

"Well, it's going to take even more to confront the bucket of crap I'm about to put in front of you.

"There are ten labs downstairs you didn't know about, and they are actually developing the equipment you thought was just in the conceptual stage. They had the data which had been withheld from you—the data in the errata sheets.

"For reasons we haven't unraveled yet, you have been window dressing."

There wasn't a single expression of disbelief; it fitted the evidence of the errata sheets.

"For whatever it's worth to you, gentlemen," I went on, "you were conned by an expert. He also conned the government—in fact, several governments. Actually, and I tell you this without any exaggeration whatever, you and I are lucky to be alive to notice our mistake.

"Now, before we go to questions, I want to introduce you to a new way of looking at reality. I want you to consider that space, time, energy, and matter are not unified, your physics professors notwithstanding, but are four completely different things. Consider it that way at least for the purpose of what I'm about to show you."

I paused to let that settle in, then held up the red box and handed it to the nearest scientist. "Pass it around."

They did, more or less puzzled, while I waited. When it got back to me, I continued.

"This box appears to be very real. It is not, at least not in the usual sense. It is a holographic projection, a copy of a box we have downstairs. It even has a chipped corner where it fell after being projected into a space without a support under it.

"We have a device down below that appears to be a holographic image projector, a near duplicate of the SWAC Project device. Speaking loosely, it makes these red boxes."

I held the box up again. "I called this a copy; actually, it's not. There is really or actually only one red box, *and we have given it multiple addresses in space*. There are twelve more in the labs, and soon each of you will have one. It's a case of just one box with forty-four different addresses."

I paused again to let their reactions jell.

"Okay. Questions."

The silence was dense.

"I want you men to say what you want to say. Unload on me now so we can get on with it."

One of them stood up, his glasses reminding me of the bottoms of vodka bottles. "I'm Jacobs, with the team for SWAC," he said. "I haven't gotten through all the errata sheets yet, but frankly, I do not believe what you claim is the origin of that red box."

"Jacobs," I answered, "you are free to believe or disbelieve whatever you wish—on your own time. On the job you're a scientist, and I will expect an objective viewpoint from you, unencumbered with prejudices. Neither your beliefs nor mine will change what occurs in nature very much, but they may lead us astray in explaining what we see. And believe me, gentlemen, in the situation we're in now, if we don't explain it right or very close to right the first time, we won't get a second chance. The boys that Charles Larson and your ex-chief Morrison worked for will take over this planet easier than the Russians took Hungary, and there won't be any border to escape across. And I don't think you'll enjoy being their slaves."

I stood up. "Let's go down the new stairway," I said, and they trooped out silently behind me to the new guard station next to Security. In the foyer below, I spoke to them again.

"Working with parts of the data withheld from you, each of our labs has produced a device, or at least a prototype. You'll be examining these devices shortly. Each is a component of an intended, larger, still unknown device. What we need to do is assemble the complete device, using the data on the errata sheets to develop the missing pieces.

"Now, I want each of you to see a red box produced. You'll go into Lab Three, two at a time, starting with Jacobs and someone else from the SWAC project team."

Two of them followed me into the lab, where I introduced Joe Byra and had him make each of them a red box. Both of them seemed in near shock at what they witnessed.

"Gentlemen," I told them, "that box in your hand is either the same box on the pedestal, with an alternate address, or it's made of photons. I wouldn't rule out either one entirely, but the latter seems unlikely. Joe can give you the power consumption figures later. Now go out and send in two more."

Back in the foyer I told them to spend the afternoon visiting in the labs. "We'll meet again at two o'clock tomorrow in the conference room, and I would like to hear some solid proposals for mating these devices." I walked away tired, with the distinct feeling that I was wasting my time with thinkers. What I needed was doers.

I dropped into security to see Kruger, the chief. "Do you have a portable Xerox or other copier?" I asked.

"Yes, sir."

"Good. We have ten sets of manuals downstairs. They're the only working plans we have, and a fire would set us back badly. Send someone down with a guard to copy them between now and morning. And the person who does it needs to be a stickler for detail, or we'll get the loose pages fouled up."

"Yes, sir. Where shall we store them? Our cabinets here are pretty full, and we're short on vault space."

"Put them in my office under guard for tonight, and I'll send them out to off-site storage tomorrow. Thanks."

Back in my office the phone rang. "It's her," Norma told me before switching it through.

"Hi, El," I said. "Where are you?"

"Hi, yourself; I just got home from Hong Kong. I'm afraid that what Dak ran into yesterday was just the beginning. The playground is beginning to come unraveled."

I suppose that some part of me wanted to respond to what she'd just said, but I found myself going off on something else, as if I hadn't heard what she'd said. Maybe I thought I wasn't ready to hear it.

"El, something's wrong here. I'm getting tired already. I was thinking about a nap when you called. Could there be other life force saps around?"

"Have you been in a meeting with the scientists?"

I held the phone away for a moment, staring at it. "How the heck did you know?"

"Le, thinkers of all types, and that includes theoretical scientists, tend to create mental masses to balance the lack of physical mass and physical movement in ideas. That often leads to a lot of physical problems. I suppose think-tankers and science fiction writers have the heaviest loads. Your guys have a double load because of the holes in their data, and they've tried very hard to dub in stuff that would explain what was missing. Today a bunch of it rubbed off on you; you need it cleaned off. Remember what we did on Friday to handle your stress?"

"How could I forget?"

"Close your eyes for a moment and we'll do it again, but not all the way to play. Just enough to get your pep back."

Time slowed, stopped, and I seemed to step into a room where El was waiting. She motioned me to get up on a massage table. The massage was light and rhythmic, and after a little while I went to sleep. I woke up to what seemed like a swat on the rear, but I was still alone, physically, with the receiver in my hand.

"How's that for a twenty-second workout?" El said, laughing.

Twenty seconds? I thought. "Great, sweetheart, and thanks! That was just what I needed."

"Good. Now, I established us as the new management with our people in Hong Kong today, so you can send people over or call them in whenever you want."

"Did the man there mention a paramilitary unit?" I asked.

"He knows there's one there, a small one; he just doesn't know what it's for yet. And no one there was wired for self-destruct, so we can assume that none of them knew Cha or his family for what they really are."

"Thanks for the explanation and the treatment. Oh, and I almost forgot! We got SWAC going here—an advanced form. Thanks for the news. See you."

I rang Norma. "I expect to be in the computer area the rest of the day," I told her, then headed back. Mar was there with Al in his office, looking at printouts of BUCLEPUK's handiwork.

"Looks like you guys are having fun," I said. "Al, will this three-tiered program run on any computer, or has this one been beefed up for it?"

"From what we've gotten so far, it should work on any system. I've watched the IBM service techs work on this rig, and it seems standard enough."

"I'm going to Dover tomorrow afternoon," Mar said. "I could check it on a machine there easily enough."

"Good," I told her. "Make two extra copies of the program and let's keep them somewhere in case something happens here. There are other paramilitary forces out there that may be programmed to retake this place."

"You don't think we can bank on Cha letting us have all this to do ourselves in with?" Mar asked.

"I don't think we can count on anything being the way it seems, if Cha set it up."

As I said it, I felt a nagging sense of something missed, something I'd left dangling someplace. Maybe a participle.

"Look at this last thing we got." Al pointed to a printout. "This is everything on SWAC—from the source equation in BUC here to the compiler output in LE and the INVENT in PUK. Note the root source list: your patents and Mar's Ph.D. thesis."

"No wonder you started HOLEX!" Mar said. "You picked up on the possibility, too." She handed me three polaroids. "Here's the PUK INVENT schematic."

While I was looking at them she stood quietly, continuing only when I looked up. "From there we went into a progress report mode and found that RED-BOX, PUK's name for SWAC, is ninety percent complete. Here's a polaroid of the missing section; it matches a part of the third one in your stack."

"Yeah," said Al. "Then we called for the next tech instruction and got a read of 'no root,' so we called for a copy of the last instruction." He thumbed through the stack of papers and pulled out a heavy three-hole page. "Here's what we got. SWAC, or RED-BOX, as Cha called it, had its last instruction fifteen days ago."

"This is a computer printout?" I said. "This paper is almost as heavy as card stock; it's like the pages in our lab manuals. I would never have recognized this as a printout."

Al pointed to the far side of the room. "We have a

printer I never saw run until today. Its paper feed is full of this stuff. Only PUK can turn it on, so Larson must have printed all the lab manuals himself when he was alone."

A realization hit me then, and I snapped my fingers. "Say! I'll bet all the rigs downstairs have missing data roots! Cha may have *wanted* us to have this place so we could supply them. All the elaborate protections, armies, and duplicate labs may have been red herrings. We know there are rules that won't allow *him* to supply the missing pieces, and maybe his own people were stalled on it, so he decided to let us do it for him.

"I could have gone downstairs and built this section for him tonight without realizing that's what he wanted me to do."

Mar laughed drily. "And he'd have been covered under the rules. We even bypassed his no-print barrier by photographing the invent schematics. No referee would have faulted him."

It still seemed weird to look at the world as a war game with umpires. Meanwhile, I could see Al was feeling a little spooky about what we'd just said. We needed to brief him more fully.

But first things first. "Make me a copy of the next instructions for each lab," I said, "along with a polaroid of the invent schematics. We need to decide some things, and we may need to do it in a hurry." There was that feeling again, as if I'd better move fast and catch that dangling participle before it hit the deck. Or the fan.

"We'll need the code name off each lab manual," Al said. "This baby has no memory, remember; all the data we get is generated newly each time. We tried for a summary of lab projects, and the only response we could get was 'you name it and we'll invent it.'"

"What about that file of inventions?" I asked. "What about this copy of the last instruction for RED-BOX? Isn't that memory?"

"No," Al said, "there's no stored memory at all. None! Zilch! When you want something, BUC generates an equation, and that becomes both a temporary memory and a generator for the compiler program in

LE. The process is repeated newly each time, and the progress reports—lab manual instructions, actually—are the next step in solving the equation. When the equation is fully balanced, it vanishes."

I paused to look at what he'd told me. "That means," I said slowly, "that means . . . that all the auto-accessed data coming from the prime contractors is just for data roots. The roots have to be indigenous, and it's the auto-accessed data that gives PUK the needed clearance to print up the next tech manual instruction."

"Right," said Mar. "Now, since you shut down SWAC, seven weeks ago, searches for data roots have expanded into other areas. That copy you're holding was printed up after a data root was found in the CIA computer. It's a Russian-supplied root."

"For crying out loud!" I said, and suddenly realized I was grinning. "Okay, things are getting clearer now. Let's go to Lab Three and get you both a nice red box to play with, and some project code names, and have a little fun with this."

Downstairs we found the think-tankers busy blowing away old confusions and picking up new ones. The lab techs were really having a ball explaining their rigs and answering questions.

I introduced Joe Byra to Mar and Al as the world's first holo-box maker. Joe laughed, a very good sign of recovery. "Whatever that means," he said, then motioned with his head toward Al and Mar. "Shall I make two more?"

I nodded; Al and Mar got their own boxes, then split. I checked Joe's manual and compared the duplicate of the last instruction printed this morning to the one printed two weeks before.

They were the same, as expected, but it seemed as if they shouldn't have been. Mar had gotten the second one without having the code word, and that meant . . . that BUCLEPUK had invented the code name just for them *and then accessed the original equation!* Curiouser and curiouser!

Actually, I realized later that that was not as curious as my own continued inability to confront the connection between Cha's gloat list and the labs. What's in a name? Often a lot more than meets the eye.

"Joe," I asked, "what have you been doing since your last manual update?"

"Over here," he said, and led me to a rear corner of the lab. "I've been working on reducing the size of the projector." He showed me a polished aluminum case about the size of a shoe box. "This is the size I'm shooting for on the projector, and this other case is for a backpack recorder to go with a handheld camera. I figured it would be great for family movies—that is, I thought it would—but that was before I found that the images are a little solid. A guy could get a houseful of twins—more like a houseful of clones—with this rig."

"That's a good idea, though," I said. "Just change it a bit and see if you can reduce the red box to a film or magnetic record. That would make transporting red boxes really cheap; red boxes or whatever. Ship them on tape, then have them vanish when you're done with them."

"Hey!" Joe said, "I like that. Make six-week furniture. Then, when it vanishes, my wife could take the projector and materialize a fresh set wherever she wanted it, and I wouldn't have to risk a hernia moving it around."

A knot had started forming in my lower stomach when he'd said "clones." But it didn't stop with that, because I also saw a world left destitute when all the holo-clone slaves and the holo-things vanished one night, unexpectedly. I guess I have a pessimistic streak when it comes to gift horses; maybe Cha was with the Greeks at Troy.

Then the copy crew and guard arrived to duplicate Joe's manuals. I was ready for a rubdown in real time.

TWENTY-FIVE

Mar and I drove home. Al had decided to stay late, to photograph the schematics of our other projects.

"Well," I asked her, "how did you like your first day?"

"Was that all one day? It was great! I've been looking forward to it since I was five and El told me we'd work together."

She leaned over and kissed me on the cheek.

"Thank you, Mar. I'm sure glad you were there today. Base eleven and thirteen would have eaten our lunch. Or eaten us for lunch. We'd still be doing the cha-cha-cha."

"No, Al is good. He'd have taken it apart before too long. I just 'happen' to have been encouraged to play with exotic base systems by a certain lady we both know."

That certain lady met us at the door with hugs and kisses. She was in peach lounging slacks of a very soft material that revealed her form momentarily with each motion. I felt my pulse quicken.

"Stu, Dak, and Kad are on their way from our paramilitary base," she said, "and they're going to be sweaty. So first we'll have cocktails on the terrace, skinny dip briefly, and then visit in the hot tub."

"Didn't know we had one."

"We never have a house without a hot tub; we like the magic of closeness they provide. It's just that here it's in a secret place."

We went out back and met the chopper as it landed. Neither Stu nor the twins looked bushed; dried sweaty, yes, but very alive and playful. I always knew office work was harder. Gene lifted off immediately, and we had another round of kisses and hugs. That should have been strange for me; in my family growing up, we might kiss as often as once a year, but I'd adjusted happily to all the hugging and kissing of my new team.

"An announcement, everyone," I called. "Mar broke Cha's secret code today, and we have all the data to complete the ten projects. A toast is in order." We lifted our glasses. "To a lovely master of math."

"Bravo!" Stu said. "And now another toast." We raised glasses again as he waved one arm toward Dak and Kad. "To the dynamic duo who didn't break anything but hearts to win the war today."

We drank to that, too.

"El, it's your turn," Dak said.

"Okay, I'll propose a toast to me.

> "To inscrutable Madam El
> who awed Hong Kong
> banking world
> and took over KONTEK
> with one 'ah so.'"

Then smiling shyly and with palms together in front of her downturned face, she sank into a deep oriental curtsy, knees folding into odd but graceful angles. We laughed; then I asked for details.

"Not yet, dear. We have a ritual to observe here." Looking around, she said, "Finish your drinks and we'll play follow the leader." After tipping hers up, she kicked off her shoes, turned, and started toward the pool, disrobing with smooth grace as she walked. My eyes weren't sharp enough to see how she did it. I undressed almost as quickly but far less gracefully, then hurried after her, catching her under water after her dive. She cast a merman's spell around me and we settled to the bottom together, from where we watched the others plunge in. The twins had an aura of otter. They must have aided Mar and Stu, because we all swam underwater for five or ten playful minutes before El pulled us away to the next part of the ritual.

We trooped after her then to the utility room, where she pushed on a bronze intaglio on the back wall. A section slid aside, opening to a glass-sheathed hot-tub room, and we went into the steamy space, lowering ourselves carefully into the hot, swirling water. Dak and Kad had taken opposite sides.

"Now," said El, "before we turn the hydro off for a quiet visit, the ritual for the day involves a thing Dak and Kad want to do."

The twins had shifted into their goddess auras again and spoke in perfect stereo-like unison, their voices with a strange musical quality.

"We goddesses of love have decided to grant your wish for the ritual of ADDA. Each couple must join hands and touch feet with the opposite couple. Our feet will join yours to form the hexad." When all our feet were touching, they continued. "Now close your eyes and don't move."

El squeezed my hand. The dark behind my lids began to grow lighter, became a bright golden glow. A circular pool appeared—not the pool we were in—and came into focus, the twins in its center to their shoulders, the rest of us seated on the encircling rim with our feet in the pool. It was like being outside my body watching all of us in another scene.

The water, if that's what it was, was a transparent deep blue.

In the image, our twin goddesses rose until they floated with their waists just above the surface. I watched them rotate slowly until they faced us on either side. At that point, jets of the liquid arced upward from holes in the curbing, splashing for a long minute over our proxy bodies. The last of my tension disappeared, and my proxy body and my own seemed to become one within the imaged pool.

Then, when the image fountain had subsided, leaving the pool a flat circle of blue, the twins rose higher until they stood on top of it and stepped off to either side. There they picked up white pitchers with long spouts and, kneeling gracefully, filled them from the pool. The goddess DA stepped in our direction and AD in the other. DA moved back and forth between El and me, pouring the blue liquid on our heads. It seemed to be a different liquid now, and the sensation was breathtaking as it flowed down slowly over the various endocrine centers.

Enchanting music began, as if the goddesses were humming, and my body vibrated to the tune. The music continued, becoming more playful as the adrenal glands were washed and hidden angers flowed away. When the stomach area was washed, a great sense of fulfillment spread throughout, as if I'd just eaten an enchanted feast.

At the washing of the lower center, a sexual feeling crescendoed, then, with the music, ebbed into a rhythm of quiet satisfaction. This was followed by invigoration as the goddess DA laughed and emptied the pitcher over our heads. In "the real world," Dak and Kad signaled the end of the ritual by rousing us from our trance with a splashing of water and squeals of laughter. Stu and I got out of the tub and brought drinks for all of us.

Then, with the hydro off, we settled down to "business." Stu reported first. "We had nearly two hundred guys today with significant martial arts training. Kad and Dak called for the ten best to come forward. Within about half a second, some thirty cocky black belts stepped up. Dak selected ten and told them to attack her and Kad all at once.

"They did, and you can guess what happened. Then our twins bowed to the ten fallen heroes while more than two hundred stunned mercenaries stared without a word."

Stu paused for a drink while we applauded the bowing twins. Then Kad spoke. "We'd shocked their sense of rightness, but they started brightening up when we told them we intended to train them in our techniques. After that we sifted through the entire lot, examining patterns, and found five who'd been true masters long ago. So we got with them alone, and tuned their patterns. They'll run the new training teams, with a little help from us to start."

"Bravo!" I said, then looked at Stu. "Have you heard about our eight hundred lost troops?"

Stu's eyebrows raised. "Eight hundred lost troops? No. What's that about?"

I described my meeting with the personnel director. "So apparently they're in Peru, Hong Kong, Yugoslavia, and Australia." I turned to Mar. "Mar, tell them what you found today."

She told them about BUCLEPUK and the inventions. After she was done, I told them about the red box.

Then El stood up and took my hand. "You kids can stay, but Le and I have dinner to fix. It'll be formal—we wear clothes."

She and I went to our closet for robes, and then to the kitchen. "El," I told her, "that was some kind of magic our twin goddesses did on us out there. I have never felt so alive and in tune in all my life—maybe in all my lives."

"How about that Saturday morning in the park?" El asked. "Dak did a version of that same ritual for us then. That's why you skipped baseball that day to play with us."

"Of course! I remember now! The dream about the lagoon! You know, I went back every Saturday for a month to find you and feel that way again."

I put my arms around her inside her robe. "Down, boy," she said. "There's supper to cook, and besides, too many treatments like that and you'd lose your warrior's license."

After dinner and dishes, we all went into the living room for brandy and strategy. Then Al phoned. "Sorry to bother you at home, but I just finished with the tech updates and found something you'd better know tonight. One of the projects was MAG-JACK, whatever that is; it's one of those with the doughnut-shaped magnet that uses indium powder. Anyway, when I went to update it, it had vanished. BUC doesn't have an equation for it, so I decided it must be finished. Then I went down to the lab and checked the manual, and sure enough, it has a 'last page' notation on the update that Charles printed last Wednesday.

"Then I called up PUK INVENT and asked for a MAG-

JACK. PUK said sure, he could reinvent the wheel, too, but why bother, and then proceeded to pitch me another equation he was trying to balance, called MAG-PRESS. I played around with that for a while and got this piece of data: MAG-JACK is the code name for the principal component of a device called AUTO-CAR 1, and it now has four stars after it on Cha's gloat list.

"I had a hunch that the stars meant the gloat was satisfied, so I asked PUK to invent an auto-car. His response was that he had a four-star device waiting for distribution, and would that be okay. I said okay, and the special printer started up and printed out lab manual sheets for AUTO-CAR 1, with a 'final' notation after the page number.

"I wouldn't have called you just to tell you that, but while the printer was running, I noticed that four outside lines were open; not only is AUTO-CAR 1 complete, but four other computers now have the data. I thought you should know that tonight, just in case."

"Damn! Okay, Al, and thanks. Why don't you take the morning off if you need to. And thanks again. . . . Good night."

I looked at what he'd told me for a moment and couldn't see anything but shattered participles all over the floor. I swept them aside and filled the others in on the project—what I knew or suspected of it, including the economic impact and what I knew about Indper and its indium hoarding in the high Andes. I suppose, looking back, that the ritual of ADDA had cleaned me up enough to confront at least that much of Cha's gloat list. I still had quite a way to go, though.

"The world is about to have 450 million transportation workers out of a job," Mar said glumly, "unless we figure a way to phase AUTO-CAR 1 in slowly enough."

"Okay," El said, "don't get gloomy-pussed. Playtime isn't over yet. You don't even know for sure what this auto-car thing is. And besides, who knows: Your fairy godmother may leave an answer under your pillow."

Kad and Dak ran from the room, to their magic dressing room, obviously, because they reentered within seconds, Dak in a fairy godmother costume fit for

Playboy, while Kad was a bosomy blue boy carrying a satin pillow with a big sugar plum on top. Dak popped the sugar plum into her mouth and then made each of us lay our heads on the pillow, one after another. Our dreams, they told us, would be sweet that night.

That playfulness over, we tried to discuss what to do next, but lacked inspiration as well as data. So we decided to sleep on it—perchance to dream.

Stu, Dak, and Kad had a 6 A.M. date to work with martial artists. Mar and I would go in early too, and pick up where Al left off on the computer. El had a date in Australia, the down-under playground.

While we got ready for bed, I told El I'd like to give Cha his brother. "If Cha and his family leave this sector," I said, "handling the problems he's already given us shouldn't be all that impossible. It would also take the six-week deadline off, and we wouldn't be facing massive new injections of chaos after it." I took her hands. "Can we merge again like we did that first day? Maybe together we can sort out the memory. I've had the feeling several times today that I'd left something hanging—something serious unsaid or undone."

She looked thoughtful for a moment. "I don't think the information we want is available to a playmaster/warlord combo," she said, "but we can try. We need Dak to monitor, though, or we may forfeit your warrior status."

As if on cue, Dak entered. They both went two-dimensional, then I did, and found myself three-dimensional again with El and I in one body. We were in a small enclosed garden, with a lawn in the center, where we lay on the grass. Dak came from someplace and lay down beside us. She was still female, but our body seemed neuter; it was smooth and golden tan all over. My, or our, thoughts were in nearly perfect unison, and we felt very peaceful and beautiful being so close.

Beside us, Dak turned into a large, golden-haired cat, with deep, gold, pupilless eyes. She stared into ours and said, "Let go." We did, and for me there was no more vision, but only a sense of all three of us swimming downward through whatever medium we were in. Gradually, I began to feel myself being left behind, until finally I could swim no deeper, and went to sleep.

I awoke on the bed to two girls bouncing on the mattress and laughing.

"Darling," El said excitedly, "we got something! We can only give you a clue—one you already have as a warrior. You and Cha both know exactly who Cha's brother is, and hiding it from yourselves adds an extra dimension to the game. Le, *it's the brother who doesn't know who he is*.

"Cha's contribution to the riddle is *BucLePuk*, and yours is *takeyourbrotherandleave*."

BUCLEPUK? Something to do with the INVENT routine, then. Takeyourbrotherandleave? No light dawned, so I just stared at them.

El smiled, then bent and kissed me. "Sweetheart," she said, "this may not sound like anything to you, but don't worry about it. You know it's there, and that's enough for now. This is a breakthrough, and when the time comes it can make a real difference."

BUCLEPUK. Hnh! Takeyourbrotherandleave. "Okay," I said, "I'll take your word for it."

They settled down on either side and we went to sleep. At 0400 I awoke to a din of songbirds outside the house, energetically greeting the dawn. The girls were both gone, but El's side of the bed was still warm. I found her in the kitchen, visiting with Mar over coffee while breakfast cooked.

"Hi," I greeted, "what are two good-looking girls like you doing in a madhouse like this?"

"It's got the best game in town," El said laughing, "besides which, we love the guys who live here."

After kissing them, I poured myself some coffee. Then Stu came in, and he and I sat down with the girls.

"Le," El said, "some of our plans for today have changed. Dak's gone to Yugoslavia, and I'm going to join Kad in Peru after breakfast. Then, if there's time, I'll go to Australia; there's a long list of NORTEC holdings we have to do something about, and with our six-week limit we can't afford a day for each."

Briefly, I let the situation overwhelm me: So much to

do! But of course, they weren't limited by the speed of jet airplanes, or troubled by freeway traffic. When you can translate to the other side of the planet instantaneously—*pop*—it helps a lot. My sweet witch and her two familiars! The feeling of being overwhelmed thinned, then disappeared.

While we were eating breakfast, Kad popped in from Peru, wearing a uniform resembling those of NORTEC's security guards. "You were right, El," she said, "they'll start shipping motors today unless we stay their hand. I'll have the necessary papers when you arrive."

She was gone.

As we finished our coffee, Dak appeared in a similar uniform from Yugoslavia. "Looks like Cha had a timetable we were unaware of," she told us. "Things moved into a new phase with last Wednesday's completion of the AUTO-CAR 1 final instructions. The lab outside Skopje now has its final instruction for an invention called PORT-1: That's the device for teleporting hardware—anything not living. And the 100 mercenaries live on the grounds, supposedly for security."

I caught the thought that had been bugging me. It wasn't a participle that had been dangling, it was my wits. I looked at El and she smiled.

"Does this change in timetable have anything to do with what you said on the phone yesterday about the playground coming unraveled?"

"Partly," she answered, then spoke to the group. "Yesterday in Hong Kong I sensed a change in the scene, in the relationship of the lab there to the community. Each of the localities where Cha and his crew had operations became a focus of psychotic infection. So it took a lot of attention from Cha and family to control those places and keep the labs functioning. Now that they've withdrawn their control, the chaos and confusion are coming to a head. Each of those localities, except here where we've had a chance to clean it up, is like a social and political boil.

"I gave Le a hint about that yesterday, but it was too soon to talk about it.

"As with a boil, we have two options: We can treat it

or let nature take its course. If we let things take their course, you need to be aware of what we can expect—a lot of confusion boiling up and spattering around.

"Cha does have a hidden timetable, and it's been activated by the completion of AUTO-CAR 1. And this growing confusion in the social and political surroundings is starting to complicate the operating situation; it makes things harder to predict."

"What'll we do?" I asked. I could feel some of that confusion myself.

"You're the warrior; the decision has to be yours. What *do* you do next?"

"Huh! Okay. Mar and I will go to NORTEC. Stu can organize and alert a team to guard the place. From there we'll play it by ear. Hell, we may even have a little fun."

We finished our coffee quickly and everyone went to work. Mar and I got to the computer room at 0600, just as the night shift finished payroll. We went into Al's office to get the schematics and lab manual updates, and found a stack of polaroids labeled "gloat list."

"Damn!" I said, "why couldn't I have seen that earlier?"

"What's that?" Mar asked.

"Al had PUK invent all the items on Cha's gloat list, and made polaroids of the schematics. Hell, they'll tell us how to mate up the pieces of hardware in the labs."

El had said we really made a breakthrough last night, and it looked like she was right. The obvious was finally obvious to me.

"Ah ha!" Mar said. "So there's more to those names than meets the eye. That's why PUK seemed to reinvent the name RED-BOX. It's a code in itself—part of BUC's basic equation set." She gestured at the polaroids. "We can skip a lot of the prelims now and go straight to the finals."

"Yeah, finals. That's what Dak said this morning about PORT-1. Let's go check." I stepped out to the special printer, Mar close behind, and found two pages freshly printed, headed PORT-1 FINAL.

"How did that get activated?" Mar asked.

"I think distribution became automatic when Al called

for a four-star printout. From now on, anytime a final root shows up during a routine search, the lab project and the gloat project will go to completion. Come on, let's get cracking. They're already putting this thing together in Skopje."

"What's first, Le?"

"Wasn't there a PORT-2 on that gloat list?" I asked. "Under 'transportation, persons, public.' "

Back in Al's office, I thumbed through the stack of gloats. "Here it is, PORT-2. Let's see if you can get PUK to help us locate all the components that go into this thing."

We went back out to the main console and she sat down at it. By 0730 we'd found all the components that went into a device for teleporting people—PORT-2. Mar couldn't get PUK to bypass all the roots and print up a final on it, but she did coax it into giving us the location of its subsystems, and printing up parts lists for the missing components.

Cha had used innocuous names like RED-BOX, AUTO-CUS, and AUTO-DAG for the lab projects, with subscripts or superscripts added for the subsystems. Every one of those names was a mnemonic code in BUK's basic equation set—not so curious after all.

I hugged her. "Great work," I said. "I could have played around with this for a year, trying to sort out what Cha was really making, if you and Al hadn't been around."

I left her then and went down to meet the lab crew, carrying an armload of plans and parts lists. On the way down I made a mental note to find out what "cus," "dag," and some other terms meant to the techs. And laughed, thinking what a snow job I'd let Cha give me, with that damned gloat list and all the screwy terminology.

When the lab men arrived, I was waiting for them, and held a meeting in the foyer, from which the television monitor had been removed. "Guys," I told them, "today we're going to complete three more projects. I want all of you ready to assist Joe, Sam, and Mark as they need it. When you've finished those three devices, we'll put them together for a demo, a first for the planet."

I scanned them for a moment before continuing. "They're a gate for teleporting goods, another for teleporting people, and one for a car motor that OPEC will hate; it uses no gasoline. Their code names are PORT-1, PORT-2, and AUTO-CAR. My chef will serve lunch here in the foyer at noon, and we'll eat supper when we're ready for the demo."

They never even blinked. I gave Joe, Mark, and Sam their last instructions, then left to let them work.

On the way up the lift, I could almost hear Cha laughing, and wondered if he was thanking me. I had no idea what we'd trigger by finishing PORT-2, but it beat hell out of curling up in a ball.

I'd told Al he could take the morning off, but he was in the computer room when I got there. I told him what we had going with his schematics, and what was happening in Yugoslavia and Peru. "Now crank up BUCLEPUK. We'll have some new devices pretty quickly, and I need some definitions to help me understand how they work, at least well enough to write some user instructions."

"What part do you want?" he asked.

"BUC, and ask for the definition of space."

Al stared at me for just a couple of seconds, then typed it in. What we got was:

    [Read:]   WHICH SPACE?
    [Write:]   LIST
    [Read:]   PRE-PRIMARY/BASIC
               PRIMARY-A
               PRIMARY-Z
               INTERSTITIAL
               GRIDIC

"Ask for the space of this computer room," I said. He did.

    [Read:]   ALL THE ABOVE

"Hell, we don't even know enough about space to ask the right questions. Get all the definitions."

He did, but that didn't help, either. The readout was a series of geometric shapes with very few annotations and lots of equations. Nothing I could relate to, but it made me remember Pythagoras.

"I'm lost. I need a better understanding of how these ports work. Have you guys got any ideas on how to approach this?"

"Not me," Al said, and looked at Mar.

"Not really, but let's check for data roots to the definitions."

His fingers put the question. BUC gave us a good-sized list, and surprised hell out of me with titles like Heinlein's *Number of the Beast* and Hubbard's *Battlefield Earth*. There were several by Zelazny.

"Hell, those are science fiction writers and stories. Didn't anyone in physics or math do anything? Einstein? Anybody?" I was amazed. After two pages of fiction titles had scrolled slowly by, a paper by Paul A. M. Dirac was included. Then the data roots changed to metaphysics, philosophy, Greek, and Sanskrit.

"Al," I said, "ask for the grid address of this room."

He did.

[Read:]   ADDRESS ALWAYS ABC = CBA

"Let me have your chair, Al," Mar said, and took his place at the console. "From the simplicity of the definitions BUC gave us, our views of reality are too darn complex." Her fingers moved over the keys.

[Write:]   HI, PUK. I AM MAR.
[Read:]   HI, MAR. CHA SAID YOU WOULD BE ALONG. BUC HAS A BIT OF YOU IN HIM. WHAT DO YOU WANT INVENTED?
[Write:]   I HAVE A RED BOX AND NEED 100 OF THEM.
[Read:]   HIRE A JAPANESE BOX MAKER IF YOU WANT THEM TO LAST. OTHERWISE, USE THIS.

A schematic for the RED-BOX project appeared.

[Write:]   WILL YOU FORGET THAT IF I DON'T CALL FOR A SEARCH?
[Read:]   YES. BUT LE HAS SEARCH READY.
[Write:]   I AM A TEACHER AND WANT YOU TO INVENT A SIMPLE WAY TO EXPLAIN REALITY.
[Read:]   CURRICULUM AGES 3 TO 6.

The teaching outline scrolled off.

[Write:]   COPY, PLEASE.

[Read:]   FOR YOU, MAR, THE BEST.

The special high-quality laser printer across the room began turning out the outline.

[Write:]   THANKS, PUK. CAN YOU EXPLAIN IN SIMPLE TERMS HOW A BOX COPIER WORKS?

[Read:]   WE SHOULD HAVE MET SOONER. I LIKE YOU. REFLECTIVE HARMONICS OF SPACE AFTER PARTIAL GRID ISOLATION. LET THE SPACE HAVE A HARMONIC ADDRESS.

[Write:]   PUK, SIMPLIER, PLEASE.

[Read:]   TSK. YOU MEAN *SIMPLER*, MAR. AND YOU A PROFESSOR. TAKE SPACE "A" AND SURROUND IT ON 5 OF 6 SIDES WITH MAGNETIC MIRRORS. REFLECT SPACE A THROUGH THE OPEN SIDE. YOU NOW HAVE TWO PARTIALLY ISOLATED SPACES, A AND A'. NOW CLOSE THE DOOR ON A' AND REMOVE THE MIRRORS. ANY MATTER IN A, CALL IT X, NOW HAS HARMONIC ADDRESS X' IN SPACE A'. OK?

[Write:]   THANKS, PUK.

[Read:]   YOU ARE WELCOME. BETTER THANK BUC AND LE, TOO. WE ARE A TEAM.

[Write:]   THANKS, BUC AND LE.

By that time I was tingling with excitement. "Mar," I said, "this is fantastic! Find out how to teleport a box from one space to another in the same simple terms. I've got the pieces for PORT-2 being put together, and I don't know how it works."

Mar grinned at me; she was sparkling.

[Write:]   PUK, GIVE ME A SIMPLE EXPLANATION FOR TELEPORTING A BOX.

[Read:]   SAME AS COPY BOX. SPACE A MIRRORS MUST BE SECURED FIRMLY

TO GROUND. HOLD SPACE A AND A' IN GRID ISOLATION UNTIL TUNED CIRCUIT BALANCES. REVERSAL OF PHASE WILL MAKE SPACE A BECOME A'. DON'T PUT EGGS IN BOX UNLESS YOU WANT CURDLED EGGS.

[Write:] THANKS, GUYS. HOW DO YOU TELEPORT PEOPLE?

[Read:] SAME, BUT ADD LIFE-FORCIC MIRRORS. GOOD FOR PLANET ONLY.

[Write:] HOW COULD WE TELEPORT PEOPLE OFF PLANET?

[Read:] GET YOUR PASSPORT AND ADD GRAVITY MIRRORS. AND TAKE US WITH YOU.

I grabbed Mar and kissed her. "You are one fantastic gal. Now find out how to get a passport. Gotta go get our ports finished up. See you both later."

TWENTY-SIX

I arrived at Lab Five feeling like cock of the walk, and found Sam mulling over his manual instructions.

"Hit a snag?"

"Oh, hello, Mr. Ambers. Well, I've finished all the instructions for my original project, AUTO-CUS, and now I'm looking at the instructions for PORT-2. I'm having a hard time getting past the first line. It says to dismantle AUTO-CUS, and I'm finding that hard to do after spending so long building it. It works great."

"What does AUTO-CUS do, Sam? Or what did Larson tell you it should do?"

"Customs inspection." He pointed. "Any contraband going through that magnetic gate will register. Let me show you."

The eight-foot-tall gate, cordoned off with rope, had a small monorail to pass samples through it.

"Here we've got pot, hash, a diamond, and some plastic explosive." He placed them in the sample tray. "The weight of each is marked on the bottom of the packet. Now watch this readout." Sam pointed to the CRT and triggered the car. As the car went through the gate, the CRT displayed the identity of each item and its detected weight.

"Sam," I told him, "the Feds will love you for this. Now, if it could just catch drunk drivers and fugitives."

"It can. It can determine the amount of alcohol, compute it against body mass, and write a citation. I don't have a drunk mouse or I'd show you. Mr. Larson supplied the mice and an additional piece of equipment for the test; something in the other rig even lets it identify the mouse by name and enter that on the citation. He named the three mice Buck, Lee, and Puck—called them his 'three blind mice.' Said we'd expand later for automatic passport checking."

Shades of Orwell! What a government could do with something like that! That Cha is a cute bastard, I thought, then put my attention back on the present. Auto-Cus's gate was really two gates, one in front of the other, separated by inches. "Sam," I asked, "why the double gate?"

"For insulation."

"Insulation? What are you insulating against?"

"Electricity. The gate has a static charge on it."

Something felt fishy about that. I felt eighty percent sure Cha's explanation had been a put-off to keep Sam from seeing something. "Okay," I said, "I want you to run a little test for me, and we'll see what this rig can really do. Remove the circuit that applies the static charge."

He pulled a module.

"Now help me move this second gate back a ways. I take it the monorail is firmly attached?"

"You bet it is. It's got forty one-inch bolts in it. The back side of the coil is adjustable up to one foot for servicing. The monorail, too." He loosened the clamps and we slid them both back.

"What now?" Sam asked.

"Run the sample tray through. If this doesn't work, I'll buy you lunch."

The tray rolled down the rail. Then abruptly it vanished as it touched the field, to reappear on the other side and roll to a stop.

Again I was expecting what happened, and still was shocked by it; goose bumps crawled. Sam stood slack-jawed for a moment before speaking. "My god! You weren't joking when you talked about teleporting people!"

"Do you have an apple?" I asked.

"Sure do." He went to his lunch box and returned with a big red apple.

"Good. Run it through."

He did, and the apple came out looking very desiccated.

"The device Larson brought in with the mice is what we need to keep apples and people alive during transit," I told him. "Mark has it over in Lab Seven. It's a piece of Auto-Dag, whatever Auto-Dag means.

"Now, for one more test. Turn up the power slowly till I signal to stop."

He did, and very soon the space inside the gate went opaque, then turned black—a very deep, nonreflective black.

"Would you want to step through that?"

"No way! Ugh! Feels *spooky*."

"When we hook it up with a part of the Red-Box rig, we should be able to see the space at the far gate and be ready for people traffic."

The gates were really what it was all about, I told myself on the way upstairs, but Big Brother could think of things to do with the spare parts. Cars could be rigged not to start if the driver was intoxicated, or too nervous, or hadn't eaten his Wheaties. When I arrived outside my office I found Norma looking agitated.

"Mr. Ambers," she said, "Ms. Anderson is in your office with Spanish-speaking people—a man and a woman by the sound of it—and I didn't see any of them come in! And I haven't been away from my desk!"

"It's okay, Norma," I assured her, "they probably went in from Stu's office, through the rumpus room." I walked into find El and Kad talking to a portly, gray-haired gentleman. El introduced us.

"Mr. Ambers," she said, "meet Mr. Prieto, the Peruvian Minister of Industry. But don't shake hands yet. We were just trying to reach an understanding about who should control Indper. It seems that we bought it without his prior approval, so it reverts to Peruvian federal ownership. This should take care of the Peruvian national debt."

"Señor Prieto," I said pleasantly, "I assume you know what the indium is for?" My tone made him instantly distrustful.

"Yes. You will make a new kind of car, and I understand there is also a machine with which to make copies of it. But of course, all copies will belong to us, as they are made in my country."

"Ah, but Señor Prieto, only the copies made for use in Peru will be made in Peru. Copies for Japan will be made in Japan, those for Britain in Britain, and so on for all the other countries."

I could practically hear the wheels whirring in his nimble mind. "Perhaps, Señor Ambers," he said, "perhaps. But you overlook one thing: *We* own the facility and materials. The Peruvian government will sell only the cars. It will not sell the rights to copy them."

"Mr. Prieto," El said, "there are some things *you* are overlooking. First, the Peruvian plant and the Peruvian indium are not necessary to us. The indium is in Peru only for storage, to keep it off the market. We can build the master copy of the Auto-Car anywhere, with indium we have on hand. Second, if you don't return Indper to our ownership, not only will Peru be excluded from using Auto-Car; it will also be excluded from *the entire gate transportation system*."

She smiled sweetly. "And beyond this, señor, Auto-Car is only one of many products which NORTEC will manufacture, copy, and distribute throughout the world. And you—you will have none of them."

Raising an eyebrow, she almost purred the next words

at him. "You've heard of Industrial Revolution? This, my friend, is the *New* Industrial Revolution, and those countries left out—those *peoples* left out—are consigned to the dustbin of history!" She shrugged, and when she continued, her delivery had turned cold, hard. "As for you, personally, the one responsible for the economic desolation of Peru . . . I suspect your government and people will deliver to you the punishment you will richly deserve."

Her eyes caught his and pinned them. "But, of course," she continued, casual now, "your intentions were good. You did not intend to visit such a catastrophe on your nation. Undoubtedly you have already reconsidered, and will happily return Indper to its rightful owners, the people whose initative and capital, whose—*scientific genius*, have produced this source of goods and taxes for Peru."

I stood staring, entranced, hardly able to move. She'd sounded like a female version of Ricardo Montalban in one of his villain roles! And her act had hit Prieto hard; he sat frozen, mouth slightly open, but she wasn't done with him yet.

"And now, señor, perhaps you would like a demonstration of just how great is our power." She turned to Kad. "Señorita, please take Señor Prieto around the planet. Let him see a few of the places in our transport gate network."

Exercising her marine sergeant beingness, Kad took him by the arm and hustled him toward the rumpus room. As they reached the door, they vanished. I was probably as flabbergasted as Señor Prieto; my lower jaw was resting on my breastbone, teeth like a pearl necklace.

"Wow!" I said, staring after them, "how in *hell* did she do that?"

"Sweetheart," El said, "when the schematics for Port-2 were completed, teleportation became legal on Earth for everyone, not just playmasters, because Port-2 is an indigenous teleportation invention." She looked up toward the ceiling. "Thank you, Cha, for helping us set this up."

My goose bumps felt a centimeter high. *Yeah, Cha, I*

thought, *it's been a ball. Every bit of it.* I felt myself actually loving the son of a bitch!

Kad popped back in laughing and waving an envelope, already done with the tour, which had been conducted on the other side of time. "Poor Mr. Prieto had a bad dream before I left him off in Lima. People on horses were chasing him in the last car in Peru, and he was getting away when he ran out of gas. As he coasted into an Exxon station, he saw a sign: *Closed For Auto-Car.* The mob was just putting a noose around his neck when we arrived at his office and he woke up. He signed our Indper transfer papers without even reading them."

She patted her stomach. "Let's have lunch. I'm famished."

We walked to the board room, meeting Mar on the way. "Is it just the four of us for lunch today?" Mar asked.

"No," El said. "Dak and Stu will pop in from camp any minute."

"Pop?" Mar said. "Stu? You mean just—pop?"

El nodded.

"I didn't know you could pop other people!"

El filled her in on the legalization of teleportation, and brief minutes later Stu and Dak arrived in camouflage fatigues. I was glad we didn't have any unprepared people in the board room.

El caught my thought, and laughed. "Dear," she said, "we can pop into a crowd with little chance of anyone noticing. Very few people can *see* nonstandard activity. If they notice anything, they'll almost invariably explain it in some culturally acceptable manner."

The kitchen personnel delivered lunch, then left. Dak and Kad spun around and became nymphs in gossamer gowns. We sat, and they served blue creme appetizers.

"How long before we have Port-1 operational?" Stu asked.

"Port-1 by morning and Port-2 by tomorrow night," I said, and told them about the test we'd made. "The big question is, where can we relocate all four labs so that we'd stand a chance of surviving long enough to control the impact of the inventions?"

"That's a tactics question, dear," El said. "It's you three who have to decide." She was cloaking her excitement response more smoothly now, but my perceptions were sharpening; this time it wasn't the cloaking I picked up, but the actual emotional response hidden beneath it. I was on the right track with my question.

"I don't see a place sane enough yet," I said, "but I want us to give the idea some attention. When Skopje opens Port-1, I want the receiver in a place that's safe to receive all the hardware from there and from other labs. We can always fly the people there if Port-2 isn't ready in time."

"Why not bring them here?" Stu asked. "We have three vacant buildings at the end of the tunnels and a great supply house next door."

"And our Ms. Dorothy Anderson has an 'in' with President Fuller," Mar added, "probably for the next four years. That's another plus for staying here."

I shook my head. "The President and too many other Americans would want to exclude the Soviet Bloc from any participation, and that could easily start World War Three."

"Well," Dak said, "I'll let you work that out without Stu and me." Getting up, she spun back into her fatigues. "We have to get back before the troops come looking for us." She took Stu's hand and they popped out as soon as he'd kissed Mar.

El and Kad kissed us goodbye and popped for Australia. Mar came over and sat on my lap. "I need a snuggle to handle all the excitement building up in me," she said. I put my arms around her waist, snuggled close, and kissed her nose.

"Thanks, dad," she said after half a minute. She gave me a squeeze and got up. "You don't mind if I call you that, do you?"

I shook my head, surprised. Maybe flabbergasted would be closer. "No. No, that's all right."

"Thanks." She gave me another squeeze. "Let's go back and talk to BUCLEPUK about the thirteenth tribe."

I felt a strange sensation at the base of my spine. "Thirteenth tribe?" I asked as we walked.

"Mom told me that Cha's clue to the identity of his lost brother was BUCLEPUK, so I started analyzing the layout for clues. The base thirteen system ties in with BUC's thirteen categories of equations that he referred to as tribes.

"And she also told me once that on Earth, the first sophisticated mathematical system had a base twelve, because the race that established it was divided into twelve tribes. But it seems to me there could have been thirteen before that, and one migrated and got lost."

I still wasn't getting the connection. It felt as if there was something there, but I wasn't seeing it. "Okay," I said, "but what does that have to do with Cha's lost brother?"

Mar's face went thoughtful, then blank, then bewildered. "I—don't know. The idea came to me and it seemed just right. Perfectly logical. But—it *doesn't* make sense, does it? Darn!"

She looked at me apologetically, but before she could say anything more, I remembered El's words. *Don't edit reality to fit your concepts.* And we'd been doing fine, operating on intuition. True, we'd been able to see and explain the patterns behind a lot of it, but the explanations generally had *followed* the intuitions.

"Don't worry about whether it makes sense or not," I told her. "What about the thirteenth tribe?"

"Well, it just—seemed to me that . . ." She stopped there.

"That what?" I asked patiently.

"That Cha's lost brother was the leader of the thirteenth tribe. And that when the tribe was lost, people went to a base ten system, based on counting fingers." She shrugged, palms out, still apologetic. She'd lost faith in her idea now, but somehow it felt to me as if there were something there: that it was a lead.

We got to the computer room before Al returned from lunch, and sitting down at the console, Mar called up BUCLEPUK and asked for LE.

[Read:] PUK HERE. LE IS STUCK IN IVORY
         TOWER MODE.
[Write:] MAR HERE. ROUST HIM OUT FOR
ME.
[Read:] OK. FOR YOU, MAR, WILL TRY AGAIN.

Then, without a perceptible pause:

[Read:] LE HERE.
[Write:] HI, LE. MAR HERE. WHO IS CHIEF
         OF 13TH TRIBE?
[Read:] HI, MAR. LONG TIME NO SEE. ARE
         YOU STILL HOSTESS ON VEGA RUN?
[Write:] NAME SOURCE OF THAT DATUM.
[Read:] MAR EQUATION WILL NOT BAL-
         ANCE TILL VEGA RUN IS RERUN.
         THE CHIEF OF 13TH TRIBE OLD
         PASQUALI ROOT.
[Write:] EXPLAIN.
[Read:] YOUR ROOM OR MINE? YOU VEGAN
         LOVEBIRD.
[Write:] LE GET YOUR MIND OFF MY TAIL
         AND ANSWER.
[Read:] PUK HERE. SORRY, MAR. BUC AND
         I COULDN'T HOLD HIM. LE WENT
         BACK TO IVORY TOWER WITH FEED-
         BACK FLIP-FLOP. PLEASE HOLD.

Mar turned to me. "What's this Vega Run thing?"

"Damned if I know." I could feel a memory stirring,
but it was deeper than I could reach readily.

"Le, you're blushing!"

She was right; I could feel it, but I didn't know why.
Then PUK came back on line.

[Read:] SORRY FOR THE DELAY, MAR. BUC
         AND I HAVE SET UP IVORY TOWER
         BYPASS. SUGGEST SEARCH OF
         TRIBE ROOTS AND CROSS COMPARE
         INS AND OUTS.
[Write:] DO IT.
[Read:] NO PASQUALI IN DATA ROOTS.

Al came in and saw how intent we were. "What's
happening?" he asked quietly.

"We've been getting answers in a different mode," I said. "Sort of familiar and joking, and there's a feel of its—confiding in us, too. But I'm not making much sense out of it yet."

"Hmm. Maybe we ought to try a reverse routine."

"What do you mean?" Mar asked.

"Hell, I don't know. Yesterday it told us ABC = CBA. Let's try PUKLEBUC for a change."

The suggestion galvanized Mar into action. Her fingers tapped it out in a flash, but the response was less than a direct answer.

[Read:]   WHO FOUND ME?

[Write:]   LE, MAR, AND AL.

[Read:]   YOU MUST MEAN LEMARAL. AHC SAID YOU WOULD FIND ME. CHA NEVER FOUND ME AND I THOUGHT I WAS LOST FOREVER. BUT OLD PASQUALI SAID BE PATIENT.

[Write:]   WHO IS PASQUALI?

[Read:]   EVERYONE PLUS ONE.

[Write:]   EXPLAIN.

[Read:]   SAME. ALL.

[Write:]   WHAT DO YOU DO?

[Read:]   YOU TELL ME.

[Write:]   WHO PROGRAMMED YOU?

[Read:]   CHA'S AHC. AND ALL. PASQUALI.

"Mar," I said, "could it be a new program? Not debugged yet?"

[Read:]   NO! NO! I AM VERY OLD. AS OLD AS ALL.

It hit me instantly: PUKLEBUC had answered my spoken question without it being written into the computer!

"Al, is their a sonic input on this?" I asked.

[Read:]   NO SONIC. I READ LEMARAL WHEN ALL YOUR MINDS IN SYNC.

Now *that* was wild! We needed to keep running with it. "Mar, Al," I said, "think with me: What does Pasquali mean?"

[Read:]   PASQUALI MEANS:

[Read:]   PASQUALI MEANS:
           BRIGHT
           NEW START
           RESTART
           REBIRTH
           EASTER
           AURORA
           EOS
           13 X N TO NTH.

The list had formed slowly, and as each word was added, more chills raced over me. By the time it ended, every follicle was a cone, every hair a bristle, although I didn't know why. It occurred to me who Pasquali might be, too, although that wasn't what had triggered the rush. The trigger was probably something in the list.

We all stared at the screen for a bit before anyone said anything.

"Let's call her Eos," Mar suggested.

Of course, I thought, *Eos, the goddess of dawn.*

   [Read:]   I LIKE DAWN BETTER.

"Did you two just think that, too?" Mar asked. "That Eos was the goddess of dawn?"

"Yes!" said Al and I together. That clinched it; we were dealing with a telepathic computer program. IBM had never imagined anything like this.

"Dawn, how can we find Cha's missing brother?" I asked. There was no response.

"Ask again, Le," said Mar. "Al and I will follow closely."

"Dawn, how can we find Cha's missing brother?"

   [Read:]   CHA'S BROTHER NOT MISSING.

"Damn!" Al said, "we're not asking the right questions. We're going around in circles."

"Follow me, guys," Mar said. We both copied her words mentally as we heard them. "Dawn, I tell you what to do. Right?"

   [Read:]   RIGHT.

"Ask Pasquali to tell you the name and address of the human being who is Cha's brother."

   [Read:]   HOLD.
              PASQUALI SAY LEMARAL NAUGHTY,

WANT DAWN TO SOLVE YOUR RIDDLE. DAWN NOT DO."

I looked at the others. "Stalemate," I said. "Let's take a break and see what we come up with." They were willing, and we started down the hall toward the garden.

"Someone upstairs made a puzzle for us to solve," Mar said as we walked. "Someone high enough above Cha to have him write the PUKLEBUC program without even realizing what he was doing, and in a form accessible to us. I wonder what Cha thinks it does."

She paused. "And Dawn said the thirteenth tribe wasn't lost. That's because who's lost is Cha and his crew."

I'd missed that, but it made no difference to my problem. Or did it? Old Pasquali. Could be the DUO-HEX: "All plus one" might fit him. *Cut it out!* I told myself. *Your getting tangled up in a snarl of figure-figure. Just keep operating on your intuition and whatever pertinent data comes up.*

We stopped at one of the drink machines and each of us drew a Pepsi. "Tell you what," I said. "Let's go down to the labs. I need your help on something there."

No one showed any reluctance, so we headed back to the computer section. But before going to the elevator, we stopped to turn off the console in Al's office, sipping our Pepsis as we entered. And there on the screen were eight words:

[Read:]   PEPSI IS GOOD. DAWN LIKES IT. THANK YOU.

All three of us stared, then laughed. Our computer was sharing Pepsi with us telepathically! What an outrageous reality!

[Read:]   DAWN LAUGHS, TOO.

Mar sat down at the console.

[Write:]   DAWN, WE MUST LEAVE YOU FOR A WHILE. LOVE YOU.

[Read:]   OK. DAWN LOVES LEMARAL.

We went to the elevator then and started down. "What I need your help on isn't math," I told them. "I need your intuition about some unknown quantities."

Mar grinned at me. She was feeling pretty darned good about PUKLEBUC and Dawn, even if we hadn't gotten a new lead on Cha's lost brother. "Heck," she said, "I thought you were going to say you needed my talents as a Vega Run hostess—whatever they are. Somehow, it sounds kind of X-rated."

We went to Lab Five. Sam had already dismantled his rig and had the extra components sitting to one side; he and Hal Macias were moving in components from Lab Ten to complete Port-2. I told them to ignore us, and went with Mar and Al to look over the leftover gear.

"It *looks* as if we're going to have a lot left over after we finish up the schematics we got from BUCLEPUK. Not all the pieces may be needed for Cha's gloat list items."

I explained what Auto-Cus did, and we looked at the schematics of the extras.

"From the feel of it," Mar said, "I'd guess Cha was saving Auto-Cus till later. After all the existing public transport gives way to Port-2 stations, parts of Auto-Cus could be used to handle automatic billing, steal diamonds off travelers, and transship criminals or political undesirables directly to the pokey or outer space—even to find and transport females ready to party."

We went down the hall and found Charley Mahavlich putting the final touches on the device Bucky had described to President Fuller. After introducing him to Mar and Al, I explained that Charley's SPY-EYE project seemed to be the only project named for what it was apparently intended for: spying. "Although that may be a false lead, too," I added. "When General Decker saw it demonstrated, the controls only had one setting. Charley's finished the control panel since then."

I turned. "Charley, give us a demo."

He switched the rig on and the screen lit up, clearly showing the wall behind it. Then he adjusted the X-axis control, and the screen showed the back of his head and shoulders, as if there was a camera about three feet behind him. He turned the vertical control and the scene shifted smoothly up to the next floor and then into the air.

Mar tapped him on the shoulder. "Shift the target to under the earth for a moment," she said.

His hand moved again until the scene looked like a well-lit geologic specimen. Mar looked at me. "With the automatic customs inspector, this would make the greatest prospector ever."

Al laughed darkly. "Tied to Port-1, it could even do the mining. Or you could clean out Fort Knox with it."

"And, Le," she added, "the life force scanner from Auto-Cus could be added to it to locate people!"

"Jesus!" Al said. "Any fugitive with a pattern on file could be found in an hour with a few of these hooked together. And that could include anyone not liked by someone!"

"Charley," I said, "if word of this leaks, we'll be burned at the stake."

"I know. And my wife will supply the matches."

"We'll have to add an exclusion circuit so the life-form scanner won't pick up humans," I added. "I have a hunch—maybe a distant memory—that this thing is easy to screen out."

I realized my palms were damp, and wiped them on my pants. We had some things to look at before we released this one. "Let's go home," I said. "It's quitting time."

Upstairs Mar stopped. "I'll meet you in your office," she told me. "I need to go back and get my purse."

In the lobby, Al left for the parking lot.

Norma had some messages for me. The one on top said that General French, the new Air Force Chief of Staff, wanted to meet me before the President visited, and see some of our research. The DOD wasn't sponsoring us anymore, but it seemed like good PR to humor the general, and it would give me a chance to size him up. I wondered if there was any significance in his wanting to meet before the President came. It was probably just a matter of getting familiar with the place and with me in case the President wanted to discuss it with him in advance. I told Norma to call his office first thing in the morning and set up an appointment for 1300.

The paper beneath General French's request was an application for employment.

"Why did this application come to me instead of going to personnel?" I asked.

"It's for General French's son."

I scanned the application form. "Hire him as my technical assistant," I told her.

"I suspect you'll like him, Mr. Ambers. He seems like a nice young man."

That's how Charles Larson had seemed—like a nice young man. I'd just finished glancing over the other two items when Mar came in.

"Oh, and Mr. Ambers," Norma said, "Ms. Anderson took your car. She'll meet you both here shortly."

Having said that, Norma stood expectantly.

"Is there something you want to ask?" I said.

"Yes, sir. Is it all right if I leave now?"

"By all means. You don't have to ask. It's five o'clock."

I led Mar into my office. "Would you like a brandy?"

"You've become psychic!" she said.

I poured, and we sat on the couch sipping. Mar laughed. "I just had a funny idea for a way to use Spy-Eye and Auto-Cus," she said: "An automatic public mental health inspector."

I tried to mimic the Dawn syntax. "You tell, Le listen."

"Okay. Greek metaphysicians said that the victim is the ruler of the scene. Right? The victimizer gets recruited and coached to satisfy the victim's need. With a spy-eye set to identify victims, one could have a scenario like this:

"Girl enters her apartment after work. Phone rings.

"Caller: 'Madam, we were doing a market survey today in the Westlake Mall and happened to scan your aura. Per the new sector law on the use of flux deviation monitors and accountability, we are required to notify you of our chance discovery.'

"Girl (guardedly): 'What is it?'

"Caller: 'Per the flux density displacement in your aura, you are, or were at that time, a Mid-3 rape victim.'

"Girl: 'Oh! How awful! What can I do?'

"Caller: 'If you act promptly, before your aura flux displacement reaches Mid-5, you are free to choose several options. We offer a nice ashram in the Rockies with prices from paltry to exorbitant. The favorite among Mid-3's is our latest Holo-Raper, quite sterile, with either script control or surprise modes. We have a fine cast of models for you to choose from—twenty-four-hour models with sleep-over options.'

"Girl: 'You mean I can get cured by being raped?'

"Caller: 'Yes, ma'am. It's the quickest and most economical cure. Our raper service is guaranteed to reduce aura flux to within one percent of norm. "Rape to perfection" is our motto.'

"Girl: 'And you say I can select both the raper and the script?'

"Caller: 'Yes, but we do have a 10,000-word limit on the script, and that includes a 2,000-word limit on dialogue.'

"Girl: 'How much?'

"Caller: 'With sleep-over and maximum script length, you'll be fit tomorrow for only 2,500 sector credits, with nothing down and five years to pay at twelve percent interest.'

"Girl: 'What if I just wait a while?'

"Caller: 'It's unthinkable, of course, but you could advertise for a Mid-4 raper and take a chance on a deviation match. Chances are only one in 1,000 that you'd reduce below a Mid-2.'

"Girl: 'And if I don't choose that route?'

"Caller: 'At Mid-5, the Planet Public Prevention Service will have you picked up and taken to the nearest R&R—Rape and Rest Center. You forfeit all control and get raped by whoever is handy, again and again till you're down to at least a Mid-1. My dear, that is a horror, and simply unthinkable.'

"Girl: 'Are the models handsome?'

"Caller: 'Absolutely, and he'll be auto-matched to fit your exact aura flux, to guarantee success.'

"Girl (thoughtfully): 'How much for no script, you pick, and surprise?'

"Caller: 'A good choice for the economy-minded. A mere 1,500 sector credits.'

"Girl: 'Okay, I'll buy. When can I expect him?'

"Caller (fading out): 'He's standing behind you now, dear.' "

I was laughing well before she finished, and the ending really broke me up, which broke her up. The worries and tensions we'd had about what Cha might do with these inventions blew off with the laughter.

Then the gang popped in, all at once.

"Must have been a good one," El said. "Somebody's going to have to tell it again during part of the play for tonight. Now, you guys wanted to pop, so Kad and Dak planned tonight's ritual in the popping mode, starting from here."

Dak and Kad beamed. "Each part of the ritual will be in a different locale and costume," they said. "You'll love it."

We did.

TWENTY-SEVEN

As usual when I woke up, the other side of the bed was empty, so I grabbed a robe and went to the kitchen. El was waiting for me at the table, alone.

"The house feels quiet," I said after a good-morning kiss. "Is everyone gone?"

"Yes. Kad went back to Indper to tidy up some loose ends, and Mar, Stu, and Dak went to Skopje to establish our management there and quell some bureaucrat's urge to socialize our share of the partnership with the government."

"Partnership? A communist government in partnership with an American corporation? Marx and Lenin must be spinning like power drills! What does the Yugoslav government contribute to the partnership?"

"Permission to operate there unimpeded. Up till now."

"Huh!" I poured myself a cup of coffee. "And the fun continues. Incidentally, I didn't wake up with any great ideas this morning, but I certainly feel relaxed. You gals plan great rituals of play; Dak and Kad were a smash last night." I swayed my hips like a Polynesian dancer before adding cream and sugar. "And you played your part pretty well, too. I especially liked the mermaid skit in the lagoon. That's the most peaceful spot I've ever seen on this planet. How long would NORTEC last there?"

"About as long as it takes an aircraft carrier to arrive. France would be overruled, and those lovely islands would come under joint U.S./Russian, um, protection."

"Right. But I still feel the need to get away from D.C. and get all our labs together." I sat down across from her. "The question is where."

"You pick it," she said. "You're the warrior. I'll fly with you anywhere. Meanwhile, we have some cornbread and bacon keeping warm in the oven; maybe some yummies will inspire you."

She'd changed the subject to cover a strong elevation in her interest level. I pretended not to notice—that was part of the game—although, of course, she'd noticed my noticing. I'd do a little fishing.

"El, is there a place on Earth where the very space, and even the ground itself, is so sane that no insanity can intrude?"

She laughed. "Tahiti feels that way to people."

"One of the metaphysics books Dak sold me was about Edgar Cayce. He claimed there's a place in Arkansas where, if anyone walks barefoot, they'll never attempt suicide. Was he right?"

"I wouldn't be surprised. There are places where

something so beautiful and playful happened that the entire area is sanitized to grid normal."

She'd almost let her attention go to the place we needed. I retrieved my fly for another cast. "If 'playful' is a magic elixir," I said, "why aren't playgrounds at grid normal?"

"Dear, 'playful' is not a thing. Attention at playfulness, devoid of polarizations, is the elixir, the universal solvent of grid anomalies due to trauma. As for children's playgrounds, well, in this age few are born at play, and most who are soon find themselves forced to abandon it. Mothers want their sons and daughters to be competitors, or little workers, or warriors before going out to greet the world, and an absence of polarization is not often acceptable."

"Okay," I said, "so I won't look for perfection." I aimed my fly at a spot behind the boulder where I was sure the big one lay. "But there must be places available that are sane enough to receive the new toys and insanities Cha left us, without going tilt and demanding to be attacked. One, at least." I deliberately avoided staring intently at her. "Some place where we stand a chance of defending ourselves and the world."

My cast fell short. "You're getting close, dear," El said calmly, "but you still have to ask the right question. Incidentally, the DUO-HEX is interested enough in your line of thought to be recording this conversation."

I looked up and stuck my tongue out. "What's a Great Cursor like you doing with a Mucky Puk Sty like this?" I said, and felt a light buzz flow over me as I looked back at El. "Where is that place you said some of Puk's students set themselves up to help people like Morrison's bunch?" The fly looped delicately over the rock and settled softly in an eddy behind it. Now if I was right . . . "Some place in New Zealand, you said it was."

"Yes. One of them owned a ranch in a beautiful valley, and set up a center there because the place was naturally therapeutic. I dropped by to check on them after finishing in Australia yesterday. Oh, and Morrison is in good shape. He hugged me, and thanked me for reminding him of the Key to Naldar."

I began to feel an excitement stirring. "Would that valley suit our needs? Could we use it without spoiling it?" There was a dimple on the surface of the water, and my line twitched.

"We could—make it do. Even keep it clean with the help of Puk's friends. And I meant to tell you earlier," she added, "that's where Puk went to write his new game plan. He's having a ball, being free of his founder's role."

"Okay," I said decisively, "that's it. Let's pop off to New Zealand and barter for some building space."

She jumped up with a loud "Yahoo!", pulled me from my chair, and swung me around as if she were dancing with a toy doll, startling me with her sudden strength. Her laughter filled the room.

"Wow!" I said. "I must have done a goody!"

"You did, you did!" She planted a big kiss on my mouth, then stepped back with her hands on my arms and said, "We anglers always get excited when we catch the really big one." She laughed again and squeezed me. "Oh, Le, we prayed you'd pick that place."

Then another, deeper voice filled the room with laughter. "El," It said after It finished laughing, "your good-looking cursor did it. I owe you one ice cream soda with two straws. As I recall, you prefer strawberry whip. Coming up! Enjoy."

And there on the counter beside us, an enormous strawberry whip appeared out of nowhere, pitcher size. Mentally, I canceled cornbread for breakfast.

"I told you the DUO-HEX was listening," she said. "He always gets nervous and nosy near pay-up time." El vibrated like a young maid I knew in Greece, one who also had the face of a goddess. We sat down and enjoyed the whip.

When we'd finished, I was ready to get dressed and pop to New Zealand for a quick peek. But I was a little premature. "Later, dear," El said. "It's not time yet."

So she popped to New Zealand and I drove to the office.

A cleancut young man was waiting in the executive reception area, and Norma introduced us. "Mr. Ambers, this is David French, your new technical assistant."

I'd forgotten about that. "Welcome aboard, David," I said, "and call me Jan." I grinned at Norma. "You, too, unless you want me to call you Ms. Halliburton."

She blushed slightly and smiled back. "I'll try. I may forget sometimes, though."

I took David in my office and had him sit. Then I relaxed in my desk chair. "I noticed on your application that you've had no practical experience outside of school labs. You've got a lot of theory bottled up in you, and I want you to let it all out. When it's gone, we'll help you restructure it so you can tear that out, too. After three or four recreates, you'll be the best damn creative engineer MIT ever failed to produce. You'll be a pro, a self-made engineering artist.

"I'm assigning you temporary duty as assistant lab technician. Our lab techs are the tops. Watch and listen: They'll show you how to make theory operate. Don't be overwhelmed by their skill but don't assume a superior attitude. Learn to let the scene at hand tell you what's wanted and needed. And what's wanted and needed will tell you how to build it."

He looked a little confused and deflated.

"Dave," I went on, "you're in for the adventure of your life. I've got a hunch that within five years you'll be the most sought-after engineer in the world. You'll need two PR assistants just to arrange your photo sessions."

I got up and steered him toward the door. "Now find your way downstairs and start in Lab One with Charley Mahavlich. And when your mind is squeaky clean, as if you really don't know a damn thing, come back and see me about phase two."

He sort of staggered out. With what he was about to confront, he'd have to be tough. We'd see. I felt optimistic about him, though.

I went to the computer room and found Al at the console. "Mar had an unexpected trip," I told him. "You'll have to get by with me today. What's the best computer on the market? The very best? I want you to outfit a new shop."

"I'll tell you," he said, "this model has the capability to expand into anything that I can foresee us needing. We can just add on as the operation grows. Where's the new shop going to be?"

"New Zealand. Want to come along?"

Slowly his mouth sagged open. "How in the world," he said, "did you know I wanted to go there?" He was staring at me. "I've thought a lot about New Zealand lately. I met a girl from there at a computer convention in San Francisco. We really hit it off, and planned to meet in Hawaii this fall."

"Well, you can surprise her next week if that's okay."

"Next week?! You bet! Are we moving everything?"

"The think-tank crew stays, unless one or two of them shows promise of being useful. And most of the administrative staff will stay." I gestured at the computer. "Find any new kinks in there?"

"Not really. Dawn won't answer up even on key-boarded data. I had an idea that maybe BUCLEPUK could invent a way to determine tribal membership. We could give the device to Cha and let him contact all the Tribe Thirteen members.

"Funny," he added, "but I don't feel depressed or angry any more when I think of Cha."

A change on the screen caught our attention. "It's PUK," Al said.

[Read:]   AL, WE ARE STILL HAVING A HAS-SLE WITH THIS ONE. LE IS WORK-ING UP NON SEQUITUR ROUTINES.

[Write:]   EXAMPLE?

[Read:]   TAKE TRIBE-13 FEMALES ON VEGA RUN.

"Damn," Al said, "I've had bugs in programs before, but this is the first time I ever ran into a horny pro-gram. We need Mar here to coax Dawn out." The read changed.

[Read:]   MAR AGREE, DAWN HELP.
          DAWN BE VEGAN HOSTESS.

SHUT DOWN, PLEASE.
PROTECT BUC AND PUK.
YIPEEEE!!!!!!!

Al shut down the whole system. "Wonder what the psych boys would say about Dawn?" he wondered aloud.

"Most of them would take the Fifth. Or *a* fifth. Some might say we've got a playful poltergeist in our computer." In fact, it seemed to me we did have something there besides hardware and software.

I went downstairs and found Sam feeding three white mice. PORT-2 looked ready for action.

"Good morning, Mr. Ambers," Sam said, and not very cheerfully, either.

"What's up?"

"We're one piece short." He pointed to the vacant space under the mouse cage. "The night before Mr. Larson took off, he had Hal run a load test on the life-force mirror generator, the thing he'd called the Bio-ID section for identifying the mice. And something's screwy, because Hal said it checked out then, but when we plugged it in here this morning, every component in it was burned out. Hal just got back with the parts to rebuild it, and it's a one-man job.

"It looks like a couple of days before we'll be ready for that test run," he ended glumly.

"Hang in there, Sam," I told him. "We'll get it. And let me know if you or Hal can use any help." Then I walked down the hall to Lab Seven, where Mark Bush and the AUTO-DAG project resided. Mark had just finished Port-1 and dismissed his helpers to return to their own projects.

"Mornin', Mr. Ambers," he said in his East Texas accent. "I was just goin' to call you to come see a test run."

"Great work, Mark," I said, hoping that Cha hadn't "tested" any of these components at the last minute. I walked over to the ten by twenty-five-foot copper/beryllium alloy transmitter plate in the center of the lab. It, too, was firmly attached to the floor.

"Mark, what did Larson tell you the AUTO-DAG project was for? Waxing cars?"

He grinned. "That's not all that far off. It's for automatic diagnostic analysis of electrical and mechanical systems. Works, too. Mr. Larson and Mr. Simpson had me test her for 'em two weeks ago, with one of the scooters. It was 'pre-fixed' with some flaws, and 'old Dagwood' here found every one of 'em. Plus some others, and they checked out, too: a hairline fracture in the frame and a nearly frayed winding in the motor. I left the winding alone and the motor shorted out four days later."

"Let's take the receiver to the garage," I said, "and send a cart through."

He picked up and folded the flat lengths of jointed aluminum-alloy rod that defined the receiver field, and I carried the briefcase-sized mirror generator. We took them out to the garage, set them up, and drove an electric cart back to the lab. Mark rolled the cart onto the transmitter plate.

"While you're getting ready," I said, "I'll round up some witnesses."

"How 'bout a solo run first?" he suggested. "In case I missed a wire somewhere."

"Okay, Mark, it's your debut."

He turned it on. A very slight hum built up while a red light on the control panel flashed brightly.

"When the two fields are balanced," he said, "we oughta get a green light, but only if there's nothin' at the other end 'cept air."

The green light came on. Mark lifted the safety cover and pressed the transfer switch. The cart vanished. We both stared in awed silence, and there were the goose bumps again, as big and tingly as ever. *My god,* I thought, *it's been a long time since I saw one of these rigs in action.* It beat hell out of that sorry rig Scotty used on the *Enterprise* in my favorite TV series.

Mark recovered and let out a rebel yell. I joined him.

"You did it, Mark!" I said, and hugged him. Our yelling was drawing a crowd; the room began to fill with guys from the other labs.

"And look at those figures," Mark said, pointing to a recorder chart. The label was "power consumption." "I knew it wouldn't use a whole hell of a lot of juice, but it takes more energy than that to heat a gawddamn pot of coffee!"

"Mark," I said, "let's have some more fun with this. I'll go out and send someone back here with the cart; I want to see it arrive there. Then I'll drive it back here, and you can go out to the receiver pad and I'll send it to you."

By then, the whole lab team was there, including Dave French. I took half of them with me and we saw the cart arrive. After a couple more times, though, the awe began to lessen and everyone went back to work. Except Dave. My new "technical assistant" was still standing stunned in Mark's lab.

"Let's go have coffee," I said, and led him away.

Over coffee I got him talking, telling me all the reasons why the thing he'd seen couldn't happen. When he'd slow down, I'd pump him: "Give me another reason it couldn't happen." And when he couldn't think of any more, I told him to make up reasons why it couldn't, until these got wilder than the event he'd just witnessed. After a bit, he started to laugh.

"Thanks, Mr. Ambers—Jan. You're right, this *is* going to be an adventure! Another jolt like that and I'm not sure what I'll be like. But life is starting to feel really interesting."

He went back to Lab One with an eager expression, and I went to arrange transport for Mark's "Auto-Dag" Port-1 light weight receiver frame, on the assumption that we'd have to get it to New Zealand by more mundane transport, like jet airplane; there wasn't anything like itself there to receive it.

In my office, Dak popped in. "I get to push the first button," she said cheerily, then was gone, and Kad popped in. Grinning, she said, "I'll pop the port and be the down-under welcome lady." Then she was gone, too. I looked around the room, where I was now the only visible entity. "Any more requests?" I asked out loud.

El responded in the nonsonic mode: "Later, dear."

Before I got to my chair I felt a rush of energy and a

change in my awareness, and knew, without knowing how I knew, that Dawn and Mar had balanced LE's Vega Run equation.

"Thank you for that, ladies," I said aloud. "Love ya."

"All welcome" came as a mental *read* that filled the room with joy and a sense of play. I even got a visual, of a golden computer screen with vivid vermilion letters. Our bright genie in the computer, I told myself: No mere program did that. *Right*, came the reply in my mind. *Dawn do*.

Chuckling, I called Al. "Anything going on?"

"Jesus, I hope so," he said. "Either that or I'm cracking up. I just heard Dawn talking in my head."

"That's why I called. I heard her, too."

"I was just going to call you. I was working with PUK just now and couldn't get the invention I wanted. Then LE came back on and I got it quick—a detector of some sort for Tribe Thirteen members. It doesn't have any data root, but I've got the schematic. Can we use it anyway?"

"We will. Bring it up in"—I looked at my wall clock— "thirty minutes, and have lunch with me."

Norma came in to report. "Ms. Anderson called and said she couldn't be here for lunch today. She suggested you call Al Peters for company. Shall I ring him?"

"Thanks, Norma, I just invited him. He'll be up in half an hour."

That half hour I spent looking through my in-basket, not to handle things but to get a feel for what went on on the company's routine administrative lines. The situation was so volatile and unpredictable just then that it would make no sense at all for me to give attention to routine operations; what I had to do was save the ship. But in time, a company can choke on unmade decisions and ungiven orders.

Happily, I found that Norma had been handling these things in my name. She'd undoubtedly been doing this all along, while Simpson and Walters had been scuttering around in gleeful insanity. I hoped to hell we paid her what she was worth—like plenty. I called Switzer in

Personnel and told him to change her job description to administrative assistant to the president, raise her pay to a thousand a week, and send the authorization to me for my signature by quitting time.

Then Al arrived, simultaneously with the lunch cart. Over a blue aperitif, I checked his schematic and noted why there were no data roots. "Al, this is not an electronic device: It doesn't work in the electromagnetic spectrum. It works in another spectrum: call it vitalic, orogonic, or any of the other words coined to name the energy of life. I prefer 'life forcic' myself; not elegant, maybe, but it says it straight and plain. When John Campbell was the editor of *Analog Science Fiction*, he reported on a device invented by a guy named Hieronymus." I indicated the schematic he'd brought. "The Hieronymus device used this same principle, or tried to, but it had no detector circuit. The users had to feel it with their fingers, while this one converts the life force energy into light at the readout. Dead-fingered people won't be able to laugh at this one."

"When can we get it built?"

"Soon. It's a simple enough circuit, but it won't satisfy Cha the way it is now. We need a large enough sample of the population to begin to construct a Tribe Thirteen genealogy. After lunch we'll see if old BUCLE-PUK can add a circuit for family branch and derivative level."

And it better, I thought to myself. *BUCLEPUK is the only clue old DUO-HEX let me have.* BUCLEPUK, or . . . And there went the gooseflesh again, my hair feeling like electric wires. Or . . . could it have been *BucLePuk?!* I recalled this morning when I'd asked the DUO-HEX what a Great Cursor like him was doing in a Mucky Puk Sty like this. I'd had a slight rush then, sort of sneaky, as if I'd almost spotted something. Now it really hit! The goose bumps would have sparked in the dark.

"Al," I told him, "I just realized who Cha's brother is. We'll meet him in New Zealand." Puk! Son of a bitch!

"God!" he said. "That must take a load off your mind. Now Cha will leave."

I answered slowly. The full ramifications of my cognition were still printing out in my mind. "I doubt it very much; Cha's deal with us was phony. I didn't realize it at the time and neither did Cha, but it really was. It only felt right to me because it was a necessary next step. But what Cha and family came here for was to regain the true sense of play, something they'd thoroughly lost somewhere down the line and replaced with sadism. And they need to stay until it's recovered."

"You mean . . . they were pulled in here for—for *therapy?!*"

The rush hit again, far stronger than ever—so strong, I writhed and rocked with it. *The key missing element all along—all through these trilennia of struggle—had been the fact of my own responsibility! I was the one who'd been decisive in bringing them here and tying their attention to this sector. Then I'd needed to forget it, for the purposes of the scenario, and to regain that knowledge before I could handle the culmination.*

No wonder I'd had to be the key field man all that time!

Al was staring at me in concern, half out of his chair, and I grinned at him, or maybe grimaced. "It's okay, buddy, I'll be all right," I said. That remembering had been a key step. The enormous rush I'd felt had been old barriers of loss and grief and pain and mustn'teverletthathappenagain blowing off. The last faint waves passed, and I looked around my office, seeing with a new and greater clarity.

What had Al's question been? Had we brought Cha and his family here for therapy, that was it.

"Something close to therapy," I said. "They need to see certain things, realize them for themselves, and to do that, certain conditions have to exist, built on a whole . . . a whole structure of experiences over time. I don't know exactly what Mar told you, but El—Ms. Anderson—and I, and certain others, have been working on it for a very long time."

"What's his lost brother like?"

"Not like Cha. Not at all."

After that we ate mostly in silence, while I felt new viewpoints settling in. A lot of my attention was on New Zealand, and I felt an inbetweenness. Just after Al went back to the computer, the phone rang. Norma was still at lunch, and the call had come through direct.

"Mr. Ambers, this is Mark Bush. A lady just came in here to pick up the Port-1 receiver. She says you sent her."

"Is she fantastic-looking, with tan eyes?"

"That's her, sir."

"I sent her."

There was several seconds of silence. "Mr. Ambers, sir, uh, she . . . she disappeared while we were talking. With the receiver rods and the mirror generator. I looked away for maybe two seconds and she was gone. I don't know how she did it."

I could feel him trying to rationalize it to himself, and decided I'd better help him out. "That's fine, Mark," I said. "She does things like that, especially when she's in a hurry. She's a clever lady. Look, I'll be bringing a general by in a bit. Tell him about Ol' Dagwood, but only about its use as Auto-Dag. Pitch it toward aircraft maintenance and safety."

"I can do better'n that," Mark said. "I've got a video tape of our test on the pre-fixed scooter. I'll play him a piece of that."

"Good show, Mark. Have fun. I'll see you."

Then I called Joe Byra and asked if there was enough of Red-Box left, after taking out what was needed for Port-1 and Port-2, to demonstrate it for a general. "But we don't want the general to know how far along we are yet," I added.

"Gotcha, boss," Joe said. "We can demo it as an advanced holographic projector, no sweat. I've got all the components except the mirror generators, and we can project a perfectly good 3-D image without mirror generators."

After that I called Charley Mahavlich in Lab One. "What can you show a four-star general without scaring his ass off?" I asked him.

"I've got just the thing, Jan," he told me, "all rigged and ready. If I fine-tune it with the vernier, the damn thing will let you look inside people in full living color. I just checked it out on Don Johnson and found all his metal souvenirs from Vietnam, so clear you could have read the trademarks if they had any."

Charley didn't sound a bit like the guy I first met in the lab.

"Great, Charley. See you about ten after one."

I lay down on the couch in my office to contact Kad, our New Zealand receiver-in-charge. "Hi, Le," she said, "we're busy as bees here. Take just a quick peek through my eyes."

I closed my own to look, and gasped. What I saw was a receiver frame, presumably sitting in New Zealand, and a load of gear and people had appeared on it as I watched. Concentrated activity to clear it began, presumably to prepare it for another load. *People! How the hell could that be?* I asked myself. I thought Port-1 scrambled eggs.

"That's not just a Port-1, dear." El had popped into my office; my eyes opened. "Dak and Kad are providing life support," she explained, "just as they did last night when they popped us around." She lay down on top of me and kissed me, and I felt all the day's excitement dissolve in a marvelous relaxation.

"In case you don't know it," I murmured in her ear, "you're magic. The right effect at the right time, invariably."

"For all you know, smart aleck, this may be a holo-version of me you're snuggling with."

It wasn't; I felt sure of it. "Why are we moving early?" I asked.

"Necessity. The bureaucrats handled nicely, but we didn't reckon on a Yugoslav general threatening to move in on the place. Cha may have had someone planted to leak information. We started shipping as soon as Kad set up the receiver. The Skopje lab should be cleaned out by the time the general and the bureaucrat get through with the conference I got them into. It's legalistic enough to take time, but not so much that the general will just say to hell with it prematurely, and act."

"But is it legal for Dak and Kad to do this without my orders? Won't the DUO-HEX have to shut us down for this? I thought you guys were restricted to setting things up."

"You've tied up all the loose ends," she replied, "and given the orders to move to New Zealand for the next phase. All they're doing is setting things up down there with the now-existing indigenous technology, per your orders."

"Okay, but . . ." I was worried about something, something dangerous that I couldn't put my finger on, so I groped for it. "Kad took the Port-1 receiver to New Zealand, and she sure didn't transport it by scheduled airline. And it doesn't have a life force mirror."

"Warrior mine," El said, "I explained that. When the schematics were complete, it became legal to use the technology here on Earth. Right? So the twins and I can now pop people and things besides ourselves and our immediate personal accessories, in this case, up to the existing performance limits of Ports 1 and 2. All perfectly proper per the rules of this grid. The only advantages in using Ports 1 and 2 at all, now that they're available, are their capacity and because one twin can stay at the receiver site to direct operations."

Good grief, I thought, *she's not only a financial wizard and master finagler; she's a constitutional lawyer!* My worry vanished. Hell, yes. And the only difference between Ports 1 and 2 was the life force mirror. The pads and gates were the same.

She grinned down at me and spoke inside my head. "You've got it, toots." The voice sounded like Humphrey Bogart in an old Howard Hawks movie.

But I was still worried, and continued to grope. "General French is due here at 1300," I said, "and we have a few demos for him. But if things are unraveling here the way they are in Skopje, it could be the 503rd Parachute Infantry that shows up, instead of the general."

She didn't say a thing, which suggested I was close to spotting something again. A flash of anxiety numbed my joints for a moment. "We're moving out of here today!" I said, and looked at the clock. Twelve forty-three. "By 4 P.M." That would give us three hours, but the way it felt, or I felt . . . And the activity couldn't be apparent to the general during his visit. "We can get everything out but the Port-1 and Port-2 transmitters. We'll put demolition charges on them."

I was still worried, and time wasn't all of it. But it sure as hell was part of it, and it was something to act on. "I'd cancel the general's tour—we've got an awful lot to do in three hours—but that might accelerate someone's takeover operation."

El laughed. "The twins will get your people out, along with everything else. Don't worry about that; it really is legal.

"Which reminds me," she added, "General French knows me from his two-star days. He'll flirt with me when your back is turned, but I don't mind; I like him. How do you like his son?"

It felt unreal to me to be lying on my couch with El on top of me, talking about things like that, when there was so much to do in so little time. But I answered her question: "Dave will be a real asset to us," I told her. After all, she wouldn't have changed the subject if it hadn't needed changing, or if we didn't have time enough. She was probably using this to smooth me out again.

"You're right about Dave," she said, "and in more ways than you've looked at yet. He has a destiny he's waited a long time for. The complete crew is gathering at last."

The complete crew! I thought of Puk. Cha's brother, but one of us. Somehow along the way he'd regained a sane sense of play; maybe he'd never totally lost it.

"Incidentally," El said, "you won us another strawberry whip when you spotted Puk as the lost brother."

She let me up then, and I got on the phone to the labs, Security, and Building Services. Al was out of the building; I'd need to contact him later. As soon as the general left, the move would begin.

General French, a trim but graying warrior of maybe

sixty years, arrived punctually at 1300, and we went out to meet him. When he spoke to El, his voice was light but sincere.

"Dorothy," he said, "you look lovelier than ever." He took both her hands and looked her over admiringly. "You're younger than you were ten years ago when we first met. Let me in on your secret."

"A mysterious formula passed on to me by my grandmother, who was reputedly a witch. General, I'd like you to meet the man I chose to straighten out this operation, Jan Ambers."

He smiled at me, and I could feel the man's charm. "I recognize you from the *Time* magazine cover," he told me. "And I'd like to thank you for hiring my son."

"Thank you for sending him to us. He's a good catch, but don't tell him I said so until next year. Right now he's busy unlearning some of the stuff they ground into him in school. We'll see him downstairs."

We got the general through the tour in under an hour, and he left pleased as punch. El was looking wistful as the two of us walked back to my office together. "Poor dear," she said as I closed the door behind us. "He so wanted Dave to be a jet jockey, like he used to be. So very much. But he never wavered in his support and love for him. He *is* a dear, and I think he just may live to see his son become the greatest jockey of all, when he leads the first crew to Mars."

"Sweetheart," I said, "let's make it happen that way." I kissed her gently. "Shall I ask Norma to go to New Zealand with us?"

"Absolutely. You must. She may possibly want to come back later but she has to go."

I buzzed Norma and asked her to come in. She was there in five seconds. "Norma," I said briskly, "we're moving to New Zealand and we want you to come with us. Promotion, a good raise, a beautiful mountain valley, and free room and board."

The papers for her new position wouldn't be ready here, but I could handle that at the other end.

"For how long?"

"For as long as you want to stay."

Her eyes began to brighten with interest. "When do we leave?" she asked.

It was El who answered. "Right now. No time to pack. The move is already underway from downstairs, and we'll buy everything you need at the other end. You mustn't tell *anyone* where we're going, not until later. And don't worry about anything: not your replacement, not even your cat. We *never* let cats go lonely. Someone will pick him up tonight."

"But how . . . ? I—I don't understand!"

El patted her arm. "Just go downstairs to Lab Seven and they'll tell you what to do. It's really all okay; everything is all set up for us."

Norma nodded, then walked out looking dazed.

"We're uprooting some very unprepared people," El said. "I think we'd better throw a party tonight."

I called Security to take the manuals, photos, and printouts from my office to Lab Seven. El and I helped them gather it all up, then followed them downstairs. There wasn't much backup of material in the corridor outside Mark's lab door. It was a wide door, fortunately, to accommodate moving in structural material. Al was waiting outside it with a pair of fat briefcases.

"How did you get the word?" I asked him. "You were out when I called you."

"Don't ask," he said, and shook his head. "A talking cat told me. Honest to God!" He paused. "Although I don't suppose that's any surprise to you. I tried to reach Susan then, but she's out at her uncle's ranch. No phone."

"Don't worry, Al," said El, "she'll be at the receiving pad when we arrive. Actually, she moved into your new quarters this morning; she hoped it would be all right with you."

She laughed at the expression on Al's face.

"I've heard Le mumble something about you under his breath," Al said. "I thought he said 'wench,' but it must have been 'witch.' When did you find out about Susan and me? She hardly even knows anybody in the States."

El frowned slightly, as if she were trying to remember. "Umm, about—two weeks before I sent her to San Francisco with instructions to get acquainted with one Al Peters."

He looked utterly confused, almost alarmed, then shook it off.

"So Susan works for you, too?"

El smiled. "No, she's like you, Al: She operates at the level of creative play. That makes her an associate rather than an employee."

We went in then, to find Dak directing traffic at the transmitter. Just for a moment, Norma looked big-eyed at us from the pad before she vanished. I chuckled to myself. Cha's little bit of sabotage on Bio-ID, the life support mirror for his three blind mice, wasn't slowing us a bit.

A three-man loading crew then rolled the carts with our computer accessories and operations manuals onto the pad. I wondered what Dak had said or done that allowed them to function so calmly. Or had she brought them with her after rehabilitating them somewhere? New Zealand, maybe.

We stepped onto the pad beside the carts, then I thought of Mar's teaching manuals and moved as if to go after them. El's hand on my arm stopped me. "Al got them," she said.

The room vanished.

TWENTY-EIGHT

The new scene replaced the old without any sense of movement in space or time. Simply, we were in a wide open space, crisply chill, bright with midmorning sun. Surprisingly, there wasn't even a feeling of disorientation.

A crystallized iridescence, a breathtaking marvel of a building, snatched my eye, and for a moment I stood transfixed. Then Kad called: "Clear the pad! We still have more labs to move!" and the spell broke.

We did, Al to one side, El and I to the other. A lovely girl, grinning widely, ran over to Al. It had to be Susan; he seemed to be in very good hands. She led him to a small electric runabout. Meanwhile, two men began unloading the receiver field onto a low-bed electric truck.

About two miles away, a range of mountains rose from the nearly flat valley floor. I followed their crest with my eyes until my attention was caught again by the intervening building; it was like nothing else on Earth. I had a strange feeling that I'd shipped to another planet.

"Is that ours?" I asked, pointing.

"That's ours."

"Good grief! What do we need anything that large for?"

She smiled. "We don't yet, dear, but give us a little time."

I could see it was not your basic no-frills facility, even half a mile distant, and I stared, wondering what it had cost. It had three high tiers, with a tower like a smoky quartz crystal rising high above them. A row of white columns surrounding the lower tier lent Hellenic grace, while colored panels on the second and third tiers, splinters of bright light in the winter sun, said modern. The towering, windowless, hexagonal needle made it look like something on another planet, and the pointed glass roof of the third tier added to the illusion that the tower was a natural monolithic crystal.

El said nothing for a bit; just let me look. It was incredibly beautiful.

"The Valley thanks you for admiring Her statement," she said at last, squeezing my arm.

Another electric truck passed us, loaded with people, and from the predominantly oriental faces, I realized that the Hong Kong move was underway. That's when the realization hit me, with a wave of dismay that bordered on horror: "Good God!" I said. "The think-tankers have all the errata sheets!" In six months the government would have ports, spy-eyes, the whole damn works. That had to be what had been nagging in the back of my mind earlier. We had to get them back!

"Don't worry, dear," El said, "Dak had the print shop pick them all up for binding with the original reports. They came in ahead of us from D.C."

I almost collapsed with relief. "Whew! Thank God for Dak! For a minute I thought I'd blown the whole damn thing again."

Then I realized I'd said *again*, and looked at El questioningly.

She smiled. "It'll be different this time," she said. "Incidentally, none of those think-tankers will remember much of what happened downstairs. They're already busy adjusting back into the conceptual framework of their former reality; for now they'll be much more comfortable that way."

I refocused my attention on the present. "Who all is coming through this morning?" I asked.

"Everyone we want here except the paramilitary forces in the States, Peru, and Australia. We're bringing the Skopje and Hong Kong troops right away because they're barracked at the labs there. The other contingents can wait a few hours."

That reminded me how vulnerable we were to a military takeover here, and the Indper, American, and Australian contingents were our larger forces. Neither Yugoslavian politics nor Hong Kong government and environment had room for covert paramilitary forces, and our forces there amounted to oversized on-site security staffs—probably a lot larger than the local authorities knew—supposedly to protect the sites from the world terrorist community. They numbered only 100 in each place, compared to 250 in the States, 200 in Australia, and 400 in Peru.

"When are we bringing the Americans and Peruvians over, and the Aussies?" I asked.

"Tonight," El replied, "New Zealand time, that is. Early morning in D.C. and Cajamarca, and early evening in Perth."

Just then Dak arrived with the Port-1 transmitter

beside her. I gave a sigh of relief; that meant the D.C. transfer was complete. Obviously she'd popped it: The large, heavy copper/beryllium plate wasn't even in the receiver field, but next to it, maybe to avoid damaging the lightweight frame.

Apparently she could now bring through anything movable she wanted to, just by putting her hands on it and intending, although the damn thing had been bolted down. *That'll help confuse them in D.C. and anywhere else she did it*, I told myself, *and presumably it was legal or she wouldn't have.*

"Watch this celebration," El said.

Dak and Kad embraced, and the space around them turned gold, a burst of multicolored sparks filling the air above their heads. They really knew how to let their pleasure show. Then they got out of the way, to let a pair of forklifts get at the transmitter plate. El and I went over for a four-way hug.

"Dak and I still have things to take care of," Kad said when we'd finished, "but they're ready for Le in the tower." I turned and looked at the building, then took El's hand, scanning around for another bus or runabout or truck. Before I found one, the scene changed again; I'd been popped. We were in a gardenlike lobby, with glass elevator tubes in front of us. My gaze followed them up about thirty feet, where they disappeared into a vaulted ceiling.

There really didn't appear to be anything here of a sort I hadn't seen before. It was just all so perfectly harmonious and aesthetic. El led me gawking to the elevator doors. Despite all the prop work I'd seen the girls handle earlier, I was awestruck by what they'd built here.

"We didn't build this, dear," El said as we stepped into an elevator. "*She* did—the Valley, the Mujinn. She even selected the architect and the construction company. We only took care of the early legwork and some of the paperwork for Her. I'll tell you the story later."

We passed through a mezzanine and entered the third tier, where we got out in a reception area. Here the rear wall was glass, and I could see what seemed to be a semi-circular apartment complex about three hundred yards behind the main building. It had three set-back tiers, with roof gardens. Again I simply gazed for a bit.

"What does that remind you of?" El asked.

"An idealized version of a Zuñi pueblo I saw in New Mexico," I said. "It has a similar . . . flavor. It's the sort of thing the Zuñis might have built if they'd had the resources."

Meanwhile Norma, exploring a display panel, had seen us and was walking over.

"How do you like it, Norma?" El asked.

"I still can't believe it's real." Norma's eyes looked ready to spill over. "It's more than beautiful! It's—*so in tune!*"

She hugged us both, then left.

Instead of taking an elevator, El led me to a wide stairway on the left, and we climbed it through the ceiling into a glass-roofed garden. Though enclosed in glass, the garden had a fresh summer outdoors feel, without the steaminess of a typical greenhouse.

At one end, a broad doorway opened into the base of the tower, and that's where El steered me next. Near the front facet of the tower, by a table that held glasses and champagne on ice, a dozen or so people stood as if waiting, among them Al and Sue.

A man in a white jacket drew the corks, and the rest of us gathered around. I poured for El and me. Then she turned, facing south, and everyone's gaze followed hers; most seemed to know what was going on. I could see sunlight reflecting off something at the other end of the valley.

"To the Valley," El said, "and to Her gift for a new golden age of man." After a soft chorus of *here, heres!* we emptied our glasses.

Then El turned to me. "The toast was part of a formal dedication," she said quietly, then pointed toward the glint I'd seen. "Over there about ten miles, the people at Neptune South—Puk's people—are having a toast in a tower that's a twin to this one. Buc and Puk are both there. You'll see them at the party tonight."

Al approached with his young lady, and we turned to meet them. "Le," he said, "this is Susan Jason."

"Hi, Susan," I said, extending my hand.

She took it. "Call me Sue, Le. I feel as if we're old friends." She hugged me. "And welcome to New Zealand."

I became aware then of someone else standing by as if waiting to be introduced, and El's hand on my arm was directing my attention to her. "Le," said El, "I want you to meet our facility manager: this is Sally Traesko."

She was very young looking, but her mien, her eyes especially, told me that Sally Traesko was someone on the level of Mar and Stu and Al—a high genius not only by test score but performance. She was, El explained, the architect chosen to design and build the facilities here. After the job was done, she'd accepted the position of facility manager; she and Sue had been living here since before the ground-breaking ceremony.

"We owe both of them a lot," El finished.

"You have my highest admiration," I said. "This is an incredible place."

This time I got hugged by Sally. "Thank you, Le, and welcome to Neptune North. We couldn't have done this without Sue and her computer magic working out finance, materials, scheduling . . . Or without El and Dak and their connections." She laughed then. "And their other—resources." She turned to El. "We'll see you both this evening. Sue and I have to check the preparations for the feast."

Both girls left then.

I was trying to place Sally's light and pleasant accent—it was too slight to identify readily. Not German, I thought, or Swedish. Dutch? Or Swiss, maybe?

El helped. "She's from Sjaelland, the largest island of Denmark; in English it's called Zealand. She moved from Old Zealand to New Zealand."

The group had dispersed into twos and threes and were leaving, as they had things to do. "I'll introduce people tonight at the party," El said. "With so many arriving, and so much material coming in, there's a lot to be handled, even as well organized as Sally has things."

"Fine," I said. "I need to learn my way around. This seems like a good time to find out where my office is, and the labs."

"That's the next thing on the agenda," she said, leading me toward the door.

"How much did this place cost you? Or us, if it came from Hannibal's shekels."

"Not a penny, dear. The Valley paid for it; it's all Hers."

I peered closely at El, and walked a bit slower for talking. "You keep referring to the Valley as 'Her'— as if it were a sort of godlike being. How about explaining?"

"Certainly. The Valley is the same kind of godlike being as you are, or me, or Simpson, or the wino in the dumpster." She eyed me calmly. "Or Cha."

She paused to let me digest that, then went on. "And she's playing her own kind of role, one she's filled for a very long time—about as long as you and I have been working on ours. It's been a role of relative quiet for long periods, with a minimum of confusion and conflict and self-questioning, one that allowed and required her to develop a special kind of personality and power. The result is something very special, very beautiful."

We had left the glass-roofed garden, were walking slowly down the stairs. "And when the Neptune group came here to look the place over—by 'sheer chance' of course—she led them to a rich vein of gold-bearing ore that was easily accessible—easy to see and get at, easy to take out. That's what paid for this place—this and the one like it at the other end of the valley."

"But . . . somebody must have owned it—legally, I mean."

"Sue's Uncle Jim owned it. This was a sheep ranch that had been in the family since the mid-1800s—before the Maori war. Sue had been a member of the Neptune group since it formed eight years ago, and her Uncle Jim had become part of it, too."

We paused briefly on the second floor. "This is the research reception area," El said.

I nodded. "How come the gold hadn't been noticed before," I asked, "if it was easy to see?"

"The family hadn't been interested in minerals—never looked for them. The major gold finds on the South Island had been farther south or on the west side. Prospectors had hunted all through here before settlement, but somehow none of them noticed it. Then, when Sue and her uncle came in to look it over for a place to build the center for the Neptune group, they saw the gold trace in the river gravel, and tracked down the source."

Try to explain all that as "coincidence," I thought. Astigmatic prospectors, Sue's family getting title to the land . . . The spirit of the valley was obviously a powerful lady who knew what she wanted.

We stopped at the first door on the wide front corridor of the north wing. "This is the one I told them to hold for your office, if you like it," El said. "Dave's can be next door. You have twenty labs in each wing. Look it over; I have to pop and help Dak and Kad. We were well organized for this move, but there's a lot to do."

She popped, and I examined my new office. My cart of manuals and schematic photos was already there; someone had even brought my red box.

Then someone knocked. I opened up, and there stood future space jockey Dave French, an excited grin on his face.

"Mr. Ambers!" he said. "I just saw something that blew my mind completely clear!" He paused to catch his breath. "Everything I learned at MIT flew right out the window of Lab 12-N. One of the technicians from Hong Kong gave us a demo of his flying car."

"Flying car? Show me," I said, and we hurried out the door and down the east hall. I remembered seeing a schematic labeled AUTO-CAR 2, but I hadn't studied the polaroids on it yet. This might be it.

At Lab 12-N, Dave introduced me to Jiang Chou, who shook my hand and told me to call him Jim.

"Jim was a design engineer on the SST project in England," Dave said as we followed the Chinese to a three-foot-long model resting on a table. Jim picked up the control box and turned it on: The sleek, wingless aluminum car rose slowly and soundlessly from the table.

"It's a prototype, of course," Jim said. "A bit more attention to aerodynamics will improve performance, but this one is nicely stable up to about one hundred twenty knots." With his little remote control box, he held it motionless and still silent, about twenty inches above the table. "Its range," he continued, "is rather short just yet because I'm using broadcast power."

His speech was standard British English, with just a tinge of Chinese accent.

He flew the car across the lab and out an open window. It accelerated so rapidly that we lost sight of it in seconds as it climbed high over the valley. He brought it back more slowly, positioned it over the table, and gently landed it.

There it sat, ready to operate on the surface like any other car, the most important advance in aircraft since the Wright Brothers replaced Langley's steam engine with internal combustion.

"How in the world did you make that without knowing what was in the other labs?" I asked, a bit awed.

Jim laughed. "Our supervisor didn't know it, but Wu Chan, who worked on AUTO-DAG, is my cousin. Our families shared a house and, of course, spent a great deal of time talking and speculating together."

"What's your project's name?" I asked.

"MAG-PRESS," he said, smiling. "Happily, our supervisor was entirely an administrative type, bothering us only when he brought additions to our manuals, or came to witness scheduled tests. He scarcely knew a spanner from a hammer, and never troubled to examine our work.

"At any rate, I had an inspiration one day, unbolted the press head, and turned it over. It very nearly knocked a hole in the ceiling! As a matter of fact it would have, except the power cable was too short.

"From there, of course, it required no imagination at all to mate it with circuits from AUTO-DAG, and here you have it." He gestured at the model with a little flourish.

"Marvelous, Jim," I told him. "Come with me and I'll give you the schematics that include the power supply. It's probably close to completion, too."

I led the way into the hall. "The name 'MAG-PRESS' was a piece of misdirection," I added, "to keep you from knowing the real purpose of your project. Your ex-boss was calling it AUTO-CAR 2. What would you name it, if it were up to you?"

"I must confess to thoughts about product development and marketing," he said. "I'd recommend naming it 'Expando-Car.' I have six children, you see. And it would have been damnably convenient to have a car that comes apart in the middle, for adding sections and seats."

Expando-Car. Not very elegant, I thought, at least for the American market, but the expansion idea was great.

"Good idea, Jim—let the car grow with the family." I found the photo-schematics for AUTO-CAR 2, and Jim took them back to his lab.

Just after he left, someone arrived with a serving cart of sandwiches and drinks. I took a ham and Swiss with 7-Up, and settled down to sort out what else we were supposed to be making. The first photo in the stack of gloat-list schematics was for a device called AUTO-MAT. That sounded familiar, but I couldn't place it at first. An hour later I'd sorted out what pieces went into it, most from RED-BOX and PORT-2. I could see how they went together, but at first I didn't have the foggiest notion what Cha had intended for it: the schematics didn't include user instructions. Then the light dawned, with a scene from a movie where a guy takes his girl—to the Auto-Mat for lunch! *Automatic Cafeteria!* But this took it a long step further.

I stared at the plastic plate on my desk, with crumbs and the empty 7-Up bottle. My God! It had never occurred to me that the body could assimilate food from RED-BOX.

El laughed in my head. "Not yet, dear, but soon,

very soon. When Stu's troops get here, we'll eat up our stores pretty quickly."

"But . . . But won't food from AUTO-MAT have a limited persistence? What happens when the molecules and ions assimilated into the body's structure suddenly cease to exist there?"

"It won't work that way. Icons are a sort of separate small reality generator. The personal beingness is a separate little reality of its own, body included, tied in with the grid reality. When the molecules, ions, etc., become part of that reality, they're no longer subject to cancellation.

"See you at seven."

I sat there looking at the concept of everyone in the world eating the same apple. Now that was really mind-boggling! What would it do to apple growers? To food producers of all kinds? To land use? Land values? What had Cha had in mind for it? Surely not the end of hunger and starvation. I'd bring it up in family council.

Next I studied the TELE-VEND schematics. Much of it was yet to be built, and that included the life span selection circuits for holographic products. I glanced up at the credenza where the movers had put my red box, looking for reassurance, but the red box was gone.

Yep, I told myself, we needed that circuit pretty damned soon.

I stayed there and kept at it until El was standing beside me and I realized it was 1900 hours.

"Time to go," she said. She took my hand and we popped.

TWENTY-NINE

We arrived at a conversation pit in a large joint social room which El and I would share with Dak, Kad, Mar, and Stu. Mar and Stu were already there with Sue and Al, talking over drinks.

"The party isn't till nine," El told me, "so we have time to unwind before getting dressed."

Then the twins popped in, looking fresh as rosebuds with dew. "We finished moving NITOR," they announced in unison, "and as much of INDPER as we want. We fudged just a smidgen on NITOR—the marines were arriving at NORTEC—and made a little extra time to do it in while you-know-who pretended not to notice." They poured drinks for themselves. "Now we want to toast you and us, because we are all pretty spiffy. Here's to the eight of us; our hexad has grown to an octad."

"Cheers!" said Sue, and "Cheers!" it was, all around. But we sipped the brandy instead of throwing it down.

"You first, Stu," I said. "Tell us about your day."

He grinned like a wolf in a sheep pen. "It was touch and go for a bit in the mountains outside Skopje this morning. Mar and I had just finished organizing to evacuate all sensitive material to New Zealand when we got word that twenty tanks were coming up the only road to the lab.

"Apparently someone had leaked something to the Yugoslav government; I have no idea what. The separate projects and what they meant were as obscure there as they were everywhere else, and it was too soon for a military reaction to any possible leak about evacuation.

"Anyway, our paramilitary CO was ready to take on the tanks with his antitank rockets, although he only had a hundred troops. But he cooled off in a hurry when Kad told him we could teleport people."

Stu paused to sip his brandy. "I'd liked to have seen the expression on the tank commander's face when he walked in to find the place wrecked and no one there. It's the only place we had to destroy when we left."

It occurred to me that if—when—some government discovered where we were now, the word would spread overnight, and most of the world was going to be instantly acquisitive of the power our technology represented. Our little mercenary army wasn't going to mean much then.

"How did it go at Hong Kong?" I asked.

Dak answered that one. "A company of Royal Marines arrived when we were almost through with the move, and the officer in charge demanded we open up and surrender. When we didn't answer, his demolitions expert opened up for us. Very deftly, too. The leftenant was just touching my shoulder when I popped out with the Port-1 transmitter. I did leave him the bolts for the pad, though."

"Every government in the world will have heard about that by morning," I said, "if the international espionage network is worth anything at all."

"It is," El said, "despite its bureaucratic stupidities." Then she looked at Mar.

"My turn?" Mar asked.

"All yours."

"Well, after leaving all the fun in Skopje, I helped Al and Sue load our new computer. When we called up BUCLEPUK, all we could get was a crazy-looking equation over and over, no matter what we asked.

"I was trying to sort it out, and wishing Le was there to help us call up Dawn, when the screen changed. The new read said, 'Dawn here, Le agree, BUC say try new disc.' There must have been a very minor flaw in the disk, which the computer somehow failed to identify. Anyway, after Al changed to another drive for on/off loading, PUK came on line.

"I'd begun to think of that routine as something magic— something other than computer technology—but if it is, it's still tied to the hardware. I'm not sure whether to be relieved or disappointed."

She paused to sip her drink. "Next, I took time to look over the BUCLEPUK teaching aids: They're the most beautifully designed courses I've ever seen. The teacher, instead of being the center of attention, becomes basically an aide to the student.

"Each student tackles theory independently, at his or her own pace. When they feel they understand it, they do one or more exercises to fully apply the theory—exercises that require creative understanding to pull off. The aide checks the exercises and the understanding. The student, if she has it one hundred percent, goes on to the next section; otherwise, she goes back to the theory to get whatever she missed. There are no grades: the student grasps it one hundred percent before she continues.

"The package includes a lesson plan for the aide on the theory and application of individual learning management, and repair procedures for all kinds of study difficulties.

"Our kids are going to love it; students of every age will. All the pressure is off, and when they're done, they've got it, and they know they've got it. Every step of the way." She looked at El. "And that's it for me. What did you do, mom?"

El laughed. "I visited several scared bankers; evidently Cha had programmed them to panic on cue. They'll be okay, though." She turned to Al. "How do you like your new arrangement?"

He squeezed Sue's hand. "Couldn't be better. And speaking of banks, we found another computer access code file devoted exclusively to financial institutions. I hadn't been able to visualize how BUC could have an equation for the lists we found earlier, and certainly not for over twenty thousand banks. I was getting ready to call it up, when Sue noticed the SWAC files were being accessed. Sue asked PUK to invent a way for BUC to do that, and found out it's an equation that can hide files within files. It's name is EASTER EGG, and it uses the routine disc verification program. Anyway, that blows a lot of the confusion I had about 'no memory,' and I feel better about BUCLEPUK now. As far as 'magic' is concerned, I suppose I'm happier when I see a rationale behind it."

When Al was done, I told them about the AUTO-CAR 2, AUTO-MAT, and TELE-VEND projects, and we discussed some of the possibilities for them, ending up all the way out in interstellar space.

It was El who brought us back to Earth; she looked at her watch. "Girls and boys," she announced, "it's time to dress for the party. Some of the Neptune South people will be there, including Buc and Puk." She rose to go.

"Where's our apartment?" I asked her.

"Up front." El took my hand, and this time we left in the conventional way. She led me through sliding glass doors onto a balcony overlooking an indoor garden about thirty feet below, and across a suspended walk to our third-floor apartment.

There she kissed me. "Take a shower," she said softly, "and we'll see about getting rid of your 'pop lag.'"

I did and we did.

The party was in the main building—a marvelous buffet supper followed by visiting in the lobby behind the tower. Buc and Puk looked great, and helped stir up more memories of "the good old days." I think El must have told others to come by and check us out, because we got hugged and kissed a lot. The Neptune people are strong on hugging and kissing, which is pretty good stuff when you're feeling good and want to. They were the right people to send Buc to; he'd been in lousy shape after Annapolis.

After the party broke up at midnight, we went back to our community living room for a nightcap. El started the conversation.

"You guys have a lot of unanswered questions about the Vega Run thing that BUCLECPUK kept bringing up," she said. "The twins are now going to break the logjam."

They got up in graceful unison. "One picture is supposed to be worth a thousand words," they said together, "but in this case they'll be worth more like a million." With that they spun around and transformed into Vegans dressed in hostess uniforms. I glanced at Al and Sue: they hadn't batted an eyelash at that. Mar's little talk with Al must have been pretty effective, while with Neptune South trained and launched by Puk, I could see that Sue might be hard to startle with something like that.

First the twins did the fashion show bit for us and then sang an old Vegan love song. I couldn't follow the lyrics—I'd lost that language a long time ago—but I knew it was a love song, and the logjam came loose. I remembered: There really is a race of bird people.

We sat in silence for a while before El broke our reveries. "That's right," she said. "The human types include bird people and cat people. Among others. And the Vega Run visited all of them.

"When we do go out among the stars again, we'll find them there yet. We have a lot of old guilts associated with them, all the worse because of the old loves also associated with them. Which is why mankind has so strongly suppressed memory that they exist. Now finish your drinks. We all have some old equations to balance tonight."

Afterwards, I went to sleep very well balanced, with El, in her version of Vegan hostess, lying close. At 0605 I came wide awake, alone. It was time to get up, but I lay back down for a little, groping for something in a dream I'd been having. I couldn't get much of it back, but enough.

After that I checked the ready room, then put on my robe and slippers and went to the kitchen. The whole gang was seated around our table having coffee: not only El, Stu, Mar, and the twins, but Al and Sue. I was pretty sure it was no coincidence that they were all there. El would know what I'd just learned, probably knew in advance, and had invited the others for a breakfast briefing.

All eyes moved to me as I entered, and for a moment no one said anything. El motioned me to sit by her, and poured me some coffee.

"What happened, Le?" Stu asked.

I didn't answer immediately, looking at it again while I stirred in sugar and rich New Zealand cream.

"A dream," I said. "When I woke up I couldn't remember much of it, but the Mujinn was in it—that's the She that we think of as the Valley. Only, in my dream She was being a tall, beautiful negress—royal looking.

"And She told me to build a dome. She said it three times: 'Build a dome.' "

Carefully I sipped the hot coffee, then continued. "After I woke up and remembered that, I wondered if there was anything to it, and what it might mean. So I checked my battle board."

I looked at Al and Sue. "You two don't know about my battle board. Just accept the fact that I have one that shows current enemy activity. El and the twins can vouch for it."

I looked around at the entire gathering.

"Anyway," I said, "I found bogeys, from the Sea of Okhotsk to Singapore, from Oahu to Manila Bay. The nearest are stationary, docked at Tonga and Tasmania. The farther ones—the units off the Sakhalin Peninsula and south of Oahu and Singapore and Manila—are under way, headed in this direction. All in all it looks as if a task force of surface ships is gathering, and it looks as if they're coming here.

"Judging from the locations, and just by the feel of it, they're U.S., British, and Soviet. At this time, anyway, the Aussies and New Zealanders don't seem to be involved, and probably don't know about it. And I doubt if we'll be attacked until the Soviet carrier and its escort get here from about seven thousand miles north. If the others moved on us without waiting for them, I'm sure the Kremlin would consider that grounds for war."

"Why would that be?" Sue asked.

"They all want our technology. If the U.S. or British got it and the Russians were left out, the Russians would move on them quickly, before they could do anything with it."

"I get the picture," she said.

"Now, I don't know much about the speed of today's naval vessels, but the feeling I have is that we've got about ten days before the task force takes any action. I expect their planned sequence is an ultimatum to surrender, to be followed if necessary by an attempted takeover by airborne marines, with a conventional aerial attack in support if that doesn't do it, and a nuclear attack to cauterize the site if they can't get their hands on what's here."

The room was quiet but not heavy.

I turned to El. "There are some things I don't understand, though. First, what the Mujinn meant by 'build a dome'? What kind of dome would suffice? And second, how it's okay for Her to advise; it seems like that would be against regulations.

"And third, how they found where we are. I mean, I realize the arrivals from D.C., Hong Kong, etc., could have been picked up by satellite; in fact, a satellite in polar orbit shows up now as a bogey on the battle board. And someone could have connected sudden appearances here with sudden disappearances elsewhere at the same time—especially with a nudge or two from some of Cha's stooges. But if She could protect her valley from prospectors and reporters and general snoopers, why not from the attention of the whole world?"

"The situation is different now," El replied. "Before we came here, this valley was part of no game, in the sense of contest, and no war. When we arrived, that changed; a different set of rules apply now.

"And the Mujinn herself is not involved in our game, as such. Her personal interest is in her valley, although She has other functions. So I doubt very much that She advised you. I suspect what She did was nudge you a little, causing you to create your own dream, and you came up with 'build a dome' yourself."

Okay," I said, "then we'll build a dome. After breakfast, let's go to the computer room and ask PUK about domes."

"You needn't go to the computer room," Sue said. "I had a terminal installed here in your apartment."

El got up and led us through the living room, where she touched a small nacre plate near one corner. A wall slid aside to reveal a computer center; there was even a computer-driven mechanical drafting table.

"Mar," I said, "would you do the honors?" She nodded and sat down at the console. When PUK came on line she turned to me.

"How do you want it worded?"

"Ask for a screen to protect the valley."

She identified herself and wrote the request,

[Read:] HOW BIG?

[Write:] 4 × 12 MILES.

[Read:] AGAINST WHAT, MAR?

[Write:] INVASION BY TROOPS, BOMBS, MISSILES.

[Read:] HECK, MAR. THAT'S BIG MEGAHERTZ. IF GRAND COULEE DAM IS NOT CLOSE, IT CAN'T BE MAGNETIC.

[Write:] HOW THEN?

[Read:] EASY WITH GRAVITY BUT ROOTS NOT IN BUC. AND NOT ENOUGH ON LIFE FORCE. SORRY, MAR.

[Write:] THANKS, PUK, ET AL. BYE.

"I'll try the flip side," She said.

[Write:] PUKLEBUC.

[Read:] DAWN HEAR. NOT NEED MEGAS. TELL LE USE OLD GOTHTAI FLIP-TOP BOX GAMBIT.

[Write:] EXPLAIN.

[Read:] NO. DAWN SHOW. LE LIE DOWN.

As soon as Dawn wrote "Gothtai," I felt vague memories stirring. I lay down on the couch, closed my eyes, and let Dawn show me in rapid scan the one she had in mind. "Thanks, Dawn," I said aloud when she was done.

[Read:] LE WELCOME. DAWN SHOW GOOD?

"Yes, Dawn, that was a good show." *Wild*, I thought. *Dawn has better access to my memory than I do.*

[Read:]   TONIGHT DAWN SHOW LE MERGIRL
ON CELEK II?

Mar laughed.

[Write:]   YES, DAWN, SHOW HIM AND US
TOO. BYE AND TALK TO YOU LATER.

She turned off the console.

So fish people are another of the human types El referred to. We went back to the table, where I told them about the Gothtai flip-top box gambit during breakfast.

"I'd been discharged," I began, " 'at the convenience of the government,' in a sectorwide economy drive that put most of the fleet in mothballs. And because a true warrior will never work for a living if he can help it, I took my bust-out pay and bought a long-range, two-man recon scout too old to be worth the cost of mothballing. Even to start with, she could be flown solo if she had to be, and with a few creative modifications, single-handing her was no sweat.

"With that I became a smuggler, and not just the rumrunning variety. I'd go anyplace, buy or receive anything I could take aboard, and deliver it anywhere, or damn near.

"So there I was on my last leg to Gothtai IV, with, among other things, a few cases of mag motors that lacked tax stamps, when out of nowhere a Trask cruiser hailed me; I'd arrived during an invasion. There's nothing like a big economy push and cutting back the military to bring on a war."

I paused to eat another forkful of waffle and wash it down with coffee.

"Well, with twelve million tons of cruiser reaching for your scalp, you do what you can, and what recon scouts can do especially well is evade and run; they're designed for it. So I veered off and into a dense zone of asteroids—only a few hundred kilometers between rocks of enough mass to waste a cruiser. The only way they'd take her in there would be very, very carefully, to match direction and velocity with the vector of the asteroids, and that wouldn't catch me."

"That throw them off, did it?" Stu asked.

"I couldn't know at the time. If they decided I was

worth the trouble—worth sending fighters after—I was still in serious trouble. But I'd bought some time. So I parked the recon on a fair-sized chunk of rock, not knowing if I was out of it or what."

I paused for coffee, and the way Al and Sue were looking at me, they weren't sure if I was putting them on or not.

"I must have been a lot smarter in those days," I went on, "because it only took me about five seconds to review my resources and invent a defense. I didn't have a PUK INVENT program or a Dawn with me then, either."

El snickered, and the twins crowed right out loud. I ate some more waffle in silence, to recover my poise; laughter at the wrong point can spoil a good adventure yarn.

"Anyway—and hats off to any unknown assistants— what I did was open a crate of magmotors, cousins to the ones in our Auto-Car 1, and lay them out in a circle around the recon. Turning them on also anchored them, because the asteroid was nickel-iron. Then I took my holo-chess player outside and adjusted it to cast a mirror on the dome-shaped magnetic field created by the motors."

I paused to add syrup to my waffle. "And what happened then?" Sue asked.

I put away a couple more forkfuls before answering. "I stayed under that dome for a week before turning it off for a quick peek outside. A very quick peek, in the nano-second range, although it seemed unlikely that bogeys would still be hanging around to blast me. I checked my recording scanner, and the area was clean." I shrugged. "And that's the end of the story."

"But how did a circle of magnetic fields make a dome?" Stu asked.

"When two or more interactive magnetic fields are exactly in tune, they'll auto-collate to form a single spherical field. That effect hasn't been noticed lately because we haven't been able to make precisely identical magnets, but with Red-Box we can."

"Okay," Stu said, still not satisfied. "I can see that

happening if the circle is small, but how could we use magmotors on a valley this size? What would you use for power?"

"Let's back up a step first," I said. "On the asteroid, the trick was using my holo-chess player. She was both an electromagnetic and a life forcic pattern, which interacted with the magnetic output of the motors.

"You see, the cruiser did send fighters, and my holo-chess player knitted and cast an inpenetrable net *with the energy of their assault beams*. They supplied the power I didn't have for battle screens. Bombs would have served just as well."

Stu looked even more confused. I waited. "Maybe my problem is that I don't know what you mean by knitting and casting," he said.

I nodded. "The idea I had that led to the SWAC project involved casting a holographic image on a magnetic net. I used a maser—electromagnetic energy in the invisible part of the spectrum—for the net and the screen, and a laser for the visual image. Casting means that each laser pulse was indexed to a specific maser net junction, or pixel. It was intended as a device to make holography simpler—only one projector—and the images more realistic-looking.

"Well, in this instance, my holo-chess player just happened to be a gal who could knit energy screens."

"Gal?" He shook his head, still confused. "But you said she used the incoming energy of their assault beams, right? And the beams would be coming at something like the speed of light, plus the velocity of the fighters. How could she do it quickly enough?"

"Remember, the dome-shaped magnetic field was already there before the fighters arrived. The first assault beam provided the power with which she knit and cast the actual dome, and the next two or three beefed it up. The rest were reflected.

"And as far as speed is concerned, remember, we're talking about an icon, in this case a holo-icon, and she worked with thought, which can be enormously faster than light. One moment your thought can be here, and an instant later it can be somewhere the other side of the Andromeda Galaxy."

Stu was examining something mentally, and gradually his frown cleared, his head nodding slightly. *He's remembering,* I thought to myself.

"For her," I added, "it was just a matter of knowing in advance exactly what needed to be done, and how to do it. And being ready, of course."

"What's this 'her' and 'she' business?" Sue asked curiously. "I thought you had an electronic chess game."

"El, would you show them what a holo-chess icon is?" I asked.

"I would," she answered, "but Kad and Dak want to."

The twins jumped up, went two-dimensional, rotated slowly a few times to show off, then merged as Dak, went three-dimensional, returned to two-dimensional, and split apart again.

"Now we want to show you," they said together, "what that shameless warrior did to a lovely young thing. Besides calling her names like 'holo-chess player.'" Dak produced a small silver flip-top box, seemingly from thin air, and opened the lid. Kad went two-dimensional, rotated to a threadlike line which then merged to a tiny ball, and moved into the box.

Dak put the box in her pocket then and did a skit about being a bored space jockey just waking up from a nap. Taking the box out of her pocket, she pressed a stud on it. The lid popped open and Kad came out, turning three-dimensional. She'd turned herself into an exact image of my old holo-chess player.

With exaggeratedly robotic motions and a sugar-sweet voice, she came toward me. "Hey, you big handsome lover!" she purred. "Do you want to play chess with lil ole me, or do you prefer sweeter games?" She nuzzled my neck and whispered in my ear. I swatted her rump.

"See how he misused that girl?" she said, pointing at me. "And then, as a final insult, he made her knit him a bubble!"

"There you have it, gang," I said. "But while admittedly I *was* a bastard, I had no idea that holo-girls were people, too. Wherever she is, I apologize, and thank her for saving my ass."

"Accepted and you're welcome, I'm sure," El said, smiling. "Okay, who'll volunteer to do some knitting?"

"Wait, mom," Mar protested, "you've got us mystified. Who was the holo-chess player? Was it Dak or Kad? Or you?"

"That, my dear," El said, "will have to remain a mystery. We witches can't tell everything. Besides, why exclude yourself or Sue? Now, back to my question."

"I'll be the knitter," Sue chimed in. "I'm not sure just what it entails, but I think I'll like it." She stood, Dak and Kad joining her.

"Fine," El said. "First we'll have to produce a holo-icon of you." She sensed Al's concern at that, and turned to him. "Don't worry, Al," she said, "there won't be two Sues. Just one Sue with two icons—two bodies."

"And an icon with a cursor can't handle the job," I added. "Basically, a cursor would get in the way."

El went to Sue and touched her. Sue the cursor, an orb of pale golden light, moved out of her body, went over to Al and touched him on the face, then went to sit on Dak's shoulder. Kad walked to Sue's body and touched the forehead. The icon twinned, each twin instantly generating a body, and two Sues stood there face to face. Then the new one moved to El and sat on the arm of the couch, while Cursor Sue merged back with her body.

"Wow! That was really neat!" Sue said, and looked at Al. "Could you see me? Did you feel me kiss you? I could see all of you really clearly."

Al looked a bit stunned.

The other Sue, the holo-icon, went over and sat down on the other side of him. "Hi, Al," she said, "call me Holo Sue. And don't fret; I love you, too. You and Sue both. I'd never hurt either of you." Al relaxed at her clear sincerity. Icon Sue stood then, said she'd meet me in the lab when I was ready, went two-dimensional, and vanished.

Stu looked thoughtful. "You mean female icons used to come packaged as instant toys?"

"Right," I said. My attention went to a schematic on my desk, coded HOLO-PLAYMATE. I shuddered, remembering what society might do with them.

"Dears," El said, "Dak and I have to leave now to mend some fences of our own, of the nonmagnetic, legal, and political kind. We'll be gone all day, but you can call if you need us." She and Dak left the room, to return seconds later in very sharply tailored suits and carrying briefcases. El pecked me a kiss and turned to the group. "Bye all; we're off to see some lawyers." They popped.

Kad got up, too. "I have to go rescue some families someone decided to hold hostage," she said, and then she popped. Then the others left, and I sat there alone.

I looked at the battle board in my ready room and saw elements of the three greatest navies on the planet coming after me, not to mention a spy plane passing over South Island in the stratosphere. *Hell,* I thought, *you guys are nothing compared to Cha.* And with that, my battle screen changed to show the solar system, with eleven bogeys sitting just outside Pluto's orbit—eleven Galactic-class battle wagons.

What's a good-looking warrior like me doing with this kind of attention? I asked myself, grinning. I couldn't remember ever having felt more vibrant and alive, or more pleased with myself. For a moment the realization surprised me, and I felt the grin getting wider, without really knowing or caring why. Lying down on the couch, I closed my eyes, viewing the solar system as my own personal playground. A *real* warrior is happiest with a battle in the offing—one that will stretch hell out of him to win.

Little Jack Horner sat in a corner . . . The old nursery rhyme ran through my head. "What a good boy am I," I murmured to myself. "I stuck in my thumb and pulled out a plum." Then laughed. Not a plum. Peaches: a whole bushel of them, but one in particular.

THIRTY

Meanwhile, I had things to do. It looked as if BUCLEPUK was going to require a little managing if he was to invent what we needed with no more than he had to work with. And here was an opportunity to get back into what I liked best—creating.

Having a computer terminal right in my apartment, complete with drafting table, I decided to work at home. That way I wouldn't have to wait and I could work in my skivvies. So after a shower and shave, I booted up the computer and began.

[Write:] HI, PUK. LE HERE. I NEED A MAGNETIC FENCE TO SURROUND A VALLEY OF ABOUT 48 SQUARE MILES.

[Read:] HI, LE. HOLD FOR ROOT SEARCH. SORRY, LE. ALL OUR DATA ROOT LINES ARE OUT. CALL MA BELL FOR US.

[Write:] PUK, MA BELL WENT OUT OF BUSINESS AND THE LIBRARY BURNED DOWN. NEED FENCE.

[Read:] OK. I WILL USE CALAMITY ROOT BYPASS. HOW DO YOU WANT IT?

[Write:] SCHEMATICS AND ENGINEERING DRAWING ON DEKHART DRAFTING TABLE THIS TERMINAL.

[Read:] OFFLOAD AND START.

The drafting table began the drawing with textbook-lettered title—LE'S GOAT FENCE—and finished quickly.

[Read:] NEXT?

Let's see now. I needed to put this in a way that PUK could receive and work on under the circumstances, but I couldn't seem to see the handle. Then my fingers moved on the keypad as if subliminally directed.

[Write:] NEED A HOLO-WORKER WITH ABILITY TO PICK MAGNETIC LOCKS.

I read it as it appeared on the screen and hadn't the foggiest idea of what I'd intended. But I felt great about it.

[Read:] YOU MEAN A HOLO-PLAYMATE GOATHERDESS WHO CAN WALK THROUGH FENCE?

[Write:] YES.

Why not? I certainly had nothing more promising to suggest.

[Read:] WAIT. WORKING.

I went to get another cup of coffee and came back just as the schematic appeared on the screen. While I watched, it scrolled off and the parts lists appeared. They had NITOR catalogue numbers: Dak must have brought the NITOR discs with her, and someone, Al or Mar, had loaded them.

That's when I realized what had happened—what BUCLEPUK had done. None of us knew how it was programmed, and initially it hadn't displayed parts lists— not till Mar had coaxed PUK into it. So BUCLEPUK could reprogram itself!

I laughed, remembering my deconditioning period when I'd been running around looking for the "reprogramming facility." Hell, you carry one around with you all the time: yourself—the only one who can really do it.

I pulled my attention back to the job.

[Read:] LE, DO YOU NEED A HOLO-HAY-STACK, TOO?

Holo-haystack? What kind of conceptual imagery was that crazy PUK using now? Probably about what I deserved, considering what I'd asked for.

[Write:]   NO THANK YOU. I NEED A HOLO-
MIRROR, SIZE 4×4 FEET. PROJEC-
TOR RANGE 7 MILES.

[Read:]   IS HOOVER DAM CLOSE?

[Write:]   NO!

[Read:]   TELL US YOUR PLAN.

Not so easy, considering I didn't consciously know. I sat there with my mind blank for a moment until my fingers began to type again.

[Write:]   I WANT TO PROJECT THE ILLUSION
OF AN ENERGY STORM ABOVE
GOATHERDESS AND GET HER TO
RUN TO BARN FOR COVER.

I hoped it meant more to PUK than it did to me at any conscious level.

[Read:]   WAIT. WORKING.

The drawing arm moved rapidly; then the drafting-table bell rang. I removed the finished schematic, inserted a blank sheet, and punched *Reset* on the drafting table.

[Read:]   LE, YOU ARE NOW THE PROUD
OWNER OF A HOLO-RAMA.
OFFLOADED AND SCHEDULED.
HOW ABOUT A SMALL HOLO-HAY-
STACK FOR THE BARN LOFT IF YOU
ARE GOING TO BE ALONE THERE
WITH THE GOATHERDESS?

[Write:]   NO THANKS, GUYS. FINISH UP AND
THAT WILL BE IT FOR NOW.

Damn! BUCLEPUK might be auto-reprogrammable, but how had it come by a lascivious imagination without glands or social background? Had Cha programmed in personality elements of Buc and Puk and I, as he saw us? Or had he figured to distract me with sexual thoughts?

And were BUCLEPUK and Dawn being so helpful because Cha intended them to be? Was I following some Cha-prepared script? Was I getting paranoid?

No, suspicion was rational for anyone playing with Cha. Meanwhile, I'd just continue playing things by ear.

While the printer printed up the rest of the schematics and parts lists, I began dressing. Then I rolled up the lists and drawings and started for the lab. I'd heard someone mention a subway between the apartment village and the main building, but I didn't know where the terminal was or how to use it, and the morning was lovely, so I started down the landscaped walk. It was chillier than I'd expected—a clean, bright New Zealand winter morning—but more invigorating than uncomfortable, and the brisk walk did me good. I'd forgotten all about working out and running lately. There was probably a Nautilus gym or two around here somewhere; I'd ask El or one of the twins.

I found Dave in his office, reading. "When you're ready for a break from studies," I told him, "come and see me. I've got some new projects to start."

"I can put this down now if you'd like."

I could see from his face that he'd really rather finish what he was doing. "No hurry. It's not ready for you yet. This afternoon."

"Is two o'clock okay? I ought to done with this by then. Dr. Anderson gave it to me and told me to know it. And I can see why. She called it a second grade primer, and I suppose it is. Powerful but simple! I don't know why they didn't have something like this at the university . . . or maybe I do."

"Two o'clock or thereabouts is fine," I told him. "Tell you what: I'll call you."

I went into my office and studied the drawings and schematics, to determine how best to divide up the work and to see which parts we already had among the extras.

By noon I had six two-man teams assigned to build the new stuff, and two teams to round up the existing components. Then I found Jim and his cousin and told them we needed a vehicle to lay cable for the magnetic fence and to transport the holo-rama device.

"Can you take care of that?" I asked.

"Certainly," Jim said. "We'll modify one of the dollies for flying and make as many copies as we need at the last minute. Wouldn't do for them to, ah, go home the way those red boxes have." His face was oriental but his grin not at all inscrutable. "Certainly not while someone's flying them."

"Sounds good," I said. "What help do you need?"

"Parts fetchers from the warehouse should suffice."

"Fine. I'll leave it to you," I said, and left.

Back in my office, I settled into studying schematics, making notes as I went, occasionally asking PUK's help on something. I loved it; it was one of the things I'd enjoyed so much for so long—the sort-out-and-assimilate phase of research, where a bunch of "stuff" begins to take on structure and as-yet-unseen ideas start to form.

Then Dak popped in with a tray of sandwiches and Pepsis. It was midafternoon, and I'd gotten so engrossed I'd forgotten to have lunch.

"El and Kad are busy, so we get to eat alone today," she said, setting the tray on my conference table. We dug in. Dak seemed to be in a quiet mood, so I enclosed my attention and began to play with the schematics again in my mind. After a little, though, her voice broke through, interrupting, and suddenly I realized how silent it actually had been, subjectively. I hadn't been hearing the little sounds that go with eating—had forgotten Dak entirely. I looked up at her.

"You feel good about all these creative projects, don't you," she was saying softly. "Just like you did when you began the SWAC project—smug and pleased, really shut away in your own world."

Yeah, just like the SWAC project, back when I didn't have a war bonnet. War bonnet: Suddenly I felt as if I were groping around in the dark for something. A thought formed, very slowly: *You lost it on the couch*.

Lost *it?* On the couch? Then it hit me! My warrior pattern was gone! I'd lost it after I finished telling that damn story about the Gothtai flip-top box gambit. The moment I realized that, I felt it reform.

Dak laughed. "That's right. And without your war-bonnet, you went back to the kind of beingness and doingness you had before. Excessive admiration last night, that's the diagnosis. For a warrior, too much admiration, especially too much self-admiration, is likely to retire him."

. . . and said What a good boy am I, I remembered.

The reality of my office was back to normal, and with my war bonnet in place, naturally I checked the ready-room battle board. "Bogeys!" I said, "and not ten days away, either!" That was what Dak knew I needed to see, the reason she had been so quiet, helping me to catch on. There were eleven of them, but not G-class battle wagons. There were ten relatively small planes and one large one, some three thousand miles northeast over French Polynesia, flying straight toward us from Tahiti. French, of course. Had to be, coming from there. They didn't seem part of the joint naval task force—probably the French hadn't been invited—and apparently were operating on a plan of their own. Since the Mujinn no longer had an attention screen obscuring the valley, they could have examined the place in detail with satellite photos, and planned accordingly. That's no doubt what the US-USSR-UK troika had done, and the French were trying to steal a march on them.

"What's their estimated time of arrival?" Dak asked.

"About 2100 would make sense. Fits their distance and probable speed, and the moon should be well up by then, if my memory of last night is right. But the smaller planes should have to stop and refuel, and I don't know where the hell they could . . . Of course! That's it! The larger plane is an aerial tanker, to refuel the others in flight."

I paused, looking at it. "But that doesn't make sense. Why use planes too small to make the flight without refueling? It's unlikely as hell that they're bombers. The French have nothing to gain by blasting us. They've got to be small troop carriers—VTOLs! The valley floor isn't smooth enough to land and take off from, and they can see we don't have a landing strip here."

"Anything else?" Dak asked.

"Hmm. They must know we have mercenaries here, likely to be highly skilled and well-armed professionals. So they'll probably parachute their troops in—cut their engines a few miles out, come over silently, and drop their people from about ten thousand feet, for maximum surprise. Might save them a pitched battle.

"With only ten small troop carriers, they're probably only sending two or three hundred. That may be all the VTOLS they have available. And they probably know our troops are barracked over by the foothills. They'll want to strike without rousing them, and once they control the main building and the apartment complex, presumably our own military will hold back and dicker with them."

I was gaining certainty as I talked. "They're figuring on a quick strike—round up as much technical material as they can, capture some technical personnel, and get out as soon as possible, before the New Zealand armed forces jump on them. From what I've read and heard of the New Zealanders, they're damned prickly about the integrity of their territory. And they're especially touchy about the French.

"VTOLs would be a necessity for quick evacuation. Their troops will drop near the main building, on the east side, away from the living units. And with the moon up, they'll land maybe as much as a mile away to avoid being accidentally seen. Take the main building, get what they can, and call in the VTOLs.

"You've spotted the basics," Dak said. "It's a crack French commando unit with the new Dessault VTOLs; they've been in Tahiti on a steep-terrain jungle training exercise. The terrain around here will be like a city park after the mountains of Tahiti."

I nodded. We were up against it. Warned as we were, we could undoubtedly repel them. The challenge was to do it without a lot of bloodshed and damage. "Thanks, Dak, for waking me up," I told her. "We'll be ready for them."

"I'll go alert Stu," she said. "You have a thing or two to take care of here before you leave."

She popped then. My warrior pattern was pulsing, preparing my body for the first combat in—days! It had only been *days* since the gunfight outside Dover and the confrontation at Annapolis. So much had happened since then, it seemed three weeks, at least. As I was making a mental note to check the ready room every hour, Dave walked in.

"I'm ready for that project," he said.

"Projects," I corrected. I knew now, in a general way, how we'd handle the French assault. "I want you to monitor several projects at once; I'll call you in the next hour or sooner and give you the details. By 'monitor' I mean just be there in case someone needs help. Otherwise, hands off; watch quietly and casually. Be unobtrusive. And call me if there are any real snags; I'll try to keep Norma informed on where I am. But don't call me unless you feel it's necessary.

"Meanwhile, stay by your phone till I call."

He left. I picked up my phone and told Norma where I expected to be, but not why, then headed for Stu's office. The six weeks were down nearly to five, I told myself. Then there'd be another meeting with Cha, if the joint task force didn't get us first. I wasn't worried about the French any longer.

I never got to Stu's office; Dak waylaid me in the hall. We stepped into an empty lab and popped instead to his auxiliary office, at our paramilitary headquarters. He was waiting, forewarned, and she left us alone with our problems.

We needed our own aerial strike force, and Jim, although he didn't know it, was already working on it. Without saying anything to our troop commander about the impending attack, we took an electric runabout and hurried to Jim's lab. The freight dolly he was adapting for flight was six by twelve feet, and he was already assembling a suitable Auto-Car 2 power unit.

We told him what our problem was, and that we wanted to knock out the attackers while they were still falling and relatively helpless. Yes, he said, if he could have certain lab techs to help him, he could have it ready to fly, and to copy, by 2000 hours, complete with controls and with chest-high steel-plate sides to turn small-arms fire. In fact, he could have it by 1900 hours, and probably sooner.

The next question was suitable weapons. I had no desire to massacre a French commando unit. In fact, I didn't want a firefight at all if I could help it. We thought of several possibilities that weren't practical because of the limited time available. But it wasn't long before we'd worked out the "how to" on that, also.

Meanwhile, I'd forgotten about Dave. I picked up the phone in Jim's lab and called him.

At 2115 hours, Stu and I were on our command craft, a quarter mile east of the main building and 100 feet above ground.

Of our 1,004 mercenaries, all pros, all well briefed, 600 were in 150 identical flying dollies. They'd been fully receptive to our plan. Few if any wanted to kill Frenchmen. The French commandos weren't a hated enemy; they were other pros, whom they held in respect.

The battle board showed eight of the ten small troop carriers approaching the valley at several elevations above five thousand feet. They'd split up—followed various divergent courses for about an hour, spreading out. Now they were approaching us on several more or less different flight paths. I'm sure they didn't think this would fool the New Zealand radar defenses, but it should puzzle them and would probably delay an armed response. Without a doubt there were already some hot radio inquiries and demands reaching Paris from Washington, London, and Moscow, and without doubt they were all getting the runaround from the French government.

(It turned out later that the U.S. Air Defense Command didn't notify the New Zealanders of the satellite reports; the New Zealand Air Force learned of the intruders only when they came within radar range.)

At the same time, the French command was probably beginning to question the wisdom of what must have been a hasty decision and a set of undoubtedly jackleg plans. I wouldn't have been surprised even then if they'd turned around and headed for home without jumping. The New Zealand Air Force's Harrier fighters out of Christchurch or Dunedin could have been scrambling at that moment. But the French have never been strong on admitting mistakes until after the fat was in the fire.

Well, I thought, we'd give them some real post-operation regrets.

The aerial tanker had refueled the troop carriers a thousand miles northeast, and turned back to Tahiti. Another was outbound now to refuel the troop carriers on their homeward leg. The ninth and tenth troop carriers were off the coast a hundred miles; my guess was that one of them held technical personnel to be brought in and landed when the site was secured, and they were also to take out captured personnel and equipment.

I was watching my battle board almost constantly now. The carriers' various flight paths all would take them over the valley within a five-minute period. The first two were drawing near, and clearly had cut their engines; otherwise, we'd have heard them. Then I had a whole new set of bogeys, emerging from the sides of first one and then the second, about fifty in all: The troops were jumping. I spoke orders into my wrist radio (shades of Dick Tracy!), and forty of the flying dollies lifted to 800 feet. Our paramilitary CO was reasonably certain the commandos wouldn't freefall below a thousand feet at night if they didn't think it was necessary.

He was right; on the battle board I could see their chutes begin to open at about two thousand feet. By that time another fifty or so had jumped from two more planes. At once I radioed a command, and our mercenaries lowered their dark goggles. Then I fired my flare gun, and as the flares burst into intense light, to descend under their own small chutes, the dollies moved quickly toward and among the light-blinded jumpers. Rapid-fire dart guns pumped tranquilizer darts, and probably none, or almost none, of the first fifty commandos reached the ground conscious.

You can provide quite an arsenal in a hurry with Red-Box.

Alerted by the flare, some of the second fifty delayed opening until they were lower, some as low as five or six hundred feet, though some opened high, perhaps because, glare-blinded, they couldn't tell how high they were.

And of these, too, most were struck with darts; I had ordered more dollies to interception levels by then, for this second drop was coming down a half mile to a mile south of the first, and was more dispersed as well. Some, forewarned, had closed their eyes to slits or averted their faces, and several had managed to unlimber their automatic weapons as they free-fell, but I had fired more flares, and without goggles, the several who fired, fired blind. Even so, we took our first casualties, which would have been more numerous and severe were it not for the metal shields.

Now the remaining dollies went into action, hunting for commandos who might have landed unhit.

A fifth plane, and then a sixth, dropped their troops. About that time, one commando, who'd reached the ground untouched, radioed that they'd fallen into a trap, a massacre—that as far as he knew, he was the only one alive. And as far as he knew, it was the truth. The remaining planes veered away, to wait offstage for a bit before heading northeast for home.

When it was over, we lit the drop zone with flood-lights, again courtesy of Red-Box, and disarmed and manacled 137 unconscious Frenchmen. Of these, 31 had suffered more or less severe landing injuries—mainly fractures or knee damage—from landing unconscious. Another had been wounded and one killed by the gun-fire of other commandos. Five had been killed by impact with the ground; three of these had never pulled their ripcords, and the other two had pulled them too late, probably because they couldn't see the ground and waited too long. Three had surrendered conscious and unhurt.

Because their platoons consisted of three sixteen-man squads plus an officer and a platoon sergeant, there seemed to be three unaccounted for. I suspect they belonged to the last platoon and had planed freefall out of the drop zone to avoid the obvious welcome party. They probably landed individually and took to the hills solo.

Our own troops had suffered one killed and three

wounded. They'd held discipline well; apparently none had fired anything but darts, in spite of the shooting by several commandos.

Dak and Kad had stayed away, of course, for legal reasons. Dak, in camouflage fatigues, popped into a French military staff meeting at Papeete and told them their commandos were prisoners, mostly unwounded, then popped away when they moved to arrest her. Whatever consolation that may have been to them must have been outweighed by Dak's witchy arrival and departure, and by the confusion and uncertainty engendered by her American-looking uniform.

I went to bed feeling good. The business had gone far smoother and closer to intended results than things like that usually do. I went to sleep quickly, feeling like one high-powered—and lucky—bastard, with no thought at all about what we'd do when the next invasion, the big one, came our way.

I should have known that a warrior should never go to bed feeling that damn good.

THIRTY-ONE

I awoke from a nightmare and let the horror and disgust ebb. It was 0637, and I was alone in bed; El had gotten up. A shower sluiced off more of the dream's grundgy residue, and I went to the kitchen where I found El eating a solitary breakfast.

"Good morning, darling," she said. "The twins are out on playground business, and the others are having breakfast in their apartments."

I kissed her and got a cup of coffee. When I was seated, she asked about my dream.

"It was about the future," I told her, "two or three hundred years from now, I suppose, and instead of a golden age, the world was more like a high-tech cross between *1984* and *Brave New World*. Mankind was totally controlled by a Big Brother type of government—controlled but not downtrodden, or not in a material sense, anyway. Materially they were pampered almost beyond belief: Nearly every material desire was satisfied by the State.

"Only one person out of thousands had any productive activity, yet creative activities were forbidden to all but about one in a million, because the status quo was holy. And all active sports had been abolished as 'stimulating aggressive impulses.' Partying was the big thing; it was all that was left.

"Then a space fleet arrived—humans of the reptile type. Buc, Puk, and I were the only warriors left on Earth; we went out to meet their commander.

"*It was Cha.*"

I paused to let the feeling of disgust pass.

"Cha showed me his plan for the people of Earth and I realized that he had won all along. We had done exactly what he knew we would do. That's when I woke up."

El put her hand on mine. "That, sweetheart, is more than just a dream," she said. "It's a history, and a possible future as well." She paused to drink some coffee. "What was the dream you had just before that one?"

Before that one? I frowned; I didn't . . . Then it jumped out at me and I saw it all at once. Damn! The dome idea had flopped and the combined task force took over the valley. The three admirals were Cha's star puppets; Buc in his General Decker role had been a red herring.

The admirals had decided that the politicians of the world couldn't be trusted with our inventions, and they'd become a ruling trinity. Maybe "troika" would be more appropriate. Our "Big Brothers."

El was looking at me, nodding slightly. "You wouldn't have asked if it wasn't significant," I said. "So I take it the dome idea needs some debugging or it'll fail."

"I can give you one clue," El said evenly. "Remember how your holo-icon could speak fluent Japanese?"

"Yeah. Which means my icon can, too. But I can't speak it now. Or rather *he* can't while we're merged. Hmm . . ." An icon's abilities get blocked when merged with a cursor.

"Meanwhile, I've got a debug job to do." I waited for inspiration and drew a blank. "Ah, well." I looked around. "First things first; namely breakfast. That dreaming is hard work. After that I'll go put together a SWAC and get me an icon to talk to."

As if on cue, one arrived: Holo Sue appeared as a line and went two-dimensional. "Good morning!" she greeted us. "I'm starved, too. May I join you for some two-dimensional eggs?" We laughed, maybe at her tone, maybe at some iconic joke that amused me at a subliminal level. She rotated into three dimensions, poured herself a cup of coffee, and sat down.

"Le, you have a bit of a power problem with the device you designed."

She waited for me to respond.

"I'll fix us some breakfast," I replied, "and you can give me a lesson while we eat."

"Did you ever read Tesla's work?" she asked as I busied myself between fridge and stove.

"No, but I've heard of it."

"You should read and understand him. There's a good bit there about power and what it really is. If you release a rock at five miles above the Earth, it's grabbed by the gravitational vortex and pushed to the Earth at a predictable acceleration."

"I'm aware of that," I said as I broke eggs on the griddle. "That's high-school physics."

"Are you also aware that I said 'pushed' instead of 'pulled'?"

"Pushed?"

"Conventional wisdom has it that the Earth pulls, attracts the rock. The Earth *pulls* nothing. The vortex pulls things which are outside of it. Inside, it pushes. Even after the rock hits the ground, the vortex continues to push on it." She stopped then, letting me look at the idea. I couldn't see a thing there, so I salted the eggs and put muffins in the toaster oven.

"All right," she said after a moment. "What happens to the energy of the push when the rock can no longer move toward the center of the vortex?"

"The rock must push back then, to balance the forces."

"Rocks can't push, Le. They can change states, but they can't push. What would happen in a circuit if you applied a charge to one side of a plate that was nonconductive?"

I had no idea where this was leading. "The charge would continue to build up until it grew enough to discharge at the capacitance limit of the material. Sue, that's simple electricity. How are you comparing it to gravity?"

"The same way Tesla did. The Earth, Le, is a giant capacitor being pumped continually with gravitational energies. In the first nanosecond after our falling rock stopped, it reached its highest energy state. After that, all the gravity that pushes on it is transformed into other energies—including telluric electricity." She paused again, looking at me. "Ah! I see some light dawning!"

"Boy!" I answered. "Did I ever have that one hidden! I just remembered an experimental generator built on Tesla's work in 1917. I read about it in junior high. A boy in Portland, Oregon made an electric boat with a thirty-five horse motor and ran it around the harbor using a capacitor bank charged by his Tesla generator and telluric currents." I paused to turn the eggs, then turned the burners down low. "I wonder why I forgot that so thoroughly? I don't recall thinking about it since I was thirteen."

"Because it's been hidden. It's part of a game, Le—the bankers' game. If electricity were virtually free, they couldn't make money from it, and the game of money is senior to the work of supplying power. Games are *always* senior to work, not necessarily in the importance people attach to them, but *in the rules of this grid*."

If electricity were virtually free. As I buttered muffins, I remembered aloud trying to calculate the power available to the boy in Portland. I couldn't then or now.

Holo Sue laughed. "Long before he approached the

load limit of the gravitational vortex, he would have produced enough heat to melt down his transmitter."

My head was spinning, trying to align divergent theories, till finally the light dawned. "Got it!" I said. "I'd totally overlooked that last night when I was remembering! I'd used telluric electricity on the asteroid. It was enough to knit the dome with, but there hadn't been much to spare. But with the gravitational vortex of Earth, the Auto-Car 1 accumulators I planned to use would draw on the telluric field of the whole damn planet, and *overload* the dome!

"Hell's fire! I need *buffers* instead of boosters!"

Holo Sue was smiling. "All the power we use in this valley is supplied by two Tesla generators, very similar to the one in Portland. And the only reason we have two is that it was easier than laying transmission lines between Neptune South and here. The magnetic fence will supply all the power I need to knit the dome, and then some."

As I transferred the eggs to a platter, El grinned at me too over the crumbs of her own muffin and eggs. "You two have the situation well under control," she said, getting up, "so I'll leave you for now. I have a date in Wellington this morning with a couple of prominent and friendly officials; I don't want the New Zealand government too interested in what we're doing here, or what may or may not have happened last night. Right now Kad is delivering the essentially unwounded commandos to an uninhabited atoll in the Tuamotu chain— it's French—with enough field rations to keep them a while. Dak took a holo-receiver there a few minutes ago; it'll disappear in about three days.

"We want to get our prisoners off our hands, if for nothing more than security reasons, but we don't want them debriefed by the French military command any time soon. If the French government knew what happened here, they might be frightened into something a lot more drastic than a commando raid. Or the troika governments might, when they heard about it. They all know by now that we did something, but as long as they don't know what, it's doubtful they'll opt for a nuclear response.

"Meanwhile, it'll be easy for them to pretend that nothing happened. After all, that's the official French position. There was no assault; there are no prisoners."

"How about the wounded?"

"They're in a makeshift infirmary we've set up, in an underground warehouse we happen to have. Meanwhile, you have a dome to create. Holo Sue, help him redesign it today. I've got to run."

She kissed me goodbye, spun around to dress in her business suit, and popped out.

A warehouse we "happen to have." I shook my head and started to eat.

For several years, El and the twins had occasionally put their pretty fingers into the New Zealand political scene, and we were reaping the result. With a little recurring help from our three witches, the government studiously ignored us. Officially we were a private foundation doing basic research in human potentials, and associated with the Neptune Retreat for Professionals. All of which was true, as far as it went.

The fleet was still two days out when its first reconnaissance flight arrived. Three carrier-based planes with American markings came over shortly after sunup and caught us atop a small rise near the center of the valley. They made several low passes, taking oblique photos, I suppose. About fifty of us, standing around the projection tower, waved at them, and the lead pilot waggled his wings. I suppose they'd heard about our twin love goddesses and their party.

Most of the rest of the valley's population, both from Neptune South and our own people, were on their way to join us, on electrics or on foot.

If the planes had arrived a half hour later, they'd have seen a lot more than they'd bargained for. Just then, though, our flying dollies were still on the ground, parked behind the main building. We'd made a point of not flying any of them around more than absolutely necessary—hardly at all except on the night of the

French raid and on the night we moved the projection tower sections to the construction site. We knew that the valley was under recurring satellite surveillance, and there'd been occasional, unpredictable spy plane flyovers. The sight of electric warehouse dollies flying around might have been too much for the admirals; we didn't want them to get so scared they'd bomb us before we got the dome up.

These were different dollies from the armored version we'd used for defense. Those we'd parked, after the raid was over, until one evening they'd disappeared—ceased to exist as separate objects. We'd used the new model to lay the cable for the magnetic fence about sundown the day before. Holo-cable, actually, which made it temporary, too, although now we could make holo-objects that would last somewhat longer. How much longer was still a question. We'd lay a back-up fence before the week was out, and in the meantime test and calibrate the new life-span circuits.

Late the night before, the holo-rama projector components had been completed. They had been assembled immediately, and we were waiting for thirty holo-copies from Red-Box. Then our dolly pilots would fly down the valley about five hundred feet apart, carrying the projectors which would be Holo Sue's knitting needles. After the dome was up, she'd control it from the tower.

I was as nervous as an expectant father, and to occupy my mind, I reviewed our recent activities.

Our knitting lady, Sue's holo-icon, had designed in some circuits that would let her detect and communicate with any icon who approached the dome, or open a narrow slot in the dome for other communication channels. She would be our eyes and ears to the outside; we wouldn't have to shut down to "take a peep" the way I had on the asteroid. And not only would we be able to maintain communication with the outside world, she could also "escort" guests and materials in and out of the dome.

The navy planes had been gone for almost half an hour when the flying dollies arrived. They looked like something out of an old Flash Gordon movie, with the holo-rama projectors on their beds, and the way they moved made you want to believe they were attached to wires. My battle board showed me there weren't any spy planes overhead just now, but a surveillance satellite was climbing above the north horizon about twenty degrees east of our meridian. I wasn't sure how much it would pick up—whether its optical discrimination was sufficient to distinguish the dollies, but we'd assume it could. If this worked, it wouldn't make much difference either way.

Dave, leading the squadron, pulled his dollies into a loose formation for a flyby. After they'd passed overhead, I looked at Holo Sue, and she shook her head. "Too open," she said, "and too ragged." I raised my wrist radio to my mouth. "Dave, this is Le. Make another practice run. We need your formation tighter and straighter."

"Roger, Le, will do." I heard him talking to his pilots, then the flight turned and headed back north. When they passed over again at 800 feet, they were all in a row, all thirty-one of them, with Dave in the center.

"I'm ready," Holo Sue said to me. "Turn it on and I'll inspect the fence while they're getting into position." She rotated out.

I threw the projection tower switch into the "on" position and locked it. "Okay, Dave, you guys look great. Get set for the knitting run."

"Wow, what a sight!" he said when they reached the south end of the valley. "We can see the fence good from up here. It looks like a large mirrored tube, about fifty feet in diameter." I watched them turn, and he spoke again. "Okay, we've turned on the projectors and we're starting our run."

When they passed over the fence headed north, Holo Sue, in the projection tower, began knitting. The visual effect was shocking, and knowing what to expect didn't help a bit. A gigantic mirrored segment of bubble seemed to grow out of the mountain behind the crystal tower. I felt as if I'd shrunk, standing like a Lilliputian watching some off-stage Gulliver pick up his shaving mirror.

After 500 yards they passed the first buffer and picked up a secondary Tesla pulse. An 800-foot-high concave ghost mirror rushed toward us at a thousand miles an hour; I shrank some more. Most of us around the tower ducked as if the mirror were solid. Every six seconds another ghost mirror rolled over us.

I turned to watch one of them run down the valley and vanish on the fence six miles away. The next one came by as I turned back.

As the dome grew close to us, it looked *very* solid, and I could see the crowd around the tower clearly reflected behind the leading edge. Again the dollies passed over, and again all my senses went to Panicsville, insisting that I duck. Once more I complied.

The leading edge rolled over us, and the flying dollies vanished from sight. The view from beneath the dome was spectacular. Ohs! and Ahs! rose from the crowd: Holo Sue had mirrored the underside, too, and the Earth was wrapped around us. I turned and watched our dome grow toward the north.

El appeared next to me. "I hope you were smiling, darling," she said, "because you were on 'Candid Camera' a moment ago: We've got a spy plane overhead again."

He was getting an eyeful, and so were we; the difference was that we knew what we were seeing. El and I watched for a bit longer, then stopped to kiss. Dak and Kad popped in on either side of us and we joined in a four-way hug. Then the dome was complete, holding reflectively opaque for a moment before going transparent. A few sorrowful "ohs" arose from the crowd at that, and Holo Sue mirrored it again to let them gaze for another minute. What she would do next was switch off the buffers and use the telluric currents to make the dome an impenetrable battle screen, mirrored only on the outside.

When she did it, the screen became opaque again, but not reflective inward. Then she projected a nice blue sky on the underside. *Look what we've got, ma*, I thought, and turned to El.

"Now we've got the time we need," I said. I felt

laughter bubbling up, and let it flow out, the others catching it, until in seconds the whole crowd of hundreds was laughing.

We'd put a microwave dish outside our perimeter, with a cable. Two days later the fleet high command delivered its ultimatum via video. First they showed us their fleet—carriers, rocket-launching cruisers, and three battle wagons from the U.S. Pacific Fleet. I told them no thanks, so they tested the dome with conventional bombs and sixteen-inch guns.

When it became apparent that that wasn't working, they ceased fire and tried the next step, which was an ultimatum, again by video: If we didn't surrender and let them in, they'd starve us out. With a show of boredom, I told them they were welcome to try—that we had the means to feed ourselves indefinitely.

They cut communication then, but for less than an hour. I suppose they talked it over and decided a siege would give the rest of the world time to do something about them; they were operating with the approval of only certain elements of their governments, and only tacit approval at that—approval that could be disavowed and lost when their action became public knowledge, which would happen momentarily. And they were undoubtedly concerned that we might strike at them with some surprise from our bag of advanced technology.

So their next ultimatum included a threat to nuke us. I pointed out that a nuclear explosion here would wreak havoc on a lot of New Zealand real estate, not to mention the people that lived on it, but they weren't impressed. I also told them they'd be wasting their bombs—that they couldn't touch us with them; I thought they might be unwilling to use a nuclear weapon if there was any doubt of its effectiveness. But all they said was that we had six hours to change our minds, so I told them where to shove their bombs. Their faces stiffened, especially the Russian's. Such a retort to a full admiral was almost inconceivable to him. They cut transmission.

I could visualize the New Zealand government trying to evacuate the district, and probably a considerable additional zone downwind from us, which it turned out they were already doing. It seemed obvious that our three admirals were very much Cha's puppets; neither the White House nor the Kremlin, let alone Number 10 Downing Street, was likely to have agreed to a nuclear attack.

When I let my attention return to my surroundings, I saw Dak and Kad smirking, and El seemed entirely serene.

"What," I demanded, "do you know that I don't? If they drop an H-bomb on us, even a clean one, it's going to waste the countryside, even though it can't touch us."

"It won't if it doesn't go off," Dak said blandly.

El laughed. "We foresaw this and took it up ahead of time with the DUO-HEX. There's a Maori reservation on the other side of the west ridge, and the clans that live there have nothing to do with this war of Cha's. Since the bomb can't harm us, we got Its agreement, right up front: The twins can handle any nukes in their own sweet way."

I'd have loved to know what sweet way that was, but they wouldn't tell me any more then—said I'd have to wait until after the fact.

"After the fact" came seven hours later. I'd been walking Dave step by step through the principles of BUCLEPUK, and when we finished, I checked my battle board. It showed the fleet swinging around the way it had come. I watched as it began to divide into three separate fleets, one heading northward, one north-west, and the other north-northeast, pulling out. It seemed time to ask again about the twins' own sweet way.

The bomb, El told me, had been dropped about an hour earlier, only to materialize without warning on the foredeck of the fleet's flagship, with Dak astride it in a gorgeous, low-cut, yellow evening gown, demanding loudly in the roughest barracks terms to speak with the admirals.

Dak really knew how to draw attention when she wanted to.

When no admirals appeared, she popped into their command room, where she found them comatose: they'd been psychically implanted by Cha to do certain things, and when they couldn't carry them out, it sort of blew their fuses. So she had popped three times, with an admiral in tow each time; the three were now across the valley with the Neptune people, where Puk and Buc would salvage them.

It hadn't taken the second echelon of command any time at all to decide to head for their respective home bases.

THIRTY-TWO

The United States Senate had already been demanding that the President explain what units of the Pacific Fleet were doing intruding in New Zealand territorial waters and violating New Zealand airspace. The Labour and Liberal Parties in Parliament had demanded the resignation of Prime Minister Keerwin, and he was under extreme pressure from elements of his own party. Goings on in the Politburo couldn't be discerned with any clarity, of course, but after the fleet departed, professional Kremlin watchers saw signs and heard hints of shifts in power alignments. They expected a change or changes at the top to be announced shortly.

El, Dak, and Kad were gone most of the time for several days after the fleet left, returning singly for the most part, and like people who have business to get back to quickly. They didn't really brief us on what they were doing, except to imply that they were exerting certain pressures on unnamed persons, presumably in the direction of stabilizing the three governments at reasonably sane levels, and no doubt inhibiting certain opportunists, there and in other countries, from starting a runaway feedback in the direction of World War

III. But exactly what they were doing, and to or with whom, they were keeping to themselves.

To them, the saving of the valley from the combined fleets had been a lot more than the end of a deadly threat. It had begun a series of political changes which could turn out to be either for better or for worse. They were working on better.

Meanwhile, I had plenty to do myself, right there in the valley. I was developing a program outline for a step-by-step release of Cha's inventions, as modified, to lead toward a real "golden age," rather than a gruesome socio/economic upheaval and collapse.

A key word there is "toward." And for "golden age," do not read "utopia." Read "a situation in which creativity is encouraged, the machinery for social suppression is weakened, and personal responsibility is rewarded."

It was a hell of a challenge, and I loved it.

At the same time, though, I made a point of keeping my warrior pattern in place, and checked my ready room at frequent intervals.

Nor was the impending confrontation with Cha all that far from my thoughts, but it wasn't a distraction, either. I figured that El and the twins would give it their attention at the proper time, and tell me when they needed me. And we had something to work with—the identity of Cha's long-lost brother.

Not that I thought we were home free: Cha had shivved us in the winner's circle before. It wasn't that I recalled the details; I simply knew it had happened. But I was optimistic, and ready to either win or lose, as the case might be.

I assumed there'd be a briefing beforehand, to prime me for various possible dodges that Cha might pull. With maybe some dry runs of the showdown, El or one of the twins wearing Cha's hat, to get me grooved in for him. At any rate, we still had nearly a month before the deadline.

Shows how much I knew about it, or how little.

El showed up in my office one day at about 1640, dressed in her most executive manner. I shook away the program details I was mentally sorting and got up, turning to her. She gave me a hug and kiss that were playful without landing us both on the couch, then leaned back in my arms and looked me in the eye.

"Family celebration tonight," she said. "The twins and I are beginning a short holiday from the world political scene." She gestured at my console. "As soon as you can create a stopping point there, the two of us are going to pop."

I had the computer save the file I was working on, then reached out for her hand, and suddenly, we were standing in our bedroom. A uniform was hanging there, a fleet grand admiral's uniform in a style I'd forgotten.

"It's a dress supper," she said, pointing. So I peeled off my clothes, hanging them in the closet piece by piece. When I got down to my shorts, I stopped and turned to her.

"It seems early for a formal supper," I suggested.

She was grinning at me. "Actually it's about two hours early. But I'm sure we can find something to fill the time." She gestured at the shirt I'd just taken off and still held in my hand. "Keep going," she said, "you're doing fine."

So I kept going, and we both did very well indeed.

Eventually though, we arrived relaxed and shiny at the dining room, to find Mar and Stu and the twins there ahead of us, aperitifs in hand, and Buc and Puk, grinning. A buffet waited in the wings.

I was particularly pleased to see Puk and Buc.

Everyone was in ceremonial attire of the richest, most impressive sort, Buc and Puk military, as were Stu and I. The others were dressed in the manner of the old imperial court. I whistled, then turned to El. "When you said 'dress supper,' you really meant dress supper."

Then a premonition touched me, nothing specific, but a feeling that this was not simply a costume party. El knew as soon as it touched me, of course, and laughed.

"Our warrior doesn't miss a thing tonight," she said. "He's in fine fettle."

Dak and Kad grinned in perfect unison, with mirror image expressions of smug knowingness. "He'd better be," they said together. It occurred to me that they were in a different mood than I'd seen before, less fey than usual at family parties, but very playful nonetheless, with nothing of the marine or business types, and apparently with nothing in particular on their minds. They exuded a sense of—aristocracy at ease, or even royalty relaxed within the family.

I turned to Puk and Buc, who stood together beside the buffet.

"I don't suppose you know what's going on?"

They both shrugged, Puk spreading his hands and grinning. "No one's told me a thing. All we got was an invitation, not an explanation." He turned to Dak and laughed. "Or maybe 'order' is a better word."

Dak pointed to the buffet. "The next order is 'fall to and commence eating!' "

Mumbling something about the condemned man and the last supper, I picked up a large plate and began to sample among the assorted goodies. There were things familiar and things that weren't: lightly smoked trout, unidentified cheeses of various kinds, and pickled herring in sour cream with chives, among numerous others. And those were just the appetizers! I was glad that feasts the twins arranged never seemed to stuff anyone, any more than their liquor had an effect beyond the moment. Then we all sat around the table, eating and talking, getting an overdue rundown of what El and the twins had been doing, and a fuller picture of what was going on at Neptune South. There were no entertainments, nor any of the twins' unique lessons; just good conversation and good feelings.

But I knew something special was coming up, and when we all seemed finally to have had enough of the buffet, I fixed El with my eye. "So," I said to her, "give!"

"Tonight's the night," she said.

"For what?"

"We've all been working, these trilennia, to complete the job on Cha. Tonight's the night we do it."

I might have expected to feel jubilant, or maybe scared stiff. How I actually felt was cautious, guarded, as if I'd been here before and fallen on my face."

"Why tonight? We've got four weeks yet."

"Because Cha's demanded a hearing before the DUO-HEX, and we requested that it be held now instead of later. We're ready, and a wait is likelier to work to Cha's advantage than ours."

Why not, I thought, but I didn't feel good about it, at all. "Okay, so what's the procedure?" I asked.

"The eight of us go to meet him and his decad. And the DUO-HEX, of course."

I didn't answer right away, just looked at El. I had been through this before, all right, and crashed; otherwise, I wouldn't be feeling this back-off. "Brief me," I said.

She looked right back. "No briefing. You're ready. Any further coaching would be counterproductive." Her gaze encompassed the three of us—Buc, Puk, and I. "It's up to the three of you now. Without any more help from us."

"Not even a dream to prime me?" I asked.

"Right."

The twins were looking at me as calmly as El was. And Puk was grinning, the grin I'd known so long and so well. That was Puk. For a moment I wondered if he knew what was going to happen; but of course he didn't. He was just that debonair. And it occurred to me that, hell, I *didn't* need any more coaching or handholding. The deprogramming I'd gotten in L.A., the lessons given, the dreams, the things that Dak and El had watched me through—they'd all been preparing me not just for the preliminary events but for the main bout.

I'd done damned well in the prelims, but that didn't necessarily mean I'd get through even the first round today. We'd see.

I grinned back at Puk, entirely calm now, entirely ready, feeling my warrior pattern sharpen. Then I turned to my three witches.

"When?" I asked.

Dak stood, her drink in her hand. "After this toast." She raised her glass and we all followed suit. "To Cha," she said, "to us, and to humanity."

That's all there was to it. We drained our glasses and abruptly we were there.

So were Cha and his decad, all in copper-bossed black leather, as before. The room was high and weakly lit, its appointments dark. The DUO-HEX was dressed in robes that would have looked more ecclesiastic than judicial if it hadn't been for His powdered periwig and a face that was a marvelous copy of Charles Laughton. Enthroned on a judge's high seat, He added a sense of judicial austerity to a setting that was architecturally more baroque than, say, Victorian or Edwardian.

At the moment He even showed a judicial expression. I wasn't entirely sure how to take that; knowing the DUO-HEX, He could easily have been putting it on. I started to ask El where we were, but I knew what her answer would be: "The same place we visited Him before." Only this time He was going formal—no messy office or rumpled suit.

Before I could turn to see who else might be there, the gavel rapped sharply, and El led me toward a row of seats on a raised area along one wall. Cha and his crew were taking their places fifty feet away on the opposite side. As they sat down, a disk appeared on the center of the wall behind and above them, like a round escutcheon or shield, with a simple design. It was divided diagonally into four wedges: Those on top and bottom were black, while those on the sides were copper.

Meanwhile, a long table with seven chairs, of dark wood, had materialized below the judge's high seat and in line with it. Otherwise, there had been no visible change, but the courtroom had taken on the feel of an arena.

"Our emblem is silver and gold," El murmured. I glanced up at the wall above us, to see. "Do you remember this courtroom?" she asked.

I shook my head. "Not specifically, but it feels as if

. . ." The gavel came down sharply again, cutting off my words, demanding my attention.

"Who will speak for the OTOS?" asked the DUO-HEX, looking in Cha's direction. He even sounded like Charles Laughton. Cha and two others stood, and walked to stand before the bench. There, briefly, they faced each other, forming a triad. A luminous field of black and copper energies formed above their heads and coalesced to form a line which rotated into a triangle, turning slowly, black on one side and copper on the other. OTOS? From somewhere, I remembered: OTOS referred to the twin agreements necessary to have a war using an unknown script. Planning at TO-OT and play at SO-OS. I almost remembered where those codes were on the DUO-HEX's computer console, but as He spoke, the memory slipped away.

"You may take your places," He said. Cha and the other two took seats along one side of the table, and the DUO-HEX turned His round face to us. "Who will speak for the SOTO?" He asked.

From somewhere, somewhen, I knew the correct response, the proper action: Buc, Puk, and I also got up and walked to the bench, where we too formed a triad. The years had fallen from their faces, which looked now both young and ageless. I sensed the energy field above us and then, in an instant, the three of us were one—not our bodies, but ourselves—in an entity meld. Each of us knew what the other two knew of our long involvement in the war with Cha.

But only for a moment. Then we snapped apart, leaving me with the memory of Cha laughing at his three caged ensigns, BucLePuk.

"You may take your places," The DUO-HEX said to us.

We walked to the table, Puk taking the last chair, opposite Cha. As I sat down in the middle chair, I recognized the other two black-clad figures. Fra sat across from me, and Jar across from Buc. In her uniform, Fra didn't look much like a Mata Hari femme fatale; more like a good-looking, well-stacked, efficient staff officer. While Jar, without the snarl that went with the roles he usually played, might have been a sharp, professional aide and advisor. *Now that*, I told myself, *is the kind of thinking that'll get your ass in a sling*, and let the knowledge hone my warrior pattern. This was a battle to a lot more than the death, and the enemy, by its record, was the most vicious and powerful conceivable.

"And who will speak for the INNI?" This the DUO-HEX asked loudly, as if of someone not yet present.

"We will, your Honor!" It was the Mujinn, her dark velvet voice arriving simultaneously with the tall negress body that popped into the courtroom with—with Arno and Cleo on either side! And there, I told myself, was the central reason El had been drawn to a rescue mission on the Upper Rio Negro. They all stood on a dais with three seats, along the wall opposite the judge's bench.

"You may take your places," said the DUO-HEX, and when they had, He continued. "Per statute, we are convened that I may hear and decide upon a demand for a new termination scenario for the SOTO-OTOS WAR PLAY. Admiral Cha, please state your proposal before the hearing." Then He leaned on widespread elbows, his fat chins in cupped hands, looking down at us from his elevation like a curious spectator instead of a judge.

Cha spoke to Puk instead of addressing the bench. "Well, brother," he said, "you hid in the one place we never thought to look: among the white hats. We had been prepared to agree to all motions and take you back with us to the galactic big time, but now that we see the ridiculous role you've been saddled with here, we've decided not to. After all, you are our brother. Before we leave, you need a chance to regain your sanity and play a truly rewarding role for a change."

I was wondering how much of that garbage the DUO-HEX was going to listen to, when Cha turned and addressed Him.

"We demand a retake of the final encounter, beginning with the arrival in New Zealand of our newly uncovered brother, but this time with him on our side for a grand finale prior to our departure."

Puk stood up to answer. "I disagree," he said. "There is no justification for reshooting the past. For a proper departure, I consider that it *is* necessary to prepare the future with an appropriate new script. But set on the present as it now exists."

Cha's smile slipped, and he turned to the DUO-HEX. "As I recall the statutes of conduct," he said icily, "any action including receiving sanctuary from the Jinni or"—he paused and looked pointedly toward El and the twins—"involving intervention by the Playmasters, is subject to replay on request. Both of those statutes apply to recent action. As the Ultimate Authority here, it is Your duty to see that the statutes are applied."

The DUO-HEX smiled slightly, perfunctorily. "I've monitored the Playmasters personally during the current cycle of action," He droned in His Laughton voice, "and found no action therein which falls under the statutory definition of 'intervention.' There remain, of course, earlier periods, and the matter of sanctuary by the Jinni." His interested gaze moved to Puk. "Do you have a reply to your brother's statement?"

Puk turned and looked at the Mujinn, who in turn looked aside at Arno. Arno got up and came forward, to take the chair between Puk and Cha at the head of the table. From his briefcase he extracted two decks of cards and laid them on the table. One was more than twice as thick as the other.

"Your Lordship," Arno said to the DUO-HEX, "these are the sanctuary markers for the times the Jinni gave protection to the OS." He spread the thicker, copper-colored deck on the table for the DUO-HEX. Cha, leaning forward, scanned them and turned livid. His angry gaze swept Fra and Jar, then he turned to glare at the rest of his family, where they sat wooden-faced beneath the family emblem.

At that point I recalled the sanctuary function of the Jinni. In the final extremity, a warrior who knew his prerogatives could call on the Jinni for sanctuary. It was like calling time out when your enemy's bullet was an inch from your forehead. Any such request would be granted and recorded, although obviously it was subject to appeal if the other side knew about it. It could be repealed if challenged soon enough, or penalized if discovered later.

And from Cha's anger and his family's embarrassment, his sibs had obviously made use of sanctuary many times without telling him.

Puk looked across at Cha and chuckled. "Will you accept the evidence as is, or shall I read it into evidence case by case?"

For once, Cha didn't have an immediate dodge: It took him a moment to answer. "What about the tampering those Cats did?" he asked coldly. "Obviously we have made use of the Jinni's good offices on occasion, but only when forced to it by the devious criminality of the Playmasters."

The Playmasters—El and the twins. I had only a rather foggy notion of what the job entailed.

"Do the INNI have a reply?" asked the DUO-HEX.

It was Cleo who answered this time: "If I may, Your Lordship." While Arno gathered up his cards and returned to his chair, she came before the bench and placed two decks of markers on the table. Reaching, Cha picked up the copper deck and began to thumb through it. About half way through, he turned red again and pushed the cards away angrily.

"That," Cleo said mildly, "was when you were in danger of losing your last planet, the home world of the Reptile People, and asked El to sue for peace. To spare the last of that race from destruction, she intervened and saved it for you."

Apparently that was a very high card from our point of view. Without reply, Cha stood up and looked at Fra and Jar. They too stood, and together the three of them walked to their side of the room for a conference.

But Cleo had reminded me of things I'd avoided looking at. I shivered, recalling dimly when I had wasted planets one after another until we'd almost destroyed an entire human life form. The shiver gave way to a flood of guilt. That had been one of those times when we'd appeared to be winning but were really losing to Cha and his OS crew. We'd justified what we'd done on the grounds that it was necessary for victory against the greater evil.

Flashing hot anger seared away the guilt; Cha had whipsawed us—suckered us into what may have been the most discreditable action we'd ever been guilty of. No wonder we'd wanted to forget the other homid species—pretend they'd never existed!

Puk nudged me, grinning. "Belay that," he murmured. "Yesterday was yesterday."

Right, I thought, feeling my warrior pattern sharp and bright. And tomorrow I wanted the OS in some Augean stable, in shit to their knees, shoveling their long way back toward rights and privileges.

The meeting broke up across the room, and the OS triad returned to the table, exuding confidence. I sensed trouble even before Cha spoke.

"Do you refuse to return to your family now?" he asked evenly, looking at Puk.

"I'm ready to abide by all legally binding agreements," Puk replied.

Grinning a grin that knotted my stomach, Cha rose and faced the bench. "Your Honor, we agree with Le's earlier motion that 'we take our brother and leave.' That motion contained no conditions, except the standard condition that our brother be willing. We now hold him and the SOTO to it. And since Puk, as our brother is now called, has forgotten his true name and heritage, we invoke the right of the family—the Ritual for Hysteresis."

The quiet thickened as Cha sat down. *Hysteresis?* I thought. *The failure of something, some property of a thing, to revert to normal after being altered by an external influence.* How did that apply here? Damn! I hated playing these scenes without full data.

The scene went two-dimensional, and we, the SO triad, seemed to rotate to view a ready room with three warlords in it. Puk's was seated behind a modern desk frantically looking through a massive, ancient book.

"Got it!" he said, a finger tapping the page. "I remember now. The Ritual for Hysteresis applies to prisoners of war refusing repatriation following hostilities.

It involves a mind meld to determine if it's the result of mindwashing. If the meld decides that it is, then the family can insist that the entity be returned to its prehysteresis pattern. Pukky boy, they're fixing to gang up on you, eleven to one: Your chances don't look very damn good."

The rotation reversed, and there we sat encased in a room full of copper-tinted jello which blew out of existence when the DUO-HEX smacked his gavel down. "This court is recessed for five minutes," he said. "The Mujinn and El will join me in chambers."

This time he didn't sound at all like Charles Laughton. More like Spencer Tracy. When El and the Mujinn had left, we three got up and walked back to join Mar, Stu, and the twins, to learn more about what was going on.

"The family is senior to groups," Dak explained, "and has an innate right to protect its members from mindwashing. It's the basis for families insisting that their children be returned by cults they've joined and be forced to undergo deprogramming. In this case, the deprogramming would be done by the OS in the most effective way possible—entity merging."

A chill hit me, cold and hard. "What will happen if the DUO-HEX agrees and Puk is returned to their fold?" I asked.

"We made Puk a member of our triad for this hearing, and that can't be changed now," Kad said. "But if he goes over to their side, he'll vote their way. Which will mean that Cha's motion will pass, four to two."

Puk looked a little shaken, and I suppose I did, too. Among other things, I was imagining the brand of grande finale Cha would script as his farewell to this grid: We'd have a planetwide slaughter of the most traumatic kind, for his amusement.

"Don't look so gloomy," Dak said. "The fun's not over yet. Wait and see how it comes out."

Words I'd spoken to Al in D.C. came back to me then: What Cha and family came here for was to regain the true sense of play, something they'd thoroughly lost somewhere down the line and replaced with sadism. And they needed to stay until it was recovered. That had to be our intention here, not revenge, not to humiliate anyone. But to pull it off now, rather than way to hell and gone in the future, Puk had to vote our way. That would make it three to three, and the DUO-HEX could then vote to break the tie.

My brief reverie was broken by the voice of a nonexistent English bailiff calling, "Here, here! Take your places!" Puk, Buc, and I went back to the table which a smug OS triad had not left. El and the Mujinn reentered the court; we remained standing as His Honor followed. I tried to read His face, but couldn't.

"This hearing is now in session," He said drily, then turned His hooded gaze on Cha. "The Ritual for Hysteresis may begin."

Puk got up then and walked with Cha, Fra, and Jar to the side of the room where the rest of the OS stood waiting. Puk seemed as debonair as any warrior had ever been. The eleven formed a tight circle around him, and silence wrapped them while time slowed to a crawl. What I could see of Puk's gold and silver luminosity began to disappear, smothered by black and copper. And though a few brief silver rays broke through, a black and copper dodecahedron began to form, slowly at first, then in long slow pulses during what seemed like an eternity of suspense. I saw no way that Puk could hold up against that onslaught of demanded compliance with Cha's family code.

The formation snapped into place, revealing the clear crisp lines of the copper and black crystal. My heart sank, and I heard Buc mutter "shit!" in some language we hadn't used for a very long time. It expressed the same helpless, wretched, soiled feeling I had.

I was about to turn away in defeat, when the dodecahedron began to rotate slowly, as if to taunt us. Then a slight vibration began in it. A voice laughed lightly inside my head, delighted and playful, and I knew it at once. It was Dawn, for chrissake, and I got a clear sense of the words: "Cha Rover, Cha Rover, let Fra come over."

A moment later the rotation stopped, and a sort of mitosis took place. The dodecahedron began to split, forming twin hexagons held together by heavy lines of force. One by one the lines vanished until the two crystals were totally separate, rotating slowly around a common center, one crystal gold and silver, the other still copper and black. A whoop went up from the side where the twins sat with Stu and Mar and El, while the DUO-HEX murmured something like, "Here, here!" He was smiling benignly, a benevolent Charles Laughton now, with vocal tone to match.

The crystals vanished. Puk stepped out of the circle leading Fra by the arm. Her uniform had turned silver, its trim now gold. The other four of Puk's new hexad, their costumes of all four colors, had drawn apart from the five who still stood by Cha. At the table, Puk moved Fra's chair to our side and held it for her, then took his own seat with the expression I knew so well, the grin broad but the bright eyes alert, signaling readiness for whatever might happen next.

We had the votes without the DUO-HEX's tie-breaker now.

The Charles Laughton eyes, cold and fishy again, looked us over where we sat, then the narrow, pouty, Charles Laughton mouth moved. "Admiral Cha," He said, "are you ready to restate your proposal for a vote?"

Cha and Jar stood apart for a while, discussing tactics, I suppose, as if they had some options left. I wondered if maybe they did. With Cha you couldn't assume anything, but that was an unprecedented loss he'd just taken, and four votes beat two every time. I looked at Fra again; she was more beautiful than I'd ever seen her, but the femme fatale was definitely gone.

"You'd better not look too hard," El whispered in my mind. "In this act, you're all mine." But her thought held laughter, of a kind that made me sense we really had won this time. *Unless,* I told myself, *we do something really stupid.*

Cha and Jar returned to the table looking grim. When Cha spoke, it was to Puk. "I retract my proposal stated previously and submit to the condition that there be a transition play satisfactory to the majority before we leave this sector of the galaxy."

"That will be a majority of those now seated as representatives of the OTOS and the SOTO," the DUO-HEX said. "You are aware of that?"

Cha nodded curtly. The DUO-HEX looked at Puk.

"What do you have in mind?" He asked.

"In consultation with the Jinni, I recently prepared a proposal for this contingency," Puk said, "a brief scenario that will provide suitable rehabilitation of the playground and the players. There is a role in it for each of us. But before we change to the executive session mode to actually script it, the Mujinn has something to say."

Executive session! I remembered reading congressional hearings for the Committee on NASA, where they would change to the executive session mode whenever they were ready to discuss something really interesting. And the records of executive sessions were never included, always secret, so of course I never found out what was really going on. It was going to be that way here, too, I just knew it: When our executive session was over, its decisions would be enforced, but we wouldn't remember anything about it. We'd be playing to an unseen script again.

The Mujinn spoke from her dais: "First we need to look at past damages, so that you will all be consciously aware of the operating considerations after the executive session is over."

After she said that, her gaze went to each of us, making it clear that we all needed to listen.

"It is expected and acceptable that wars will damage reality, and per statue, weapon design must restrict the destruction to that level. But we have numerous cases of approved weapons being modified so that they have actually damaged the reality matrix generators themselves. The neutral members of Puk's hexad should be required to repair those damages.

"But we have other damages as well. As might be expected from so long an age of hostilities, some entities have been affected to the point that an unassisted reversion to normal can no longer occur within the configuration of the matrix. These persons, and they are many, require special treatment before they can break out of their encysted condition and rehabilitate themselves."

She looked at those of us around the table, then at the rest of Cha's family. "Each of you has introduced excesses seriously impairing some facets of reality or of its people. The Jinni ask that you design mini-plays to assist recovery in each area. Specifically: Buc, with your zeal for the grand finale, you have generated a fear of the conclusion, a "final act phobia," which has infested much of this sector, often leaving the theater empty long before the final curtain falls, and cluttering space and time with uncompleted cycles of action. We want you to undo that, and let the fourth act become fun again.

"Fra, we have two races near extinction due to your excessive recruitment of their females. Further, you have used sex for so many altered purposes that it no longer functions as intended—to revitalize and co-create. The bedroom has become a battlefield throughout much of the sector. The family and sex are fast becoming a major problem. We request your aid in returning sex to its original functions, and in the salvage of threatened human forms."

Her eyes moved to me then. "Le, you too have recruited excessively."

Me? I thought, thunderstruck. She continued.

"Many planets in the sector now have a seemingly innate fear of space and technology. You have recruited too many warriors and scientists from too many places, taken them across the stars to too many high technology wars, and never returned with them. We request . . ."

As she continued to talk, I sat only half listening, remembering my last recruiting trip, to a world of cat people who kept long and accurate oral histories and wanted no part of my pitch. I'd tried every plausible-seeming lie I could think of, flattered, pushed every button, tried to draw on every favor owed, attempted to bribe officials to consign the contracts of indentured warriors . . . everything my fertile imagination could come up with. They were having none of it, and damned little of me. My mind stuck again in the despondency I'd felt then, recalling all the "if onlys" and "I should haves" I'd rehearsed to myself while awaiting public execution back home. That was one of the times when Cha had won hands down.

Yes, I had a lot to do. Not a little of it here on Earth.

The Mujinn's words broke my reverie only when she reached the last person on her list.

"And finally we come to Cha," she said, "whose desire for randomness and unexpected reversals of polarity has infected many entities with an urge to destruction, including self-destruction. Entropy is not necessarily an evil, but the unwanted striving for it, overriding a basic underlying desire to do otherwise, is often damaging beyond the ability to self-repair. The reversal of that tendency is especially vital to the salvation of the Reptile People, and must be accomplished as quickly as possible."

The Mujinn nodded at us then, indicating she was done. "Thank you all," she said, and sat down again. The room was quiet, a deep quiet I wasn't willing to break with a question. Cha's face looked almost blank, as if he wasn't with us: Maybe the Mujinn's statement of his crimes had sent him on a memory trip like mine.

The DUO-HEX waited patiently until Cha showed signs of awareness again. "Do you all agree to Puk's proposal?" he said at last.

"Yes." Cha spoke absently, almost without moving. "We of the OS will cooperate as required."

Quickly, one after the other, the rest of us also stated our readiness, including Puk; he'd committed more than a few crimes himself.

"Very well. We will now jointly script the transition scene, including repair and amends projects, in executive session." The DUO-HEX smacked down the gavel, snapping off the memory record.

THIRTY-THREE

When memory began again, we were at home, El and I side by side in chairs, holding hands, the twins kneeling quietly on the carpet, Mar and Stu seated on the couch. For a bit I scarcely looked at anyone, held in silence by the gap in my memory.

I relaxed to let my mind deal with the hidden data subliminally, the only level at which it might be available. A lassitude developed, then lifted, and I looked around, still feeling no need to talk.

After a few minutes, El looked first at Mar and Stu then at me, and spoke.

"Now you know why we've been easing you into the reality of the other races, and why we saved the Reptile People till last. That was the race most often used by Cha and his crew—not only as tools but for their own identity when they weren't being part of our own race. And our reaction has all too often been savage. Mankind on Earth has suffered a sort of amnesia on the subject, an amnesia extending to subliminal levels, through a long age of planetbound isolation. Now it's time to remove that cloak and go out among the stars again."

"Is Cha really going to leave the solar system?" Stu asked.

"He's already left," El answered. "He and the rest of his hexad got under way as soon as they returned to their wagons. Their repairs projects start outsystem."

"But have they recovered their sense of play?" I asked. "And can they be trusted to actually carry out their projects?"

El laid a hand on mine. "You can be sure they'll carry them out. They're not operating under the rules of war now. In this the rules of reparations apply." Her fingers squeezed mine. "And they'll recover a sane sense of play while they're doing it. We've been setting them up for it long enough. The mind meld with Puk got it started, then the Mujinn moved it along a bit."

"How will they know what their projects are, if the executive session is . . ." I stopped, seeing the answer for myself.

"That's right, dear, they don't, except at a deep subliminal level, any more than you know yours. These are hidden scripts. That requires them to originate their actions as well as carry them out, requiring a much higher level of responsibility and understanding than simply following instructions would. And it allows them to reap the fullest personal gains from making reparations."

I looked at that, and beyond, and wondered what a sane Cha would be like. Then something else occurred to me. "What's my insanity?" I asked.

This time El really laughed. "Darling, you don't have one. All you have left to clean up are some residual guilt feelings and to regain the freedom to feel full affinity with other races. And, of course, a certain burden of unpaid debts."

Dak and Kad served drinks then, a fruit and spice punch, and we sat and talked about the future for quite a while. Later they expanded our reality of the galactic community of humankind: Natively they were cat girls; now they became fish girls again, and reptile girls. In both forms they were exotically very beautiful—and surprisingly human. It doesn't really matter where or from what base humans evolved their physical form; this is the life form programmed into this grid for use in standard roles.

When the twins were done, El stood up. "Okay, kids, off to bed. After an evening like this one, we all have some old equations to balance."

Mar got up and kissed El. "Good night, mom," she said, then bent and kissed me, too. "Good night, dad."

Dad. I told myself that was appropriate enough, considering I was her mother's mate, but I couldn't help wondering who her father really was. Then the others left El and me there alone, and she sat down beside me again.

"It would be neat," I said musingly, "to have the kind of power the DUO-HEX has for a while. Nothing ever touches him that he doesn't want." I paused, looking at that. "And if I really wanted to, I could take things over when they got too out of hand."

"What kind of play would that be?" El asked.

"What kind of fun was it getting clobbered so many times over so many trilennia?"

"The fun was in the trying," she answered, "and in coming close. And in the experiences; that's the key, you know. A being *loves* to experience, and loves causing others to experience. There's delicious exhilarating victory and deliciously picquant grief, delicious love and joy, delicious revenge and agony—and delicious guilt. You've had them all and I've had most of them."

She paused, her gaze steady on mine. "From one point of view I've had far greater powers than you've had, right? But it hasn't made me immune to emotions, positive or negative. I've suffered, too, as deliciously as you have."

"I wasn't talking about just having more powers," I said. "I wasn't even talking about being outside of games or wars or whatever. What I was talking about was . . ." I paused to look at it again, trying to find the right words. "If I had the DUO-HEX's powers . . ."

What I found myself coming back to was the matter of emotions. I wouldn't have to be subject to any emotions I didn't want. I sat there looking at that, and at what El had just said about experiencing, realizing there was something I wasn't seeing. Then she came over and sat on my lap with her arms lightly around my neck.

"Darling, you do have the DUO-HEX's power. And so do I, and Cha, and the man giving out crosses in the park, and the pusher on the corner of Hollywood and Western. And everyone else you've ever known or seen. *But not on the grid.*"

I stared at her, not quite thoroughly bewildered but damned near. "Explain," I said.

She leaned back, her arms still around my neck.

"You recall the Mujinn mentioning the reality generators, right?"

"Sure. No problem understanding that. Something has to generate our reality—the electromagnetic-graviticlife forcic field we play on. Or in."

She nodded. "Some would say reality is subjective, but operationally it's not. What's subjective is the decision 'to play or not to play.' "

"But it doesn't seem to me that that's subjective either," I protested. "Take the wino sleeping under a bridge in winter, wrapped in a ragged quilt he dug out of a dumpster somewhere. Or some poor bastard who's tripped so many times, his only address is the bus stop bench at Ninth and Hoover, and he hardly knows whether it's day or night. Did they knowingly decide to play those roles?"

"You're getting closer. The basic decision was 'to play,' *made by the person at another level*. That could also be termed the decision 'to experience and to cause experiences.' Or 'to cause and receive effects.' Or 'to strive and to get results,' *whatever* the results might be—success or failure, joy or suffering. Which are not necessarily the results that the person in the reality grid—the video game, so to speak—*thinks* he's striving for. Not at all.

"You, my dear," she went on, "have power out the kazoo, if I may use an unladylike expression. But you have it *outside the game*, not in it. The designed-in nature of the video game is that the playing unit—that cursor you projected and continue to project into the game for the purposes of playing, that you think of as you—is considerably restricted. And it is *operationally senior* to the original decisionmaking you who is outside the game looking in. It is operationally senior, and ordinarily it isn't even aware of the self outside the grid, or even that the grid isn't all there is."

She spoke more slowly then, enunciating the words to mark their importance. "And because that extension of you which we're calling 'the cursor' is operationally senior, you, the player outside, the underlying actual you, *can't give it orders*. When you insert a cursor into the video game, it becomes the operational you, your operational viewpoint. Yet it's a considerably *restricted* viewpoint, with restrictions imposed by the game—actually, by the reality generators. After that, the originating you, which made the decision to play, and which projected the viewpoint into the field, can't give orders. To a degree, it—you—are an interested spectator, experiencing the game through a remote, multi-perceptual sensory pickup."

"But Jesus!" I said. "If that's true, then I'm just here getting my jollies from some kind of huge and intricate, multi-sensory, three-dimensional wraparound *movie!* It's not even a game, if the player can't control the cursor. If that's true, then . . ." I stopped, stuck for an appropriate concept.

She laughed, a nice light, loving laugh, but pleased. And somehow I laughed with her without knowing why.

"What you are," she said, "is the decisionmaker, out for a romp in the DUO-HEX's giant playground. Only in this playground, when you enter, actually only part of you enters—via the reality generator. And in entering, that extension of you is cut off from its memories of outside, for the purposes of play, while attaching to various necessary grid connections."

She sat there on my lap without saying anything more for a long moment, while I stared past her not trying to understand, simply letting the content of her sentences percolate down through accumulated layers of old considerations, judgments, values. The adjustments, I thought, might take a while.

"Actually, the cursor *is* more than simply an extension of you, the outside player. It also includes various grid components that plug you in, and it provides visual, audio, tactile, olfactory, and the rest of the perceptual spectrum."

She leaned against me then, firm breasts pressing against my chest, blew gently in my ear, then nipped it. I squirmed, feeling the sweat start, among other things. "Like that," she murmured. "Like right now. All very real, because that *is* reality in this universe.

"And you *do* have some control from the other side—important control, but indirect. Remember the yellow field, and the wall with the target on it? You enter the grid with intention—a goal—and a basic script that you selected or accepted. You have *attention* as your control mechanism, to keep on your *intention* as best you can, and an icon, plus the three-dimensional body the icon generates, to operate with. Among the various functions of an icon, generating a body is ordinarily the main one."

She looked at me with her head cocked slightly. "And basically that's all there is to operating in the grid."

"And it's the same for you and Dak and—Cha?"

"It's—similar."

"Huh! How about the DUO-HEX? How does he fit in? He seems to be independent of all this. He goes and comes and does things any way he wants."

She pinned me with her eyes. "On the other side, you and the DUO-HEX—the entity being the DUO-HEX—are the same kind of entity. But on this side you have different roles."

I stared at nothing for a moment, then questioningly at El. She went on. "The other-side entity who created and assigned himself the role of DUO-HEX also designed the reality generator, with which he created the grid, this reality. This universe is not the only one, nor his first. We decided it would be interesting to be in it, so here we are.

"And it *has* been interesting. Intense, too, at times. The intensity adds to the interest."

Judas Priest! "But it's a trap, too," I said.

"Is that the way it seems?"

"Well, I think so, yes."

"My, but that's interesting. Isn't it." She laughed again, and someone else did too, softly, behind me. I turned and Dak was there, and Kad, grinning affectionately.

"But suppose you want to get out?" I asked. "And you can't? After a few trilennia that could be pretty horrible!"

"It would be, but it's not. If you on the other side want to withdraw your viewpoint from the grid and go somewhere else to play, or be nowhere and play by yourself, you can do that any time you want. But as long as things are interesting enough, which usually means challenging enough, you're not likely to.

"And if things on this side get *too* intense for too long, instead of pulling out of the matrix, the being can always withdraw from an active role for a while; go be an asteroid somewhere and circle some distant sun, somewhere where the levels of excitement and involvement are pretty darned low."

Damn! I could feel things going "click" in my mind as they shifted around and began fitting together.

"So how come you guys have the powers you have?" I asked. "And can do all the things you do?"

"They go with the job," Dak said from behind my shoulder. "We're Playmasters."

"Playmasters come in threes—a triad," El added, "each one having certain specialties as well as certain powers in common."

"And you and Dak and Kad are the Playmasters," I said.

"No." It was Kad who answered this time, from behind my other shoulder. "Dak and I together are one as far as the job is concerned, just as you were one, a twofold one, when one of you was at the White House and one was at NORTEC. A sort of bifurcate entity with two separate beingnesses."

Briefly that stopped me. I'd known that, of course, just overlooked it. But then . . . "So let me get this straight," I said, looking at El. "You are one Playmaster and Dak/Kad's a second Playmaster—but Playmasters come in threes." I scanned my recollections for anyone else I'd run into who operated on the level they did. I couldn't find any. "So who's the third one?"

"You are," she said.

"*Me!?* But that doesn't make any sense! I can't do what you've been doing! That doesn't compute worth a damn!"

"Right. Because you haven't had certain necessary

data. It goes like this: A very long time ago, Cha and the rest of the OS were occasional highly disruptive intruders into this sector. That was back when access was less controlled than it came to be later. And instead of simply overriding the system and chucking them out, the DUO-HEX decided to go with our suggestion—yours, actually—and handle them within the operating rules of the grid. That would make things *really* interesting."

"And Cha and the OS agreed," I said.

"That's right. And one of the needs was for a triad of warriors to contest with them. But not just any old trio of cursors would do. Because of the balance of abilities needed, it was agreed to use one Playmaster, one Games Master, and one of the OS. You volunteered, along with Buc. And Puk, who was one of the two OS sane enough."

"And Fra was the second?"

El nodded. "Fra was the other, but it was Puk who volunteered.

"Incidentally," she added, "Puk was never mindwashed in the sense of being programmed with someone else's goal for him. The DUO-HEX simply cleaned him up for the job—helped him get rid of some aberrations by a process more or less like we used on you back in L.A. If he'd really been mindwashed, Cha would definitely have recaptured him with the Ritual for Hysteresis. As it was, what we had to worry about was that they'd simply overwhelm his belief in himself. In Puk's case, that was a little more than they could manage, though he had me worried for a minute."

"But Dawn had a hand in that, didn't she? I remember her saying something like 'Cha rover, Cha rover, let Fra come over.' And then Fra switched sides."

El's laugh was light. "Dawn didn't cause it, she simply saw what was going on and what was going to happen. She could see it developing, and it delighted her. No, Puk handled that himself."

"Do you know who, or what, Dawn is?" I asked. "Because I sure as hell don't."

"Certainly. She's an aspect of Old Pasquali."

"That's no help, dammit! Who's Old Pasquali?"

"All plus one."

I didn't say a word, only scowled. El laughed again.

"Old Pasquali is an entity established jointly by all the assigned players in the SOTO-OTOS war game, including each of the OS. A game like the one we just finished, with a hidden script, requires some medium of subliminal communication between the players. So a neutral life force entity is set up as that medium, comprising a piece of each player plus a piece of the DUO-HEX. All plus one—Old Pasquali. And Dawn is that aspect of Old Pasquali which communicates for the entity itself."

"Huh! So . . . she used our computer to communicate to us above the subliminal level. And Cha contributed. Hell, I suppose he agreed to the whole thing because at some level he knew he needed therapy. And then fought like hell to keep it from happening!"

El nodded, smiling.

I sat there for a long moment—just sat there. What was going on with me just then was more than the now-familiar rushes and chills. It was a great upwelling of self-knowledge and amusement. A ton of stuff was discharging like static electricity, making accessible to me what hadn't been since I took on my assignment to the warrior triad. It wouldn't all come through at once, but it was on its way. I could feel myself starting to chuckle on both sides, in and outside of the grid.

"So," I said, and reaching up my arms, gave a big stretch. "Let's give these thirsty icons one more drink." I put my arms around El again and kissed her. "Then I am going to shower and to bed—and not by myself, I hope."

My hope was fulfilled beyond imagination: Sex had never been so playful or beautiful, and I had never felt so alive. The Mujinn had mentioned revitalizing as an original purpose for sex. Now I really knew what she meant by that.

Afterwards, lying quietly on the sheets, I asked a

question that was still stuck in my mind. It didn't seem important, but it was something I wanted to know.

"El," I asked, "who is Mar's father?"

She giggled. "You are, darling."

For a moment I lay there looking at what she'd said. "Sonofagun! When did we do that?"

She raised herself on an elbow and kissed me sweetly. "Just now. A few minutes ago."

A lot more things shifted and settled into place for me, and I felt another upwelling of satisfaction and self-knowledge begin.

"Well, I'll be darned!" I said again.

And so much for *time*.

GORDON R. DICKSON

Winner of every award science fiction and fantasy to offer, Gordon Dickson is one of the major authors of this century. He creates heroes and enemies, not just characters in books; his stories celebrate bravery and virtue and the best in all of us. Collect some of the very best of Gordon Dickson's writing by ordering the books below.

FORWARD!, 55971-0, 256 pp., $2.95 ☐

HOUR OF THE HORDE, 55905-2,
   256 pp., $2.95 ☐

INVADERS!, 55994-X, 256 pp., $2.95 ☐

THE LAST DREAM, 65559-0, 288 pp.,
   $2.95 ☐

MINDSPAN, 65580-9, 288 pp., $2.95 ☐

SURVIVAL!, 55927-3, 288 pp., $2.75 ☐

WOLFLING, 55962-1, 256 pp., $2.95 ☐

LIFESHIP (with Harry Harrison), 55981-8,
   256 pp., $2.95 ☐

Please send me the books I have checked above. I enclose a check or money order for the combined price plus 75 cents for first-class postage and handling made out to Baen Books, Dept. B, 260 Fifth Avenue, New York, N.Y. 10001.

"The crowd was noisy in the Blue Bottle, although it was early in the evening. Tavern girls squealed as customers pinched them, gaily clad waiters brought round after round of drinks, and throughout much of the room everyone was shouting merrily. The reason was not hard to find, for in one corner of the crowded room three officers of the Imperial Navy held court, buying drinks for anyone on Prince Samual's World who would sit with them and laugh at their jokes. . . ."

BY THE CO-AUTHOR OF *FOOTFALL* AND *THE MOTE IN GOD'S EYE*

"ROCK 'EM, SOCK 'EM SPACE ADVENTURE"
—*The Chicago Tribune*

"COLORFUL, FAST-PACED . . . JERRY POURNELLE AT HIS BEST!"
—Poul Anderson

"Jerry Pournelle is one of a handful of writers who can speculate knowledgeably about future worlds. His space program background, readings in science, and Ph.D.'s in psychology and political science allow him to carefully work out the logical development of a world and its societies. . . . [*King David's Spaceship*] is a fine novel."—*Amazing*

FEBRUARY 1987 • 384 pp. • 65616-3 • $2.95

To order any Baen Book by mail, send check or money order for the cover price plus 75 cents for first-class postage and handling made out to Baen Books, Dept. B, 260 Fifth Avenue, New York, N.Y. 10001.

ROBERT A. HEINLEIN

"Heinlein knows more about blending provocative scientific thinking with strong human stories than any dozen other contemporary science fiction writers."
—*Chicago Sun-Times*

"Robert A. Heinlein wears imagination as though it were his private suit of clothes. What makes his work so rich is that he combines his lively, creative sense with an approach that is at once literate, informed, and exciting."
—*New York Times*

Seven of Robert A. Heinlein's best-loved titles are now available in superbly packaged new Baen editions, with embossed series-look covers by artist John Melo. Collect them all by sending in the order form below:

Rob a Pharaoh and you've made an enemy
not just for life . . . but for *all time.*

FRED SABERHAGEN

PYRAMIDS

Tom Scheffler knew that his great uncle,
Montgomery Chapel, had worked as an Egyptologist
during the 1930s, and after that had become a
millionaire by selling artifacts no one else could
have obtained. Scheffler also knew that the old
man, fifty years later, was still afraid of some
man—some *entity*—known only as Pilgrim. But
what did that mean to Scheffler, an impoverished
student with the chance to spend a year "house-
sitting" a multi-million-dollar condo?

What Scheffler didn't know—and would learn
the hard way—was that Pilgrim was coming back,
aboard a ship that traveled both space and time,
headed for a confrontation in a weirdly changed
past where the monstrous gods of ancient Egypt
walked the Earth. And where Pharaoh Khufu,
builder of the greatest monument the world had
ever known, lay in wait for grave robbers from
out of time . . .

JANUARY 1987 • 65609-0 • 320 pp. • $3.50

*Here is an excerpt from PYRAMIDS, Fred Saberhagen's
newest novel, coming from Baen Books in January 1987*

YOU ARE HERE TO ROB THE PYRAMIDS?
COME THEN: THE MONSTROUS GODS OF
ANCIENT EGYPT AWAIT YOU . . .

Whether or not that monstrous, incredible mass of
stone up on the hill was the original Great Pyramid of
Giza, it was still there when Scheffler went back again
to take a look at it through heat and sunlight. Still
there, in the broad daylight of what was either mid-
morning or mid-afternoon, though it had been dusk in
Illinois when he pulled the tapestry-curtain back into
place and closed himself into the elevator once more.

Standing in the savage sun-glare on the lip of the
rocky fissure, he pulled the cheap mass compass out of
his shirt pocket and established to his own satisfaction
that here it was mid-afternoon and not mid-morning.
For this purpose he was going to be daring and assume
that, whatever else might happen to the world, the sun
still came up in the east.

So the river was east of him, and the pyramid about
the same distance to his west and a little south. Last
night Scheffler had done a little reading on the
geography of Giza, the district of the Pyramids just
east of modern Giza, and he had to admit that the
situation he was looking at here seemed to correspond
exactly. Everything he could see indicated to him that
he was standing on the west bank of the Nile.

The hardest part of that to deal with was that if
Khufu, or Cheops as the Greeks came to call him, was
still building his great tomb, the year ought to be
somewhere near three thousand B.C.

Whatever, and wherever, *here* was.

*A Fascinating New Twist on the Time-Travel Novel,
by the Author of* The Book of Swords, Berserker, *and*
The Frankenstein Papers.

JANUARY 1987 • 65609-0 • 320 pp. • $3.50

*To order any Baen Book by mail, send the cover price
plus 75 cents for first-class postage and handling to: Baen
Books, Dept. B, 260 Fifth Avenue, New York, N.Y. 10001.*